L.L. LOVELAND

Entanglement

The Landlord Series · Book One

LOVELAND BOOKS

AN INDEPENDENT PUBLISHING IMPRINT OF L.L. LOVELAND

Copyright © 2026 by l.l. loveland

All rights reserved. No part of this publication may be reproduced, stored, or transmitted in any form or by any means, electronic, mechanical, photocopying, recording, scanning, or otherwise without written permission from the publisher. It is illegal to copy this book, post it to a website, or distribute it by any other means without permission.

This novel is entirely a work of fiction. The names, characters, and incidents portrayed in it are the work of the author's imagination. Any resemblance to actual persons, living or dead, events, or localities is entirely coincidental.

l.l. loveland asserts the moral right to be identified as the author of this work.

l.l. loveland has no responsibility for the persistence or accuracy of URLs for external or third-party Internet Websites referred to in this publication and does not guarantee that any content on such Websites is, or will remain, accurate or appropriate.

Designations used by companies to distinguish their products are often claimed as trademarks. All brand names and product names used in this book and on its cover are trade names, service marks, trademarks, and registered trademarks of their respective owners. The publishers and the book are not associated with any product or vendor mentioned in this book. None of the companies referenced within the book have endorsed the book.

AI Training & Data Use Prohibited

No part of this book may be used to train artificial intelligence technologies or systems, including large language models, without the express written consent of the author. This restriction applies to all text, characters, concepts, and original expressions contained herein.

First edition

ISBN: 979-8-9937850-0-4

Proofreading by Rebecca Buck
Proofreading by Mandolin Marie

This book was professionally typeset on Reedsy.
Find out more at reedsy.com

To my husband and boys,
Thank you for loving me through the drafts of endless writing, the oversized notebook I dragged everywhere, and the hours that this entire process stole from us.
Your patience, hugs, and encouragement, gave me room to bring the book I've been dreaming of writing for twenty years—to life. The time and space you gave, allowed me to create from my heart and soul.
This book came to life because you believed I could write it.
I love you all, the most.

Acknowledgments

My mom and sister—

Thank you for pretending to care every time I launched into another story breakdown, character crisis, or "wait... just listen to this one scene" moment. You deserve medals.

I love you both for putting up with me (and all 90,702 of these words)

Alicia Davies—

Thank you for being more than just a friend throughout this journey. Your encouragement, insight, plot-hole patching, and willingness to dive into these pages with me means more than you know.

This book carries your fingerprints in all the best ways.

Rebecca Buck—

I'm so grateful you stepped in and filled the final missing pieces of this novel. Your proofread gave me the confidence to release this book into the world. Your skill and friendship are unmatched; I'm lucky to know you and honored to have you in these pages.

Mandolin Marie—

I found you at the final hour. Some relationships come when you least expect them. I can't express how thankful I am for you—coming in and fixing the final errors. You have an incredible talent for precision and detail. You're truly a heaven-send.

Content Notice

This novel contains mature and emotionally intense themes, including:

· Infidelity and betrayal
  · Emotional abuse and gaslighting
  · Physical abuse (choking)
  · Religious guilt and faith-related trauma
  · Sexual content (consensual, but emotionally complex)
  · Psychological manipulation
  · Psychological distress
  · Obsessive behavior and stalking
  · References to alcohol and substance abuse
  · Grief, isolation, and identity crisis
  · Suicide-related themes

While this is a fictional story, many of the emotional experiences are rooted in real and painful truths. I wrote this book to reach people at many different points in their lives. I hope it meets you where you are.

— L.L. Loveland

Prologue

I could start at the beginning. When Maya convinced me to go to Homecoming with Dominic—the rebel who smoked pot behind the bleachers, the thrill-seeker who drank beer in the parking lot during lunch, the boy who was loud enough to own a room and wild enough to be talked about for days. I could tell an entire story about how our opposite lives collided, and somehow made sense. I could go on about the secret we kept, the tenderness no one else saw.

But my story starts somewhere darker.

It doesn't begin with a dance. It begins with a slow unraveling—one gaslighting word at a time. One emotionally abusive thread pulling loose the version I believed myself to be, until only scraps remained. I didn't know then that beneath the wreckage was a woman I had never met, but would come to know intimately.

There was more of me to become.

The good girl raised to be righteous. The one who lived by every standard, who prayed, obeyed, sacrificed—she would be torn at the seams. Shredded. Restitched into someone unfamiliar. A woman I didn't know I could be. A woman I didn't know I might want to be.

The standards I held myself to.

The standards the church held me to.

The standards my family held me to.

All of it began to split. To rot. To release.

PROLOGUE

Not because of my delinquent husband.
Not because of the boy I married to stay pure.
But because of the choices I made.
Because of the temptation I let slip through the door.

The landlord entered my life during the weakest, rawest season of my undoing, and I didn't resist.
I opened.
I leaned in.
I let myself want.

And just when Dominic believed he had me contained, controlled, owned—that was when I finally learned who he really was.
The dance could have been the start of everything good.
Instead, It was the breaking.

And this—right here—is where I began to shatter.

One

Spring 2004

The dryers drone in the background, steady as breathing, while I glance down at my vibrating hand. The air is thick with shampoo and damp fur, heavy enough to taste. No one warns you how sin can look like rescue. How danger can step in wearing steel-toed boots and a possible wedding ring. Through a curtain of golden strands, I sweep my eyes toward the ladder.

He moves with quiet confidence, muscles in his arms flexing as he reaches overhead working like he's done this a hundred times before. Sculpted and focused he could have stepped out of a Renaissance painting—the modern-day David come to fix the air conditioner.

The whir of my clippers snaps the spell. I refocus on Gizmo, the ebony Pomeranian blinking up at me like he knows my thoughts have drifted somewhere they shouldn't. I mutter a quiet, "Thank you," to the dog instead of God.

Through the veil of my hair, I watch a bead of sweat slide down his temple. It traces his cheekbone, glides down his neck, then rolls over his chest. The high-endurance ball of sweat continues to crawl its way down each of his individual ab muscles until it crashes against the leather of his tool belt, slightly above the low line of his jeans.

Stop staring, Sarah. I tell myself, but it's impossible.

He climbs down the ladder, voice as confident as his build. "That should fix it."

ONE

I snap my eyes back to Gizmo, forcing myself to focus on an uneven patch of fur, pretending I hadn't been looking. "Great," I manage, pretending I wasn't memorizing the curve of his mouth a second ago.

He smiles slightly, and my heart misfires.

Heaven help me, *this is our new landlord.*

My mom, Linda, laughs from across the shop, her voice rising above the noisy whirl of the fans. She's talking to him, probably about rent or renovations, but her words dissolve into the background. The only thing I can hear is the uneven rhythm of my own pulse and the barking of the dogs in kennels.

Attraction surges, fierce and impossible to deny. I force a laugh, pretending the idea is nothing, but something in me already knows—I won't walk away from this unchanged.

Just as I finish trimming Gizmo's paws, the door opens. Mrs. Callahan shuffles in, her cardigan button askew, her eyes illuminating the moment she spots him.

"There's my handsome boy." She cries, her voice quivering with delight. Gizmo practically leaps from the table, his tail wagging furiously. I set him into her arms, and she brushes her cheek against his fur, kissing the top of his head over and over.

"Oh, Sarah, you always take such good care of him," she breathes, mist forming in her eyes. "I don't know what I'd do without you."

Warmth pulls me back to myself, softening the tension of the moment before.

"He's always a joy," I confide honestly. She beams, pulling a small tin from her purse. "I made fudge for you. Don't argue, take it. You deserve it."

I chuckle softly, gratitude threading my tone. "Thank you. You really didn't have to."

"Hush now," she chides tenderly, still clutching Gizmo like he's the most precious thing in the world. "You spoil him, so let me spoil you."

She departs with Gizmo nestled in her arms, and I can't help grinning as the door jingles shut behind her. These moments remind me why I love what

I do. Why this shop, chaotic as it is, feels like home.

Laughter drifts through the doorway, light, unguarded. And his name falls through it like a match struck in a dry field.

"Thanks, Spencer," Linda repeats earnestly for what feels like the tenth time. "We're so grateful you bought this old place."

I don't need to look up to know he's still here. Or that trouble has found me.

The dogs bark on as Linda gabs cheerfully.

I call my mom "Linda." The reason? My Grandmother is stamped with the name "Mom." My oldest brother started referring to her as that when he was a toddler, mimicking Linda calling her by that name. I know it sounds backwards but it's always been that way.

No one calls the business by its official name anymore; to everyone, it's simply *The Dog Shop*. Linda launched it in 1995.

For years, the building was owned by an older man named Cleed. When he could no longer keep up, it changed hands, and until today, I'd never met the new owners.

It doesn't matter that I've never encountered Spencer before. What matters is this:

I'm married.

Seven months ago, I tied the knot with my high school sweetheart. We wed shortly after graduation, following the path I was always taught was "right." I'd never strayed from expectations. I never wanted to disappoint anyone.

Raised in a strict LDS home, I grew up believing that sex before marriage was forbidden. While I didn't always live up to those standards, I still believed in them.

That belief is part of what rushed me into marrying Dominic.

But what I once thought would be a perfect marriage has come to feel like penance.

ONE

After seeing Spencer today, I can't stop measuring everything, my choices, my vows, the man I promised myself to.

It's complicated. Or maybe it's becoming clearer.

I love Dominic, or I did, when I said *I do*. But in the months since, he's changed. He's become more withdrawn and impatient. His cruelty seeps through even in the simplest moments. What's worse is his constant dishonesty, the quiet lies that rot everything underneath.

For months, I've refused to face the truth. But lately, it's becoming impossible to ignore.

My pulse stumbles, a reckless rhythm I can't command. An uninvited conjuring of the image of him—the landlord. A love-at-first-sight moment I never asked for.

I'm caught between guilt and curiosity, and both are winning.

I need to know more about this man.

The urge to ask Linda prickles at my tongue. I need to say something, anything, but I swallow it down. I can't let her see what's spinning in my head, what I'm already questioning.

I notice she's pulling her blonde hair into a ponytail, her hands working swiftly. She's thirty-three years older than me, but we share the same distinct green eyes, scattered freckles, the same small frame, though she stands a few inches taller at five-foot four, and my hair is much longer, falling to my waist. Even with the differences, she's still the mirror I measure myself against.

I chew the corner of my lip, still debating. Then, finally, I blurt it out, trying to sound natural.

"So... what do you know about the new landlord?"

She explains, her hands still busy, that Spencer and his business partner, Mike, recently bought the building. Mike handles the office side—paperwork and finances—while Spencer manages the hands-on work—contracts, tenants, employees, and repairs.

"If something needs fixing, he's the one who tackles it," she remarks.

"They don't just own this place. They've got other ventures too. One's a heating and air company based at the far end of our building. People whisper about more businesses, but they keep them quiet."

Excitement ripples within me, knowing Spencer might come back. It shouldn't, but it does.

Tonight, the contrast sharpens, daylight temptation giving way to the cold reality of my marriage. I crawl into bed beside my husband, resting a hand on his waist. He doesn't flinch.

He never does.

I stare into the dark beside the man I once would have sacrificed anything to save this marriage with, but doubt gnaws at me—I can't fix this alone.

He won't even offer me the courtesy he gives strangers, and that's what I feel more and more—we're becoming strangers.

The heaviness in my chest settles, pressing me into the mattress. Restless whispers tell me this is all it will ever be, bound by vows, ensnared by silence, settling for this.

His softness, once a comfort, now repulses me. The drinking has changed him, his skin tinted a sickly pallor, his frame bloated by it.

My loyalty loosens. Spencer's image intrudes, uninvited, detailed. His firm abs. His dark, skillfully trimmed waves. The leather tool belt slung low on his hips. Every detail floods back with perfect clarity.

I turn from Dominic, seeking solace in sleep. But my mind spins until Spencer finds me again—in my dreams.

Two

The day opens bright, the light air carries the sweetness of blossoms from the garden. Their colors blaze against spring's awakening.

The trees we planted glow with neon-green leaves, shimmering in the early sun. Branches sway like dancers in the breeze.

To the east, the mountains rise—vivid, rugged, and snow-capped against the sky. The lower slopes pulse with life, while the summits remain stark, clinging to the last traces of snow. No matter how often I see them, the Rockies always steal my breath.

Linda arrives a few minutes later, a grin lighting her face as she begins to chat about the day's lineup of adorable dogs we'll be grooming. Her enthusiasm is contagious, and we share a spark of joy over the little fur balls waiting to be pampered.

The soft jingle of the doorbell cuts into our chatter, signaling new visitors. A flutter stirs low in my belly as Spencer and Mike step into The Dog Shop. An unexpected surprise—but not unwelcome.

Blood climbs my cheeks. I smooth my smock, as if I can tame the restless energy building inside me.

Spencer's presence awakens something unfamiliar.

Mike ventures, his tone easy. "Mind if we steal a minute of your time?"

Spencer stands beside him, relaxed, his eyes flicking toward mine for a moment too long. Gravity tugs me toward him, but I break the stare, forcing composure into my face.

Linda and I exchange a glance. "Of course," she replies smoothly, as we step into the small foyer. The door closes softly behind us, muffling the cacophony of barking dogs and leaving a quiet, charged silence in their place.

I try to focus, but being this close to him unsettles my calm.

Mike exudes charm, his tone light and friendly, but there's an undercurrent of superiority that sharpens each word.

Spencer doesn't speak.

His silence carries a weight, a formality that's edged with arrogance. But it's more than that. There's a sharpness in his stance, in the way he's steering the moment. I can't tell if I'm intimidated by him—or drawn to him.

Either way, I feel out of place as the conversation flows around me.

Meanwhile, a single question loops. *Are they married?* I don't know why it matters—only that it does. I keep rehearsing ways to ask without sounding like a lovesick teenager with a crush.

Finally, as the conversation shifts from remodeling the shop to lighter banter, I gather the nerve.

"So... are either of you married?" I blurt, my tone light as I point between them, hoping the question lands without suspicion.

"Yes," they reply in unison.

Damn. The air rushes from my lungs before I can stop it. Just like that, the fantasy I barely allowed myself to entertain vanishes. The thought of running my hands over Spencer's rock-solid abs? *Gone.*

I recover quickly, masking the storm inside. "Do you have kids?" I ask next, my tone steadier than I feel.

Before they respond, my thoughts tumble.

Kids? That's a curve-ball I hadn't prepared for. A future I'd never imagined, certainly not one I ever intended.

"Yes," they say together.

"Two."

"Three."

They toss out the numbers simultaneously, so I can't decipher who said what. My brain scrambles to make sense of it.

Two kids... I could handle that. I clear my throat. *Three? Maybe that's manageable.*

Pointing to Mike, I ask, "So you're the one with three?" It makes sense, he looks years older than Spencer, so naturally I would assume the bigger family belongs to him.

He shakes his head, "No, I've got two."

My gaze flicks to Spencer. "Then you?"

Spencer, however, answers before I finish my thought. "Yes, three," he admits, his voice dipping deeper, as if fatherhood itself is stitched into his identity.

Spencer isn't just married, he's a father of three. There's no room in his life for the idle fantasies of a married girl like me.

He'll always be the unattainable landlord, distant, older, off-limits.

I force a polite smile as if this revelation doesn't send a pang of disappointment through my chest. Whatever fantasy I had entertained, however briefly, is nothing but a fleeting spark, one that should vanish as quickly as it flared.

But then I glance at him again, the sharp cut of his jaw, the brush of his skin against the deep navy of his shirt, and I *know it won't*.

The only way to chase the image away is to escape to my mountains, to lose myself in the trails until my mind is as clear as the sky.

Three

I drag myself home after a long, exhausting day at work, my body aching from hours of grooming and cleaning. It's been weeks since my last encounter with Spencer. I've tried not to think of him, yet I catch myself making subtle attempts to cross his path. I can't tell if I'm relieved or disappointed that he's been nowhere in sight.

I've developed a habit of glancing toward the far end of the building, where his HVAC company runs. But he's never there. With nearly 60,000 square feet across our businesses, finding him feels like searching for a ghost.

As I pull into my garage, watching the door creak open, I spot Dominic. One hand rests on his head while the other digs throughout the shelves, his movements sharp and restless. He looks frustrated. I approach cautiously, knowing anything I say could fuel his irritation, but hoping he'll soften.

"What are you searching for, Dom?"

"My fishing pole. I'm going fishing."

I ask lightly, "Can I come with you?"

"Nah, I'm good."

He slams the tacklebox down more forceful than necessary, the sharp clang of metal making me flinch.

An empty beer can lies on the ground; another sits on the shelf. My eyes catch on his hands instead, trying not to stare at the cans.

"Right," I say, backing away slowly.

His jaw tightens.

"Why do you always do this?" He scrubs a hand down the auburn shadow

THREE

on his jaw. "I say one thing and you twist it into something else."

"I—I didn't mean anything," I stammer. "I thought we could spend time together, we don't do that very much anymore."

He turns, his eyes fixed on me with a stare so cold it chills my blood. "I said I'm good. Don't push it, Sarah."

For a beat, we both go still. The energy shifts to sour, volatile.

It isn't disappointment curling in my gut.

It's danger.

I nod quickly and step back, my muscles locking tight, every instinct screaming to retreat before the storm inside him breaks.

But as I close the door behind me, a thought strikes: *Ugh, I forgot to change the laundry over at the shop.*

Needing space from Dominic, and not wanting the towels to smell sour in the morning, I grab the excuse and slip back out.

Hopefully he's gone by the time I return.

Once I arrive, I toss the towels in the dryer and lock up again.

Ready to head home, my luck takes a turn. Scanning the traffic for a safe crossing of the two-lane road that parallels the shop, a low growl of an engine throttle catches my attention.

Spencer.

He rounds the corner on a dark blue motorcycle, his chrome pipes gleaming under the fading sunlight.

Of course he has a motorcycle.

The sight of him, hands firm on the handlebars, body balanced with easy control, makes me seize up.

He slows, rolling up beside me at the curb. His eyes sweep the area in quick, calculated glances. As though secrecy is second nature.

Probably checking for Nick.

Nick, Mike's younger brother, recently moved back to Utah after years in Florida. He's the nicest guy in the building since Spencer took over. And yet, annoyingly, he's always around when you least expect it. At the shop.

In the lot. Even days I swear I haven't seen him go inside, somehow he's just... there. Watching, maybe. Or maybe that's just my imagination.

But right now... it's just me and Spencer.

Shit.

He can't see me like this, sweat, dog hair, and nerves.

Of all times for him to stop...

I fluster, seeing him lift his helmet off, revealing those piercing blue eyes and flowing waves. He tucks it under his arm.

"Are you off for the day?" he approaches.

"Am *I* off for the day?" I repeat back to him like an idiot. *Oh my gosh, who else would he be talking to?*

"I—yeah, I guess so." Leave it to me to stick my foot in my mouth.

"So... when are you going to take me for a ride on your bike?" My voice is playful, my heart pounds.

Spencer tilts his head, an amused smirk creeps across his lips. "Now, you know I can't do that. You've got to earn it."

A nervous laugh slips.

"Then maybe you should put me on the list to earn it," I manage with a playful banter. "Just one ride. That's all."

What the hell is wrong with me?

I'm shamelessly pressing, knowing exactly where it could lead.

"Careful what you ask for," he warns.

He leaves just enough hope dangling for me to cling to.

Before I can respond, he slides his helmet back on, revs the engine, and disappears in a blur of leather and chrome.

I stand rooted, air caught in my throat, my fingers twitching a faint wave goodbye.

I can't stop the image from blooming. *What if I'd climbed on that bike?*

My arms snug around his waist.

My palms spread across his abs.

Maybe more.

I swallow, a tingling sensation rising up my neck. I surprise myself by crooning under my breath: *"Next time."*

Four

Linda and I decided to expand our dog grooming shop into a full-fledged boarding business. Mike and Spencer have been working closely with Linda to map out the logistics. We're gaining more indoor space to board dogs, and the most exciting addition is the outdoor dog park.

An artesian well runs beneath our building, and we've chosen to incorporate the stream into the outdoor area. It'll keep the dogs cool in the summer, offering fresh, moving water to drink and play in, an oasis for our four-legged guests.

We're making progress on the fencing. Linda, my brother Shane, tall and broad-shouldered but quiet as ever, and my sister Amber are measuring, digging, and setting posts. Amber is the classic middle child: quick to joke and fill the silence. Always determined to be noticed in the shuffle. Her strawberry-blonde ponytail is silky as she tosses it back with a grin, like she's on stage.

"Hold it straight, Shane," she teases, tilting the tape measure in his hand.

"It is straight," he grumbles.

"Not from this angle," Amber insists, her voice full of mock authority. She glances at me with a wink. "Tell him, Sarah."

Shane exhales, muttering something under his breath, but adjusts it anyway. Linda laughs, shaking her head. "Alright, enough bickering. How long should the fence line be?"

Shane squints down the stretch of ground. "Hundred feet, give or take."

Amber cuts in, "A hundred and twenty. Dogs need space to run, not shuffle."

"A hundred and ten, then," Linda mediates, already pulling a pencil from behind her ear to mark down.

Their chatter drifts as they move toward the far end of the yard, still debating measurements.

I spot Spencer near a trailer, and with them preoccupied, I seize my chance. I drift from the group.

Trying to sound laid-back, I ask him, "What are you up to?"

Without hesitation, he says, "Getting ready to take my mistress camping." *What?*

I blink. "Your mistress?"

I don't believe I misinterpreted him. It wasn't a slip, it was a test. An invitation. My mind, like kindling, catches instantly.

I force a friendly tone, suppressing the sear rising in my chest.

He smirks, an unfamiliar chuckle escaping him. "No, I'm going scouting, for deer, gotta get an early start."

"Cool, well, that sounds like fun. Have a great trip," I offer, keeping the rest locked behind my teeth.

He subtly signals his need to finish packing.

I don't know much about hunting, except that my husband goes on a week-long trip every year. I guess Spencer goes hunting for at least a week each year, too.

I don't stick around. I can't. Not if I'm going to play this right.

Even as I turn to walk away, desire weighs heavy. *I need him to notice me.*

We finish work at the dog park and I head back to the condo I bought a few months ago. Home.

I signed the papers this spring, wishing Dominic had been there but he wasn't. He's checked out of everything that matters.

When I open the front door, I'm hit by the clean, still-new aroma of the place. But something feels off—Dominic's here. He shouldn't be.

"Why aren't you at work?" I question, with unmasked surprise.

He answers too quick, too rehearsed. "We finished early today."

Tension rises. Same excuse. Same smooth words. I sense it in my gut—he's lying again.

Maybe he's always been this way. Or maybe I've refused to see it. But one thing I know now, Dominic lies. Trust has been eroding for some time. Yet, I stay.

I remind myself he's a good man in many ways. I've done everything I can to overlook his faults, to shove down the doubts that have crept into every corner of our marriage.

But the voice in my head, the one I use to convince myself to stay, is growing fainter with each passing day.

Dominic and I eat dinner, trading hollow small talk neither of us cares about. His words are flat. We move past the motions like strangers sharing a table.

He pushes his food around the plate more than he eats it.

"Long day, huh?" I question.

He mutters, his eyes fixed on his plate. "Same as always."

"Did the job finish early? You said you'd be home late."

His fork scrapes the plate. "We wrapped it up early."

The glow from the TV flickers across his face from the other room, softening the edges I've grown used to hardening against. His hands are clasped on the table, not in prayer, but tight, like he's holding himself together by sheer will.

When his eyes meet mine, they aren't sharp or accusing. They're tired. Lost.

"I don't sleep anymore," he admits, voice low, as if saying it too loud might make it real. "Every time I close my eyes, I see bills piling up... and me failing you."

My throat stings. Vulnerability isn't something Dominic gives away.

"You're not failing me," I say, shaking my head. "We'll figure this out together."

I lay my fork down and cross the space between us, resting a hand on his shoulder. He still doesn't lean in, doesn't reach for me, but he doesn't shrug me off either. For one suspended heartbeat, it feels like maybe we're still on the same team.

Then, just as quickly, he drags a hand over his face and pulls back into himself. "Forget I said anything. I'll figure it out." His tone clips shut again, back to the Dominic I know.

The reflection of that moment, the crack in his armor, sits with us as we finish dinner in silence.

Afterward, I shower, letting the scorch of the water burn away more than just the day. The steam fogs over the mirror, blurring my reflection until I can't tell who I'm supposed to be anymore, the wife who yearns for her husband's vulnerability, or the woman who can't stop picturing another man's touch.

When I slip into bed, Dominic reaches for me. It feels less like want, more like habit.

His hands are on me, but his eyes are far away.

So are mine.

"Dominic," I whisper, searching his face. "Is your mind here, in this marriage?"

He lays a kiss against my neck. "I'm here."

An intrusive thought pulls me from the moment.

Spencer's voice plays on a loop—

Getting ready to take my mistress camping.

Dominic slowly releases his breath, pulling me closer. "You're so quiet. What's wrong with you?"

"What do you want me to say?" My voice sharpens despite myself. "That I feel miles away from you even when you're right here?"

His jaw tightens. "You always twist things. Can't we just... be normal for one night?"

I want to. Damn it, I want to.

My fingers tangle in Dominic's thick auburn curls, but I imagine Spencer's inky—almost black waves. As my hand trails lower, I find him and stroke him gently, picturing a man I've never touched, a body I've only imagined.

He groans before climbing on top of me, moving inside with mundane

FOUR

rhythm.

I stay silent, he's never liked the sound of moaning.

I try—*fuck, I try*, to keep my thoughts tethered here. But they slip back to Spencer. His nearness. His dominance.

Dominic's touch is too soft, too familiar, sparking no fire within me.

Disappointment pools low and heavy as my arousal fades.

"I can't," I whisper, pushing him away gently.

For a moment, he pauses, staring across me. Then he rolls onto his back without a word. He doesn't ask why. He doesn't care to know. His breathing evens out, heavy with drink, already drifting. Maybe that's the only mercy in all of this, his drinking makes moments like this easier to escape.

I lie beside him, wide awake. Shame burns but so does desire.

Spencer has already taken root in places I swore belonged to only Dominic.

Five

I recently had a photo shoot for my nineteenth birthday, after winning a drawing from a local photographer. As a bonus, I included my dog, Evie, because leaving her out would feel like leaving out a piece of myself.

She's cloud-like and cuddly, with her creamy curls framing a permanent little smile. She's my constant companion, following me to the shop every day and keeping the dogs in line.

Now that my photos are back, an idea has been simmering, something bold, reckless, even.

Spencer has another scouting trip coming up.

We've shared a few glances, a handful of words, and one more failed attempt to get on his motorcycle. But this... might change that.

I've put together a small care package: jerky, candy, and a few daring shots from the photo session.

Tucked between the harmless snacks, the photos show me leaning against the frame of a motorcycle, one foot on the peg, and an arm draped on the handlebar. My golden hair sharpened in the light, my body aligned just right, my gaze locked on the lens, carrying intent. Suggestive without being explicit. Enough to resonate in his mind.

I don't know how he'll react. That's part of the thrill. The trepidation. The possibility.

Hopefully, this gives me the perfect excuse to get him alone and have a quiet moment to hand over the package and let the gesture speak louder than words.

FIVE

I step through the sliding door onto the patio. The smell of smoke and charred meat hangs in the air.

"Smells delicious." I say, forcing lightness. "What's for dinner?"

Dominic stands at the grill, a wedding gift from my brother James, flipping burgers without looking at me. His stance is slack, his movements mechanical. The tongs clink against the grate in a weary rhythm.

I don't waste time. "Are you happy?"

He pauses. "Sure," he says, finally. "Aren't you?"

It's not an answer; it's a deflection, tossed back at me like a challenge.

"That's not what I asked. I want to know if you're happy Dominic."

Only then does he glance over, clouded, like he's surfaced from a fog.

His voice says *yes*. His eyes say *no*.

And I know the truth: he isn't happy.

But, neither am I.

Sometimes, when I'm at church and I catch myself staring at the other Mormon girls, the ones who never seem to falter. Their hair pinned neatly, their dresses pressed, arms linking as they head toward the chapel like they belong there, radiant with certainty. A feeling of refinement I've never had.

That should be me. And what's more...

I should be stepping through temple doors, claiming the life I was told to want, the life that was supposed to make me whole. But instead, I'm here, in a marriage that feels thinner by the day, with questions I don't dare voice out loud.

It's not just about Dominic. It's about me. About the distance between who I was raised to be and the woman I'm becoming, restless, caught in the crossfire of shame and desire.

Six

Days later, Spencer rolls in on his motorcycle, looking like sin in leather. He's wearing his vintage jacket, cream stripes running down the sleeves. The man knows exactly what he is doing. Every time he pulls up to the shop, it's like he owns the world, and damn it, I notice.

I test the waters again, nudging for a ride, but he doesn't take the bait.

Instead, he does something unexpected. He steps closer, eyes dark with intent.

"Come on," he says, voice low and enticing. "I want to show you something."

He waits, giving me a chance to refuse, but I don't.

"I think you'll like it," he adds, the corner of his mouth curving, "It's quieter, in there." He signals toward the building.

The invitation landing somewhere between a challenge and a promise. I blink once, pulse hammering, and follow.

I let him lead.

"I've never been unfaithful," I whisper, unsure if I'm saying it to him or myself.

Spencer stops and brushes his fingers under my chin. His mouth tightens, the hint of a smirk tugging at one corner as though he's fighting some private thought. His brows lift, amusement shadowing his face before he reins it back.

"Not yet, but you're here with me, aren't you? Begging me to test you."

Heat creeps up the back of my neck.

He tilts his head, studying me with an expression that feels equal parts knowing and amused, as if he's already counted me among the guilty. "Besides," he adds, "thinking about it is almost the same as doing it. Don't tell me you haven't thought about it."

"I have," I admit, with a small voice, "but the only thing I've ever cheated on was a history test in the eleventh grade."

"I'd say it's been too long then." He dares me before continuing to guide me.

This hunger for him, a man I barely know, is shaking everything I thought I believed.

I know it's wrong. I know I should turn back. But it's too late. I'm with him, now.

The building stretches around us, dark, vast and foreign; the air hangs damp with musk and faint gasoline. A slow, rhythmic drip echoes in the distance, water falling on concrete, pooling in the silence.

Every step sounds louder than it should, bouncing off the stripped walls, like an abandoned museum.

I question—*is this real?*

Then, Spencer stops and turns.

His eyes lock on mine, and suddenly I can't breathe.

I can't do this. I can't cheat. But fuck, I'm starving for this.

My willpower splinters the moment he reaches for me.

His touch is electric, igniting something primal inside.

"I should go," I whisper.

But I don't.

He consumes me.

His strong, work-roughened hands—built for labor, not tenderness, find my waist.

He lifts me like I weigh nothing, settling me onto something I don't recognize at first. But then the narrow, flat vinyl, is cool through my shorts. The solid shape beneath me isn't a bench or a ledge. It's a machine. The back of a four-wheeler. The sensation jars loose a memory of mud, engine noise, and Dominic. But I ignore it. I can't let it intrude now.

Tension crackles between us, reckless and consuming.

He's everywhere.

His hands slide up my flanks, over my chest, and cradle my face. Claiming me before his lips meet mine.

"May I?" He asks, his voice, careful.

My heart hammers into my ribs. I speak a quiet, "Yes."

* * *

SPENCER

Her eyes hold mine. Unflinching. She doesn't move away.

She's the sin I shouldn't taste. The thought is sharp, immediate, but it shatters on contact with her. With the way she looks at me. Like I'm something more than I am.

My hands lift her petite body while inside I'm unraveling. She stiffens, then yields. That's all it takes. A moment so small, it feels like the ground giving way beneath my feet.

I lower my voice, barely holding together. "May I?"

Her answer is almost a whisper. "Yes."

The word ends everything I've been resisting. The chains I've carried snap clean off.

I lower my mouth to hers.

The kiss is wildfire after lightning, splitting me wide open. She tastes like something I'll crave until the day I die. Her mouth is soft, her breath sultry, her skin carrying the faint scent of vanilla. Ordinary to anyone else. Unforgettable to me.

Her fingers clutch my shirt, drawing me closer. And fuck, her cool touch feels like surrender, but I'm the one undone. The feel of her is a revelation. She's smaller than me, yet in this moment she holds all the power.

The last of my discipline breaks.

I know—whatever this is, I'll chase it until it kills me.

SIX

***

SARAH

Our mouths collide, gentle, unhurried. Like they were always meant to connect.

Heat pulses as his mouth parts, inviting me deeper, consuming me whole.

Another man's lips.

A first.

Damn, it's thrilling.

His mouth is molten, tender, and cinnamon-laced.

His tongue grazes mine, a tremor races down my spine.

Is this my real-life romance-novel moment?

My fingers trail up, finding his jaws sharp angles, rough skin. *A man.*

This is my first real opportunity to feel him, flesh and heat and everything forbidden.

And now I know: his skin, the sharp cut of his cheekbones, the firmness of him pressing into me.

Dominic's name flashes at the edge of my mind, a shadow trying to rise.

But I silence it away, keeping this moment sacred.

I won't waste this chance to see what lives beyond the confines of my marriage.

And suddenly, the thought slams into me:

I'm married to a boy.

All this time, I've been waiting for Dominic to become the man I've needed. But hoping has only wasted my time. *Because this, Spencer, is what I've been craving.*

I wrap my legs around his waist, pulling him closer. His body leans solid into mine.

His hands brush over my chest again, this time lingering just enough to drive me mad.

The first touch had been *too* quick. Too fleeting.
I need to feel the weight of his desire, every bit as much as I feel my own.
Our mouths move in perfect rhythm.
Time warps, stretching endlessly. My breath shakes.
I've had a taste, now I can't stop.

The room narrows to him, the consistent drip of water somewhere far away, irrelevant.

Reality crashes back in.
I whisper, "I'd better go... we're going to get caught."
Spencer smirks, his lips still damp from mine. "Until next time?"
"I'll be waiting," I rasp, breathless.
Before I can react, his mouth finds the curve of my neck, dragging his lips along my skin.
His hands grip my hips, removing me from the ATV with ease.
My legs clamp around him on instinct.
He carries me a few steps, his movements confident.
When he sets me down, my back hits the cold, rough brick.
Wasting no time, his hands pin mine above my head, fingers locked tight.
He drives into me, solid, demanding.
He towers over me, and I feel impossibly fragile.
I'm completely at his mercy.
Even through the barrier of his pants the relentless grind of him is intoxicating.
If he kept going a minute longer, I might come undone right here. I arch toward him instinctively.
This is wrong. But I don't pull away. I don't reach for him.
I simply let him lead.
Then suddenly, he lets me go.
The absence of his touch is jarring.

My hands fall to my sides. I could walk away.

But I don't.
I don't want to.
I need to stay here, lost in this moment, and him.
But I know—it has to end.

His mouth skims over my ear with a whisper meant only for me.
"Careful, Sarah. Next time, I won't stop."
Breathless, I challenge him, "Maybe next time I won't let you."

I wipe the taste of him from my lips, smoothing down my disheveled hair. My hands tremble as I adjust my shorts, grounding me in the reality of what just happened.
He steps into the open air first, his exit practiced.
He slips outside without another word.
I stay a moment longer, waiting for the space to fill between us.

Seven

Summer 2004

Spencer leaves for another scouting trip tonight.

I catch him out by his truck, the tailgate down, a spread of gear already stacked in neat rows—rolled sleeping bag, worn boots with the laces loosely lying. He moves with purpose, every item checked and re-checked, like there's no room for mistakes out there.

"I almost forgot," I say, holding out the small care package.

He pauses mid-motion, hand still on the cooler he'd been about to slide in. His brows lift, and then he takes the package from me, fingers brushing mine.

"What's this?"

"Snacks. And... a surprise."

His mouth softens, the hard edge slipping for a moment. "Appreciate it. Now I can't wait to see what's inside."

I'm hoping, the small surprise I tucked inside will keep him thinking, wondering, about the possibility of me.

While he's away, I try to keep busy, errands, grocery shopping, anything, to keep my mind from wandering too far.

Still, unease curls in my gut. Dominic's been off work again, a pattern I don't understand, but can't ignore. And now things in the house are vanishing.

It first happened before we got married. Small items disappeared, unex-

SEVEN

plained. Then it stopped. Until now.

At first, I chalked it up to forgetfulness. A misplaced twenty-dollar bill, a bottle of medication.

But lately, it's been happening too often. I'm not losing things.

They're *disappearing*.

Today's missing item?

My silver charm bracelet.

Linda gave it to me when I was little, adding a new charm every time she traveled. Tiny pieces of her adventures strung together, wrapped around my wrist.

I never leave it lying around. And yet, it's gone.

I think I'm going to be sick when realization dawns; there's only one common thread.

The missing items.

The timing.

The silence.

Once early in our marriage, the house we rented was ransacked, torn apart, while I was at church with my dad.

At the time, I believed what Dominic told me: that it had been a random break-in. But now, as the missing pieces start falling into place, the memory doesn't sit right.

A seed of suspicion blooms into something darker.

It was him.

My husband.

The man who vowed to love and protect me has been the one terrorizing me all along.

I didn't see it then. But now? The signs are too loud to ignore.

Dominic isn't only an alcoholic; he's something far more threatening.

A man who blacks out and forgets the damage he causes. A man who weaponizes suicidal threats to trap me in a marriage I no longer want to be in.

I can't leave him. Not only because of my vows.

But because if I do—
He says he'll end his own life.
He reminds me of this often.

Needing to talk to someone, I pick up the phone and call Maya.

It rings enough times that I almost hang up, but then she answers in her perfectly pitched, feminine voice.

"Hello."

"Hey, Maya," I say, trying not to let the frustrated quiver be noticed.

But she instantly notices.

"Sar." Her tone sharpens. "Your voice... what's wrong?"

"Everything." I press a hand to my forehead. "Dominic's barely working. The lies, the drinking, the way he manipulates me. And now... I think he's been stealing from me."

Stunned silence. "Stealing?"

"Yeah. My bracelet's gone. The one Linda gave me when I was little. I never leave it lying around."

"It's him. It's always been him." Her certainty confirms my feelings.

"I know." My throat tightens.

"How long do you think this has been happening?"

"For years." I sink against the sliding glass door. "I even tried putting him on a strike system. Three strikes and I'd leave. But the strikes weren't small infractions. They were serious. Getting blackout drunk. Calling me a bitch. And now stealing. And still... I've stayed."

Her voice lowers, almost bitter. "Because he promised to change. But promises don't mean anything, Sar. Not from him."

"I see that now."

"So tell me... if you're done with Dominic, what do you plan to do?"

"...Spencer." I whisper his name before I can stop myself.

"Spencer?" she sounds shocked. "Another man?"

"He's not just another man." I say, maybe a little defensive. "He's my new landlord."

She laughs. "Your landlord? You're insane, but you have to tell me the details."

"He's strikingly attractive. Older. Married. With... children." The words nearly choke me.

"You can't be serious."

My fingers twist the hem of my shirt. "I can't explain why I'm so pulled into him."

"This is crazy. Do you hear yourself?"

"I know. And yet, I can't stop comparing him to Dominic. He is everything I'm not supposed to want."

"Sarah..." Her voice softens, weighted with worry. "Your excitement for Spencer can be heard through the phone and you're fear of marriage with Dominic is present at the same time. Which one's louder?"

"I'm scared of what I'm becoming." My chest tightens. "I wish I could be fully invested in my marriage. But Dominic's hard to be with, and part of me wants Spencer." I pause, reflecting on the first moment he touched me. "I... I hate that I want him so much."

"You've just been surviving." She exhales into the phone, firm now. "You deserve to feel alive again, even if it's messy. Messy means you're breathing."

"Yeah, but feeling alive shouldn't feel like I'm burning everything down."

"Sometimes things have to burn before you can build anything new." She pauses, then her tone's light, teasing. "And for the record? If he's half as good-looking as you say, I need to meet this man for myself."

A laugh escapes me despite everything. "Come over. I'll tell you everything."

"Perfect." I can hear the smile in her voice.

Eight

Spencer's due back any moment, and I'm counting down the hours.

He never gave me exact details. He hardly said a word before he left.

He doesn't owe me anything, but I wish he had at least told me what day to expect him.

He said about a week. It's Monday now—which means his work week is waiting for him.

I don't see him on lunch break, but I hang onto hope that he'll show up before the day ends.

The hours crawl.

The thought of him gone a week—living a life outside of mine—gnaws at me in ways I can't explain.

And then, as I'm leaving for the night, I see him.

He's on the sidewalk outside my shop, approaching me.

My pulse spikes, nerves flaring.

He looks striking. Too good. And suddenly, my confidence falters.

I push through it. "How was your trip?"

"It was great."

"Did you take your mistress?" I tease, testing the waters.

He laughs, "Yeah, she ended up in my candy."

I blink confused, until I realize what he means. The photos I'd tucked between the snacks. A secret thrill rushes through me at the thought of him finding them.

"Joking aside, I went with my buddy, Ken."

EIGHT

"Sounds like it was a fun trip."

I grin, unsure why I suddenly feel like I should've been there.

Maybe if I were the mistress, he would've had more fun.

Neither of us knows quite how to carry the conversation from here—until he cuts straight through the silence.

"Why don't you meet me here later? I'll show you what I do with my mistresses."

Caught off guard, I question him.

"Where did that come from?" My voice is sharper than I intend. "You wouldn't dare."

"I would, and I will." The weight of his words settles between us, thick and unshakable.

"Okay then," I breathe, a buzz tickling me inside. "See you at eight-thirty tonight."

This is my chance.

The fact that we're both in committed relationships makes it feel safe... and infinitely more lethal.

The possibility hangs heavy, that we could be entangled in lives that no longer feel like ours, caught somewhere between what's right and what we *want*.

He looks me in the eyes, holding my gaze with quiet intensity—no teasing to be noticed.

Only certainty.

"I'll be here." It sounds like a promise.

"Okay," I say, turning to head in the opposite direction, like it's no big deal. As if I'm only joking.

There's no actual *way* I'm going to meet him tonight. I tell myself that because it's true.

"See you later," I toss my hair over my shoulder.

His voice follows me, soft and sure. "You sure will."

I hold my kitchen barstool with my foot, running the paintbrush along the slat. Maya eyes me suspiciously over the rim of her brush.

"You've been wandering around like you've got a secret," she says, "spill it."

I pause, my brush hovering over the wood. "It's nothing."

"Nothing?" Maya arches a brow. "Sarah, I know you. What's the secret?"

"Okay." I bite down on my smile. "The guys at the shop started calling me something new."

Her brush stops mid-stroke. "Okay, now I need to hear this."

"Princess."

Maya's mouth drops open. "Princess? You?"

I nod, my cheeks warming. "I guess that's the name being thrown around. Nick, Spencer's employee, told me that's what they all call me. My window shades say 'princess,' and since they didn't know my real name, they just... stuck with it."

Her grin widens. "Honestly, I kind of love it."

"But that's not the secret I've been dying to tell you." My cheeks flush hotter, a mix of heat and fear. "He kissed me, Maya. And it wasn't just a kiss, it felt like my life's changed forever. It's like he saw me in a way no one else ever has."

She sets her brush down, eyes shining. "And you're only telling me this now? Sarah!"

I duck my head, brushing with careful strokes just to keep my hands busy. "I know. I probably shouldn't even smile about it. But when his lips touched mine," my voice dips lower, shaky, "it was fire."

Maya lets out a low whistle, shaking her head like she can't believe what she's hearing. "Fire? Sarah, you've been holding out on me."

I giggle nervously, dipping my brush back into the paint. "I know it's wrong. I shouldn't even want this."

"Please," she says, rolling her eyes, "you're grinning like a teenager who just got kissed behind the bleachers. Don't tell me it didn't mean something."

"It meant... everything. Like for one second the rest of the world just disappeared."

EIGHT

Her brush slows, and she studies me. "Then don't downplay it. You deserve to feel that. Even if it scares you."

I glance away, tracing strokes along the stool leg, afraid she'll see too much in my face. "Scared is an understatement."

She nudges me with her foot. "Yeah, well, sometimes the best things are the ones that terrify us. Just promise me you'll be smart about it."

"I'll try," I admit, though the memory of his lips makes "smart" feel impossible.

We fall into silence, the rhythm of paint brushes sliding up and down on wood fill the kitchen. By the time the last barstool is drying, our hands are streaked with color and our cheeks ache from laughter we didn't mean to share. For a while, it almost feels like I'm allowed to hope again.

Nine

I've been buried, caught up in the never-ending renovation of the new boarding shop and Spencer's most likely been busy too.

Tonight, after hours, I'm caring for a few boarding dogs. We're running a soft launch for a few of our favorite clients, a trial run of the overnight service. Since we don't groom on weekends, the days blur into late nights more often than I care to admit.

The shop door swings open, releasing a wave of August swelter that clings as I step outside.

The sky bleeds color as the sun kisses the mountains goodnight.

I pause, breathing it in. Savoring the quiet moment before I head to my car.

Then, out of the corner of my eye, I spot Spencer's truck.

My breath stutters, pulse catching. After two months, just the sight of it is enough to make me nervous.

My feet pause on the curb before I veer down the sidewalk, drawn toward the back end of the old, red brick building.

When I round the corner, I catch him as he's closing a door behind him.

"Hey you."

The words tumble out. Too loud, too eager.

Spencer jolts, his body tense as his eyes snap to mine.

"You scared the hell out of me."

I bite my lip, barely holding in a laugh. "Well... that was hilarious."

He exhales sharply, shaking his head.

"Yeah, for you maybe."

Silence settles and his gaze locks on me, steady, like he's searching for something I'm unable to give. I shift my weight from one foot to the other, suddenly aware the space between us is exposed—waiting to be broken—and how desperate I am to close it.

"Sorry, I didn't mean to scare you," I say, tilting my head. "What have you been up to? I haven't seen you around."

"Why did you stand me up that night? You know, the one we were supposed to meet up?"

His tone is neutral, but his eyes tighten.

I study him closely, unsure if he's serious.

"I didn't know you were serious," I admit, forcing a grin. "Honestly, I thought we were teasing."

"*Of course we were,*" he says, but there's a sharpness under the words.

Guilt stings. "I'm sorry, I didn't realize..." I stall, unable to form words. Then I introduce the idea again, "How about tomorrow night—let's say nine?"

His jaw sets. "Why? So I can get stood up again?" His arms cross, his expression intense.

I rush to explain, panic brewing on the inside.

"I'm sorry," I blurt, stumbling over my apology. "I didn't know. But I do now. Tomorrow night, I'll be there. No excuses."

He tries to keep his response nonchalant, but doubt shadows his voice. "Maybe."

I step closer, lowering mine. "Don't make it a maybe. Make it a promise."

He raises a brow. "Alright, Princess. I promise." His voice dips lower. "But you better show up... because I'm not letting you off easy this time."

And for a second, I see a little flicker of hope in his eyes.

I thought it was me who had been anxiously awaiting.

But maybe... maybe he's been waiting, too.

The day crawls.

Every moment stretches under the weight of what's waiting for me tonight.

As I groom my customers' dogs, my thoughts drift to the moment we'll meet.

Will I taste the cinnamon on his lips again?

Will he kiss me with the same urgency, the same hunger? Or will he pull away—punishing me for standing him up?

The idea unsettles me. If he doesn't chase me, *will I have the courage to chase him?*

The barking of dogs fades into the background, a dull buzz against the storm in my head.

Linda chatters beside me, oblivious to the tangled mess I'm creating for myself.

Her daughter has her own drama chasing after the new landlord. A possible disaster waiting to happen.

I almost laugh at the irony.

"Never mix business with pleasure," they say.

But here I am, longing for something wild.

Linda and I keep it light. Business. Dogs. The possibility of hiring extra help.

She listens when I vent about Dominic, his laziness, his disappearing acts. She agrees with my concerns. And yet we both know the truth: I'm not going to leave him.

She's supportive. She doesn't judge. But she doesn't know about Spencer, and maybe she never will.

For now, Spencer and I exist in a solitary stolen moment of passion. A spark suspended in one perfect moment of tension. A kiss.

Nothing significant has even happened.

Maybe it never will.

Maybe *it shouldn't.*

I don't want to ruin his marriage.

I don't even know what his marriage really *is.*

NINE

And yet... I can't stop thinking about him.
About us.
About what it all could mean.

Ten

After an entire day of debating, I finally settle on my excuse.

"I'm heading out. I'll be back later," I say quickly, already halfway to the door.

I chose the easiest lie: nails.

As expected, Dominic stirs from the couch, his expression is glazed over in a drunken haze; he doesn't meet my eyes. He just stares at the TV. "Why the fuck are you getting your nails done so late?" His voice has bite but is lazy, still refusing eye contact.

I don't engage.

"I'll be back later," I repeat.

He hears me. He just doesn't care. So I leave him to his too-loud commercials.

I slip out the door, closing it behind me with a quiet click, and take a deep breath.

Freedom brushes past me. Quick.

Weightless.

My car waits in the garage, the engine cool.

My body trembles.

Adrenaline fires within my veins, my grip tightening around the gearshift.

The familiar feel of it in my hand is oddly grounding, a small anchor against the storm inside me.

The reality of what I'm about to do lands heavy on me like a hammer.

Am I prepared for this?

TEN

To cheat. To lie. To fall.

My mind spins, but my desire speaks louder.

I don't think. I move.

My body overrules my mind, commanding every move.

I press the button. The garage door groans as I reverse, the decision already made somewhere deep inside me.

I shift into first, pressing the gas pedal, as if accelerating will leave my conscience behind.

A sharp right takes me out of my condo complex, and I head south; bypassing second gear, I push into third. The city blurs past, darkness swallowing the streets.

On any other night, the eerie quiet would rattle me, but the low-crime neighborhood and security system guarding the dogs ease some of my tension.

No lights glow from inside the building—only the dull halo of a single streetlamp over the two-lane road.

I slow near the shop, creeping along the side until I reach the dog park in the back.

Pulling into the farthest corner, I hide my car from view.

The last thing I need is Spencer's business partner, Mike, or anyone for that matter, spotting me and asking questions.

I cut the engine and let myself breathe.

My eyes drift to Spencer's Chevy Silverado.

It's the kind of truck I'd expect an old man to drive, boxy, longer than I'd ever find attractive, but undeniably masculine.

Like him.

My fingers rest on the door handle before I slip out as quietly as I can, shutting the door with a near-silent click.

Gravel crunches beneath my five-dollar flip-flops.
With each step, suspense cinches tighter.

Tonight, everything changes.

Thirty paces in, I stop at Spencer's office door.
I lift my hand to knock, and the door creeps open, as if some unseen force is waiting.
I step inside.
My breath hitching.
Wow.
The door closes behind me. The sound barely louder than my heartbeat.
He's shed the crisp shirt from earlier, still in dark slacks, skin lit by desk lamp.
I'm disarmed by his provocation, dressed in restraint; for a moment, it feels like the whole office bends toward him.

This isn't what I pictured. Not at all.

The office is nothing like the old red brick exterior suggests.
It's massive and pristine. A towering picture window dominates the front wall, filtering in the glow of the street lamp outside.
The lambent haze drapes the room in shadow, softening every clean line.
A pale loveseat sits poised against the far wall. To my left, an executive desk—sleek, wooden, yet effortlessly timeless, anchoring the room. Underfoot, old pallet planks, carefully refinished, their worn texture telling silent stories.

He leads me toward a staircase swallowed in shadow. The steps ascend steeply, vanishing into the unknown above.
As we climb all thirty-two stairs, the room below fades, each turn winding me deeper into something unnamed. My pulse accelerates with every step. *Where is he taking me? And why does the question sit in my stomach like pleasure*

TEN

rather than fear?

We reach the top. Before I can gather my thoughts, Spencer moves, swift and resolute.

In an instant, he turns me in his arms, pressing my back against the nearest wall. His touch ignites. His mouth, a mark I'll never forget. No second-guessing. He claims me in a way that tells me he's been thinking of doing this again, for too long.

The taste of cinnamon explodes on my tongue, mingling with the faintest trace of something uniquely him.

My sheer blouse is no barrier to his touch. His strong, calloused hands slide up the delicate fabric with ease, leaving lines of fire in their path.

His right hand finds its way to my back, and with a swift snap of the clasp, my white bra gives way.

How the hell did he do that?

He's smooth. Experienced. Powerful. Dominant.

This isn't fumbling—this is a man who *knows*. Who *takes*. Who *claims*.

And I let him.

Eleven

In a whirlwind, Spencer yanks my top over my head, the fabric fluttering to the floor like a scene from a movie. *He must watch a lot of rom-coms — or maybe he just knows exactly what he's doing.*

My hair spills over me like silk, veiling the swell of my breasts though the tips press forward through the strands.

Cool air skims over my bare skin, sending a chill rippling through me — not only from the sudden change of temperature, but from the way Spencer takes me.

Hunger simmers in his gaze as he nudges me into the wall. His solid frame holding me in place.

His hands move with intention, sweeping my hair aside, exposing my bare my chest, inch by inch.

His fingers trace my curves, cupping the soft weight of my breasts. A deep, satisfied sound rumbles in his chest as he presses them together.

He lowers his mouth, parting his lips to take both hardened peaks at once. A gasp escapes me as I arch into him. His tongue flicks, teases — *devours*.

"You look at me like that again," Spencer growls, his breath hot against my skin, "and I'll ruin you for anyone else." He drops to his knees, the site of it sending a charge into me.

"You've been under my skin all day," he rasps, the words low, certain — like a truth he can't contain.

My cheeks burn with desire as his hand glides past my navel, fingers grazing above my waistband.

With another masterful flick of two fingers, my jeans loosen, the button undone as if he's done it a thousand times.

"Say my name," he commands, voice rough and dark. "Say it, or I stop."

"Spencer…" a breathless whisper ghosts through the air.

"Louder," he demands.

"Spencer." I repeat, with more power.

But as he moves to lower, I catch his hands, guiding him back up to my chest.

His eyes flicker up, searching, uncertain, asking.

I trail my fingers along his jaw, pulling him in.

Our lips hover close, breath colliding, hesitation knotting around me like a vice.

What am I doing?

Months of stolen glances, secret thoughts, restless nights infused with fantasies of *this very moment,* and yet, now that it's happening, I'm forced to pull back.

Did I think we could stop at a kiss?

Set ourselves on fire, and walk away unscathed?

Desire wars with reason.

It's not guilt.

It's timing—the worst kind.

I kiss him harder, pouring everything into the way our bodies fit.

His hands roam, exploring me, striking parts that have always been dormant.

But beneath the fire is a flicker of dread, not emotional, not about us—physical. A reminder. My body won't let me forget.

"There's something you should know."

My fingers curl around his waistband, pulling him closer. I don't want to kill the mood. But I need him to know.

"I'm… it's that time of the month."

I don't step away. I don't break the spell.

The words sit between us, fragile. A part of me braces, afraid this will be the thing that pushes him back, that he'll see me differently, less desirable.

That this truth will make him step away.

My cheeks burn as I add quickly, voice trembling but firm: "That doesn't mean I want to stop."

His teeth graze my ear, his voice a husky growl, "Good... because I've been starving for you, and I won't let you go until I've had every last taste."

I guide his hands to my hips, drawing him in, needing him to feel how badly I still want this—want *him*.

And when he doesn't flinch, relief crashes through me, loosening something tight inside.

My fingers fumble with the button of his slacks, my confidence slipping when it refuses to budge. I let out a frustrated laugh. He smirks, amused by my struggle, until my persistence finally wins. I pop it open, feeling the fabric loosening beneath my touch.

And still, I hesitate.

Only because reality, annoyingly, has its limits.

Sensing my pause, he pulls back just enough to search my face.

"I'm sure." I whisper.

Pushing his pants lower, letting them drop to his ankles. He steps back, removing them and his loafers in one fluid motion. Now, standing before me in nothing but his briefs, he looks powerful.

He tips me backward, lowering me onto the floor with surprising grace. The moment my back hits the plushness beneath me, I register the contrast—unexpected comfort against the tension coiling inside.

My hands skim the fabric, velvet beneath my palms.

"Is this?" I manage, momentarily distracted by the sensation.

"Yes, Sarah, it is." He breathes my name against my neck and I can't think.

He explores, mapping my curves with reverent hands. His kisses leaving invisible ink across my skin. When his fingers inch my pants lower, I flinch.

I already told him once, quietly, hoping he'd take the hint, but he didn't.

He pauses now, voice thick. "Why not?"

"I told you earlier."

His tone shifts, curious, concerned.

There's a stillness, then a nod, understanding dawning in his eyes.

ELEVEN

"Right... gotcha. Let me take you to the restroom."

Rising with a quiet resolve, he extends his arms, lifting me upright.

"I should have listened before," he offers. "I'm sorry."

Not needing more, I pull my pants back up, instinctively wrapping my arms over my chest, suddenly aware of how exposed I feel.

At the bottom of the stairs, he directs me with a gentle touch down an extended, dark hall. Finally, a small placard bearing the silhouette of a woman indicates that I've reached the right door.

Inside the pitch-black restroom, the automatic light flickers on, revealing my reflection in the mirror. My make-up appears untouched. In the near darkness, my flushed skin doesn't show itself to him, but here in the light, I see what he can't.

I carefully lower my pants to retrieve a single delicate string of cotton. It's clean—no trace of my cycle. With no extra thought, I dispose of it, draw up my pants, and wash my hands.

Stepping out, I find Spencer waiting, a quiet sentinel.

He turns, offering no words, just his presence, then leads me back through the office, up the staircase, back to the room where I'd been.

The space holds echoes of the past moments. I sink into the blanket, reclaiming the intimacy we'd only just begun.

Twelve

His voice teases, his tongue brushing the shell of my ear, while he unfastens my bottoms, again. "I think we were here." His touch is slow as he peels them away.

With the gentle care, he slides the white lace thong down my legs, its design perfectly matched to my bra.

Each glide of fabric feels like an unveiling, not only of my body, but of every guarded part of me.

I'm not only exposed; I'm choosing to be seen.

Spencer's touch carries more than desire. It's a confident guidance, threaded with tenderness.

My hand drifts across the fabric of his briefs, fingers curling around the elastic band until slip them off, one leg at a time.

While I lie exposed physically and emotionally, with a man I hardly know, I'm fully aware of the forbidden nature of our encounter.

Tethered to separate lives, each bound by marriage, we dare to share a connection that defies convention.

Spencer moves to explore the uncharted territory. He gently parts my legs, inviting a vulnerability that is both exciting and terrifying.

"Do you... have a condom?" I stop him.

He's surprised. "No," his brows rise, as if the notion had never crossed his mind.

Guilt glints in my tone as I ask if he's been with anyone else besides his wife.

"No, not for a while. You still wanna...?"

TWELVE

I cut him off before he can finish his question.

"If you're good with it, then so am I."

He wastes no time tracing a scorching path along the slickness of my core.

Driving his palm against my clit before his fingers take over, probing with a rhythm that makes my legs quake.

He explores me like a man intent on learning every secret, coaxing gasps with each measured swirl. His touch dances between torment and pleasure, alternating between feather-light teasing and deep, dragging strokes.

He rolls and rubs with obscene skill. Dismantling me with ease.

He knows *exactly* where to press until I'm teetering on the edge.

No one's ever touched me like this. Not with this kind of hunger, with this brazen confidence.

Is this what a man who knows what he's doing feels like?

My hands glide down the ridges of his abs until I find him, thick, hot, and impossibly hard.

I wrap my hand around his shaft; it twitches in my palm. My fingers barely meet.

I stroke him slowly, dragging out his breath as I squeeze and glide, watching his jaw clench when I twist at the tip.

I guide him forward, pulling him toward the aching space between my legs, spreading for him, needing him to engulf me like only he can. My hand shakes as I line him up, the blunt head of his cock pressing against my entrance.

"Don't tease," I whisper. "I need you inside me."

His presence is overwhelming. His body a tower of need, his arousal pressing hard, demanding space inside me. He's so big. A flash of panic zips through me.

Can I even take all of him?

I imagine Dominic discovering what I'm about to give Spencer. His size alone feels like a secret too massive to keep.

Will Dominic feel the difference? Will he know?

Spencer's hands sweep across my body, tender yet assured. I relax beneath his touch, craving the raw fullness he brings.

We fumble a little. The moment isn't cinematic; it's messy. It's real.

I laugh, my breath coming in short gasps. "This is going to hurt," I whisper with a half-smile. "It's like I'm a virgin all over again."

Spencer giggles, mischief flickering in his eyes. "Well then let's get that cherry popped." He teases.

Inch by inch, my body yielding, his thick cock splits me open until my toes curl.

It's *perfect*.

I clench instinctively around him. Pain and pleasure blur together until I can't tell which cuts deeper into me.

He pauses, halfway, his breath ragged. "You okay?"

I inhale, gripping his shoulders. "Yeah, stay. Let me feel you."

He does, letting me savor every throb.

Then, he moves again, this time deeper.

The stretch is unforgiving.

"So fucking tight," he groans.

I've always muffled my pleasure, trained myself to be quiet, because that's how Dominic preferred it. Controlled. Contained.

But Spencer is chaos. Freedom. Fire.

My restraint shattered the moment his name tumbled from my lips.

His hands clamp around my hips, dragging me closer, anchoring me to the length of him.

"God, you're perfect," he rasps, barely holding himself together.

When he begins to move—slow, deep, brutal strokes—I realize I won't last long.

Each thrust drives deeper, pushing me to the edge, desperate and unrelenting.

Pressure coils, searing, while pleasure whips into a frenzy. I feel him unraveling too, his muscles trembling as he struggles to hold on.

And then he shifts.

His length slams into me—and I combust. Grabbing his shoulders,

TWELVE

grounding myself as he bottoms out, buried so deep I swear I can feel him in my throat. My back bows beneath him as pleasure detonates inside me. I cry out, nails clawing his back, legs wrapped around him.

He's right behind me, chasing his own release.

A deep groan tears from his chest as he locks against me. I feel him spilling into me, like a torrent surging through my body, unstoppable. No man has left his claim inside me like this.

Dominic *always* used protection, or left the mess on top of me.

Spencer doesn't.

And somehow, that makes this moment feel unforgettable—like it's not just sex, but a claim.

He collapses, breathless, forehead pressed to mine as we both float in the aftershocks.

The air is thick with the scent of sex and surrender, clinging to my dampened skin.

I don't only feel satisfied; I feel taken—desired.

"There's something about you..." he says under his breath, his tender touch trailing down my arm.

"It feels like it's meant to be."

The words slip out before I can stop them, leaving me embarrassed.

"Something like that..." he agrees, his voice saturated with tenderness.

My hands roam over him, unable to resist the sculpted perfection of his chest. I pause at the dark hair that fans across his pecs, curious as wings sweeping outward. The shape tugs at my attention even as my fingers drift lower, tracing the planes of his abs.

"Does your wife tell you often how hot you are?" I ask with a playful nudge.

He chuckles, his eyes dropping to meet mine. "No, to be honest, I don't get many compliments," he says, surprising me.

How?

How could someone like him, this beautiful, magnetic man, not hear it every day?

"Well," I reply, placing my palm firmly on the balminess of his chest, "I'm not sure I can stop saying it."

The words come easily, because they're true. Every syllable drips with admiration; hoping they sink into the part of him that needs to hear them.

"*This...*" I whisper, "This is the best night of my life."

"You haven't had a very fun life then. We need to change that." He smirks, lying beside me.

"My life hasn't always been like this... successful, fun," he says quietly. "We didn't talk about feelings. Morality wasn't a priority in my house. We were poor, and survival came first. I had to figure a lot out on my own."

I turn toward him, my fingers brushing his jaw. "That sounds like a heavy burden."

"It was—but it made me strong. I rebuilt myself. I made mistakes, but I learned. And now... I know what matters. Steadiness, building something solid."

His words press into me as surely as his touch. "That matters more than anything," I tell him softly, "not perfection, just someone real."

I trace lazy circles on his chest, needing him to feel my attention. "You don't have to survive with me. Not like that. I don't need *tough*."

His eyes flick toward mine, guarded but softening. "That's harder than it sounds."

"Maybe it is," I say quietly. "But tonight, you don't have to keep it all to yourself."

"You have no idea how hard it is for me not to."

"Then don't." My voice trembles, not with fear, but with the weight of how badly I want him to say the things I've been feeling too.

He exhales almost a laugh, almost a surrender. "You're not just beautiful, Sarah. You undo me. Being near you feels like the only thing that makes sense."

"You think I don't feel the same?" My throat tightens, but the words break free anyway. "You've been in my head from the beginning."

He exhales, voice low. "We haven't... been close in months. Not once in half a year, me and Vanessa."

My breath stills. "Not even once?"

TWELVE

He shakes his head. "Eight years, Sarah. Eight years of marriage, and the passion's gone. What's left isn't love, it's habit. Loyalty dressed up as intimacy."

"Habit can still look like love," I say carefully.

"It looks right from the outside," he admits. "But inside... it's hollow. We smile for photos, host dinners, keep our routines. But when the lights go out, there's nothing left."

I whisper, "A flame that never burned the way it should have."

His eyes catch mine, heavy with unspoken truth. "Exactly."

My imagination careens, trying to place this man, this disciplined, desperate-to-be-loyal husband, beside the confession he's just given.

"So why did you marry her?" I finally ask.

He swallows hard. "Because it's what I was *supposed* to do. Fresh off my mission, everyone expected it. She was safe. Good. A virgin. She was what I was *encouraged* to marry."

"She was never the *right* one?"

He doesn't answer right away, just runs a hand over his jaw. "Right on paper. Maybe never right in here." He presses a hand flat to his chest.

He might be the most captivating man I've ever been near. Steady, yet scarred. Guarded, yet open.

When I ask him to tell me two things that he loves, his answer is immediate.

"Black coffee and morning runs."

Possibly what I love most already... is that he's ambitious, motivated. A man of routine.

He's solid in a way that makes me feel safe enough to share pieces of myself I've never voiced before.

I draw in a breath, startled by my own candor. "I married too young. I thought I was doing everything right, checking all the boxes. But somewhere along the way, it stopped feeling like *my* life."

He studies me, his hand warm over mine. "You don't have to explain. I know what it's like to live by the rules that don't fit anymore."

The quiet between us feels safe enough to risk another truth. "I used to have these dreams... big ones. Like owning horses—one black, one white." I laugh, embarrassed. "It sounds ridiculous when I say it out loud."

"Why ridiculous?"

"Because dreams like that don't happen to people like me. They belong in some other world—some other life."

He shakes his head. "Not ridiculous. *Possible.* I can see you with them."

I search his face for any trace of teasing, but find only certainty. "You actually believe that?"

"I wouldn't say it if I didn't. You'll have them someday. And when you do, you'll know you were never asking for too much."

The weight of his conviction sinks into me, permission I never knew I needed. For the first time, my dream doesn't feel foolish. It feels real.

I smile, letting his certainty settle in me. "No one's *ever* believed in me like that before." His hand tight around mine. "Then they didn't really see you. But I do."

The words lodge deep, stirring something undeniable.

We stay like this, cocooned in stillness. His weight grounding me, his presence charging the silence with something honest, too powerful to ignore.

I've never felt anything as intense as this moment, here and now, not even my wedding day—eleven months prior.

Thirteen

Fall 2003

Getting married this young is not only a tradition—it's a path.
But right now my path is about redemption...
I'm standing at the first wedding I've ever attended, and it happens to be my own. I'm only eighteen, still more girl than woman, with expectations that feel like blank pages I've yet to write.

Our wedding is a dream woven in lace and old-world charm, nestled in the small town where Dominic and I grew up. The venue is nothing short of magnificent.

Sunlight pours in from large picture windows, casting golden beams across the rustic floors and illuminating every detail. At the center of the main lobby stands our wedding cake, a towering, elegant creation that immediately draws the eye.

Each tier is wrapped in smooth ivory fondant, adorned with delicate handmade flowers. Tucked within the petals are tiny pearls and glittering diamonds, catching the light like morning dew.

Ivory candles flicker among small floral arrangements on each table, their flames dancing in the breeze that drifts in from the open barn doors.

The air carries blossoms and sparkling cider. It feels alive with love and possibility.

Yesterday's rain cleared, unveiling a flawless September afternoon. The sky is a pristine blue, interrupted only by the occasional cloud, with light spilling gold over the horizon. Autumn leaves, kissed by burnt orange, gold, and blush pink, rustle in the evening breeze.

With a stutter in my heartbeat, my grand entrance unfolds—a scene torn from the pages of a storybook.

Four powerful Clydesdales draw my white carriage to a halt, their glossy coats shimmering in the sunlight, sweat beading like diamonds across their shoulders.

My fingers clutch at the folds trailing behind my wedding gown, as I step carefully down, the carriage cradling my hesitant descent, like something conjured from a dream.

My eyes sweep across the crowd and I take note of everyone I know in attendance, until my eyes finally find Dominic.

My soon-to-be husband.

He stands centered, his smile stretched with nerves and love.

I clutch my bouquet, an extravagant spill of exotic blooms I can hardly pronounce. It cascades like something picked from a royal garden, more opulent than any small-town wedding.

Beautiful, yes. Too much? Never.

This moment is pure magic. The kind of scene little girls are promised in bedtime stories, the kind captured in films.

Then—our song begins. That slow, country melody. *You're still the one.*

Our song—the one we claimed—stirs memories we carved out together in the quiet of our secret drives. My eyes flood. Love boils at the edges, threatening to escape me.

I slide my arm into my father's, his grip the only thing keeping me from floating away. I breathe in slowly. This is the man I choose.

Dominic is kind and loyal. He treats me like I'm everything he's ever wanted—*most of the time. Isn't that what love is supposed to look like?*

As if summoned, another memory surfaces.

Weeks ago, his mother pulled me aside. Her voice had been gentle but firm.

It's okay if you don't want to go through with it.

THIRTEEN

Her words repeat now, more a burden than a comfort. She meant them with love, I know. Her sincerity was never in doubt. But instead of easing me, they lodge deep, like a splinter I can't expel.

The Church says marriage is sacred—the cornerstone of family and faith. Today, marrying Dominic is meant to keep me on the path toward eternal happiness, a life of purpose and devotion.

But there is a shadow tucked inside my soul, a secret sin I can't outrun.

I gave myself to Dominic before marriage.

My body, meant to be pure, saved only for marriage, has been marked. The second gravest sin—next to murder. Yet marriage, they say, can cleanse. This covenant, this ceremony, restores my vows before God. Once I become Dominic's wife, I will no longer be lost. No longer a sinner. I will belong.

I cling to that promise as I move toward him, trusting Dominic to *guard* my heart, my mind, my body. To stand strong where I am weak. To make my life right for both of us.

At the altar, my heartbeat drums beneath the lace of my gown.

My father's hand squeezes mine and when he presses a kiss to my temple, his silence says what words cannot: that he loves me, that he is proud, and he entrusts me to Dominic now.

I turn to Dominic, my husband-to-be, and my eternity waits. His brown eyes as warm as earth after rain, find mine, and for a moment, everything else dissolves. The guests, the music, the weight of expectation—there is only us.

Our vows entwine, sacred words binding us in *forever*. Promises of love, devotion, unwavering faith. *For better or worse. In sickness and health. For time and all eternity.*

As the words leave my lips, a sense of peace settles deep inside. Tears rise, not from sadness, but from joy and devotion.

I imagine our life: full of laughter, shared burdens, quiet moments of comfort in each other's arms. Nothing else matters now.

I am ready to love Dominic as a wife should. Ready to care for him, to stand beside him, to *serve him* in every way. To make him happy. To be *dutiful*. To build the life we were told we were meant to have.

This is what I'm *supposed* to do.

* * *

Three months into my marriage, everything I once believed about love and commitment had begun to unravel.

Dominic, once charming and full of promise, shifted before my eyes.

The mood swings came first. Then impatience, and yelling. He never hit me, but somehow everything became *my* fault.

When he drank, the man I knew disappeared. In his place stood someone darker, unpredictable, even frightening. His words cut sharp and deep. His presence was suffocating.

I wanted to believe love and faith could keep him from destruction. But I was wrong. They couldn't.

He sank lower than I imagined.

Blackouts. Threats of ending his own life when I wouldn't comply with his demands.

Manipulation masked as desperation.

"You make me act this way," he'd snarl, eyes wild. "If you'd just listen, I wouldn't lose my temper."

Later, he'd sag against the wall, voice breaking into something almost tender. "I'm sorry. You know I love you, right?" I clung to those apologies like lifelines, even as the words lost weight with every repetition.

If I returned home late, or someone in my family said the wrong thing—he would explode. And somehow, I was expected to make peace.

It drained me.

But still, I stayed.

Not because I was blind. Not because I was weak. But because I had made a vow. I wore the weight of that promise like a second skin.

"You're worthless without me," he'd spit, venom sharp enough to slice through any illusion of love. Minutes later, when the rage cooled, he'd say weakly, "I'm sorry. You know I don't mean it. You just push me too far."

And somehow, I believed the second part more than the first, because I needed to.

Even when he pulled away. Even when I felt like a ghost in my own home.

I once dreamed of the future where we were a team, two hearts striving together, building a sanctuary saturated with love and purpose. But what I live is not that dream.

Despite the distance, I clung to the vows I made on that autumn evening, and to the man I *thought* I knew.

And for fleeting moments, Dominic tried. He was gentler. Softer. But it never lasted.

Within weeks, the same patterns returned, darker, sharper, more frequent.

The day he legally stepped into a bar, something in him fractured, and nothing was ever the same again.

I had hoped to be sealed in the temple with him one day, to secure not only a lifelong commitment but an eternal one. I trusted that if I followed every teaching, even avoiding caffeine, I could lead by example. That my obedience would spark transformation.

Instead, I found myself in a quiet war—fighting for a man that didn't fight for me. Married to someone who rarely treated me with the respect every person deserves.

But still I pray. I beg for God to steer me in the direction I'm meant to go.

I love Dominic through the silence, through the cold shoulders, through the nights I cry myself to sleep. Even in the mornings when I wake up pretending everything is fine.

Fourteen

Summer 2004

My vows lie shattered beneath my feet as I step out into the night, an evening that feels unforgettable.

The weight of what happened hasn't fully sunk in, and it feels like I've been lifted from a depth I never realized was drowning me.

Outside the building, I turn to Spencer, his figure strong beside me. He centers me in a way that feels like the refuge I've been searching for.

Without thinking, I wrap my arms around his solid frame, pressing into him with a meaningful embrace. The kiss lingers, not born of habit, but of a desperate need to cling to something real.

"I'll see you tomorrow," I stammer, my throat constricted.

"You certainly will." he assures me, while holding me tight.

Reluctantly, I take a step back.

Not because I want to. But because I have to.

I don't look back.

I can't.

Because if I do, I'm afraid I'll run straight back into his arms, into the honesty of what I found in him. The contradiction of the lie that breaks every vow I've ever made, but somehow feels more honest than any promise I've ever spoken.

After only one night with this man, something lasting is already taking root.

I was stunned to learn he's eleven years older than me; I would never have

FOURTEEN

guessed.

He carries himself with the vitality of a man in his prime, and yet he's already planning retirement, not in vague daydreams, but in real timelines. Ten years. And I believe he'll do it. He's that focused, that determined.

I see him differently now, not as someone stepping outside his vows, but as a man who let rules and expectations steer him too long. He met her—his wife—weeks after he returned home from his mission, and they moved swiftly toward marriage, toward a life that seemed right. But maybe never quite felt *right*.

I don't know why this short-term affair feels worth the risk of losing everything we've built individually, but somehow, it is.

And now here we are. Two people who did everything we were supposed to.

Two people who, in our past, made promises before we truly understood what we were giving away.

But now have cracked each other open without shame.

Driving back to my house, the reflection of the street lights washes over the windshield in shadowed waves. My heart still races with memories of Spencer, his touch, his words, and his eyes that seemed to see all the parts of me I had forgotten. However, every minute that passes brings me closer to home and Dominic—the weight in my chest grows heavier.

I rehearse the words I've chosen, lips barely moving as I whisper them aloud to the empty car.

"I was at my mom's, after I got my nails done. You know Linda lives all the way across town. It took forever to get back."

I pause, glancing down briefly at my hands on the steering wheel. My nails haven't been touched in days. But Dominic isn't one to notice small details.

He barely looks at me, let alone studies the shape of my cuticles or the freshness of a polish. The truth is, he's stopped seeing me as a whole person. I've become background noise in his life, a fixture, not a flame.

The lie tastes bitter, but manageable—a necessary thread in the tangled web I've been weaving in silence. I'm not lying to hurt him; I'm lying to survive. To breathe. To feel something beyond routine disappointment and fading vows.

I don't know what Spencer will tell his wife—if he'll tell her anything at all. That part is a mystery I've accepted, for now. Our lives are both complicated, stitched together by duty, guilt, and silent longing. *But tonight, with him, it felt like something real. Something worth keeping.*

The porch light is still on. Everything looks exactly as I left it, unchanged, as if the night never happened. But *I* am changed. There's a version of me that only Spencer knows now. A version lit from within.

Uneasiness wraps around me like ivy, tightening with every step I take toward the front door. My hand trembles on the knob, not from the cold, but from the unknown. I'm never sure which version of Dominic I'll find on the other side. Angry. Drunk. Silent. Or worse—chipper, pretending nothing's wrong.

I turn the handle as quietly as possible, pushing the door open. If he's asleep, I don't want to wake him. If he's not, I don't want to alert him that I'm this late.

The hinges creak, and I peek inside.

The midnight-blue sofa where I left him is empty. My eyes dart to the TV stand; it's closed. Relief loosens within me. He's tapped out for the night.

I step in, shutting the door behind, and scan the condo. From here, I can see nearly the entire main level. The kitchen behind the family room is cloaked in darkness. No dishes in the sink. No low hum of the dishwasher. Just stillness.

I tiptoe to the landing up the stairs, passing the guest room door. At the end of the short hall, our bedroom door stands wide open.

There he is. Dominic. Tucked tightly into bed, chest rising and falling with the rhythm of sleep.

Thank goodness.

A sigh escapes before I stop it, my body slackening.

I change quickly, slipping off clothes that still carry Spencer's scent, trading them for a T-shirt and shorts. My side of the bed, always the furthest from the door, feels cold, but safe. I slip under the covers and pull them up to my shoulders, the sheets too clean, too crisp, like a lie tucked in tight around me.

I want to pray, but the words stick in my throat. How do I confess something that felt holy while it was happening? Maybe God turned away, or maybe He watched and pitied me.

I close my eyes, and Spencer floods back—his touch, his voice, the way his eyes stayed on me like I was something sacred. The sensation of his touch still tingles across my skin.

His words, too, low and rough: "Do you feel that? That's what you do to me, and there's no undoing it now."

I curl into myself, a smile tugging at my mouth.

But then... the guilt strikes.

Dominic's breathing only sharpens it. What does it mean, that I could have the best night of my life with someone who isn't my husband?

I roll onto my side, facing the wall—the core of me split wide. Spencer gave me something tonight that I've never felt before. But Dominic still wears the ring. Still holds the vows. Still takes up half this bed.

And I'm left lying somewhere between the ache of what I'm missing... and the ache of what I've found.

Fifteen

I'm ripped from sleep not by the gentle wake-up I crave, but by a single defiant ray of sunlight piercing through the wooden blinds, slicing across my face like a spotlight on guilt. My lids flutter open, but I want to shut them again, to vanish back into the darkness where last night still lives like a secret I don't want to face.

If the sun weren't so insistent, I'd keep sleeping, keep pretending.

Instead, I roll over, and that's when I feel it.

The tenderness.

A raw, aching sensitivity in the deepest parts of me, a physical echo of Spencer.

I can still feel him on me, the memory clinging like a signature scrawled across my skin, visible only to me but blazing in neon guilt.

I try not to panic, but my mind races.

How am I going to look Dominic in the eyes? Will he see it in my face—in the way I move?

I push back the covers, my movements stiff and careful. It's like my body is glass, if I move too quickly, I'll shatter beneath the weight of what I've done. Instinct takes over, I head to the shower.

The hot water pelts against my skin like needles, and I scrub hard. Too hard. I lather again and again, as if soap could absolve me. I focus on the rhythm of the washcloth the roar of the water, the fogging mirror—all of it a futile ritual. I'm trying to wash him away.

But I don't want to.

Every inch of me burns with memory of Spencer's hands and his taste—the way he looked at me, as if I were something more than a wife going through the motions.

I don't want to let go of that feeling. I wish I could bottle it up and live inside it. But I can't.

This *has* to be a one-time thing.

I made a promise. I stood before God and family and pledged myself to Dominic.

Spencer has a wife. A home. A family.

Separately, we are tangled in responsibilities we can't ignore. Promises we were raised to honor at all costs.

This has to be the end.

I'll stay away from him. I'll resist the magnetism, the electricity, the way everything disappeared when we were together.

But as I rinse the last bit of soap and shut off the water, I know the truth: I can't wash him away. Not completely.

Spencer is a part of me now.

And no amount of scrubbing will ever erase that.

Sundays are my mornings to care for our boarding dogs. With the new dog park, the business has taken on fresh meaning. Linda and I have been busy transforming the space to keep up with the demand. Spencer and Mike recently tore out walls next to our grooming shop, creating an open layout that will soon include a large kennel area and a cozy indoor playroom.

For now, we are taking a few boarding dogs. They rest in chain-link kennels which will soon be replaced with vinyl fencing for individual, secure spaces. Linda and I lead them from the indoor play area to the dog park, where they stretch and play.

While I'm standing outside with the pups, the early morning air brushes against my skin, I spot a familiar white work truck pulling in. Spencer.

Great. He should be at church since he's a Mormon. I shrink into myself, confidence fading like breath on a glass. I compose myself as he steps from his truck, broad shoulders, worn denim, a sureness in his stride.

Trying not to look like a deer caught in headlights—or worse, a stalker—I glance his way and force a smile.

He moves toward me, hands in his pockets, casual as if last night never happened.

"What are you doing here so early?"

I shrug, brushing hair behind my ear to hide the flush in my cheeks.

"Taking care of the dogs," I answer, aiming for nonchalance, like I wasn't tangled with him less than twelve hours ago. "What about you?"

His lips slant faintly.

"Work," he says, with dry humor. "One of my guys bailed, so I'm playing technician today, making people happy."

He tosses me a wink. One wink. That's all it takes.

My mind flashes back to last night.

I shift my stance, and the movement reminds me how sore I am from the hours we spent breaking every rule.

"Okay, well, my dogs are ready to go inside," I say, hinting that I need to leave. I don't want to, but the weight of what we shared last night hangs awkwardly.

"I better get them their breakfast."

"When are we going to get together again?" He questions like it's a given.

As much as I fight the urge to stay away and tell myself that I will, I'm not sure I can. He wants to see me again, alone.

Of course we would... wouldn't we?

I'm thrown. Last night was supposed to be a one-time thing. My gut screams I should never cross that line again, but my soul aches for more.

I cave within seconds after promising myself I wouldn't.

"I don't know. Next week?" My voice lifts, giving away my eagerness.

"That works. Any day, any night. You name it."

His enthusiasm tells me everything. I'm not the only one hijacked. Whatever this is, it isn't fleeting. It isn't a fling. It's undeniable... real.

He must have wanted it as much as I did.

He's as drawn to me as I am to him. I know it from how easily we fall into each other's orbit. It isn't just chemistry. It's gravity.

Our lives have aligned in a strange, perfect way, and even though I know I should run, protect myself, protect what little is left of my marriage, I also know, there's no escaping Spencer.

"Thursday evening?" My question is carefully curated in tone. I don't want to give away too much, but waiting any longer feels like asking the moon not to rise.

His face lights up. "Sure, see you at 8:00? Here?"

"Yes, that's perfect," I reply.

"I'm glad I ran into you today."

"I'm here every week."

A low ripple of laughter passes between us.

"Well then, I might miss church every Sunday if it means seeing you." I drop my head shaking it shyly.

With that, I turn back to my responsibilities, leading my clients' dogs toward the shop. I sneak one last look over my shoulder as Spencer climbs into a different truck and drives away.

After spending the morning taking care of the dogs, I head back to Dominic. He's on the couch, a can of beer already cracked open, even though it's barely noon.

"Where were you last night?"

Blood rushes to my face. *Shit. He noticed.*

Thinking fast, I calm my nerves. "I told you, I went to get my nails done. After that, I went to my mom's."

The lie slides out too smoothly. It makes me sick.

"What nail salons are open after eight?" He asks, not really wanting an answer. He shrugs, takes a sip from his can, and turns back to the TV.

That's it.

That's the first time I've flat-out lied to him.

I'm instantly transported back to childhood, breaking a porcelain statue and blaming my brother. That same churn of guilt bubbles up now.

What if Dominic finds out? What if he knows?

If my integrity unravels, so does everything I stand for. I've always believed truth is the only thing worth speaking. But I let him believe my lie.

In a way... maybe it's his fault he doesn't know me. If he looked closer—he'd see my nails aren't done.

A desperate part of me keeps hoping he'll notice.

That he'll care enough to call me out. Not because I want to be caught, but because I want to be seen.

I think I've been fooling myself into believing Dominic cares, only for the sake of our marriage.

For the *idea* of love.

Because I *love*, love.

I've always been that way, a hopeless romantic, dreaming of fairytales and forever. I believe in marriage. In holding on.

I've never understood how people could fall out of love.

How couples who once adored each other could turn bitter, resentful, cold.

But I'm starting to understand them now.

Sixteen

I steady my voice hoping Dominic will want to come with me. "What do you want to do today?"

"Maybe we could go to my dad and stepmom's for dinner?"

I glance down at the drink in Dominic's hand as he shrugs.

"Nah, I'm good. You can go alone. I'll hang here and watch TV."

"All right," I force cheer into my voice.

"I'll take a nap before heading over there later."

I trudge upstairs, every step heavy. My body still aching from last night with Spencer.

I flop down onto our old, queen-sized bed, Dominic's bed from before we married. It's overdue for replacement.

I've been trying to save money for a better one, but it's difficult, especially since I'm paying the mortgage on my own.

Every time I feel like I'm finally getting ahead, something happens.

Dominic gets injured again, and the medical bills land in my lap. He refuses health insurance, claiming it's expensive and unnecessary.

For me, no insurance is manageable. I'm healthy. I take care of myself. I take minimal risks.

Dominic? He's a walking, emergency room visit.

A thrill-seeker who loves pushing limits, especially in the terrain park. Once, he nearly sliced his thumb clean off.

He hit a rail, botched the landing, and his ski broke free from his boot. Of course he wasn't wearing gloves.

When he reached for the ski, it slipped and sliced the webbing between his thumb and index finger, all the way to the tendon.

Injuries aren't rare for Dominic. They're a pattern, each one draining my bank account and patience.

At first, Dominic was the main provider. But things changed the moment I bought my condo. He had no interest in helping me purchase it, and he slowly stopped contributing altogether.

I rest my head on the pillow. Now I'm caught between the extremes: floating on a high of Spencer's happiness. And sinking under the weight of Dominic's neglect.

Spencer has raised the bar in ways I didn't expect.

The contrast is suffocating. With Dominic, everything feels smaller, dimmer. With Spencer, it feels like breathing for the first time.

And now, I find myself silently asking: H*ow could Dominic possibly meet expectations he doesn't even know I have?*

I know it isn't fair to him. I'm pulling away, becoming more distant, and he has no idea why. It's a set up for failure, for both of us.

But then again, he's been failing me for months. His disinterest, his lack of effort, his daily devotion to alcohol and weed—it feels like he's already chosen his escape. He's been unfaithful to me, not with another woman, but with his addictions.

As I stare up at the ceiling, a single thought echoes in my mind: *How am I going to get out of this marriage?*

Even if Spencer walks away tomorrow, I still can't go back to the life I had with Dominic. What Spencer awakened in me isn't just attraction, it's awareness. It's knowing what it feels like to be wanted, cherished, seen—not tolerated. He made me realize I'm capable of being loved in a way that softens instead of bruises, in a way that makes me feel alive instead of small. And now that I've felt that, tasted tenderness and been touched like I matter, I can't unknow it. I can't return to starving just because I'm used to hunger. My choice isn't about Spencer. It's about me, finally choosing more than the bare minimum.

I don't want to be married to Dominic anymore.

I made a mistake marrying him.

And I need out.

After I wake from a much needed nap, I head for the stairs. Out of habit, I count them—twelve. I always count stairs. *I'm* not sure why anymore. I've done it my whole life.

Dominic's in the kitchen when I reach the bottom. Another drink in his hand. Same posture, same silence, same tired scene. I pause in the doorway, already knowing how this will go, but I ask anyway.

"Are you sure you don't want to come with me?" My voice is careful, though a quiet plea lies beneath it. I feel like I should give him a fair shot, if only to say *I* tried.

"No, it's all good. Have fun. Don't be out too late," he says, eyes fixed on the kitchen counter.

The words land like a leash. Casual on the surface, but I know better. He's not wishing me a good night, he's setting boundaries, silent curfews.

"Sounds good. See you later."

I already know what he's doing. He's mentally setting a timer, tracking how long I'll be gone. He won't say the limit out loud, but I can feel it ticking in his mind, like a countdown I never agreed to.

Driving to my dad and stepmom's, my mind drifts, restless, unsettled. I start replaying the past, tracing the reasons I committed to Dominic in the first place, and the reasons why I've stayed.

I try to lay it out logically. A simple pros and cons list.

Pros:
· He's familiar. Comfortable.
· I married him because marriage is forever—God redeems me if I stay.
· He can still make me laugh.

Cons:
· His values don't align with mine.
· He lies about work, about money.
· He avoids responsibility, especially the big decisions.
· I'm no longer attracted to him.

· And the biggest con—the one I've never spoken aloud is what happened last fall. He went hunting with his dad at the cabin. It's nestled beside a massive body of water, in the kind of setting people write about, quiet, serene, charming. But also volatile. The weather shifts in an instant.

The lake and Dominic have that in common.

I always knew his father was a drinker. What I didn't know was Dominic would take after him in that regard. And on that trip, something ugly happened between them. I don't know what. I just know it pushed Dominic to a corner I never imagined he'd face.

Driving home alone and intoxicated, he lost consciousness behind the wheel. Somewhere along the dark mountain road, he pulled over. Then he reached under the seat, took out his handgun, and pressed it to his head.

He told me later, eyes wet, voice breaking. "I had the gun in my hand. I wanted it to end. But I couldn't do it. I couldn't pull the trigger."

He broke down and sobbed like it was still living inside him. "I don't even know if I wanted to die, or if I just wanted the pain to stop."

Then he drove the rest of the way home in the middle of the night and crawled into our bed without saying a word.

I lived with his silence for three days, questioning myself, replaying every word and gesture, wondering what I had done wrong. And when he finally did speak, well, I've been carrying it ever since. Alone.

I haven't told anyone what he said. Not Linda, or even Maya for that matter. Some truths feel too heavy to share, like they might become more real once you speak them out loud. And maybe, in some sick way, I've been protecting him, his pain, his image, our marriage. But the truth is, carrying it has been undoing me.

Trying to hold together a man who doesn't know how to heal has meant breaking myself in the process. He keeps hurting himself, and me.

It's not what he almost did that night. It's what it revealed.

Before we got married, he threatened to end his life more than once—three

SIXTEEN

times, to be exact.

The pattern started long before marriage. I was sixteen, tired of him tearing me down for how I dressed, how I laughed, even how I existed. That night, I told him we were done. We were standing in the parking lot outside the high school. He had graduated but wanted to take me for one of our rides. I still remember the cold bite of winter against my skin.

"You dress like a boy," he snapped, his voice cutting. "No guy will ever want you but me."

"Then maybe I don't want any guy at all," I shot back, my voice trembling, though I willed it not to. "I'm done, Dominic. I'm tired of feeling small every time you open your mouth."

His face darkened, and for the first time, I saw something like desperation under the anger. "Don't be a bitch Sarah. If you leave, I'll make you regret it. You won't just ruin me—you'll have blood on your hands."

I didn't believe him at the time. Not fully. But the seed of fear planted that night—never left me.

That was the beginning of the trap, love tangled with fear, affection warped by threats.

Both times he threatened suicide after that, were when I tried to leave.

So I stayed out of fear, guilt, and confusion. I didn't know how to carry someone else's darkness while still trying to grow up.

He's the only relationship I've ever known. In dating and early marriage, I convinced myself this was love: messy, dramatic, painful. I thought passion wrapped in chaos was intimacy.

But everything changed after that night in the mountains.

*That image—him, alone on the side of the road, gun in hand—*etched itself into my mind and never left.

What if he had pulled the trigger?

Worse—*what if he'd killed someone else driving drunk?*

Since then, I've had nightmares, vivid, terrifying repeats of the same scene: the shower. He raises the gun, pulls the trigger, and the bullet passes through him—into me. I wake drenched in sweat, my chest heaving, gasping for breath. I've started avoiding going upstairs when he's in the bathroom. *What if it happens? What if one day, he actually follows through?*

What if I'm the reason?

Those are the thoughts that surface every time I consider leaving.

But here's what I'm learning—slowly, painfully: love shouldn't feel like fear. Companionship shouldn't feel like captivity.

I crave more.

More than walking on eggshells.

More than pretending I'm fine when I'm crumbling inside.

More than managing someone else's storm when I'm barely weathering my own.

I long for romance.

I ache for passion.

I need tenderness, laughter, intimacy, and safety.

I hunger for the kind of fire that ignites something beautiful, not the kind that burns you to ash.

Now I see it clearly. I've talked myself through the fog of my own crisis, guiding myself to exactly where I stand.

I'm tired of disappearing.

It's time.

I need to tell Dominic I want a divorce.

This clarity has been building for a long time. It was never a matter of *if*, only *when*.

I pull into my dad and stepmom's house tucked quietly in the country. It's where I lived until I was fourteen, and every time I see it, my soul settles. The red brick exterior stands proud, the white marble accents around the windows catching the afternoon sun.

The neighborhood is like a page from a perfect suburban dream, neat lawns, dignified homes, each sitting on an acre. Years ago, it was quieter, more open. Now it's filled in, but still charming.

The scent of Sunday dinner greets me from the front door, wrapping around me like a familiar blanket I didn't know I was craving.

SIXTEEN

Inside, the polished floors under my feet shine, and the weight I've been carrying finally lifts. From the kitchen, I hear my dad whistling his usual tune while shaking his watermelon belly back-and-forth. Somehow it makes me smile.

He brings the last of the roasted chicken, mashed potatoes with brown gravy, and vinegar-sprinkled broccoli to the table, just as my stepmom, Betty, sets down a pitcher of juice.

"Perfect timing." I smile and take my usual seat.

"Yes, glad you decided to join us," Betty says, tapping my shoulder with her delicate hand.

"How was church?" I ask, trying to sound casual, but the words ache in my throat. I miss it, the steadiness of faith, the sense of being held by something stronger than myself. But with the new boarding, the dogs need me.

"It was great," my dad, Frank, answers reverently. "The spirit had a strong presence today."

My throat tightens unexpectedly. That's what I need, something divine to guide me through the quiet chaos building in my chest. The kind of strength that speaks without words. The kind that might help me face what's next.

Should I tell them? Should I say it out loud, what I'm thinking about divorce?

But I haven't even told Dominic yet. I've only hinted and warned. He knows he's on thin ice, strike *one* has already come and gone. And he knows exactly what that means.

Still, saying it to my dad and Betty feels *too* soon. Too heavy. They might not understand. They believe in marriage, and fighting for love even when it hurts. Despite my dad's divorce from my mom, they will do everything possible before divorce is an option. I don't know if they'd see my pain as enough.

I absorb the words that sit bitterly and heavily on my tongue. I smile instead, listening to the soft clang of utensils against our plates. Letting the safety of this home hold me a little longer.

I decide to carry the secret for now, keeping things light during dinner instead. The two of them always have a way of lifting my spirits, even if it's for a short while, so I let that peace remain.

My brother James couldn't make it tonight. He was pulled away by his fiancée's family. Still the evening feels complete.

After we finish eating, I slip outside and make my way around the property. I don't do this every time I visit, but something about today makes me want to linger. The breeze is soft, and the sunlight is beginning to dip, casting a glowing hue on the grass and the old brick.

This place raised me. I remember summer nights when we played kick the can in the cul-de-sac until the street lights came on, and winter evenings skiing at the resort until closing. I spent Friday nights watching TGIF, while waking early to glue myself to Saturday morning cartoons.

Summers were spent poolside while Linda worked extra hours to buy passes for swimming in the summer and skiing in the winters. My parents rented out condos for income, always working hard to give us more than enough. They divorced when I was seven, though I didn't fully grasp it until years later. That's how peaceful it was, how intentional they were about protecting us. They were civil, even kind. They never fought in front of us. *Never put us in the middle.* Their love for us was always greater than their differences.

When I was fourteen, my dad married Betty, and she blended seamlessly into our family. Even now, she joins us for the holidays at Linda's, Christmas, birthdays, all of it. Our family stayed stitched together, even when frayed.

And I love spending time with them, which makes it sting more that Dominic avoids them at every opportunity. He makes excuses, mumbling half-reasons, choosing to stay behind. My gut tells me it's not shyness or awkwardness. It's guilt, he's hiding something, and maybe he knows he wouldn't hold up under the weight of their honesty, their kindness, their expectations. He can't look them in the eyes, not like someone with nothing to hide should.

Drifting around the safe haven that shaped me, I feel even more the weight of clarity settling in. Dominic will never be able to give me the life I've known, the life I was raised to expect, the life I deserve. He pales in comparison to the man my father was to my mother, and is now to my stepmom. I was

SIXTEEN

brought up around stability, effort, strength, and love. Dominic offers none of those things.

My family wanted more for me than what I settled for. I see that now, so clearly it hurts. My sister Amber, seven years older and always a few steps ahead of me in life, saw it before I did. She despises Dominic. She tried to warn me, but *I didn't listen.* No one could tell me anything—not even his mother, who quietly cautioned me not to marry her own son.

She knew, just as I'm beginning to accept, that he would never meet my standards.

Still, I convinced myself that marriage would fix him. That being his wife would somehow inspire him to rise to the occasion. But in truth, it did the opposite. It made him worse.

He's not Mormon. His values, his endgame, his standards—they've always been misaligned with mine. I thought we could find a middle ground, but we never did.

Now, I'm standing at the edge of my marriage, holding only the pieces of a future I no longer want.

I don't know how I'm going to tell him. I don't even know when. But I do know it's coming.

Soon.

Seventeen

The dogs are playing in the park, soaking up the sweetness of a perfect summer day. They dart in and out of the grass, wagging tails, splashing joyfully in the cool stream that cuts from the front to the back of the property. It's chaotic, but a little magical.

We still haven't finished the inside of the main building. Temporary kennels hold us over, but progress has been steady. Most of our time has been eaten up by remodeling the shop itself, and what's left goes to whatever else we can knock out in a day.

But the dog park's a different story.

It's already perfect.

Towering trees stretch along the West end, throwing generous shade over the stream. We've added kiddie pools for the pups that are too shy or too small to brave the current, and the area is scattered with every kind of ball and squeaky toy imaginable.

With Labor Day coming up fast, we're getting slammed with last-minute bookings, grooming, boarding, you name it. Everyone wants their dogs fresh and groomed, ready for family gatherings and backyard barbecues. It's also prime season for "camping haircuts"—short, manageable trims for the little fur people heading into the woods with their humans.

For our first Labor Day, we are hosting a group of dogs we already see regularly. A small trial run before the grand opening.

SEVENTEEN

The front room is fixed up for comfort, plush couches, soft lighting. A TV cycles through soothing animal shows to help the dogs relax, like they're still at home.

Most clients enter through the foyer, where we greet them. That's where I learned Spencer is married, a moment I haven't quite unpacked yet. Past the foyer, a row of kennels stretches, giving dogs space to relax in privacy. The walls still need framing, and insulation, but we're getting there. Spencer should be here any minute, fulfilling his landlord duties—just to get it finished up.

Just after I've finished putting the dogs away for the night, Mr. Dreamy strolls in. Of course his shirt is already off, ladder and tools in hand. He looks like a chiseled dancer straight out of a Vegas revue, leather tool belt in place of a bow tie.

I follow behind him toward the back of the kennel area, unable to resist watching his raw, masculine glory.

I long to talk to him. We don't get enough quality time together because life's been hectic, and phone calls are too risky. Before he starts, he double-checks we're still on for later.

"8:00 tonight, right?" he says, adding a wink that hits me like it always does, fast, flirty, completely disarming.

Gosh, he knows exactly what he's doing.

"Yes!" I answer, a little too quickly.

He works to set up his ladder.

"You ever think about what this would be like... if we weren't sneaking around?"

I blink, caught off guard. "You mean, like, normal?"

He shrugs. "Yeah. Us, out in the open. No lying."

I crave that more than I'll admit.

He doesn't wait for an answer, he positions his tools on the concrete floor, then wraps his arms around me, *I melt into them.*

His lips crash into mine, cinnamon and spice. I press closer, my body begging, pleading, for his.

I'm seconds from surrendering, from giving in to every wild thought when...

***

SPENCER

Her lips are still on mine when the voice cuts into our moment.

"Spencer. Spencer."

Sarah jerks back, confusion flashing in her eyes. She doesn't recognize it, but *I do.*

In an instant, the ground tilts. The charge of her mouth still burns, vanilla clinging to the air where she stood. Then it's gone, ripped away by the cold snap of reality.

She slips from my arms and vanishes out the back before I can speak. The slam of the door behind me echoes like a verdict as the front door swings open. Vanessa steps in, composed, polished, her gaze sweeping the shop.

The shift cuts down my spine like a cold blade.

I force the switch. I mask the lover in me and expose the husband—now standing in place. My tone shifts, playing the part.

"*Vanessa, honey.*"

***

Sarah

Spencer freezes. A woman's voice, sharp and *unfamiliar*, ricochets off the walls of the building.

My entire body locks up.

At first, I can't process what I've heard. My mind spins, searching for logic, some way to rationalize what pierced into our stolen moment. But there's no mistaking it.

She said his name.

Not once—but *twice*. Louder the second time.

SEVENTEEN

My heart skips a beat. Blood drains from my face. That voice doesn't belong here; it doesn't belong to *anyone* who should be calling for Spencer.

He stiffens too.

I question.

Who is she?

My vision narrows. I don't look at him—I can't. If I meet his eyes, I'll lose time. Time I might not have. I need to move.

I don't wait to see who it is.

I know it can't be good—not for me, not for us.

A primal instinct takes over. *Run. Hide. Don't be seen.*

I bolt.

Slipping from his grasp, I duck out the back door into the dim hallway behind my boarding room. My chest tightens as I hurry down the hall, barely breathing, nerves strung taut like wire.

I make an exit from the building, rushing down the sidewalk, head low, avoiding eye contact, and loop back to the front of my shop. I gather my things and leave Spencer with the woman's voice I still haven't placed—the stranger who remains with him—*in my shop.*

Spencer knows the job that needs to be done. He's already familiar with my shop. He doesn't need my help.

And because he's a fully capable man who doesn't need to be babysat, I lock the doors behind me and head back to my place.

Eighteen

I've told Dominic that I need to let the dogs out for their nighttime potty break.

It's a lie that's growing easy to tell.

I shower and apply makeup, something I rarely do anymore. Not because I don't want to feel beautiful—but because I've almost forgotten how.

On the rare days I bother, it feels like a mask that melts under the humidity of the dog hair and shampoo steam.

But tonight, I feel like someone else. Someone Spencer will ache to touch.

He's always so perfectly put together. His clothes are expensive but not showy, well-tailored, and he wears confidence like cologne.

I spray myself with toasted vanilla sugar. It settles on my skin, reminding me of who I used to be, back when I still believed romance could rewrite everything.

I slide into a denim skirt and pull a jacket over my arms, hoping the layer will keep me toasty, knowing that it won't last long.

Then, without stalling, I head down the shop road...

Shit! Spencer's truck *and* his business partner's are still here.

So much for our escape. I park in my usual spot and wait, unsure of what I'm even hoping for.

I flip through my CD mix—filled with love songs from the 90s.

Each one is a whisper from the past, each lyric a reminder of what love is supposed to feel like.

After what feels like forever, Spencer appears in the doorway. His expression is unreadable, but when he spots me, he gestures for me inside.

EIGHTEEN

I rush to meet him in the foyer bathroom.

"Sorry," he mutters, running a hand through his hair. "Mike decided he wanted to stay late to work on accounting. I got roped in."

The irritation in his voice is low and simmering.

"Meet me at the end of the two-lane road."

And just like that, I'm in drive, chasing a fantasy that feels barely within reach.

I speed past the last small cabin and into the dark. The night is still, rural, and silent. Ten minutes later, his headlights sweep across the field. He pulls in beside me, cuts the engine, and slips into my car without a word.

The moment the door clicks shut, his hand slides up my thigh, slipping beneath the hem of my skirt. His touch is firm, impatient, hungry. The pressure of his fingers dig in enough to make me ache.

"I've missed this body," wet lips graze my ear, the sound of his voice instantly soaking my panties. "I missed the way you taste—the way you sound."

A whimper slips from me as he pushes the fabric aside, fingertips grazing my bare slit. I'm already slippery. My hips buck into his hand with aching need.

His mouth takes over mine, his tongue forcing its way past my lips, demanding control. I moan, gripping his shoulders as a finger slips inside me, curling it just right while his thumb works circles over my clit in an experienced rhythm.

"Fuck, you're already dripping," he growls before sucking my bottom lip between his teeth. Pulling back, he tears open his belt. The scrape of metal sends a shiver through my body. He frees his cock, thick, hard, already dripping, and my mouth waters from looking at it.

I pull the handle, leaning the seat back to straddle him. My knees dig into the console, and I grind against the length of his shaft.

As I peel off my shirt, my breasts brush against the stubble on his jaw.

"It's been too long," he rasps, cupping them before pulling one into his mouth.

"Too long," I repeat.

After he's done taking his time exploring my body, his hands full of unspoken hunger, I reach for the hem of his fitted polo. I tug it upward in one smooth motion, forgetting about the buttons. The shirt snags at his face, catching around his chin and ears as we both laugh.

"Oh, crap," I tug it back down. "Round two. Let's try that again."

"One... two... three," I count aloud, fingers teasing open each button, tension building with every pause. I lean in, kissing him slow, before sliding the shirt from his shoulders. He lifts his arms to help, his eyes never leaving mine.

I fold the shirt carefully and place it on the driver seat like it's sacred. No way I'm letting it hit the floor—not on my watch.

"Let's move to the backseat," I whisper. My voice dips, low, inviting, daring. "I know it's small... but I think we can make it work."

"Oh, I *know* we can." He says.

One by one, we scramble into the backseat, hunched over and squeezing ourselves into the tight space. I crouch behind him as he shifts, struggling to get comfortable in the cramped quarters. When he settles, one leg drops to the floor, the other bent against the seat back. He makes room for me, his silhouette broad and commanding in the low light.

Even with the windows bare, the car sinks into shadows. There's no dome light to provide clarity, and the night sky above offers no assistance. No streetlights reach this far. Discretion is the entire reason behind choosing this secluded location.

"Okay, I'm ready for you, baby," he smacks his lips in a playful kiss.

He's how I would imagine a giant folded into a toy car, his back against the window, legs stretched wide.

Once he's settled, I shimmy out of my skirt, clumsy in the cramped space between the seats. I'm grateful for the dark, it disguises most my insecurities, ones I'm not yet ready to share. But being naked again with Spencer—in a moment I've craved and unsure it would ever happen—excites me in ways I don't fully comprehend.

Things usually feel so natural with him, but a strange mix of unease and desire swirls within me.

"I'm glad you're ready," I whisper, "because here I am, in all my glory."

I climb onto his lap, straddling him. My right foot stays planted on the ground for balance, while my left leg curls around his bent one. There's barely room to move, let alone any foreplay. Not that we need it. I'm already aching with desperation, soaked from the moment he pulled me close, stirred by his sweet cologne and cinnamon kisses.

I wrap my hand around him and guide him to the place that's been aching since his first touch. I press his tip against my entrance. Gradually, with deep breaths and control, I manage to guide the thick, swollen tip of his cock past the threshold of my opening. Once again, he doesn't slip in easily. *He's not Dominic.*

The pressure is instant, tight, a little painful. I wince, "Sorry."

He giggles under his breath, teeth grazing my ear. "Don't apologize. unless you're sorry for making me wait this long. You feel incredible."

After a few teasing strokes, I lower myself onto him, and with one firm push, he's fully inside. Deep. Stretching me with that perfect, delicious ache. I cry out, part pleasure, part shock, and he devours it with a kiss.

His hands grip my ass, guiding me as I move, our rhythm catching fire.

His cock is thick, unfamiliar, so different from Dominic's.

Inside me he feels impossibly large. Every ridge pressing against my walls overwhelms me. Our skin's flushed and balmy, breaths fill the windows with fog. But right now I don't care if the whole damn world is watching.

I trail kisses along his neck. His breath halts when I suck at the sensitive spot beneath his jaw. Spurred by his reaction, I bite harder, marking him in ways I hope won't leave too many traces.

"Easy, tiger. I've got to face people tomorrow. It's difficult to explain hickeys during a staff meeting."

His sarcasm only makes me bite harder.

"That's it," he mutters, smirking between ragged breaths. "Destroy my reputation one bruise at a time."

He drives me to the edge, my body aching with more desire than I've ever known.

Giving him this part of me, letting him feel every inch of me wrapped around him, and the way he revels in it, ignites me as much as the pleasure itself.

The harder I take him in, the more his breath stutters—like he'll never get enough. His sounds grow louder, more unrestrained.

I grind my clit to his pelvis, chasing the stimulation I need. It's *too perfect*. The way my body molds to his makes me dizzy with pleasure.

He's so big.

The thought loops like a mantra. He stretches me in every way, pulling moans from my throat, tightening each nerve inside me. With him buried deep, my climax surges forward, so fast I can barely brace for it.

My lips find his ear, words tumbling out: "Fall apart inside me, don't hold back."

I don't know how long I can hold out, how many seconds until he spills into me—but I know this: I've never let anyone else do this. This intimacy, this kind of release, was kept guarded. But tonight, I give him everything.

The desire builds, unstoppable. Every grind of my hips rips a guttural cry from my throat.

"Ah—!" I shudder as wave after wave slams into me. My hands clawing at him, my thighs quaking, my entire being pulsing with need—then breaking open in release.

"Fuck! Keep going!" His growl rumbles in the steam-thick air as he drives harder, chasing every flicker of sensation. His body tenses, then breaks, abandoning himself with me. His pulse throbs, hot and thick inside me. I gasp at how right it feels to let him fill me completely.

He's the only man who's ever left his heat inside me—twice now. This type of intimacy had been my secret fantasy. In my mind, only the closest, most bonded couples ever reach a moment like this. That's what I believed. That's why I always held back, but with him the fear dissolves. For once, I don't stop it.

There are no risks with him. No consequences. Only connection.

Spencer made sure of that long ago. After his third child, he had a vasectomy, something he mentioned during our first intimate night together, after I admitted I'd always dreaded the possibility of pregnancy.

I'd been naïve, assuming vasectomy meant removing the testicles. His laughter had been warm, not cruel, and he looked at me as if I was the most adorable woman he'd ever met. That moment stayed with me, his amusement, my embarrassment, but more than that, the tenderness in his eyes.

"Shit, Sarah," he grinned, eyes gleaming with mischief. "You really thought they just cut them off? What did you picture, men wandering around like Ken dolls?"

Heat rushed to my cheeks before he kissed the top of my head, still chuckling, adding, "Trust me, sweetheart, if I'd been neutered, I wouldn't be making you moan like this."

I'd never encountered someone with a vasectomy before, at least not someone I had been intimate with. The fact that I thought he'd been "fixed" like a house pet proved how naïve I was. And maybe still am.

I shift against him, still straddling his lap, my body wrapped around his as he adjusts to sit up.

"Next time, remind me not to fuck in your car," he mutters, voice strained. "My neck's cramped."

I groan, laughing. "My leg's on fire."

We both giggle, exhausted and aching, tangled in the ridiculousness of what we just did. But no matter how cramped the space, I wouldn't trade this moment. Not for anything.

He tugs me closer, pressing my chest to his, brushing my hair back with a lazy sweep of his hand.

"I can pull it into a ponytail if you'd like," I offer, always keeping a hair-tie around my wrist, just in case.

"No, I love your long hair. It's like a security blanket you always wear. It's beautiful." He runs his fingers through it, then twirls it at the ends.

He kisses between my breasts, inhaling deeply, as if memorizing my scent.

If I'd known love could feel like this, I would never have rushed into marriage so young.

This doesn't feel like an illusion. It's too authentic, too intense. No one could fake this kind of care—the way he touches me, the way he listens, the way he breathes me in. It's too sincere to be anything but real.

Still, doubt needles in: *is he feeling the same way? Or is he just a man who knows exactly how to mimic what makes a woman fall in love?*

"Have you been unfaithful to your wife with others besides me?" I ask.

His gaze holds mine. "Yes," the word lands without flinch, quiet honesty cutting deep.

"How many?" I push, needing to understand. "How serious was it? Were you just playing? Or is this—"

"Shhh." He presses his finger against my lips. "Slow down, cowgirl. I'll answer all your questions." He pauses before answering.

"One, a few years back."

He speaks in slow, measured words, open, willing to lay bare the parts of himself that might break this.

I listen, weighing every sentence for truth, searching for where I fit in this story.

"How many times?" I press again. "I need to know whether I'm a phase or something more."

He traces his fingers, tickling the outside of my arm.

"Maybe once a month, for six months, give or take." He says.

"We ended things about a year ago. She wanted something serious. But I didn't want more than sex. I had a family, and at the time, I was still trying to hold on to my marriage."

"And your wife?" The word feels foreign in my mouth. "You don't want to be her husband anymore?"

He exhales slowly, the weight of the question bending his posture.

"I do. I did. But now... I feel like I'm at a crossroads. I'm leaning toward leaving. I haven't been happy in years."

Spencer's voice grows heavy with frustration.

"This past year, I poured my heart and soul into making our marriage work. I tried making her feel loved, valued, happy. But I've realized something: nothing will ever make her happy. She lacks the ability to find her own joy, and I am not the one who can rectify that. I've given her time, attention, children, money, everything I have, yet it is *never* enough."

He falls silent, the truth hanging between us. "She has to figure out what happiness means for herself. I can't keep breaking myself to define what happiness means for her."

I'm motionless, absorbing his honesty, his exhaustion.

He huffs out a humorless laugh. "Guess I should add 'professional joy consultant' to my resume." His lips twist, the sarcasm sharp but brittle, masking the ache underneath.

"I don't want to talk about it anymore," he says, voice flat. "It kills the mood."

There's an awareness in his eyes, the kind that comes from years of emotional labor and quiet resignation.

But something about his confession stirs me. His clarity, his vulnerability, it opens a space in my chest I wasn't expecting. He's on the verge of something else, maybe walking away from her—maybe toward me.

And that thought pulses in me like a secret thrill.

The idea of being what she couldn't be.

I'm aware of my twisted logic. These thoughts, these desires, are only mine, and I excuse them because I haven't acted on them. Not yet. *It's possible it's not truly wrong—right?*

"It's okay," I say quietly, kissing the corner of his mouth. "We'll talk more later, when your..." A nervous laugh slips out as I shift off of him, suddenly aware of the mess between us... "...when your dick isn't slipping out of me."

Looking around, I realize I'm unprepared, no towels, no plan. Spencer doesn't seem bothered.

"Once I get home, I'll shower," he says, with a shrug. "Assuming tonight's not the night Vanessa decides she's in the mood for the big D." He half-jokes, but the bitterness behind it is sharp enough to taste.

Perhaps he's like me. Maybe, the more he's with me, the less he wants her. The way I feel about Dominic—after every moment with Spencer—I desire Dominic less and less.

"Yeah, hopefully my husband won't expect sex tonight, either."

Spencer grins, proud. "Well, I know you won't. Not after this."

"I wonder how many days I'll be reminded of you," I say, still flushed from the ache between my legs. "Last time, I was sore for days."

"Really?" His smile deepens, smug and satisfied.

"Yes, really."

"Good. Then you won't want anyone else."

He raises a brow, flashing that cheesy, confident grin.

I can already feel the bruising from our time together this round, but I still tease him, hoping it inflates his ego enough to keep him hooked.

"I guess I'll see how many days it takes to recover," I say, lightly. Maybe if I feed his confidence, it'll keep him coming back—so I give him the affirmation he clearly thrives on.

Before he pulls his shirt on, I reach out one last time, sliding my hand down his chest. The hair there is just enough, masculine but not overwhelming, and I can't help but admire it.

"You're so damn sexy," I exclaim, my voice thick with longing. "I can't get enough. I need more. When can I have more?"

His eyes sharpen, amusement sparking.

"Careful—keep talking like that and I'll never let you leave the car."

His tone shifts, excitement bubbling to the surface. "Actually, I've got a surprise for you next weekend. Saturday, 6 p.m. at the shop. Wear jeans and a t-shirt. You might want a jacket, too."

"Where are we going?" I ask.

"Don't worry about it. You'll love it. Just show up."

Secretly jumping with joy, I agree to see him again. "Okay, I trust you. I'll be there."

We finish getting dressed and settle into our respective seats. Spencer reclines on the passenger side with a contented sigh.

"Aaah, so much better than being cramped in the back."

"That it is." I agree, before I rev the engine.

"Good night, sexy." He leans in, stealing a kiss, lips lingering like they don't want to let go.

"Sleep tight," I whisper against his mouth before he slips out. The sound of his shoes fades into the night, leaving me both empty and full at once.

Nineteen

Pulling back into my condo, I feel disheveled and off-kilter—nothing like the composed woman who walked out earlier tonight.

I'm later than I should be. My mind races, frantic. Urgency propels me the instant I step inside. I need to shower before Dominic catches even a trace of Spencer still clinging to me.

Without greeting him, I bolt upstairs, barely registering his voice calling me from the kitchen. I strip off my clothes in a rush, the weight of my choices pressing down hard. I crank the water on high, craving anything that might smother every trace of what I've done. I want it to be a scalding inferno, to burn away the evidence.

But standing here, waiting for the temperature to rise, *I know I'm not fooling anyone, least of all myself.*

The water can't erase what I've done. *It won't.*

I don't want this life of infidelity. The guilt is suffocating. I need to think of a way to tell Dominic I'm finished—that the marriage is over. But the thought terrifies me. How do I break him without causing irreparable damage?

I don't want to hurt him more than I already have. Worse, I can't risk fueling his temper. That could be catastrophic—something I might never be able to undo.

The shower hisses around me as I slip inside, letting the scalding cascade wash away every trace of my betrayal. But the word clings to me like a brand. *Affair.*

I'm having an affair.

The realization strikes again, as if it's the first time I've allowed myself to admit it. *Honest, loyal me—how did I end up here? How did I fall so far from the person I swore I was?* I never imagined betraying anyone, least of all my husband. I thought I was incapable. Yet, here I am, drowning in what I've created.

Maybe if it means I end up with Spencer, I'll accept the consequences.

I've stepped willingly into this chaos, and walking away from Spencer isn't an option anymore. *The desire for him has already become an addiction.*

I've surrendered to the pull of this man. He hits me like a force of nature.

He's everywhere now, flooding me with toxic need that nothing can stop.

Like last time, I rinse off the stain of what I've done. But this time, I don't care if it sticks.

The rules are clear—don't sleep with a married man. And yet I've already broken it, so now all bets are off.

The only rule that matters now is not to get caught—and for once, I don't need to be in control. I'm tired of being the perfect girl, of living up to everyone else's expectations.

I've played the good girl easily enough. But this affair? It's challenging. And for once, I welcome it.

Fuck my angry, drunk husband.

The thought spikes inside me with clarity as I scrub my skin, desperate to erase the remaining traces of Spencer.

But it's futile. I can't wash away what's inside me now. I'm marked. I'm no longer the girl who fits neatly into the box I once believed I belonged in. I've crossed the line, and there's no going back.

I scrub my hair and face harder, letting the water attack me as if could drown out the guilt. But it can't. If anything, it drags it to the surface. The rebellion inside me is both liberating and terrifying. I try to compartmentalize my thoughts, to cage the chaos, but it keeps spilling free.

I'm going to live for me.

I'm going to keep fucking Spencer.

Whenever and wherever I want.

I will do whatever it takes to have him be mine.

And only mine.

NINETEEN

After rinsing away the remnants of my betrayal, I yank back the plastic shower curtain. A cool blast of air lashes at my damp skin as the bathroom door creaks open. I reach for a towel, but before I can step over the tub wall, Dominic blocks me. He plants himself in front of me as if to say: *tonight*, he wants to make love.

I'm done with indulgences. My evening with Spencer was everything I needed. I'm satisfied, both physically and emotionally. The thought of enduring any more of Dominic's halfhearted gropes, or his perpetual *"I'm not in the mood,"* is utterly repulsive.

Despite the nagging urgency in his eyes, I reach for the towel, brushing off his protest. He counters. He's aroused, his cock straining in front of me. Exhaustion and irritation snarl inside me, but I know there is no easy escape from this obligation.

With quiet sass, I mutter, "Fine, I'll pleasure you." Even as I speak, a bitterness festers inside me. I don't want him there, not when Spencer still clings to me like a ghost.

I move toward Dominic, snatching the towel to blot at my skin. I quickly dab at my body, my mind a whirlwind of regret and resignation, until I let the towel fall.

He steers me into position. Kneeling before him, bare and unwilling. I begin the act without passion. My mouth isn't entirely full; I move mechanically, my hands limp at my sides. Dominic isn't tall, so my mouth meets him with ease, but as I look at him, a grim truth hardens: his pallid, almost ghostly skin, a grotesque contrast to the vivid, burning desire I've known with Spencer. I can't recall when I first noticed the change; but now his very appearance is repulsive.

Time drags in a blur of obligation until he finally grinds out a command to shift. I obey. I crawl across our unmade bed, feeling the fan's cool air sweeping over my wet hair, tugging at it, as if the strands themselves resist being dragged back into this bed. In this moment, my jaw locks, shoulders stiff, my body refusing to bend even as I obey.

I love what I'm doing with Spencer. His laughter still hums in my ears, a sharp counterpoint to Dominic's muttered command. I hate that I've trapped myself in this cycle of deceit. If Dominic ever discovered Spencer's imprint on me, I'd be branded a *traitor*—but *I'm not the bad* guy. *He is.*

As he draws nearer, his hands clamp around my waist, and I feel him slipping in with remarkable ease. His arousal, perversely feeding off the ghost of a better man.

"You like sucking my dick, huh? Got you all wet," he grates—bold, for a man who is usually silent during sex.

"You don't talk like this," I breathe, startled by the sharpness in his voice.

"Maybe I should have all along," he bites back, his thrusts sharper now. "Maybe then you wouldn't look so... bored."

Heat rises to my cheeks, anger mingling with shame. "You think this fixes anything? You barely even touch me unless it's about you."

He laughs, low and bitter. "And yet here you are—still opening your legs. Don't act like you're better than me, Sarah. You're not."

I respond with silence.

He starts to move with more vigor.

My body arches and trembles, caught between sensation and the weight of everything I don't want.

"Look at me," he grits, pressing harder. "You think you can hide from me? You're mine, Sarah."

His words snap like chains, dragging me deeper into a reality I don't want to claim. I force myself to picture Spencer, his hands, his heat, his laughter, anything to escape this suffocation pinning me down.

Dominic thrusts harder, his voice breaking through labored breaths. "Say it. Say you're mine."

I bite my lip until I taste blood, refusing. My silence is answering enough.

His frustration sharpens, but he doesn't stop.

Inside, I crumble. His used breaths fill me with revulsion. His limp form makes my skin crawl. It's torture—a living nightmare, reminiscent of a medieval punishment.

When my resolve hardens, Dominic suddenly withdraws, releasing across me in a final, messy claim. It's detestable, a defiant punctuation to a routine that never fails to disgust me. Usually careful, pulling out or using a condom, he now leaves behind an indelible mark, an imprint I'm desperate to erase. I flinch at the streak he leaves behind, one I can't wash away fast enough.

"Sarah..." The low timber of his voice settles somewhere deep in me. "I know I've pushed too hard. I just—" he exhales, feigning defeat. "You make me crazy. Because I love you too much."

The words land like a trick blade, dull on the surface, sharp underneath. A part of me wants to believe him, to fall into the illusion of a husband who cares. But my skin still crawls from his touch, my body still aches with the memory of Spencer. The apology feels rehearsed, another lie dressed up in love.

Sliding off the bed, trembling, I mutter, "I'm getting back in the shower." I turn away before he can say more, clutching for the towel willing it to be a lifeline. The shower hisses back to life, drowning out whatever words he throws at me. I don't care. I won't let them stick.

Behind me, his voice shifts into something smooth.

"Sounds good. I'll be in after." A casual mask, as if nothing happened—as if he hadn't just tried to spin poison into affection.

He doesn't realize this is the last time he'll ever touch me.

The *disdain* I feel for him is the feeling I was supposed to have for Spencer, but I don't. I feel it for the man I once vowed to love for life.

The good girl I once believed myself to be, the one who kept her vows and lived within the lines, has vanished. In her place stands a woman awakened by secrets and the ecstasy of dis-obedience.

My secret has become my liberation; it belongs to me, Maya, and now Spencer. Only three people know it. *And I will guard it fiercely.*

Twenty

With the boarding dogs settled, the shop is finally calm, and I'm alone.

At least, I think I am.

Gravel crunches behind me.

"Hey," a voice calls.

I spin around.

Nick stands a few feet away by the corner of the building, holding a thermos and looking like he's barely off a job. His shirt is wrinkled and untucked, his hair mussed from work. "Didn't mean to scare you," he says with a small smile.

"You didn't," I lie, pressing my hand to my chest. "I wasn't expecting anyone."

He tilts his head toward the yard. "Saw you out here last night. Looked like you were by the stream?"

I freeze. "You... saw me?"

"Yeah. I was checking the exterior cameras for Mike. Got a glimpse of you walkin' around back there." He shrugs. "Just sayin', probably not the best idea to be out here alone after dark."

I glance toward the fence line. "I wasn't out long. Besides, I didn't know there were cameras."

"Yeah, Mike just had 'em installed. Gotta keep an eye out on the vehicles in the yard."

He says it casually before continuing. "This area is quiet. Safe even. But still, people know there are women workin' here late."

TWENTY

His tone carries confusion I can't place. Concern? Warning? Something else?

"I'll be careful," I force a smile.

He gives a small dip of his chin and heads toward his truck.

As he crosses the work yard, my stomach knots.

He saw me.

Good thing it was only *me*—and not with Spencer.

But I can't help but wonder *how many times have I been on camera before.*

Maya pulls into the lot across the two-lane road, and the second I spot her from the other side of the street, a smile spreads across my face before I can stop it.

She steps out of her car like she owns the place, moving with that effortless grace that's always made me feel proud to call her my best friend. At five-foot-nine, her frame is willowy and fluid, the kind of build most girls only dream of. I've never envied her beauty; I've always known my own. But standing beside Maya, I'm reminded of how different our strengths are. Hers, in the way she commands a room. Mine, in the way I go after what I want, and refuse to let it go.

She's graceful, her posture flawless, her movements confident without ever tipping into arrogance. She could own a runway in Milan, yet here she is, crossing the cracked sidewalk to meet me.

Her skin is radiant, saddle brown, glowing in the late-afternoon sun. She doesn't wear much makeup, she doesn't need to. Her beauty is natural, earthy, magnetic. Her long, light-brown hair flows like silk, catching little glints of sunlight with every step. Each ripple trails behind her, wind-swept even when the air is still.

There's something ethereal about her. High cheekbones, a soft jawline, and full lips. But it's her eyes that stop people in their tracks. Big, round, and deep honey-brown, they stare straight into your soul.

And when she speaks, her soft voice rains like grace. Gentle but firm, threaded with certainty that makes people listen. Always. Maya is the kind of beautiful that doesn't only turn heads, it roots you in place and makes you forget what you were doing before you saw her.

"Hey, girly." I call, opening my arms wide for the hug I've been waiting on all day.

She rushes into me with the same energy, hugging tight. "Hey, Sar." Only she calls me that. Since Sarah is already short, nicknames for me are rare—but somehow Maya's always had her own version of me. She's been calling me that since kindergarten, and now it feels like a name only she's allowed to use.

"You ready for the grand tour?" I pull back, grinning at her like no time has passed.

"Always. Show me what you've been building out here. I want the full story."

Maya has always been my number-one supporter. Through every loss, every new beginning, every version of myself, she's stood beside me, never once flinching. She's the kind of friend you can trust with anything. No filter, no fear, no judgment, just that ever-present kindness and loyalty.

I take her through the shop, showing her every corner we've updated. She listens attentively, asking thoughtful questions and smiling the entire tour. By the time we reach the new outdoor park, her eyes light up with the same magic Linda and I feel. We wander the length of it together, soaking in the beauty.

On the stroll back to the main building, I spot Spencer through the window, concentrating on paperwork.

"Do you want to meet Spencer?" I ask.

She doesn't hesitate. "Of course. I've been waiting for this."

"I think his business partner has left, so we should be fine. No one's going to see us go in."

Maya claps her hands together, grinning. "From everything you've told me, he sounds dreamy. But... maybe a little intimidating too?"

I laugh, shaking my head. "You'll be fine. Trust me—he should know you. My best friend and my boyfriend.... those worlds were always going to collide."

TWENTY

She lifts a brow. "Boyfriend now? That's a promotion. He's officially moved up from 'booty call' to the big leagues?"

"Yep. But he doesn't know that's what I think of him yet," I say with a wink. "So mum's the word."

She gives me a look of certainty. "Got it."

Opening the door to Spencer's office, I see it clearly for the first time in daylight, it steals my breath.

Last time, it was dim—the situation distracting. But now, bathed with soft sunlight pouring through the wide windows, it's stunning, sophisticated, intentional. From the exposed brick wall behind his desk to the sleek black leather chairs facing it, everything is curated. Floor-to-ceiling bookcases flank an oversized matte-black monitor, glowing like the centerpiece of some futuristic control room.

It's masculine and modern, but refined. Like a luxurious cigar lounge collided with a high-end design studio.

Spencer's eye for style is everywhere, elevated, minimalistic, powerful. The room reflects *him*.

I glance at Maya, who's soaking in the same view, her wide eyes scanning the room with quiet appreciation. She's impressed. I can tell by the slight curve of her lips.

And then there's Spencer.

Sitting behind his massive desk, radiating command. He peers up from his screen, jaw cut sharp as his lips climb up into a smile that reaches his eyes.

For a beat, his gaze burns into me like I caught him off guard, before shifting to Maya.

"Surprise." I announce, stepping further inside.

"Hey." His voice is molten steel, smooth but edged. "What are you two doing here?"

"I wanted you to meet Maya. She came to see me at the shop, so I thought— why not introduce her to *you* too."

He rises, smoothing a hand across the top of his desk like he's brushing away invisible wrinkles, every movement sleek, confident, effortless. He makes his way over to greet her.

"It's great to finally meet you," Spencer says, his warm, rich voice laced with sincerity. "Sarah speaks so highly of you. It's nice to put a name to such a beautiful face."

Of course, he'd lead with a compliment—classic Spencer. But the way he says it doesn't feel rehearsed.

Maya, never one to fluster easily, responds with grace. "It's nice to meet you too."

They exchange a polite hug, appropriate—quick. The perfect length to mark mutual respect. But when he pulls back, his eyes flick to mine again, so fast Maya doesn't notice. That fleeting second feels like a claim, hidden in plain sight.

After the introduction, Spencer casually strolls to the door and with a click locks it.

He doesn't seem concerned about having the two of us in his office. But, I can't help thinking about what someone might assume if they saw us all together in here after hours.

"Have a seat." He gestures toward the plush chairs near the desk.

We make an attempt to maintain a natural demeanor, pretending the electricity between us isn't charging the air.

To break the tension, I blurt, "Want to try something fun? I found this quiz online. It supposedly reveals your canine personality."

Spencer's lips part as he swivels toward me. "Let's do it." Already he's pulling the site up on one of his oversized screens. Two screens, of course.

Because Spencer doesn't do basic. Ever.

The three of us lean in, taking turns answering the quirky questions. Laughter fills the room—Spencer sharp and energetic, Maya soft and melodic. The tension thins, dissolving for the moment.

Spencer's result: Jack Russell Terrier. We all burst out laughing. It's so accurate it's almost prophetic, energetic, bold, sharp, relentless. He's the kind of man who sniffs out bullshit from a mile away and digs until he

TWENTY

exposes it. He's never still. Driven by instinct, but not reckless. He's tactical. Alert. Dominant.

Mine flashes on the screen as a Golden Retriever. Loyal. Friendly. Safe. Predictable.

I laugh, but there's a sting to it. That used to be me, but now? I'm sneaking around, risking everything for this secret. Golden Retrievers don't dive headfirst into fire. I do.

Maya's result: an Afghan Hound. Elegant. Graceful. Regal.

It suits her. She radiates composure, admired without trying. She's still smiling, oblivious to the identity crisis happening in my head.

Spencer leans back in his chair. "So, it's settled. Sarah's the loyal retriever, Maya's the elegant hound, and I'm the relentless Terrier. Sounds about right, doesn't it?"

I circle Spencer's desk and slide onto his lap. He turns the screen so all of us can see, but the real claim is in the brief squeeze of his hand at my waist—hidden under the motion of the mouse.

He's polite enough not to ravish me in front of Maya, *thankfully*. Yet sitting here, pressed against him, inhaling his warmth, makes me yearn to be closer.

I love this moment. My boyfriend, my best friend, laughter, comfort, fun. The only thing missing is the truth. And that truth is... none of this is normal. This is all borrowed, stolen.

Still, my chest hums with a happiness in doing something ordinary with Spencer. *This is what right should feel like.*

Maya parts her lips as if to say something.

Just then, the handle rattles and a knock thumps.

A bolt of shock shoots through me, but Spencer glances at me with composure across his face. As if to say, *I've got you.*

I scramble off his lap and drop into the chair beside Maya.

Then a knock comes again. This time louder, more urgent. It pounds in my chest, each strike like thunder landing.

Meanwhile, Spencer, cool as a cucumber, turns his screen back to face himself, stands, smooths his slacks, and unlocks both the deadbolt and the lever handle in one easy motion. Right before opening it, he glances at me with an even expression as if nothing unusual is happening.

The door swings open.

I don't recognize the person standing there.

But Spencer does.

I peer over to Maya, hoping for a read. Her wide eyes lock with mine: *holy shit.* I can practically hear her thoughts mimic mine. *What is going on?*

Then I hear it.

"What the hell is this?" the woman's voice spits out, accusatory.

My body drops a flush of blood. I *know* that voice.

Fuck. Fuck. Fuck. My mind screams.

Maya has no idea who the woman is *yet.* I turn to her, giving her silent *holy-fuck* eyes, silently begging her to catch up—fast. Her sharp mind kicks in. I see it click. The posture, the tone, the shock. Maya realizes exactly what's happening.

Spencer doesn't flinch. He allows the woman to step inside like it's any other day. Like his *wife* isn't now standing in the same room as his *mistress,* and her best friend.

"Sarah, Maya," He gestures casually, the corner of his mouth curved in the faintest smile. "This is my wife, Vanessa."

He introduces us like we're meeting at a dinner party, not ground zero of a nuclear explosion. His composure is flawless, terrifyingly so.

I sit straighter, forcing myself to look natural.

"Sarah is my tenant. She runs the grooming shop next door. She's here to drop off rent." He answers Vanessa's question with an unruffled tone, doing everything in his power to appear unbothered.

Maya's hand brushes mine under the desk, the smallest lifeline. She's processing it, too. Piecing it together in silence.

"Why was the door locked?" she snaps back, arms folded tight across her chest. Suspicion hardens her voice.

"Locked?" he repeats, amused. "Oh, yes. I didn't want any customers wandering in and keeping me here later than I already need to stay."

Great excuse. I almost believe the lie.

Vanessa tilts her head, eyes narrowing, but she buys it, or pretends to.

TWENTY

That's Spencer's gift: he makes women believe. He makes *me* believe him, even as he lies right in front of me. And I excuse it, because *I want to.*

He's told me he's done everything he could to make it work with her. He's not a quitter. I believe him when he says that.

"Oh, Okay. Well, I was on my way home from a friend's and thought I'd stop in and say hi."

"Sounds good. Thanks for stopping by, honey," Spencer replies smoothly.

The chair under me pushes back as I stand. Maya mimics my movement without a word. Spencer leans in, kissing Vanessa right in front of me. It's not a dagger; it's worse. A slow, twisting burn that hollows me out from the inside. I keep my face still, but inside I'm screaming.

I *understand* why he kisses her; he has to. But understanding doesn't make it hurt any less.

Vanessa is the kind of beautiful that doesn't have to try. Her presence alone makes my connection with Spencer feel smaller, like a secret I invented in my head.

She's nearly as tall as Maya, but carries herself with her own subtle elegance. Today, she's in a soft sundress that glows against, olive-toned skin. Her bare shoulders and collarbones shimmer under the light, framed by the delicate gold chain of her purse. She sweeps her jet-black hair over her shoulder with one fluid motion, revealing a face that could sell shampoo.

Standing next to Spencer, they look too perfect. Like a power couple cut from an editorial spread. Their beauty feeds off each other, infuriatingly seamless. She makes "normal" appear grand.

But if you dropped her in our small town alone, she'd stick out like a red sequin dress at a barbecue. Our area is more earth and grit than glam and gloss—Vail without the Oscars. High-end, sure. But more boots than ballgowns.

I should feel intimidated standing in the same room as her. Most women would. Especially with the added humiliation of being forced to witness their shared kiss. But strangely, I don't.

Because deep down, I know I'm the one he truly desires right now.

If he wanted her, he wouldn't need to invent little lies to be with me.

He claims to have tried to make it work with her, but she's too wrapped in herself to notice his deeper need for connection. That's how I see their relationship. Spencer is a gifted salesman, and as long as he keeps telling me his story, I'll keep believing him.

He says she's pulling away, that being with her feels forced. That's where I come in—his escape, his life raft. And the strangest part is, I don't even hate her. Honestly, if the circumstances were different, I could probably like Vanessa. She's sharp and seems like a kind person. It's... unfortunate we're on opposite sides of the same lie.

I offer a polite smile. "It's nice to meet you," I say, pretending I don't already know her name.

Vanessa studies me, her guarded expression softening now that Spencer has given her reassurance. "What was your name again?" I ask, faking ignorance.

"Vanessa. It's really nice to meet you," she says. "You're running the grooming shop. Spencer said it's been keeping busy."

"It has," I say. "But not too busy. We were just on our way out." I add quickly, grabbing Maya's arm. "Have a great day. Vanessa. Spencer." I give a nod to them each individually. My eyes catching heat with Spencer's before we exit.

"Nice to meet you," Maya adds with her usual grace, polite as ever.

"Drive safe, girls." Spencer has the last word.

My hand trembles on the handle as I pull the door shut.

We've narrowly escaped being caught red-handed.

"That was close," I announce.

Maya lets out a long, drawn-out breath. "Girl, I wasn't even breathing in there."

She flicks her hands a few times to release the nervous energy, and we both laugh—uneasy but relieved. "Good thing Spencer locked the door when he did," I add, a hint of pride sneaking into my voice. "He's always one step ahead."

"And that rent excuse?" Maya raises a brow. "Clever."

TWENTY

"I'm just glad she didn't walk in while I was still on his lap," I joke, still riding on the adrenaline.

"You do love to play with fire." She teases.

"Guess that makes me the girl who forgot her fire extinguisher."

We both break into another laugh, looser now, the tension finally bleeding off.

"What did you think of her?" I ask.

"She's obviously beautiful," Maya's smile softens, "but he doesn't look at her like that."

"Like what?"

"Like the way he stares into you. That man's orbit changes when you enter the room."

I blink, trying not to let the words settle too deep. "You're seeing things."

"Maybe." She tilts her head, smirking. "But if I'm wrong, you're still glowing, and it's not from fluorescent lights."

We hug, laughing again, both pretending this day hasn't left its mark.

"I'll call you later, thanks for stopping by."

"The shop is looking amazing, Sar. And Spencer..." Her grin turns knowing. "He's trouble. The kind that makes mascara bleed."

"You're not wrong." I say.

"You never have gone for easy."

"Wouldn't know what to do with it." I agree.

She laughs, waving as she heads for her car. "Love you, fire hazard."

"Love you too."

Returning home to my sanctuary, nerves still looped tight, I can't shake the feeling of exposure after what just happened.

I spent time face-to-face with my boyfriend's wife.

The silence in the driveway greets me like a small mercy. Dominic's truck is gone. This brief reprieve lets me gather myself without an audience.

Inside, the house feels hollow. My stomach growling in protest. I've ignored it all day. I pop a tamale into the microwave, my go-to when I'm too tired to cook or bother. The scent of spiced pork and masa fills the air, stirring the hunger within me.

Now it's close to 6:30 p.m. I don't know where Dominic is, or when he'll be back. I don't ask anymore, and tonight, the distance feels like a gift.

I round the kitchen counter and sink onto the barstool instead of sitting at the dining table. I need something less formal, less committed. My mind drifts while I eat. There's no surprise where it lands. Spencer. Us. His hands, his mouth, the magnetic pull of our bodies like they are made to fit.

But the cold slap of reality crashes the fantasy: Vanessa.

Gosh, she's beautiful. So composed. *So flawless.* It almost hurts to think about her. That golden dress. That impossibly shiny hair. The kind of woman men don't just want—they keep.

And then there's me. The girl he hides. The secret he reaches for when he needs to feel alive again.

He'll never leave her for me. I've told myself that a hundred times, yet it still slices clean. I'm a detour. Something shiny to escape the monotony. Maybe I'm delusional. Maybe I'm falling too fast—too hard. But when I'm with him, it's like a part of me locks into place. It feels *right*.

I close my eyes and let the truth settle over me like a weight I don't want to lift. Deep down, I believe we're meant for each other. I *feel* it.

My heart doesn't lie—not about this.

Twenty-One

I arrive at the shop with a light jacket in hand, per Spencer's request.

When I pull in, his reflection flashes in the glass, and there he is. *Damn*, he looks good in that leather jacket, gloves on, legs straddling his motorcycle.

He glances up, that half-smile already undoing me. With a tilt of his head, he motions for me to hop on.

"Really?" My voice lifts with giddiness. "Is this my big surprise? Do I finally get the ride I've been begging for?"

"Maybe." He pauses. "You'll see. Put this on."

He hands me a dark-blue helmet, its paint matching his bike. I slide it on, the padding cool against my cheeks. He does the same.

"Safety first," he says, his voice muffled behind the shield.

This is it—the moment I've asked for over and over. I swing my leg over and wrap my arms around his chest, my fingers splaying across the leather.

Tucked in close, I feel the vibration surge as the throttle opens, propelling us out of the shop. Wind tears at my jacket, cool and wild.

It's my first time on a motorcycle, and it feels both romantic and terrifying. We fly from the city, devouring miles toward the canyon where I grew up.

My dad still lives there, in the valley on the other side. The house I visit some Sundays.

I start to wonder if Spencer knows, but I can't ask, the engine's roar swallows everything except the rush of speed and sound.

I hold on tighter, savoring the ride, the cars blurring past us in streaks of color. Each turn pulling us tighter together.

The river winds along every curve, framed by towering mountains. The rush of fresh wind tangling my hair, the pavement thrumming beneath us. My focus stays locked on the man guiding us through it.

Then, suddenly, the canyon widens into a sunlit valley. A deep blue lake sprawls before us, a mirror of sky and memory.

We call it *The Dam*. The placid waters are dotted with boats, inviting everyone to gather for summer celebrations.

The Rockies cradle the lake and homes in every direction. This hidden valley stays cooler, higher, untouched compared to the crowded city where I live now.

It was once a quaint little ski town until the Olympics came. Now the edges sprawl with new money, but the heart still feels like home.

And suddenly, I realize where he's taking me.

Bright, colorful balloons rise in every direction, drifting into view across the late-afternoon sky. The Hot Air Balloon Festival in full swing.

As a child, I never missed it. But I grew older, and the festival faded into the background. Now people travel from everywhere to see it: floating globes glowing against the mountains, food, music, and laughter spilling into the valley.

The balloons lift gracefully, some from the carnival grounds, others already high above, their silhouettes catching fire light as the pilots heat the air within.

Spencer pulls the bike close to the edge of the crowd, parking where the gravel meets the grass, and we roll into a spot that isn't technically a parking space.

I suppose that's one of the perks of riding a motorcycle.

Not knowing how the helmet unlatches, Spencer helps loosen the straps, his fingers grazing my neck, sparking a shiver beneath my skin.

He drapes his jacket across the gas tank and stuffs his gloves into the pockets.

"You're going to leave your jacket here?" I ask.

TWENTY-ONE

"Well, where else am I supposed to put it? I'm not lugging it around all night."

"You're daring to trust no one will steal it."

"Nobody wants my old motorcycle jacket. Trust me."

He kisses my forehead, our fingers finding each other and leads me through the carnival.

We weave through the crowd until we reach the largest balloon on the field. It's a stunning swirl of dark colors, patched together at an angle, reaching toward the sky. The glowing fire bellows. Hot inhales and exhales infuse the air, lighting the rainbow oval.

Spencer reaches into his pocket, presses something into the pilot's hand. I catch only a glimpse. Maybe folded cash, or a piece of paper.

"We'll be back in an hour," he says.

Shock clings to me. Spencer, the man who hides everything, taking me to the most public place in town. Even with people arriving from all over, it's still a small-town festival. Everyone knows everyone.

What if someone we know sees us?

If Dominic or anyone from my old life saw us, there would be no explanation good enough.

I'm uneasy, and I should be. Most of Dominic's old crew still lives in this valley—people like Dustin.

The odds of being seen with Spencer instead of Dominic are dangerously high. Still, I let my guard drop. I'm too thrilled to resist showing him off in public. We wander hand-in-hand like any couple, sampling lemonade and caramel popcorn, pretending nothing exists beyond this crowd.

The fastest hour of my life passes, and Spencer leads me back toward the hot air balloon where he handed the man something earlier. I still don't know what it was, but the man clearly trusts Spencer, and so do I.

"Are you ready?" Spencer asks, eyes gleaming.

"Ready for what?"

"For this." He gestures toward the balloon basket.

I laugh. "For *this*? You're not serious."

"Yes," he grins. "You wanted an adventure, so here it is."

My jaw drops. "No way. We're actually going up in that?"

His smile widens. "Would I lie to you? I usually save my dishonesty for taxes." He winks.

I push his shoulder. "You're impossible."

The balloon pilot offers his hand to help me climb in. I take it, stepping inside. His grip holds a second too long, his thumb brushing my palm before he lets go.

Spencer's already beside me, his hand closing possessively at my waist. His voice cuts low, sharp enough to sting. "He held on a little longer than necessary, don't you think?"

"He was helping me in." I whisper.

Spencer's jaw flexes. "Didn't look like just helping."

He climbs in after me, pulling me in tight against him. Heat bites into my hip, a silent claim. He buries his face into my hair as the burners roar to life.

Leaning against Spencer's chest, I feel him gaze down and press a kiss to the top of my head.

The earth falls quiet as the balloon drifts upward, slowly, reverently, as though even gravity has stepped aside. The only sound is the hiss of the flame, a breath of fire melting into the silence.

The wicker creaks beneath our feet. Up here, fate agrees, this is where we're meant to be.

Wind brushes my skin, cool and clean, carrying the scent of grass and pine. Suspended between heaven and earth, we drift as though time has paused only for us. No turbulence. No chaos. Only peace.

The horizon glows in hues of apricot and rose, clouds painted in soft strokes of light. The sun hovers low above the earth, casting a warm haze across his face. I can't help but stare at him and think he's never appeared more beautiful, serene and quietly strong.

In the moment everything falls away: the noise, the stress, the guilt. Up here, it's only us, floating in a space untouched by the weight of everyday life.

Below, the land softens into a watercolor painting. The people shrink to dots, roads to ribbons, cars to toys. Grasslands fade into a patchwork quilt of greens and golds across the valley floor.

Balloons drift past like bubbles in a steel sky, silent, held up by nothing but air.

I glance up and find Spencer watching me, his expression unreadable-yet-glowing. He brushes a strand of hair from my cheek, his fingers linger long enough to send tears pricking my eyes.

The serenity of it all overwhelms me. It's the most romantic moment I've ever known. Spencer has outdone himself.

"This is incredible!" I whisper.

"So are you," he says softly.

"Have you flown before?" I ask, wondering if he's shared anything like this with someone else.

"Nope. First for me too. Feels like I'm on a magic carpet." A rare laugh escapes him, cracking his usual calm exterior.

"I have one last surprise." He leans in to say against my ear.

"This is surprise enough," I say, shaking my head, as I turn toward him.

He smiles. "I know you don't need anything else, but I *have* something for you."

From his back pocket, he pulls a small black box and sets it into my hand.

I open it. Emerald stud earrings catch the fading light, gleaming in quiet perfection. "They're gorgeous," I whisper. "But I can't accept them."

"Yes, you *can*," he insists gently. "And you *will*."

"They're too much," I protest. "We've barely been dating. Are you trying to buy me?" I add, teasing to lighten the moment.

A flicker of vulnerability crosses his face. "I'm trying to remind you that you *deserve* beautiful things."

After a split-second pause, I agree, "If you insist—they are my birthstone after all."

I slide each earring from the box and fasten them into my ears.

"They're perfect on you," he says, twirling the earrings between his fingertips. "You are the real beauty, and these come close." He cups my face in his calloused hands and pulls me in for a kiss.

I must be dreaming. *Where does this man come from?*

We drift for the remainder of time, laughing, trading stories, and stealing quiet touches as the balloon floats.

I show him my childhood home, and point to the swimming pool where I used to swim summers away. He was unaware his surprise flight would turn into a personal tour of my past.

After the most romantic hour of my life, we finally descend.

I scan the crowd, pulse quickening, terrified someone might recognize me. No familiar faces. Not yet. Only us, suspended in our secret.

A band starts warming up nearby, one I grew up listening to. Spencer did too. Even with years between us, our taste in music is the same.

We find a spot on a grassy knoll, side by side.

While we wait, we discover that we both love to people-watch, laughing at little dramas unfolding around us. Spencer leans back on his hands, relaxed, and I follow his gaze as he watches families spread blankets and kids dancing near the lights.

Then a hand lands on Spencer's shoulder. He turns, and a couple is standing behind us.

"Jackie! So good to see you!" Spencer jumps to his feet. I follow.

"Tom, nice to see you," he adds, his tone shifting to measured and cautious.

There's no hug, only a simple handshake with Tom. Strained smiles cross our faces. The kind that cover secrets.

The woman, Jackie, glances between us. Her eyes catch mine, sending unease crawling under my skin.

When they finally move on, I ask, "Who are they?"

"Jackie. We've been friends since high school. She's close with Vanessa too. The worst part? She's our neighbor."

"You're kidding." Reality rushes in. "Shit, is she going to tell Vanessa?"

"I don't know," his reply is low. "I hope not. Probably not. She's been my friend longer than Vanessa's. She might not even mention it. We weren't doing anything."

TWENTY-ONE

He tries to joke, but his eyes give him away. "You could've been my little sister, for all she knows. My sister's almost ten years younger. My friends and I never paid attention to her."

"Right," I say. "Because you always bring your sister to concerts."

He tries to laugh it off, but it dies quickly, swallowed by the thrum of bass and conversation. "I guess time will tell," he says, forcing a smile.

The music swells, mercifully breaking the tension. A familiar melody begins. One I loved as a child—about fishing in the dark. Spencer pulls me back against him, swaying in time with the beat. His arms tighten around me, possessive and protective all at once.

Although this feels like a dream finally come true, I keep watching the crowd, waiting for Jackie's dark hair to reappear in the sea of strangers.

But she's gone.

Even still, I can't shake the feeling she took something with her.

Twenty-Two

Fall 2004

Labor Day is quickly approaching, and I have no plans.

I'll need to come in to board the dogs, as the holidays are always our busiest time of year. I won't be grooming, just managing the boarding schedule.

We still need to finish the kennel area, so all week we've been staying late, painting, tackling one task after another to get it done.

Today, though, I need a break.

I decide to track Spencer down and see what his plans are for the weekend. I've learned to arrive a few minutes early. By now, I know if he's not around by 8, he's gone for the day—and often, he's not even in town.

Today, I get lucky.

I spot him loading work trucks, sleeves rolled up, sun catching the shimmer of sweat on his arms.

I park, throw my princess shades on the dash, and head across the two-lane road.

He sees me and I motion for him to meet me in the lobby.

Inside, I walk straight into the lobby—the same place where I first discovered he had a wife and children. There's a bathroom tucked away beside the area where Linda and I work.

When I hear the front door close, I ease it open barely enough to signal him in.

He slips inside, and before the lock clicks, I grip his shirt, dragging him

TWENTY-TWO

into me, my mouth claiming his with desperate force. No words, only need. He answers with equal urgency, his palms pressing over my chest, clutching as if he can't get enough.

"As much as I should, I can't stop," I whisper against his mouth.

"I've got a full day," his breath crosses my lips, still kissing me. "But while I've got you..."

His hand trails down, before the warmth of his palm covers me. He pulls me in tighter against him and enters one finger, then two.

He drags his lips along my neck, leaving trails of lust.

"You're cruel," I murmur.

His voice drops. "And you like it."

"Maybe," I breathe, using his word against him. "When can we meet again?"

"Soon," he promises, pushing me against the wall.

"No, not now," I say, catching his wrist and pulling it up.

He lifts his hand to his nose and inhales, eyes gone dark with hunger. "You smell too good, I could devour you."

"You'll get your chance—if we don't get caught first. Do you have plans this weekend?" I ask again.

"No. Vanessa will be away with our kids. Come to my house a little later, once the neighborhood settles. I'll let you know what time to meet me once she's left."

The mention of her name still stings, but I agree to go to his home anyway.

I cut his attention short and return to work, still buzzing from his provocations, every nerve alive.

Twenty-Three

After a week of long overtime hours finishing our new dog boarding area, I'm finally ready for a *real* night with Spencer. It's my first time in his territory, and honestly, I have no idea where he lives. All I know is that his business partner is building a massive estate on top of the hill, and by "hill," I mean as far up as a mansion can be built on a 9,700-foot mountain. It's designed to sprawl over twenty-thousand square feet with panoramic views over the city. From the shop, I've watched it rise from the dirt, practically shouting *look at me*.

But Spencer isn't that kind of flashy. He prefers keeping his wealth quiet. No ostentatious car, no loud displays—just understated elegance. A single Rolex instead of a different designer watch every day. But his hair? That's a barber who charges more than I make in a day.

Come to think of it, maybe he's more high-maintenance than I gave him credit for. I'm not one to chase trends, but I'll admit I have a weakness for good perfume and the occasional new purse.

One last spritz of my signature scent. It drifts through the air and settles against my dress, simple, soft, but shaped to tempt. The fabric hugs my waist and moves when I move. *If the outfit doesn't get his attention, the scent will.*

I hook my white sandals in one hand as I take the stairs. Once I reach the bottom, I step into them, my size-five feet now dressed for the night.

Spencer told me to meet him at the end of the two-lane road, where I'll follow him into his territory. At nearly 9:00, the timing feels perfect. It's dark enough that the night itself feels like an accomplice.

I pull off to the side of the road and cut the engine. The stars flare brighter than I remember from childhood, scattered diamonds across the black silk sky.

My mixed CD plays, a ballad about a man standing on a mountain and bathing in the sea. Classic 90s love song, exactly the kind of song that makes bad ideas feel like a good idea.

Headlights approach from the opposite direction. Spencer slows, rolls down his window, and grins. I lower mine. Our eyes hook and hold. My pulse skips.

"Are you planning to admire the stars all night, or will you let me steal you away?" he teases.

"Steal me? You'll have to catch me first." I wink. "Come and get me."

It only takes a minute to pull my car into a hidden spot along the tall grass. Hidden by the darkness and the curve of the road, no one would ever know it's there.

Moments later, I'm climbing into his truck for the first time. It's taller than I expected.

I grab the handle and haul myself up. The passenger seat swallows me, and his scent—strong, masculine, impossible to ignore, envelopes me before he even speaks.

His truck is spotless, like it just rolled off the showroom floor. I'd expected it to be slightly disorganized, but everything is curated to fit. Even his matte-black Maui Jim sunglasses rest neatly in their case inside the console.

Searching for something to say, I glance down. "What's in here?" I ask, flipping the latch.

He shrugs. "Check it out for yourself."

I open it to find a pack of cinnamon gum, a ballpoint pen, a Bible, and the Book of Mormon.

The cinnamon hits me first. He remembers.

That scent sparks something deep, the same pull I felt the first time he kissed me.

"Do you still attend church regularly?" I ask, because we share the same faith.

"Yes," he says, easily. "My family and I go almost every Sunday. If we miss, it's because we're out of town or something important comes up."

I can't remember the last time I prayed without bargaining.

"I guess I have a lot to learn about you." I say.

"Indeed, you do." He reaches for my hand, but before our fingers touch, red and blue lights explode in the rearview mirror.

"Shit, I wasn't speeding," he mutters.

Panic squeezes tight. One wrong word, one curious cop, and our secret could unravel.

"I don't know why I'm being pulled over." Spencer's voice shakes. I glance at his hands clamping the wheel, knuckles white.

He eases the truck to the shoulder. A suffocating silence looms until the officer approaches.

He rolls the window down.

"Good evening, officer," he greets him, his tone forced, straining to sound polite.

"Evening. Where are you folks headed tonight?"

"Home," Spencer says.

My mind sprints. What if he thinks I'm underage? What if he questions me, about us?

"Do you know why I pulled you over?" His question rings firm, not unkind.

"I'm not sure. I wasn't speeding." Spencer's words wobble.

"No, you weren't," the officer replies. "But your tail light is out. You aware of that?"

"No, sir. I'll get that fixed right away."

"License and registration." The demand is clipped, all business.

Spencer reaches into the glove box, retrieves his wallet and papers, and hands them over.

"Sit tight," the officer says, before returning to his cruiser.

Relaxing, Spencer's shoulders sag.

I glance at him, "You don't get pulled over often?" I whisper.

TWENTY-THREE

He shakes his head. "Not when I'm driving straight," he teases. "I've actually never had a ticket. Let's hope tonight's not my first."

Of course he hasn't. Not even a ticket. Everything about him is spotless, polished—the kind of man who's untouchable. The man who never leaves fingerprints on his mistakes. Meanwhile, I sit beside him, praying the officer can't smell the guilt radiating off me.

Tap, tap, tap. The officer returns, rapping his flashlight against the window. Spencer lowers it three-quarters.

"I'm going to let you off with a warning," the officer says. "But get that tail light fixed."

Spencer swallows. "Yes, sir. Thank you."

The officer gives a curt nod and hands back the paper and ID. "Have a good night."

"You too," Spencer replies, his voice steadier now.

Only when the cruiser pulls away does Spencer exhale hard, like the fear has sunk claws into him, too.

He pulls back onto the road, confidence already sliding back into place.

He chuckles. "We're not far now, good thing I didn't know the cop."

"Do you know a lot of them?" I ask, half-joking, half-fishing.

"I know a lot of people," he replies. "My presence in the community is strong. I own the largest building in town."

I roll my eyes at the arrogance, though I can't argue.

"So, our affair's going to be tough to keep secret, huh?" I question, letting the teasing mask my nerves.

He glances over, unreadable. "Nah, I know what I'm doing. Don't worry, no one will see us. We're turning onto my road now. I'll kill the headlights. Follow me to the door, okay?"

I agree, my nerves shooting little shots of fire.

As we drive between the dark silhouettes of the mansions, I realize how far I've stepped out of my world—and into his.

Twenty-Four

Wow, I breathe, unable to hide my surprise. "It's beautiful!"

"It is, isn't it?" Spencer's lips curve with confidence.

"I built it myself. I'm a man of many talents. One of them, being a contractor." He lets another piece of himself slip, though I sense it still isn't the secret he's keeping.

The opulent dwelling looms ahead, more commanding with every turn of the driveway. Recessed lights glow over the roundabout fountain, silver ripples scattering across the stone.

The front door towers above me, heavy mahogany polished to a dark sheen. The place is a statement: three-car garage, RV bay, and a driveway patterned in stone that leads us straight to its threshold.

Through the windows, I glimpse a white grand piano, ivory keys catching the faintest light. This isn't just a house—it's a declaration.

Spencer strides ahead and pushes open the massive door. I count the steps under my breath, a nervous habit disguised as composure as I enter.

The air shifts the second I step inside. It's laced with a fragrance I can't place. It's inviting, like summer colliding with the spice of holidays. Lamps spill golden light across the textured floors, painting the space with warmth. To my right, the grand piano dominates like a centerpiece. Above, an ornate ceiling rises toward the loft, every detail lined in crown molding. To my left, a sweeping staircase winds upward, its cherry wood railing catching the light before curving into shadow.

The foyer stretches wide and open, windows framing the lit valley beyond. The ceiling soars higher than anything I've seen outside a temple.

TWENTY-FOUR

"You play?" I gesture toward the piano.

"Among other instruments," he replies with a hint of pride.

"What other instruments?"

"Guitar, violin... maybe even the banjo," he admits with a twinkle of amusement.

"Wow, a man of many talents," I tease, though I'm secretly impressed. The thought of him playing pulls at something in me; I want to hear those hidden pieces of him.

"Oh, you have no idea," he teases, alluding to talents beyond the instrumental. "But, one of these days, I'll play for you."

"I'll hold you to that."

My gaze drifts over the lavish space, every detail feeding both awe and unease.

Despite its grandeur, the house feels intimate. Family photos line the walls, a glimpse into the man behind the mystery.

As a child, I used to imagine my future husband: his presence, his stance, the way he would command a room. Spencer embodies every piece of that vision.

But Spencer's not mine. *I'm not here to break up a family. He'll never leave her. He's done this before and he's willing to risk everything. Well, so am I.*

He takes my hand, pulling me deeper into the heart of his home along an unimaginably long hallway. Moonlight streams through tall windows, mingling with the illumination of ground-level fixtures, shifting shadows across the floor's grain.

I can't stop staring at the quiet elegance, wondering how his wife keeps everything so flawless.

How could I ever compete with her?

She's beautiful. A mother. An impeccable housekeeper. This flawless home is proof of her presence, of her hold on him. Every detail whispers that I'll never measure up.

Shit, I want to marry her.

We stop at three wooden doors, all closed, except one. The open doorway feels like a line I shouldn't cross, yet my body moves anyway.

I step inside like an intruder. I stand frozen, unable to wrap my mind around the idea that people live like this. *How did Spencer end up here? He has secrets. He must.*

The thought of stepping into someone else's most private space, the room that they share with their partner, sends adrenaline into every vein.

Spencer is a man of many layers, talented, successful, and very well-connected. Yet the thought nags at me: *Why me? Why would someone like him want me?* The question haunts me as I stand in the midst of this impeccable home, surrounded by a life I can't comprehend.

To the left, an enormous king bed, piled high with throw pillows in precise symmetry. Beyond it, a bay window stretches across the wall, a custom-built seat tucked into the alcove beneath. Pillows spill there too, from cotton to silk, every detail curated.

My gaze flickers right, struggling to keep pace with the luxury. Beyond the bay, French double doors with large glass panes hint at a hidden terrace. Ten steps farther, a narrow hallway disappears into shadow.

The wall opposite is lined with shelves, staged with an assortment of decorations. A clear glass bowl rests on a book, white geraniums inside. I notice a crystal award engraved with words I can't make out. A photo of Spencer and Vanessa embracing on a mountain top twists webs inside me. The unspoken reminder: I'm intruding on a perfectly constructed life.

A TV sits on a low cabinet stretching wide, in front a large wall. On the end of the stand, a red light blinks from a camera, quiet and watching.

I glance at Spencer. "What's that?" I ask, pointing toward the camera.

"Nothing," he replies with a shrug. "Home videos I haven't put away."

"So this is where the magic happens," I tease, a playful smile tugging at my lips, though a small part of me burns with jealousy, imagining Vanessa in this space.

TWENTY-FOUR

Spencer's grin is wicked. "Yep, all eight inches of magic." Pride flickers in his eyes.

I laugh, shaking my head. "Do you always make the bed when your wife isn't around?" He shrugs again, "I guess so. She likes it that way, so it's become a habit."

His response, paired with the way he moves around the room, only deepens my fascination. He's a pleaser, a man who thrives on details. It's clearer now why people admire him.

Turning to face him, Spencer steps closer, his towering figure now inches from mine. He threads his fingers with mine, a wave of comfort seeps into me. He wants *me* here.

I push aside the questions clawing at me. Right now, I feel like the prize he's been reaching for, set high on a pedestal only he can touch. The way his gaze settles on me, hungry and unyielding, pulling me deeper into his gravity.

In a flash, his hands are on me. He lifts me like I weigh nothing, carrying me to his bed. My dress rises higher as I curl my legs around his body, drawing him closer.

"What next? What do you want?" I whisper.

"I know what I want, do you want it too?" His tone is low and enticing.

With restraint, I murmur, trailing ardent breath along the curve of his neck. "Maybe this is what I want."

"Like this?" his hands answer, tracing boldly down my sides.

Warm air skims my shoulder, stirring a few loose strands of hair drifting behind me.

Then his mouth claims the curve of my neck, a slow drag of current against my pulse. His grip tightens, pinning me in place, his chest pushing solid against mine. A shiver overtakes me—his strength holding me still, his lips coaxing me into unraveling.

I've ached for this, for a man who can be both relentless and tender in the same breath.

His damp lips trail lower, kissing a path from the valley between my breasts down to my navel. He pauses, his mouth hot against my skin, covering me in goosebumps. "Should I continue with this?"

His hands slide beneath me, cupping each cheek.

"Or how about this?" His nose presses into the thin fabric that still separates us, fervor coursing into me, reaching my most sensitive spot.

"Yes," my desperation pleads. "I want more of this. Whatever *this* is."

He inhales slowly against my skin. "I fucking love the smell of you," he whispers, lust heavy in his tone. One hand slips from beneath me, dragging down the curve of my hip before finding its way between my thighs. He applies pressure to my personal area with his cupped hand, tenderly making small circular motions.

I lean back on my arms, giving him space to explore every inch of me. My head tips until my hair spills across the bed, my face turning toward the ceiling.

Spencer strokes me once more, taking a deep breath before withdrawing his other hand, only to slide both palms along my sides. His touch persists, promising more, until his fingers hook the strings of my panties, easing them off.

I tremble, aching to know where he'll go next, surrendering to the control he's taking over my body.

With Dominic, I'd always felt forced to lead, to carry the weight, to mask my femininity. But Spencer doesn't let me hide. He places me in the role I've desired—his woman. He knows exactly how to draw out the softest parts of me.

His tongue meets its craving by flicking across my clitoral mound, each stroke unleashing ripples of desire that wash over me. I'm captivated by the fearless control he exudes, within the most intimate depths of my body.

He slides his middle finger inside. I find myself dripping, perhaps more than during our first encounter.

"Let me know what you can handle," he teases, pressing me further in the most delicious way.

A second finger joins, pushing me higher, pleasure surging until my back

TWENTY-FOUR

arches off the bed. I absorb him completely, every nerve lit by his touch.

Then his tongue replaces his fingers, unyielding, relentless. He sweeps over me again and again, from trembling entrance to aching peak. No one has ever ventured this far south, or claimed me this way.

Whatever secret craving he's feeding, I love it.

"You taste so good."

"Stop," I demand. Not because I want him to, but because I want to touch him too.

His lips glisten, breath heavy, wild even. Like a man after his feast, he looks sated.

"Come here," I whisper.

Bracing himself, he climbs my body. His mouth crushes mine, his chin slick with me. For a moment I'm unsure if I want to taste myself on his lips. Doubt dissolves as desire takes over. I kiss him harder, the taste of us searing my senses. What started as unfamiliar becomes something I thirst for.

I'm still uncovering his darkest cravings, how much he enjoys filthy foreplay. I never knew it existed in my sheltered Mormon bubble. But now, I crave more.

His fingers skillfully release my bra in one effortless motion. But as I embrace his easy touch, something catches my eye—the faint blink of a camera light on the table.

"Tell me that's not on," I plead for reassurance—I'm not being filmed.

"It's not," he says, dismissive, his attention fixed on me.

I press again, needing to be sure. "Are you sure? Why do you have it out?"

Evidence like that would ruin us. We don't even text for fear of leaving a trace.

His answer comes, reassuring but firm. "No, it's off." Then he carries me further onto the bed—Vanessa's side, I realize before he lowers me down. It Stirs a strange blend of satisfaction and unease.

Now, fully bare, I part my legs, a decorative pillow propped behind me. His eyes blaze as he kneels between them, hunger radiating off him. His fingers tug at the buttons of his shirt until it's free of his shoulders. I reach for his belt, and unfasten it with less grace, desperate to match his confidence, to pretend this feels as natural to me as it does to him.

I drag my touch higher, tracing the sculpted line of his abs.

My hands explore the cut of his chest, the dark hair patterned like wings, until my fingers curl at his neck. His jaw is solid beneath my palm. He looks at me like I'm the only thing he's ever needed.

He strips his pants with a fluid motion, folds them neatly, and sets them at the foot of the bed. *Of course he does.* Even now, he's deliberate. The detail makes me smile to myself until my gaze drops lower, all sense of humor evaporates.

As much as I ache to take his thickness in me, I thirst every bit as much for his pulsing length in my mouth, to unravel him, the way he's been undoing me all along.

His thick, pulsing length stands before me, hard, demanding, impossible to ignore. It's the first time I've truly seen him. Before, darkness veiled the details, leaving me with silhouettes, shadows, and the feel of him. But now, with nothing between us, I can't look away.

"You want this cock, don't you?" he teases, dripping with arrogance.

"Yes. Yes, I do. Right now."

I pull the elastic from my wrist, gathering my hair back, readying myself for what's to come. This little band is always present with me, ready whenever my hair demands to be tamed.

My fingers wrap around him, fitting like my hand is molded just for this. The size, his ardor, the twitch beneath my touch make me ache.

"You're so sexy," I say quietly.

I trace the thick veins along his shaft, my touch feather-light teasing, testing. I want to memorize every ridge, every silent plea his body releases. The power in holding him like this, knowing I could ruin him with a single flick of my wrist, emboldens me.

"You're killing me," he mutters, his voice strained and half-feral. The hunger in his eyes is possessive now, his control slipping with every second

TWENTY-FOUR

I delay.

In one smooth move, he straddles my sides, his stiffness poised in front of me. I lean in, daring, taking him with a bold sweep of my tongue. His taste—salt, heat and sin—floods my senses, all power and want.

With a need that's been held in for too long, I open for him, welcoming his solid weight into my mouth. A broken sound rips from his chest, something between a moan and a curse, and it pushes me deeper into him.

My rhythm builds, slow and methodical, my tongue coaxing him deeper with every stroke. His body tightens, answering every pull of my tongue.

I continue to move in a slow sensual glide: up, down, deeper, savoring the way he shudders, how his body reacts to every inch I give him.

When a soft gag catches in my throat, I pull back just enough to breathe, wrapping my hand around his base and stroking it in perfect harmony with my mouth. I work him with relentless focus, letting the wet, lewd sounds roll across the room. My jaw aches, but I refuse to stop. I want to be the reason why he loses his perfect composure.

A sharp pop reverberates when I release him.

He tangles his fingers in my ponytail, not roughly, but with purpose, guiding me back down with a slow, controlled pull. My ponytail comes loose in his hand, strands falling over my face as he takes in the mess he's made of me.

With his grip still in my hair, he feeds himself back into my mouth, inch by inch, as if staking a claim. I moan around him, the sound vibrating from his length, earning a growl from deep in his chest. There's power in this—for both of us. He leads. I follow. Yet I hold his pleasure in my mouth, like a secret only I get to keep.

Cradling him with both hand and lips, I swirl my tongue along the sensitive underside, coaxing new tremors from his thighs. He's thick, too thick for me to take fully, but I try. Gosh, I try. I spit, licking him up again, determined to reach deeper the next time. And still, that inevitable choke comes, gentle but insistent, reminding me I'm only human. My eyes water, and I welcome it, loving the wreckage we're making of each other.

"Take that cock," he growls, his tone a heady blend of dominance and authority. With a tug on my hair, he forces my head lower, groaning at the sound of my gag that escapes my throat. I push past it, relishing the burn as the tears prick my eyes. There's something intoxicating about testing how far I can go.

Flashes of my past cut through me. My husband's love was routine, predictable, missionary. A dull cycle.

There was that one wild day in high school that we made a rebellious escape; he ripped my pants off as we snuck out of class for a forbidden rendezvous in the theater room. Though that moment of reckless abandon was brief, it ignited a passion within me that I've since suppressed. More often, our clandestine meetings took place in the quiet confines of his truck. He was intoxicated, and I sat silently beside him. A painful sacrifice of my morals to be in his presence.

But Spencer? He doesn't simply want me—he commands me. With every explicit word and every firm touch, he draws out a version of me I'd vaguely known existed. With him, I'm who I want to be.

With a gentle tug of my ponytail, he removes my mouth from him before laying me onto my back. With careful restraint, he flips me on top of him.

Glancing around the room, I catch sight again of the camera recorder's flashing red lights, making a mental note of its presence.

Then, without missing a beat, I surrender to the passion.

I trace my hand down his chest—my voice a low confession of how much I want him. His response is wordless. He lifts me with ease, lowering me onto the hard length of him until the only sound left is my gasp as he fills me.

I'm open for him, but he's still almost too much. His size stretches me, and so does what I feel for him—something vast and terrifying.

He grinds against me, his thick length parts my lips and nudges inward, the tension in me holding him at bay.

The moment he presses in, a deep, intoxicating stretch splits me open

TWENTY-FOUR

steadily, a fraction at a time, and I gasp, sharp, raw, breathless, as my body struggles to accommodate his impossible size. "F-fuck... you're huge," I whisper, my voice a shattered mix of disbelief and desperate need. The pressure mounts as my slick passion clings to every vein, every ridge, my body adjusting to the delicious invasion with trembling surrender.

Spencer groans, his grip biting into my sides.

"Damn it, your pussy feels like heaven."

His words ignite something primal in me.

I move over him in slow, circling waves, each shift sending sparks through my veins. I rock forward, then back, as his hands clamp down on my ass, his bruising fingers dragging me harder, deeper, grinding against me with punishing precision.

"Oh fuck... don't stop. Fuck me harder." He's desperate now, his thrusts rise to meet mine, losing the last thread of restraint.

Something untamed rips inside me, slamming my hips down with frantic need. My nails dig into his chest for balance, but he is the one controlling everything. He guides me, dragging me down deeper, until I cry in sweet agony.

I moan loudly and unfiltered, the sound ripped from my throat as he pounds into me from below. "Fuck yes," he groans, his tone rich with pleasure. "Ride me. Just like that. Take every fucking inch."

My body responds instinctively, chasing the rush, bouncing on him with wild abandon. I'm soaked, shaking, stretched to my limit, yet it's still not enough. I want him deeper, until there's no space left between us.

His hands grip my ass tightly, his fingers digging in as he matches my rhythm, grinding me against him with deliberate force.

"Oh fuck me, more," he growls, desperate with need.

My cries climb higher, spilling into the charged air with every pounding. His hold steadies me and bruises at once, dragging me against the merciless drive of his thrusts.

Everything disappears except the tug and slide of his body against mine, the dizzying pressure clenching tighter. And before I break, he flips me in one swift motion, throwing me onto my stomach, maintaining control.

With intentional force, he slams back inside. His fingers tangled in my hair, yanking my head back with sharp control.

"Do you like that big cock?"

The question burns low and rough, and for a heartbeat, I can't speak, only breathe him in.

I bite my lip, trembling under the weight of his command. "Yes."

"Good," he rasps, one hand sliding down to anchor my hips. "Do you want more?"

"Yes."

He thrusts into me unyielding with each pulse, my body propelling forward over and over. My moans intensify, blending with his heavy, raspy breaths. I savor the pleasure of his powerful thrust, each movement fulfilling deep, concealed desires. Desires I never knew existed until my vagina met his cock.

I brace on my hands. Wasting no time he slides his tongue up my spine before breathing me in at my neck. Then he pounds his huge cock unyielding into me. "Damn it." I squirm beneath him.

I didn't know sex could be like this. *Is this what I've been missing all along?*

His pumps are hard, powerful, forcing my body to drive forward, making my arms tremble beneath me. With every collision, my ass ricochets against him, his pace punishing.

"I love this." I whisper, breathless.

"You haven't even had a real fucking yet," he taunts.

"Then fuck me harder," I challenge and dare him to unravel me in the same breath.

And he does. His rhythm sharpens, brutal and merciless. My pussy clenches around him, each thrust branding me from the inside out, marking me as his.

His hand seizes my throat, tightening just enough to remind me who's in control.

A full-body tremor grips onto me, and the world dissolves into heat and stars. It's blinding, involuntary, like my soul had been dragged out and kissed back to life.

The bed rattles beneath us, the sound of flesh against flesh echoing off

TWENTY-FOUR

the walls.

"You're mine," he snarls.

His restraint is slipping.

"Take this hard cock," he demands. "Harder."

"Harder," I repeat.

And with that he smacks my ass, soft the first time. The second time, unforgiving. And the third time, I shriek out loud.

"Mmm... I love making your soft little ass pink." He's ruthless with his pleasure.

I'm coming undone, spiraling forward, the unleashing is intense and uncontrollable.

His fingers toy with my clit, stroking in maddening circles until I'm gasping, desperate, seconds from detonation.

"That's it." His lips ghost over my neck. "Let it go."

"I'm coming," I cry out, the climax crashing like a tidal wave, every muscle clenching tight around him.

"Me too," he growls, voice unraveling as he drives into me one final time. He spills inside with a low, guttural sound, heat surging into me as our bodies crash together, breath mingling, skin slick, what's left of the moment spilling down his shaft.

My thighs quiver from the effort. Our hearts race in sync. Neither of us moves—only heavy breaths and the afterglow anchoring us together.

We shift eventually, curling onto our sides. His semi-stiff length remains nestled inside me, a surviving reflection of the chaos we created. He exhales softly, lips brushing my temple. "You're an incredible fuck," he whispers, reverent.

In his arms, I feel soft, cherished, but still aching in the best possible way. What happened was more than physical. It broke me open and rebuilt me all at once. My skin's still buzzing, every nerve humming like a struck chord.

I summon the nerve to ask, "Do you always have sex like this, aggressively?"

"Not always. The first few times, I was gentle with you."

"I mean in general. Once it's not new—do you prefer it rough?"

"Yeah... some of the time. Is that alright with you?"

"Yes," I say with a soft, wry smile.

"Although this speed and intensity—it's new for me." I pause, my voice lowering. "I've never had a man take control of me the way you do."

After a beat of silence I ask meekly, "Would you... maybe want to do this again? Sometime soon?"

I turn toward him, searching his eyes.

"Absolutely. I will have my way with you anytime you want." He gives a slight wink.

Then, after a beat, his voice drops with quiet promise. "I'm going on a work trip. Come with me."

I shift closer, tucking my arm beneath the pillow as my leg drapes over his torso—tangled, skin to skin.

"And where would you be taking me?"

"Park City," he replies.

"And what's your plan for making sure your wife doesn't find out?"

"She won't," he assures me. "It's just a furnace check. I'll send one of my emloyees to fix it after I diagnose the issue. Vanessa never asks about work. She doesn't care as long as the money keeps rolling in." He pauses, brushing my hip with his thumb. "We'll make a weekend out of it. Come with me."

"When?"

"Next month. For a weekend."

"Let me see if Linda can take care of the dogs at the shop," I say, considering it. "I'll try to come. I know we've been careful not to text, but can I message you a yes or no?"

"Sure, message during work hours so my wife won't find it on my phone."

"Gotcha." I agree to his terms.

My fingers trail up the grooves of his back, then over his jaw, already my favorite part of him. I cradle his face in both hands, tracing slow strokes across his jawline.

"Something about this just does it for me." I whisper.

TWENTY-FOUR

A mischievous smile tugs at his lips as he cups my breast, giving it a playful squeeze before pulling gently. "And something about you gets to me," he teases back.

I pull his mouth to mine again, drinking him in. This time, it's not remnants of me—it's all him, thank goodness. We kiss deeply, tongues moving in a slow rhythm. I nip his bottom lip; he draws my tongue into his mouth possessively.

He's stiffening beneath me, his arousal pressing hard between my thighs. My clit throbs, aching with renewed need.

I kneel, giving him space.

"Sit on my face."

I obey, lowering myself onto him, my thighs straddling his head. His hands grip hard, guiding my movements where he wants me.

He pulls me down before his tongue plunges deep into me. Hunger radiates from him—each breath shudders against me, breaking and catching like he can't get enough.

He's not only tasting; he's drinking, savoring me like a prayer.

I move against him, each shift a surge of reckless pleasure.

He's relentless, his tongue flicking, swirling, lapping from my entrance to my clit and lower. My body tenses with each stroke; my mind unravels in his rhythm.

It should feel wrong, but the way he worships me makes it feel effortless, almost pure.

One of his fingers slides inside as his tongue flicks over my clit, the combination pulling gasps from me. He starts slow, easing in, swirling teasing circles. I know he's building toward something, and I ache to find out what.

When he lifts his face, his lips glisten with the mix of us. He wipes it with a towel.

Where did that towel come from? Of course—always prepared.

He doesn't pause. His hands catch my hips, guiding me down onto him again.

I straddle him upright, savoring the stretch and slide of every thrust.

Then, shifting, I lean back, gripping his ankles for support, my arms stretching to hold myself up. My breasts bounce freely, my body arching as he takes me. There's friction where our skin meets. Every sensation crackles electrically.

His hands rise, claiming what he wants, a rough pinch of my nipples that pulls another sound from my throat.

The other hand finds its way between us, thumb tracing where I'm already slick and trembling. I moan, my body stuttering as the teasing ignites an unbearable tingle inside me. His firm grip on my nipples and the friction against my most sensitive spot sends bright, jarring flashes beneath my skin.

It's almost too much.

I lean forward, bracing against him, my fingers catching in the dark hair that smells like him.

I keep going, chasing the peak, until my thighs burn and my arms tremble from the strain.

The climax builds fast, crashing over me like a dam breaking, pleasure spilling from every nerve ending.

Spent and trembling, I collapse against him, my body molded to his.

I burrow my face into the pillow between us, drained, my limbs heavy with exhaustion.

"I'm sorry... I couldn't stop myself. You're too damn sexy."

He laughs softly. "Don't tell anyone how sexy I am."

"I won't," I promise. "Because then they'd all want you."

"Of course they would."

He shifts, his body still tout with need, a wordless invitation. I press a lazy kiss against his throat, tracing the line of his collarbone with my fingers.

"Give me a second," I whisper, stalling while savoring the way we fit together.

His warmth and the way he holds me like I was always meant to fit here.

Lifting my head and rolling to the side, I tuck one arm beneath me for balance support while my hand drifts lower to his still-firm cock. He's slick with our release, the wetness clinging to him as my fingers glide over him. A hush settles between us. With a tender touch, he brushes back a loose strand of hair that broke free from my ponytail.

I love the way he feels in my grasp, solid, weighted.

"You're... big." I murmur, grabbing hold of him.

"Is it really that big?" He asks, voice low, while I stroke him slowly. "I mean, I knew it was decent, but no one's ever told me it's as big as you say it is."

I tighten my grip slightly, emphasizing my point. "It is."

Shifting my position, I slide between his legs, centering myself to give him my full attention. With one hand, I work his length; with the other, I cup him, rolling the balls gently.

His muscles tense, his body instinctively fighting the urge to thrust into my hand. He's close. I can feel it. I transition from drawn-out, deliberate strokes to short, rapid ones, aiming to push him to his max. The slick sounds between us make me self-conscious for a beat, but his response dissolves the doubt. He revels in every moment of it.

Leaning up, his panting grows ragged. He wraps his hand around the base of his shaft beneath mine. Together, we stroke him. My fingers tease the sensitive tip while his firm hold moves along the lower half. The sensation of working in tandem, sharing control, is exciting. It's a deeper level of connection that we haven't explored together before. Our rhythm quickens, and his winded breath grows uneven.

"Let me finish on you," he groans.

"Where?"

"Your tits." He's certain of where he wants to empty himself.

I release him and lie back, pressing my breasts together with both hands as he kneels over me. His strokes turn frantic, his body clenching with each motion.

His abs flex, his jaw tightens and with a deep moan, his release comes hard and fast. Hot ropes wildly spill over my chest and hands, the sheer force and amount catching me off guard. Spencer works the last drops from his length, then grabs the towel, carefully wiping me clean before tending to himself.

His touch now is gentle.

Spent and weak, I sink into the mattress, feeling the continued pulses of our time together. My body settles with satisfaction, my mind tangled in the contradiction of him being dominant yet tender, predictable yet full of surprises.

Untangling ourselves, we lie in silence. My fingers idly trace the familiar arc of his chest hair, and I can't help the hook tugging at my lips.

Twenty-Five

We remain still, our bodies sunk into his mattress.

"I enjoy spending time with you," he says suddenly.

"Me too." I say. "I hope I can see you again, but I don't know how. Not while I'm still married to Dominic."

"I need you to come on my work trip. Please, find a way."

I decide now is the time to reveal my plan. "I'm going to tell Dominic that I want to divorce. Once he's moved out, all of this will be easier. You can come to my place."

"You're serious." he sounds excited and surprised. "In the meantime?" he asks, tilting his head toward me, intrigued.

My shoulders sag in quiet surrender. "I guess we keep sneaking around at the shop."

A slow grin spreads across his face. "I'll come see you at work. Meet me in your lobby bathroom."

I scoff. "Right. Because that won't appear suspicious at all. My mom is never going to believe me when I tell her I'm following the landlord into a tiny bathroom to 'talk.' "

I lift my hands to make sarcastic air quotes.

Spencer shifts, propping himself up on his elbow. "Maybe it's time to tell her?"

"No," I say quickly. "We can't. Not yet."

His lips press together in thought. The wheels seem to turn behind his eyes.

"Fine. Come to dinner with me, then, before my trip next month. Two weeks from now, on Thursday, does that work?"

"I think so," I reply, mentally checking my schedule.

Our plans always have to be set ahead of time because of the limited contact we're allowed.

"Thursdays are my day off. Where do you want to meet?"

"The Market on 16th? Near the Mine? Less chance of running into someone we know. I can drive you from there. Let's say 7:00?"

"Perfect." I say, certain he's already thought it through.

He stretches and glances at the clock. "I better get you back. It's late."

"Or early," I remark, seeing the time beside him. It's already past one.

"Shit," I mutter, a nervous laugh slipping out. "How am I going to explain this to my husband?"

I joke, though the tension beneath my smile is undeniably real.

Spencer smirks but doesn't offer a response. Instead, I shift the conversation. "Hey, quick question, when's your birthday?"

"November twenty-fifth," he answers easily. "What about yours?"

"May third," I say, locking the date into my memory. "Yours isn't too far away. I won't forget it."

Another question sits in my mind.

"Why don't you wear your garments?" I ask.

It's the layer of clothing Mormons wear after they've been sealed in marriage at the temple—a symbol of faith and commitment.

"You're supposed to wear them day and night. They're meant to offer protection, at least that's how we're taught. I mean, they are important to you, right?"

I already know the answer, but want to hear it from him.

He threads his fingers through my hair, answering slowly. "I usually do wear them. They do what they are meant to—protect. But when I know I'm going to be with you, I take them off. I shouldn't... but they're sacred. And I wouldn't feel right wearing them with my mistress."

His answer makes sense.

I love being his little secret, but I wouldn't mind being the wife he wears them for—so I don't push the subject.

"This is..."

His thumb pauses, circling the mark on my hip.

"A birthmark?" he asks, softer now. "I've never noticed it before. It's kind of perfect. Like a hidden signature."

I smile faintly.

"Well, it's been there my whole life."

"Now I'll never forget where it is," he says.

He remains by my side, one arm draped lazily across my waist, fingers tracing over it.

I've never felt so close to someone. So claimed by someone.

My eyes are half-closed when his phone buzzes on the nightstand.

He doesn't move at first.

Then it buzzes again.

The screen lights up.

Vanessa—Wife.

I freeze.

He exhales slowly and reaches for it, glancing down before turning the screen face-down.

"You're not going to answer?" I whisper.

He shifts, brushing hair from my cheek.

"Not right now."

I nod. But something sharp lodges in my chest.

Another buzz. A voicemail. Silence stretches between us. I turn onto my back and pull the sheet up to my chest.

"What does she need?" I ask, trying to sound light.

"Probably about the kids. Or the schedule. I don't know."

I don't want to be the reason he lies. But I already am.

And as I lie here, wrapped in another woman's sheets, in another woman's house, seeing that other woman's name flash across his phone... jealousy crawls up my spine.

Then, it rings again.

He picks up the phone *for her*, like he never can for me, leaving me feeling unseen.

"Hey, honey," he answers. That must be his nickname for her. He's used it in front of me twice now.

My eyes stay locked on the ceiling. I suddenly feel naked in the worst way.

"Yeah, I just walked in, we worked later than usual," he lies, voice smooth but strained.

Vanessa's voice cuts through the quiet—crisp, clear, composed. "I emailed you the spreadsheet and the doctors invoice. I need you to respond before five this time."

"Okay, work caught up to me," he says, his voice lower. He sits up slightly, dragging the sheet with him. "I'll take care of it. It's too late to be talking about this. It can wait."

"And about this weekend—"

"I already told you, I can't."

"You mean *you won't*." Her voice sharpens. "You've missed three back-to-back recitals, Spencer. I'm not doing this again."

His voice is bristled with irritation. "I said I'll figure it out."

She doesn't yell. She doesn't need to. "Keep your promises. To them, if not to me."

The line goes dead.

He drops the phone onto the mattress beside him, frustration tightening in his face.

"Sarah..."

Just my name. No apology. No explanation.

I sit up slowly, pulling the sheet tighter around me. "Do you always answer when she calls, when you're with your mistress?"

"Not always." His expression's unreadable.

"But tonight you did."

He shakes his head. "I didn't want it to seem suspicious."

I understand, but the pressure in my chest stays. Immovable.

He was inside me. I was wrapped around him. I was whispering things I've never said out loud.

And now I feel like I don't exist.

I reach for my bra. "I should go."

"Sarah, don't."

"It's fine," I lie. "I'm used to disappearing."

Maybe I'm just a pause in his real life. A beautiful mistake he won't admit to, until it's too late.

But then he looks *at me*. Not through me. Not like I'm a mistake. And my anger unravels.

I kiss him anyway, hating that I can't stop myself. The feelings won't let go, no matter how much I want them to.

After getting dressed, Spencer leads me out to his truck, to drive me to my car. Reluctance clings to me like static as we step outside. I'm not ready to leave this stolen world. Across the street, a bedroom light glows. It hadn't been on before.

The rest of the residence is dark, which seems strange for this hour. I don't mention it. Instead, I keep the conversation going, pulling trivial details from him, hungry for every piece.

By the time we reach my car, I've relaxed, or maybe I've just become numb. It's easier to pretend I'm fine than admit how much that phone call cracked something open.

It's his wife. Of course, he's going to answer the phone.

Our goodbye stretches into a drawn-out embrace. I don't want to let go, but eventually, I have to.

Driving back, I make no effort to come up with an excuse for Dominic. I don't have one, and honestly, I don't care to.

Slipping quietly inside, the bathroom light clicks on. I wash my face before I prepare for bed. Crawling under the covers, I instinctively roll toward Dominic's side, but this time, it's empty.

Dominic isn't there. I hadn't noticed his truck missing from the overflow parking.

He always throws a fit if I'm ten minutes late returning from my mom's, yet he can't bother to call when he's the one gone all night.

For a moment, I climb onto my high horse.

He's a hypocrite. Then again... *so am I.* The difference?

He forced this side of me to come out. He comes by it naturally. And right now, he's at some bar, drowning in it.

That thought alone makes my evening with Spencer feel even sweeter.

Twenty-Six

* * *

SPENCER

The house feels wrong the second she's gone—the walls know what I've done.

I locked the front door out of habit, though it feels pointless—as if locking out the truth could undo what we just did. Her scent still moves through the air: a sweet shampoo and vanilla. I run a hand through my hair, and slide into my slippers.

She looked back before getting in her car. Just a single glance punched the air out of me.

I walked through the foyer, past the framed family photos—Vanessa happy, the kids grinning with melted ice cream on their hands. I can't stare at them for long. It's too much like being watched.

My reflection catches in the mirror above the photos. I don't look like a man who's just cheated. I appear as the same man I've always been, aside from something in my eyes giving me away, there's a quiet tremor of knowing that this time, I've crossed a line.

Vanessa's voice from earlier plays in my head—the clipped, restrained tone she uses when she's tired of pretending we're still the same. "You've missed three recitals, Spencer."

Yeah. And now I've missed something else entirely. The version of me I thought I still was.

I head for the kitchen, pour a glass of water I don't want, and lean against the counter. The rattle of the refrigerator fills the silence. The familiar sound should feel solid, but it doesn't.

Do I feel guilty?

Yes.

And no.

I could convince myself it's not really cheating, not when my marriage has been running on fumes for years. Not when Vanessa and I stopped touching each other without duty behind it.

But that's the oldest lie in the book, isn't it? Infidelity with justification stamped on top.

I set the glass down too hard, water splashing over the counter. I wipe it with my palm, because cleaning up a small mess feels easier than facing the big one.

I picture Sarah, the way she trembled under my hands, the way she looked at me like I was the only man left on earth. No judgment, no expectations. Just need. And for a moment, it felt holy. Like redemption dressed up as sin.

But it isn't redemption.

It's hunger, the kind that's been starving for too long and finally got fed.

I walk down the hall to the bedroom, the same one she was just in. The sheets are rumpled, the pillow still warm from where she lay. I should strip the bed, wash away what's left of her. But I won't. Instead, I sit on the edge of it and drop my head into my hands.

I've built this life brick by brick, the businesses, the house, the family. And yet, one touch from her made it all feel like dust.

Was I unfaithful?

Yes.

But it doesn't feel like a betrayal of Vanessa, not exactly.

It feels like a betrayal of the man I promised myself I'd be.

When I finally move, it's automatic. I undress and crawl into bed, the clock

TWENTY-SIX

reads 2:14. I lie there staring at the ceiling, trying to decide which lie I'll tell myself in the morning.

That it was a *mistake*.

That it meant *nothing*.

But the truth is, she wasn't a mistake.

And she doesn't mean nothing.

Twenty-Seven

***

Sarah

Dominic didn't come home for the weekend. He claimed he was staying at his friend Dustin's until Monday. I didn't care. Bigger, more important things were on my mind.

This week at the dog shop is an important time for Linda and me. We are soft-launching the boarding aspect of the shop, extending it to all grooming customers. While we have been boarding a few of our clients' dogs, it's only been a select few, as we wanted to make sure it runs smoothly.

I'm proud of myself for managing to keep things separate, careful not to let Linda suspect anything about Spencer. I never mention him. But she hears plenty about Dominic, and that's enough to make her hate him on my behalf.

Linda is the best mom—supportive, sharp, open-minded, and brilliantly business savvy. I've learned more from her than I can measure. Honestly, I couldn't have purchased my house when I was eighteen or managed a budget this well without her. She runs the numbers; I chase the vision. Together, we make it work.

Our human clients love us, and our dogs adore us even more.

The bell over the shop door jingles, and I glance up with a practiced smile,

TWENTY-SEVEN

expecting another regular. Instead, a man storms in, red-faced, dragging his shaggy retriever behind him. His voice booms before the door even closes.

"This is ridiculous. You butchered my dog's haircut. I want my money back."

Heat rushes into my cheeks as other customers in the lobby swivel toward us. The retriever looks perfectly fine to me, brushed, trimmed, and wagging its tail. But the man jabs a finger at me like I've committed a crime.

I force a smile to stay put. I can't afford to lose my composure in front of the crowd.

"I told you I wanted *just a trim*. Do you people even listen? This is the worst cut I've ever seen."

"Sir, I followed the instructions your wife left, maybe you should talk to her. Your dog is beautifully groomed and well cared for..."

"Don't argue with me," he snaps, slamming his hand down on the counter hard, enough to rattle the treat jars. "I've been coming here for years, and this is how you treat me?"

The lobby goes still, customers shifting uncomfortably, eyes darting between us.

Before I can answer, the door opens again.

Spencer steps inside, his tall frame casting a shadow across the man, dark stubble roughening his jaw. His voice is even but firm, carrying authority that silences the room.

"That's enough. You can be heard from outside."

The man's eyes flick toward him. "Who are you?"

"The owner of this building," Spencer replies coolly. "And you will not come in here yelling at her. If you're unhappy, take your business elsewhere. But you don't get to treat her this way."

The man blusters, sputtering about wasted money and unfair service, but Spencer takes a step closer, unflinching.

"Get off my property," he says, "And don't come back."

The man's face mottles with rage, but under Spencer's gaze he falters. Tugging on the retriever's leash, he mutters something under his breath and storms out, the bell clanging violently as the door slams shut.

For a long moment, everyone is still. My heart pounds, my hands tremble as I stare at the counter. Then Spencer's demeanor softens. "You alright?" He asks quietly.

I confirm with a quiet gesture, though my chest still stings from the man's words. Spencer holds my gaze a beat longer, making sure I am okay, before he turns and leaves as quickly as he came.

Only after the door clicks shut do I finally exhale.

For every person like him, there are a dozen others who remind me why I love what I do.

I press my palms to the counter, grounding myself. Just another man who thought yelling made him right.

Spending time with our customers has been one of the greatest rewards. I've heard their stories. Tales of families fractured after loss, health scares, adoption struggles, financial hardship, and even regret over not having children, the last perhaps leaving the most impact.

Getting to know them, while loving and caring for their animals, has been a pleasure.

My mom and I built this place from love, and sometimes that's what keeps me going.

I also love that my mom and I share not only a devotion to animals, but also so many of the same friends and acquaintances. Over time, Linda has become my built-in best friend. The only person, except for Maya, that I confide in about everything, except my affair. I know I'll have to tell her eventually, just not yet.

We talk about the angry customer for a moment, laughing off his tantrum, but Linda's smile fades when I mentioned Dominic's carelessness with money.

"He's been slacking in the financial department," I admit. "And the drinking... it's worse than ever. Sometimes, it feels like I'm carrying the whole marriage by myself."

Linda studies me quietly her sharp eyes softening. "Sarah, you don't want to lose everything if he gets a DUI. One wrong night and it's not just his

TWENTY-SEVEN

life—it could be yours too."

The words hit me harder than I I'd like to admit. "I know," I whisper. "I'm scared he'll drag me down with him."

Her gaze drifts for a moment. "You know, my dad—Pop—came home from the war a different man. I didn't know him before, but mom said he used to be bright and full of life. By the time I was old enough to remember, he was already drinking too much. At first it was just to take the edge off. Then, year by year, it was all he did. The drinking covered everything else, his pain, his temper, his sadness. And in the end, it took him from us long before his body gave out."

Her voice lowers. "Living with an alcoholic wears you down in ways you don't see until you're the one drowning with them. I watched my mom spend her whole life trying to hold it together. I don't want that for you."

Her story clears the fog, I can't drown with him.

Linda reaches for my hand. "You deserve better, Sarah. Don't let his choices decide your future."

She's right, I know she's right. And sitting here, across from the one person I trust most, I realize I'm not as alone in this as I'd thought.

"I'll help you," she adds firmly. "Through the divorce, through whatever comes next. You won't be doing it on your own."

Her promise settles into me like a lifeline, filling me with the confidence I've needed to finally tell him the truth.

Now, I can only hope she'll accept Spencer in my life when the time comes.

Twenty-Eight

I pull up to the Market on 16th, Spencer already waiting to take me to the Mine.

It sits outside the narrow canyon where we took our motorcycle ride earlier in our relationship. It's an old Western-theme steakhouse, dimly lit, with antique lanterns, mining cars, vintage stoves, irons, and various rustic décor pieces.

Our table is tucked in with a low-hanging light and enclosed like an old covered wagon—secluded, discreet, perfect for an illicit affair. No one can see us clearly, making discretion easy.

On top of that, the ambiance is undeniably romantic. The scent of grilled steak mingles with warm bread and the faint tang of whiskey from the bar. Silverware clinks against plates around us, muted beneath chatter. That quiet charm sets the stage for what I already know will be a passionate evening.

"Hi," I say, as I slide into the booth, pressing myself against the wall.

"Hello there," Spencer responds smoothly, settling in close beside me instead of across the table. The brush of his shoulder warms my arm, startling in how intimate it feels.

I blink. *Weird.* Dominic never sits next to me in restaurants. This must be something mature adults do. I lean in instinctively, welcoming the closeness.

Clasping his jaw on both sides, I turn him toward me. His baby blues glisten in the overhead light. The faint smell of cologne clings to his collar, and when his lips part slightly, I catch the warmth of his breath against my cheek. I'm sad and nervous to tell him, so I go straight to the point. "I need to tell you this before we begin our night."

His face softens with concern. "Should I be worried?"

"No, no. Nothing serious, don't worry." I continue. "I can't go to Park City with you. As much as I'd love to, I can't get away from work. The timing falls too close to the grand opening of the boarding shop."

Relief flushes his face. "You had me worried. That's it? I mean... not that that's it... but I'm glad that it was nothing more serious—like you don't want to see me anymore."

He releases a deep sigh. "That's fine. I will make it a quick day trip then. No big deal. Though it would be better if we had a full night together."

"I know, it would be amazing. But this time I can't make it work. Next time."

The corner of his mouth lifts, and his thigh presses against mine under the table, a quiet promise of patience. I leave the door open for him to invite me again, hoping he will.

We're both famished from waiting for our meals, but as the evening progresses, we eventually get to the point where we've nearly devoured our meals, my plate holding very little, only remnants of steak, crab legs, a perfectly baked potato, salad, and a heated roll slathered in the most delicious fresh-made raspberry butter.

With each bite, I begin to understand why Spencer brought me here and why he chose to sit next to me instead of across. The upscale atmosphere, the intimate setting, everything feels intentional.

My little black dress hugs my body. It's thin, one-inch straps barely cling to my shoulders and pair with my silver and black heels, making me feel elegant and seductive. The dangling necklace resting against my collarbone catches the low light, glinting softly every time I move.

For what must be the hundredth time tonight, my eyes lock with Spencer's. With hunger sated, the craving shifts to something else.

The energy between us hums. At some point, my leg drapes over his, instinctively seeking contact. Touching him is a reflex.

His hand rests on my thigh, fingertips tracing slow, unhurried paths up and down. My hands are busy with the last of the crab legs. These pesky buggers take a while to feast on.

Then, Spencer shifts, slipping a hand into his pocket. The lighting is subdued, so I don't bother trying to see what he's doing. I lift my glass of lemon water, then pause at the subtle buzz against my skin.

Soft at first, then stronger, it tickles the inside of my thigh. Then it begins inching upward.

My breath hitches. I catch his wrist, my voice hushed, half-amused, half-curious.

"Is that a vibrator?"

"Maybe," he whispers, his fervent breath against my ear as he kisses the tip.

"Is that what you want it to be?"

His hand slides beneath the fabric of my panties, now slick with arousal. My veins thrum with energy. I'm sitting in a public restaurant, unforgivably turned on. Spencer is full of surprises.

His fingers press the toy against my panties, sending a jolt ripping through me like lightning.

I fight the urge to moan, to squirm, to climb onto his lap right now.

The toy drifts lower, teasing, before he slips into me.

"Oh, fuck," I whisper, barely able to contain myself. He leans in, a devilish curve tugging at his lips.

"Did you say, you want to fuck?" His voice drips with sarcasm, but the hunger in his eyes says otherwise.

"Yes," I rasp, thighs pressing together in desperation, as the waitress materializes out of the dimly lit room.

"Do you need any refills?" she asks, her voice pulling me from the haze. I swallow hard, forcing composure. "No, we're good," I manage, though my voice cracks.

"Can I take any plates away?" she asks, standing there too long.

Spencer flashes her a polite smile. "No, we're doing juuuust... fine, you can leave them." He casts me a devilish look.

"All right," she nods, "I'll check back in a bit."

TWENTY-EIGHT

She doesn't move, clearly waiting for more conversation. My nails dig into Spencer's leg, my body tense from the relentless thrum still working inside me. *Go already*, I scream silently.

"Do you guys need the check?" she finally asks.

"Sure." His tone is smooth, calm, while I'm barely holding it together. He knows exactly what he's doing, enjoying my torment while the waitress takes her sweet fucking time.

Meanwhile, the intensity inside me builds.

I clutch Spencer's leg tighter, silently begging for release. *Get the hell out of here*, I plead internally while the waitress asks another round of pointless questions.

The second she's gone, I let out a low, shaky moan, my body trembling.

Spencer doesn't miss a beat. His hand slips beneath my dress again, fingers pressing against the silk fabric of my panties.

He rubs slow, practiced strokes along my clit.

I bite my lip, fighting the inevitable, but I'm losing.

Then, without warning, Spencer grips the small toy still nestled inside me, and gives it a sharp, teasing thrust. Another. And another. I gasp, gripping his wrist tighter. It only takes a few more before the pressure becomes unbearable, and with a quiet, shattering breath, I let go.

My body melts, my head tilting back, revealing my exposed neck, ripples of euphoria jolt through me.

Spencer leans in, his breath hot against my ear. "Good girl."

He stamps a few soft kisses to my neck before he carefully, removes the bullet from inside me. With ease, he wipes it off with a cloth napkin from the table and slips the slick metallic toy back into his pocket as if this is normal.

"Well, that was... orgasmic," I tease while straightening my dress.

"The food?" he questions, his sarcasm pouring out, while a wicked grin stretches across his face.

I scoff. "You know exactly what I mean."

"It was, wasn't it?"

I narrow my eyes at him, shaking my head.

"You take pleasure in torturing me, don't you?"

He shrugs, his devious smirk still in place.

"Maybe."

Maybe. A word he wields like a shield, always dodging direct answers, always keeping me guessing. I tilt my head, studying him, my curiosity getting the best of me. "Okay, mystery man... I have to ask. What's your last name?"

"Hawthorne," he replies.

I raise an eyebrow. "Spencer Hawthorne. So proper and fancy."

His lips twitch. "And yours?"

"Vaughn."

The tone of his voice rises with approval. "I like that. It has a nice ring to it. Sarah Vaughn—wait, is that your maiden name or your married name?"

"Maiden," I answer.

"Well, what's your married name? Didn't you ever legally change it after you tied the knot?"

"Velasquez. I never actually changed it. I suppose instinctively, I knew our marriage wouldn't last long."

Spencer studies me for a beat, then nods. "I suppose so."

I smile, trying to lighten the moment. "Well, at least we finally know each other's full names. Took us long enough."

"Exactly," he says, flashing his charming grin. "Now, let's get out of here."

We both head for the front door of the restaurant and he stops to pay the check. Sitting on the table near the exit is a small bowl brimming with hard cinnamon candies. I can't pass up an opportunity to grab one, pop it into my mouth, and flash him an exaggerated, cheesy grin.

Spencer huffs quietly, "You're pretty cute, you know that?"

The words stick to me. Cute. Not perfect. Just... cute.

He takes my hand as we walk along the antique-filled hallway, his fingers lacing through mine.

Outside, he opens the door to his truck, giving me a little boost as I step up.

"I should call it a night," he says softly, once we're parked near The Market.

TWENTY-EIGHT

"Gotta grab some milk for the kids in the morning."

I try not to let my disappointment show. "Of course. Go be the responsible one."

He smiles faintly. "Someone has to be."

I reach for the handle, but before I can step out, he catches my wrist and draws me back in. The space between us narrows. The sweetness of his lips melt as we share the remaining heat of my cinnamon candy. We embrace the slow, mind-numbing kiss, for a few seconds before he finally pulls away.

"I hope you enjoyed my little magic trick tonight," he teases.

"Thoroughly," I grin, "sorry we didn't have more time for me to return the favor."

"Tonight was about you, Princess."

I freeze for a split second. "Princess?" I ask. "Do we have pet names now? You have called me that once before."

He shrugs. "I guess we do."

"I like it, Buster," I quip.

Giggling under his breath, I can sense his enjoyment.

"Goodnight, Sarah."

"Goodnight," I whisper back.

When I step out of the truck and close the door, contentment seeps into my chest. I take a deep breath, soaking the moment up. It feels like we've reached a significant milestone in our relationship. My plan to get him to fall in love with me seems to be working perfectly.

Twenty-Nine

Sunday morning unfolds like any other. I let the dogs out, fill their food bowls, and refresh their water. But then the unexpected happens.

Spencer.

It's been a while since I've seen him.

He steps inside, still dressed in church clothes, looking completely out of place, yet somehow effortlessly perfect. In one hand, he holds a drink. In the other, a bouquet of red roses. Without a word, he sets them down on the counter, nudging the drink toward me before carefully arranging the flowers. I raise a brow.

"For me?"

He teases. "No, for the dogs." Then, softer, "Yes. I left church while Vanessa and the kids were still in class to come see you."

A mix of thrill and guilt overtakes me.

"Won't they notice you're gone?"

"Maybe," he says, unfazed. "I couldn't stay away. I've missed you."

I step closer, brushing my fingers over the cool condensation of the root beer. "You remembered."

"Of course, I remember you don't drink caffeine. And the flowers... they don't hold a candle to you."

I bite my lip; happiness takes hold. "Are you like this with all your mistresses?" I tease, trying to get a feel for who this man really is.

He chuckles, eyes glinting with mischief.

"No, only the ones I like."

TWENTY-NINE

I don't know whether or not to believe him, so I decide not to overthink it.

"I have to go," he says, "but I had to see you, even if for a minute."

"I wish you could stay," I say, following him to the porch.

It would seem like a high-risk location for being seen, and usually it is. But on a Sunday morning, there's almost no traffic. The town's mostly made up of Mormons, most of whom are either getting ready for, or already at church.

Spencer studies me for a second before wrapping an arm around my waist and pulling me close. I loop my arms around his neck, rising on my toes as I hold him tight.

"You smell incredible," I brush my lips against his. "What cologne is that?"

"A new one. Do you like it?"

I inhale deeply, letting the scent consume me. "Love it."

"It said on the bottle it would get a reaction out of whoever smelled it," he teases. "Did it work?"

"Yes."

"Good. Then my job here is done." He presses one last kiss to my lips. "Now you'll have something to hold onto until I see you again."

"You're a tease," I reply with a note of frustration.

"Good, I'll continue to tease you later."

"I don't want you to go!" My clingy side emerges.

"I have to before anyone notices I'm missing." He pushes my hands down to my sides, so he can step back.

"See you soon, Princess."

Thirty

Mondays tend to be one of our busiest days, and today is no exception. Customers have been in and out all day, boarding dogs returned after the long weekend, and anxious pet owners awaiting to get their pups groomed. It's organized chaos, and I'm still catching up.

Linda steps out into the foyer to use the restroom. Shortly after, the shop door opens. Expecting another customer, I turn, ready to deliver a greeting, but no such luck. It's Vanessa, and another woman who looks vaguely familiar, her dark hair twisted into a messy bun with loose strands falling around her face, both standing at the front counter of my grooming shop. My pulse skitters. I move to greet them politely.

"Sarah," Vanessa says brightly, her tone too smooth to be genuine. "I was just giving my friend Jackie a tour of the building, and thought I'd bring her by your shop too."

Jackie's smile doesn't quite reach her eyes. "You've done such a nice job with it."

"Thank you," I say, forcing a small smile. There's something oddly familiar about her name, a memory brushing just out of reach.

Vanessa glances around, running her fingers along the counter like she's testing for dust. *Good thing she'll only find dog hair.* I joke to myself.

"Honestly, I haven't ever been in here, not even since Spencer bought the building. I've been meaning to see what all the fuss is about. He's been so busy with work lately."

Her words sound casual, but her tone carries an undercurrent, part curiosity, part warning.

"I'm sure he's been proud of his hard work," I say carefully, trying to sound neutral.

"Yes, he's been talking about it nonstop."

Jackie drifts a few steps away, studying the walls and the grooming stations. Her eyes linger a little too long on the framed photos of me with the dogs. When I look her way, her focus is already elsewhere.

Luckily, the dogs are extra loud today, and the general commotion makes it uncomfortable for anyone to hang around too long. I excuse myself, saying I need to get back to work, and they leave shortly after.

The bell above the door rings as they go, the sound a little too light for how heavy my chest feels.

They seem nice enough, but I can't help wondering what their real intentions are. Something about Jackie's calm smile won't leave my head even after they're gone. Women like that rarely do anything unannounced without a motive.

Moments after the two of them depart, Linda returns from the restroom.

"Do you know who came into the shop?" she asks, her eyes sweeping across the shop, noticing no dogs have come or gone.

"Vanessa and Jackie. Spencer's wife... with her friend. You missed out on getting to meet them." Sarcasm bleeds from my voice.

"Oh, what were they here for?"

"Vanessa apparently wanted to show Jackie the building. She hasn't been here before. I'm sure with how materialistic Vanessa is, the shop is another feather in her superficial cap."

Linda studies me quietly, maybe hearing the tension I didn't mean to reveal.

How would I know anything about Vanessa and her materialistic ways?

Hoping Linda doesn't catch onto what I know, I continue grooming, but she wears a thoughtful expression, as if trying to piece something together.

"I heard them chatting in the foyer while I was in the bathroom," she says, watching me too closely.

"Aaand?" I prompt, pretending to be distracted with the dog I'm currently brushing.

"I couldn't catch everything, but one of them seemed to be here for you. She was here to look at your hair. Do you know why they would need to do that?"

Uncertain of what that means, or why they would be interested in my hair, I pause. I wonder if now's the moment to tell Linda that I've been spending time with the landlord. We're solid now. I'm confident neither of us will be ending the affair anytime soon, unless we get caught. Besides, Spencer is like a drug to me; he's all I think about when I wake up, eat, sleep, and work. It's been killing me to keep all of his gloriousness to myself.

"Actually," I reply carefully, "I might know why they came." I swallow hard. "It's odd they would show up here, but... there's something I need to tell you." I pause, my voice dropping to a lower tone as the weight of the situation settles in. The words taste unstable, and I'm scared to mix my work life with my private life, but it's too late for that. She might as well know the danger she faces too.

She *deserves* to be informed. It could affect her if my relationship with Spencer fails, which, statistically speaking, it might.

I've been researching the odds of affairs turning into lasting marriages. Only about 5% of affairs end up in marriage, and nearly 75% of those end in divorce. But Spencer feels different.

"So... I've been spending time with the landlord—Spencer," I admit hesitantly. I sneak a furtive glance her way to gauge her reaction. Linda's eyebrows shoot up in surprise.

"Really?" she asks, her tone a mix of concern and curiosity. "So what exactly are you doing with Dominic then? Is this just fun with Spencer, or are you planning to leave Dominic like you've hinted before?" She hits me with several questions all at once, with no time to respond in between the curiosity.

I attempt to sound convincing as I explain, "My relationship with Spencer is still new, so my decisions regarding Dominic aren't based on what's happening between us now," I pause, suddenly unsure who I'm trying to convince, Linda or myself.

THIRTY

"Dominic isn't holding up his end of our marriage, and I've made a conscious choice to pursue happiness with Spencer."

She brings the conversation back to where it started. "So, why would Vanessa bring her friend, or neighbor, here?" she asks.

"One night, Vanessa went out of town, leaving me to spend the evening at Spencer's. As I was about to leave, I noticed the neighbors' light on inside. It was peculiar, especially since it was past midnight." I pause to gauge her reaction to my revelation. She listens attentively, but her expression remains impassive. Whatever thoughts are crossing her mind, she's not revealing much.

"One of them said her *hair* was longer. I'm not sure what that meant."

Like something mechanical snapping into place, I realize I've seen Jackie before. Not once. Not twice. Three times.

"She was the woman at the balloon festival who touched Spencer's arm like she knew him. She was the neighbor with the light on when I left his house after midnight. And now, here she is, smiling politely in my grooming shop, like a stranger being introduced for the first time. If she's putting it all together... *we're so unbelievably screwed*," I whisper, mostly to myself but also for Linda.

"But why would she say your hair was longer if it was you?" she asks, linking things together like a detective. She's already trying to help me keep this secret. She's always had my back.

"I'm not sure," I admit. "I did get my hair trimmed, but only a few inches." I pause, considering the possibility. "Maybe Jackie did recognize me or didn't want to call me out in front of Vanessa. Or... maybe Spencer had another woman over."

I don't want to entertain the last thought. I don't believe that's the case, not for a second, but if he's willing to be with me while I'm with another man, it's not impossible there could be others.

"Either way, it doesn't sound like she fully identified me," I say, reassuring both of us. "So I think we're in the clear. Spencer and I need to keep some distance for a while, making sure the suspicion fades." I exhale, relieved. "I'm glad I told you. It was hard not to."

Linda gives me a loving look. "I'm glad you told me too. Spencer seems great." Then she grins mischievously. "Does this mean we get free rent?" We both laugh, letting our tension ease, relaxing into shallow gossip about Spencer's wife and her mysterious friend, as if that can keep the walls from closing in.

Thirty-One

Today marks the grand opening of our new boarding shop. I've taken the day off from grooming to focus entirely on introducing our services and amenities to the stream of visitors. Our advertising and banners have paid off.

There's a solid turnout, and the energy in the shop is buzzing. The area we live in has a large pet population, and many well-off families are scattered throughout the mountains. There's no shortage of people willing to invest in quality care for their animals. The shift from the heat of summer to the crispness of fall is perfect for showing off the cozy setup we've created for our boarding customers.

After our trial run, over the last few months, we made an official decision: small dogs and cats only, no big dogs. Big dogs are wonderful but they're too much to handle walking back and forth from the outdoor dog park.

During the open house a man pushes through the door holding a massive bouquet of flowers. I barely glance up, assuming they must be for someone else. But then he asks, "Is there a person named Sarah here?"

"Ummm... that's me. Can I help you?"

"These flowers are for you." He steps forward and hands them to me.

I set them down on the counter and pull the small card from the envelope tucked inside.

I open it.

Sarah, congratulations on your new shop. I wish I were one of the dogs, so you could put me to bed too. I miss you, Spencer.

A rush of happiness floods me. He's thinking of me—he misses me.

After I told him about Vanessa and her little adventure in my shop, he agreed that distance is necessary for the time being.

I force myself to remain composed as I continue greeting customers—giving tours, and answering endless questions. Despite my efforts, I can barely focus, as his words keep replaying in my mind.

Hours later, the day winds down and the open house comes to a close. Spencer arrives with Mike, Nick, and their employee, Cooper.

Spencer's presence sends a charge through the air.

The sexual tension between us is thick, impossible to ignore. When our eyes lock, the moment stretches longer than it should. We want to embrace. *Desperately.*

How no one else sees the storm between us is beyond me.

Nick and Cooper are attractive in their own right, handsome and confident, but they're not Spencer. *No one is.*

Nick stands at least six feet tall, thin, with dark hair, blue eyes, and an incredibly kind demeanor. He's around thirty, the same age as Spencer. Over the past few months, I've gotten to know him while he's been putting the finishing touches on our shop. He's helped with several projects, always reliable and easy to be around.

Cooper, on the other hand, seems close to my age or a little younger. He doesn't have the same stature or build as Spencer, but he's not difficult to look at—especially when he smiles, it's perfection. Whoever his orthodontist was needs a raise.

"Congratulations, you guys." Spencer's voice breaks any tension in the air. He stands near the bouquet of flowers I received earlier, his presence magnetic.

"How was the showing?" Mike asks, standing round in stature.

Linda responds first, her voice full of excitement. "It went better than expected. We signed up several new clients, and the holidays are booked solid."

I chime in, still buzzing with adrenaline. "It was absolutely a success."

Nick watches me with an unreadable expression. There's something

THIRTY-ONE

behind it I can't quite name.

"Nice flowers," Nick says, glancing at the arrangement, then back at me. His smile pulls tight.

"They're beautiful," I say.

"Must be nice," he adds, and something in the way he says it makes my skin prickle.

"Excuse me?"

He shrugs, unbothered.

"You know, sometimes the guy giving the flowers doesn't get the happy ending." Then he turns to grab a soda from the snack table provided for the guests.

Cooper stays quiet, observing everything, taking it all in, sizing up the space.

Linda and I spend over forty-five minutes chatting with the four men about their upcoming projects and the ones they have recently finished. Most of the conversation revolves around Mike's new house, which broke ground in May and is expected to be finished by November.

"We have to go see it," Linda says, her voice appeased.

I agree, knowing how much work Spencer poured into it. "Definitely. It sounds incredible."

I move to the door to flip the open sign to "closed," and a chill slips down my spine. I glance out the window, my heart catching for a second. I could've sworn I saw someone standing across the street—watching. My brain instantly leaps to Jackie. She's seen me too many times now. Maybe she's spying on us here.

I blink, and the spot is empty. Maybe it was nothing, just my paranoia creeping in.

Mike's becoming less intimidating, not as uptight as I initially thought. Cooper is a cute kid. If he were older, I might actually be interested in dating him. But I've always preferred older men, and of course, there's Spencer.

He isn't the scary, unapproachable guy I first assumed he was, though his dry sense of humor still keeps me on my toes. Half the time, I can't tell if he's being serious or not.

What's driving me crazy, though, is having Spencer so close yet completely untouchable.

As the guys wrap up their conversation and begin heading out, Spencer pauses near the flowers again.

"Pretty flowers," he remarks, his eyes fixed on them. "Who bought them for you?"

"My husband," I reply, with a smooth voice.

His expression is unreadable. "He must think highly of you."

"Something like that," I say, with a twinkle in my eye.

With that, the group heads outside. As soon as the door shuts behind them, Linda turns to me with a knowing look.

"He bought you flowers," she states matter-of-factly. "I felt the chemistry between you two. He couldn't keep his eyes off of you."

Linda starts, "Nick and Cooper might be interested in you too. Nick kept looking in your direction, and of course you didn't notice."

"I noticed he was looking at me differently today. I've never recognized him doing that before now. Regardless, I think Cooper is more attractive than Nick. Still, none of that matters right now. I need to get divorced so I can actually explore my options. But honestly? All I want is Spencer. And I believe he'll be my husband someday."

Linda raises her brows. "Is he getting a divorce?"

"He hasn't said it outright," I say, "but I know we're meant to be. I don't see how he couldn't feel the same."

Linda says thoughtfully, "I'm sure you'll end up with the best person for you. We know at this point that's not Dominic."

That I can't argue with.

With the shop finally empty, we turn our attention to cleaning up after the successful day of dog showings. The turnout was incredible, far better than we expected.

"I think our boarding business is going to do great," Linda remarks.

"I agree."

"Word of mouth will take care of the rest."

"Yeah, I'm excited."

As we finish up, Linda glances at the bouquet. "What do you want to do with these?"

"I need to leave them here. If I take them back to my place, Dominic will ask questions. Honestly, I'd rather keep them at the shop anyway. This way, I'll get to see them every day, sitting right here on the desk. A little reminder of Spencer..."

Alone in my bedroom, my body aches with desire for the touch of Spencer. Dominic's away for at least another hour, and my thoughts of him staring into my eyes earlier replay.

I collapse onto my bed. Flashes of him on top of me wind in my mind. I reach for my vibrator, buried deep in my nightstand. I've never used it before. I don't even remember how I ended up with it.

But right now, I'm grateful it exists.

Thoughts of Spencer awaken me, so I let them run wild, spiraling through my core, as I think about the things he's done to me.

Pulling my shirt up slightly, I let my fingers graze my skin, imagining they're his instead. I flick the switch to on, the soft hum sending a shiver across me as I trail it over my body, teasing myself with the thought of him and the way he claims me.

My body reacts instinctively, growing slick with longing as I press the toy to me. I arch, gasping at the sensation. It's not him, but it will have to do.

Touching my breasts, I do my best to imitate his hold, caressing me. My hips rolling with the vibrations, the pleasure building as I let my imagination take over.

Inserting this imitation of Spencer into me is a new tingle, similar to the bullet he left inside me at dinner. This one though is stronger, more potent.

Dreaming it's Spencer above me and inside me, I lose myself in the moment.

Pleasure crashes over me, sharp and consuming. My body tenses, releases, pulsing with aftershocks of satisfaction.

As I catch my breath, the thought settles deep in my chest. I can't stay away from him much longer.

And I don't want to.

Thirty-Two

Too much time has passed since we decided to keep our distance. I break down and text Spencer late, probably too late.

The thought of him lying with Vanessa is eating me alive. It's been too long since I've seen him—really seen him outside of the fleeting moments at work. The distance is suffocating, and a terrible fear is beginning to rise in the pit of my stomach.

What if he's done with me? What if I'm only a short-term fling?

I don't know how I would handle it if he simply moved on. I keep telling myself I'm prepared for that outcome, that I could accept it if he stays with his wife. But the truth is starting to crack through me. The idea of Spencer choosing her over me doesn't feel like something I could recover from. I'm more attached than I meant to be. More tangled than I ever planned. And admitting that terrifies me.

My fingers move slowly over the keyboard before finally typing out the message. "Are you awake?"

I hit send and pray Vanessa doesn't see the screen light up beside him. Dominic, asleep beside me, never checks my phone. He would never suspect me of being anything but faithful. His trusting, goody-goody wife.

I stare at the screen, waiting. Then seconds later, a light flashes across the display.

"Yes."

Relief washes over me so intensely that I feel lightheaded. "I miss you. I need to be with you." I respond.

"Same."

"Come see me tomorrow," I say, inviting him to my place.

He's never been here before. The thought is a little nerve wracking.

I type out my address and time. "7:00 a.m. Dominic leaves at 6:30. Come before work."

I release tension, my body finally relaxing after weeks of stress. He's coming—and he still wants me. Finally, I can sleep knowing that in a few hours, he'll be mine again. At least for a moment.

Dominic heads out for work first thing in the morning. I pretend to be asleep, avoiding the obligatory morning kiss. I do that often now.

The second the door shuts behind him, I grab my phone and text Spencer.

"The front door's open. Come upstairs."

I wait in bed while the minutes pass, then thirty. But, as doubts start to creep in, I hear the door open and softly click shut.

But then... silence.

I frown, listening. Five more minutes pass, and I begin to wonder what's going on? *Did he get nervous? Did he leave?* He's never been here before, so maybe the reality of it hit him. I give it a little longer, but when nothing happens, I throw on my shorts and a tank top, then quietly make my way downstairs to investigate.

The moment I turn the corner into the kitchen, I freeze.

Spencer's standing there. A grapefruit, neatly cut in two halves, sits on the counter. Beside it is a steaming cup of hot chocolate. He peers up at me, completely at ease.

"What are you doing?" I ask, surprised by the unexpected sight of him in my kitchen, effortlessly finding everything he needs.

"Wanted to surprise you."

Warmth floods my chest. I step into the kitchen in seconds, wrapping my arms around him in a deep, comforting hug.

"I've missed you so much," I can't restrain myself from getting as physically close to him as possible. So much silent time has passed. I doubted I'd ever hold him again. My lungs expand as I draw him in, and for a moment, I feel like I'm exactly where I'm supposed to be.

THIRTY-TWO

"Same. It's been too long without you." He doesn't rush himself as he slowly wraps his warm arms around my shoulders, pulling me close.

"I love grapefruit," I murmur, touched by his thoughtfulness.

"Good," he says. I slide onto a stool at the counter while he remains standing. We eat together. He sips coffee. I drink hot chocolate.

"I've never met a Mormon who drinks coffee," I tease, raising a brow.

His lips curve. "It's my vice. I don't exactly follow the Word of Wisdom all the time."

I let out a small laugh, nonjudgmental of his indiscretions. After all, we are both committing adultery, the second worst sin, next only to murder. That's what we were always taught in the Mormon religion. Unless we repent, we're both headed straight for hell. *At least we'll be going there together*, my reckless mind muses. The thought disappears the moment our eyes lock. I take his hand and lead him upstairs. "I want to show you where I sleep—my bed," I tell him softly, "so you can picture me here the way I picture you."

In my room, we lay on the bed, fully dressed.

"This is it. This is where I lie at night and envision you," I say proudly.

"It's similar to the way I thought it would be—the way I stroke myself imagining you lying in your bed." He wraps his arm over my waist.

"You think about me like that?" I press for more. The thought piques my curiosity and I secretly love the idea of him wanting me when I'm not with him.

"Maybe... have I said too much?" he questions aloud, as if he let his thoughts slip without realizing that he let me into his mind—when maybe he wasn't ready for me to.

I smile and give him a peck on the cheek, "I love that you think of me. Someone's got to. So why not you?"

"I'm happy to be that guy." He relaxes after letting his feelings for me be known. "I have to head out, I'm glad I was able to stop by and see where you live. It's adorable."

"I don't want you to go," I whisper, my voice carries the slight whine that comes out on occasion.

"I know," he says.

"I don't want to be needy," I admit, "but I can't help it with you."

Something about him turns me into a different version of myself. I'm independent in every other part of my life. But with him? I become subservient.

"There's never enough time," I say, staring up at the ceiling, trying not to pout.

He shifts beside me and says quietly, "Let's make this a regular thing. I'll come over in the mornings after your husband leaves."

"I'm not going to say no to that," I say, elated at his suggestion.

He gets up reluctantly, straightening his clothes. I don't want to let him go, but I do— because now I know: he'll be back.

"I'll miss you, Buster," I say, unable to keep the whine from my voice.

His lips curl up, the confidence in his response resonates in me. "I'll miss you too, Princess."

The shop is quiet. Only the hum of dryers in the back of the shop along with the tick of the clock above the counter. The French bulldog lies curled up in my lap on a folded towel, her breathing shallow, chest rattling with every rise and fall.

I stroke the velvet of her ears, whispering nonsense words repeated since her very first grooming appointment years ago. "You're my pretty girl. Always my beautiful girl."

The note her owner left is folded in the drawer, a single line I can't stop hearing: *if she declines, make the call. Let the vet handle everything.*

But there's no call to make. No time for decisions. Her little body is already slipping away while I sit here helpless. Tears spill hot and unrelenting, and I rock her against me like I can bargain with God, like love and faith should be enough to keep her here. But her body is too old to stay until her owners return.

Tears burn my eyes as I press my cheek to her fur. She exhales once, twice—then stills.

And just like that, she's gone.

I stay beside her for minutes, maybe longer, my arms wrapped around her like I can anchor her spirit, like I can keep her tethered to me. My chest aches with the weight of it, the unfairness, the loneliness of dying in someone else's arms because the person who loves you isn't there.

And the thought hits harder than it should. This tiny blunt reminder that time runs out, whether we are ready or not. Lulu didn't die alone. But she died without the person she belonged to. Without the one who mattered the most. And suddenly I'm struck by how easy it would be for me to do the same, to spend my young, breathing years wrapped up beside someone who doesn't notice me, doesn't choose me, doesn't treat me the way I deserve. Wasting the best of myself on a life that feels small and quiet and wrong, while the one person who makes me feel alive isn't mine at all.

It rips me to pieces. She wasn't just a customer. She was mine in some small way. The dog who wiggled every time she saw me. The one who bounced balloons off her nose during playtime and the one I bathed with extra care, because I adored her.

When I lay her down, the towel beneath her is too cold. To clinical. I whisper a goodbye no one will hear. And as I wipe my face, I know I'll carry this with me, another secret grief tucked inside, where no one thinks to look.

I sit at the edge of the bed, hands still trembling from the day. The image of Lulu, lying lifeless in my arms—won't leave me. My throat feels raw from holding back tears at the shop, from pretending I could keep it together until the last client left.

"She was old," I whisper to Dominic, voice breaking. "I did everything I could, but... she passed away. Right there in my arms. Her owner asked me to care for her while he was away, and now I have to tell him she's gone."

For a moment, I thought he might soften. That maybe, just maybe, he'd say something kind. But Dominic only scoffed, shaking his head.

"Figures," he muttered, setting his beer down on the table with a heavy thud. "First you lose a customer, now you lose someone's dog. You really think people are going to trust you with their pets after this?"

The words hit like ice water. "It wasn't my fault," I say quickly, my voice too sharp, too desperate. "She was old. They knew it could happen while they were gone. I..."

"You should've tried harder," Dominic cuts in, his tone flat, dismissive. "If it was me, I wouldn't be handing you another dime. You can't even keep a dog alive."

I stare at him, disbelief tingling with fury, with grief. "You're cruel." I whisper.

He shrugs. "It's reality. Maybe you're not cut out for the boarding thing. Grooming, sure. But keeping something breathing? You're in over your head."

The room feels smaller, pressing in. My hands curl into fists in my lap, nails digging crescent moons into my skin just to keep from breaking apart in front of him.

I want to scream, to hurl something, to make him feel even a fraction of the pain ripping through me. But I do nothing, because fighting back would only give him another chance to tear me down.

Thirty-Three

Spencer's been coming over the moment Dominic leaves for work. We make incredible love in the short time we have, our passion urgent and quick. Luckily, I live close to work, allowing us to steal these precious moments together.

Today is no exception.

We've finished cleaning up and gotten dressed when I hear the front door open and close.

My blood runs cold.

"Fuck. Fuck. Fuck."

Spencer looks at me, confused, still tugging his shirt down over his head. He doesn't recognize the subtle differences between my neighbors' sounds and the unmistakable presence of someone *inside* my home. He doesn't know what I've heard.

I can barely breathe. My pulse hammers in my ears as I cross the room in two frantic strides and shove him into the closet behind a row of long dresses.

"My husband is here," I whisper anxiously. "Stay here until I come back."

Spencer's eyes widen to say *holy fuck!* He doesn't argue.

By the time I shut the closet door and pull myself together, Dominic is already coming up the stairs. I force a breath through my nose, praying he can't hear the wild beating of my heart.

"What's going on?" Dominic asks, stepping into the bedroom.

"Nothing. I'm getting ready for the day." I inject a note of casualness into my voice that doesn't match the chaos inside me. "Why are you back so soon?"

"Forgot my tool belt," he replies, scanning the room.

I pray he doesn't notice the trembling in my fingers, the scent of passion still clinging to my skin. The room smells like us. *Does he know?*

"Oh, that sucks," I say, feigning sympathy. "Did you find it?"

As subtle as possible, I shift my stance, steering him slightly away from my closet.

Dominic pauses, his gaze narrowing. His instincts prickle. He knows something's off. His eyes sweep the room. "Is there a man in here?"

My stomach flips, but I keep my expression locked down. "What?" I let out a dry laugh. "No! Why would you even ask that?"

He doesn't answer right away. Instead, he moves, checking behind the bedroom door.

Then the bathroom.

Every breath I take feels like a countdown.

He's suspicious.

"I don't know... I felt like you were hiding something," he finally says.

I shake my head, forcing out an exasperated sigh. "I'm getting ready to go grocery shopping. It's my day off. I always run errands and clean. I may even watch a Lifetime Murder Mystery." I roll my eyes. "Seriously, Dom?"

He exhales, slow and long, shaking off his paranoia. But my heartbeat hasn't slowed. Not even close.

"Now," I say, trying to sound upbeat, "let's find your tool belt. Any idea where you left it?" I ask him, again trying to divert his attention anywhere but toward the closet.

"I'm not sure. Possibly downstairs, or in the garage."

I latch onto the excuse. "Yeah, you should go check there."

After scouring the room, he turns toward the door and leans in for a peck. I barely register it before he shuts the door behind him.

The second he's gone, I sprint upstairs and yank open the closet.

Spencer steps out, visibly shaken. So am I.

"I'm so, so sorry," I whisper, voice cracking. I apologize over and over. "He's never come back so soon after leaving for work. That was way too

THIRTY-THREE

close."

Spencer runs his hands along the sharp edges of his jaw exhaling with irritation. "Yeah. No kidding."

The tension clings to us. The adrenaline still racing through the both of us. When he moves toward the door, I don't stop him, as I normally do. We both know he needs to get out of here.

"I think we should find somewhere else to meet for a while," I say, feeling embarrassed for putting Spencer in this uncomfortable situation.

I quickly see him out after making sure Dominic has pulled away. We can't risk Dominic coming back for something else, only to find Spencer standing in the living room, or worse, on top of me.

I spend the rest of the day trying to shake the lingering fear, but the close-call has done more than rattle me; it's left me with even more crystal-clear clarity—clarity I may have already had, but had been too afraid to face.

I don't want to keep living like this.

The only time I feel alive is when I'm with Spencer. It's unfair to keep stringing Dominic along when my heart is somewhere else. And it won't be long before Dominic messes up again. And when he does, three strikes will be reason enough to finally walk away.

I stroll into the kitchen, pop a tamale into the microwave, and lean against the counter, while I wait. I haven't eaten since 11:00 a.m. Linda and I took an early lunch at work, as we usually do. Our schedule is predictable: bathe the morning dogs, eat, bathe the second batch, and groom the first one while the second dries. The cycle continues until all the dogs look perfect.

Now, it's late, and I have no energy to cook a full meal, especially not when I don't know if or when Dominic will return.

I pull the tamale from the microwave and sit down to eat, absently picking at my food while my mind wanders.

I think about Spencer. About the incredible love we've been making. About how easy it feels. How natural it is to be with him.

My mind replays our passion. My dream of floating in the hot air balloon, a night of intimacy without ever needing to touch. The way my body melts for him. How when we're together, it feels effortless.

Then, self-doubt creeps in.

Vanessa is beautiful. Classy. Untouchable. And me? I'm possibly a young, temporary thrill. A secret. *What if he never leaves her for me?*

My thoughts spiral, my appetite vanishes. *I'm being ridiculous.* Our relationship has only deepened in the past several months.

Deep down, I know we belong together.

My heart recognizes it. My soul does too.

But how do I make him see it too?

Or worse, what if he already does and it changes nothing? I don't have the answer yet.

I scrape the last bit of my tamale onto my fork and push back from the counter. My body itches from the long day of grooming. Showering is always the first thing on my post-work agenda. I cross through the family room passing the couches and the coffee table, heading toward the stairs, when the front door suddenly opens.

I take a quick step back so it doesn't hit me.

It's Dominic.

For a second we stare at each other, both surprised like neither of us expected to be face-to-face right now.

"Where have you been?" I ask, annoyance rising.

"Work," he says, flatly. "Had to stay late."

I narrow my eyes. *Liar.*

The excuse is weak. I can sense it—in the way he's standing, the slight tension in his voice. I know him well enough to tell when he's feeding me bullshit.

I pull my arms across my chest, blocking his way between the door and the armrest of the couch.

I'm done. So done.

I didn't plan to do this today, but suddenly the words are on the tip of my tongue.

We hold eye contact, tension hanging between us. My mind races, yet my body is frozen.

"What's wrong?" he asks, his gaze searching mine.

I open my mouth, but stop. I could say it now. *I should say it now.*

But I can't.

Instead, I shake my head, dropping my eyes to the dark-blue couch. I don't move.

Before I can find my voice, he says it.

"You don't want to be married to me anymore, do you?"

It's not only a question—it's a statement.

He sounds weak. Defeated.

A beat of silence passes. I shake my head, "No," I answer quietly.

"Okay," he says, his expression unreadable. "I'll have my stuff out by this weekend."

I blink. That's it? No argument? No fight?

I expected anger. Denial. Begging. Questioning. Something.

But instead, he's making it easy.

That's when I realize, maybe he's been wanting this too. Maybe he's felt the distance between us as much as I have. Maybe he's known, deep down, that we've been over for a long time.

I think about the way he always smells like booze. How he exists in his own world, one that no longer includes me. Maybe it never did.

Mine certainly doesn't include him either.

I have to face it: we were never built to last.

I didn't expect it to end so quietly. Where's his anger? The threats? The thrown objects? The venom! *None of that happens.*

Instead, Dominic is eerily calm. He stands there, quiet, composed—so unlike himself that I almost don't recognize him.

"What stuff will you be taking?" I ask, arms crossed, still on guard.

He answers like he's already planned this out. "I'll take the bed. The dining room table. The grill. My clothes. And the couches."

Although I love my brand-new couches, my brows furrow, confused. "That's it?"

No argument over the condo? No threats to take half of everything? I closed on this place earlier this year, yet he doesn't even seem interested in fighting for it.

"Great," I say, unable to hide my disbelief.

He nods, unfazed. "I'll start getting my stuff tomorrow. I'm staying at my sister's tonight."

Did he have this all planned? Did he already pack his clothes for tomorrow, or are they waiting in his truck?

Most likely not. He's always been the guy who can crash comfortably anywhere and wake up in the same jeans from the night before.

I study his face, searching for any sign that he's bluffing, or that he might lash out. But he's serious.

And just like that—it's over.

A wave of calm settles over me. I relax. I'm confused. I silently question. *He's happy about getting divorced?*

I am.

He leans in to give me a final peck on the lips, a strange, empty gesture.

"I'll file the paperwork soon," he says, before turning toward the door.

I take a step back as he twists the knob, and the familiar flicker of the entryway light comes on as he lets go. The door glides open. He steps through it, pulling it softly shut behind him.

And then he's gone.

I exhale, suddenly motionless in the silence of my home. *My home.*

I'm free.

Free of his anger.

Free to visit my mom, without getting in trouble for staying too long.

Free from his threats to end his life only to manipulate me.

Free from his lies about going to work when he seldom brought in a paycheck.

Free from having my things stolen and him blaming it on some random passerby.

The house is silent, no TV, no shouting, no chaos.

Just peace.

Just freedom.

Thirty-Four

I head down the sidewalk lining the building, rent check in hand, toward Spencer and Mike's offices. Along the way, I pass Cooper and offer a cordial hello, maybe even a teasing look that hints at more. It's fun to flirt a little.

I step into Spencer's office, where I find Spencer and Mike deep in conversation, both in high spirits.

"Hello, Sarah. What can I do for you?" Spencer greets me in his upbeat voice, masking the unspoken intimacy between us.

"Hey, I'm bringing the rent over a little early for next month. How are you guys doing?" I say.

"Great!" Spencer says.

Mike chimes in, "We were talking about the Christmas party I'm hosting at my new house." He sits proudly in the leather chair facing Spencer's desk.

Then, offhandedly, Mike adds, "By the way, my little brother who works for me—Nick? He mentioned asking you out on a date before. Would you be interested?"

I pause. Nick, who's been helping out around the shop and now lives with his big brother? Nick is nice enough, handsome, friendly, but I have no desire to get involved with him. I'm glad Mike doesn't suggest that I come to the Christmas party with Nick. Still, I can't help but wonder how Spencer feels about that. And more importantly, how does Mike already know that I'm separated from Dominic? I suspect someone has let it slip, but I can't know for sure.

The thought of Spencer at a Christmas party with his wife while I'm on a date with Nick leaves me feeling inherently conflicted. I feel a twinge of jealousy at the mere idea of Vanessa with him. Those moments they share are the ones I long to experience with him.

I want to be the one curled beside him on the couch after a long day. The one whose hand he holds in a dark theater. The one who goes to parties with him.

It sinks in that I'm not the one—that I may never be.

Before I can dwell further on these thoughts, I force myself to wrap up our conversation. "Sure, tell Nick to call me or catch me after work. I'll plan on it." A lie, maybe. But I say it with a smile, hoping Spencer's watching.

I glance over, trying to read his reaction. I can't tell if he cares, but a secret hope stirs inside me that agreeing to Mike's suggestion might spark even a tiny flash of jealousy from him, something that would only reaffirm his feelings for me.

I take a deep breath and force a smile as I hand Spencer his rent check. "Here's your rent."

Heading out of the office, I feel a bittersweet mix of apprehension and excitement about my first potential post-divorce date. I'm new to the dating scene, and I'm not sure what to expect, but one thing is clear—it's the start of something new.

Spencer came to see me this morning before work. I no longer need to worry about Dominic catching us together since we are separated. Our only worry now is Vanessa, especially after her little visit to my shop with her friend Jackie. But it seems things have calmed down since our break, no more tension. No more close calls.

Earlier this week, I found the perfect surprise for Spencer. His birthday is coming up on Thanksgiving. Of course, he'll be spending it with his family, indulging in turkey and potatoes. I bought him something expensive—he's been wanting it for a while. Even though it stretched my current budget, he's worth every single penny and I hope he thinks of me each time he sees

THIRTY-FOUR

it.

We share a brief but meaningful hug and a quick kiss, a quiet exchange before work. I waste no time handing him his huge, wrapped gift box. I'm thrilled to finally give him something special.

He settles onto my brand-new rustic leather couch. I had to buy these after Dominic took my comfy blue ones away. That was something I was extra bummed about. In the grand scheme of things, it's a small sacrifice—he didn't fight for the condo or any money, so I feel like I've come out pretty well in the separation. And with our boarding business taking off, I'm finally earning enough to exhale again.

"Happy birthday!" I exclaim as Spencer slowly begins to open the gift. I could scream watching him unwrap it. Why is he one of those people who carefully peels the tape instead of tearing the paper? It's a little obnoxious, but since it's him, I wait patiently for him to reveal the gift.

"You didn't need to get me anything," he protests softly.

"I know. But I think it's perfect, and Vanessa won't suspect that it's from another woman. It's subtle." I say, a little proud of myself.

He pulls a small pocket knife from his pocket and carefully cuts the tape along the top of the box. As he lifts the lid, his eyes light up. He freezes-then smiles. Gently, he closes the box again and looks at me.

"You shouldn't have gotten these for me. They're too expensive."

"I got them to show you how much I love you," I blurt, as shock and disbelief widen in my eyes.

Shit. I let the three words slip out... Trying to pull them back, I stammer, "I... I mean I really like you."

I can't believe I said it first. But I did.

He doesn't answer right away.

"Damn it, you love me?" He teases, his tone a mixture of shock and delight. Leaning in, he gives me a passionate kiss. I'm embarrassed, yet relieved that he now knows how I feel.

"Yes, like I said, I really like you."

"No, no, no, you can't take it back." An excited energy animates his whole face.

Though he doesn't return the words, I'm okay with that. Why would he say it back, only because I blurted mine out?

He turns back to the gift and pulls it out of the box again. "These are the coolest saddlebags I've ever seen," he says, his eyes bright with excitement. "I love the studs on them, they're so rad. They'll be perfect for my motorcycle. Thank you."

He wraps me in a soft, lingering hug.

"You're welcome." I smile. "Remember our hot air balloon ride? We both needed a place to put our things, and I didn't want your jacket to get stolen. Now we'll have somewhere to stash the extras when we go on rides this summer."

In response, he playfully kisses me all over. While he doesn't explicitly say he loves me, I feel it in the way he touches me.

"I wish we could stay together all day," he laments, rising to leave.

I cling to him, as I always do during these stolen moments.

He kisses my forehead with his smooth, confident charm—then winks.

"See you," I say regretfully, watching him leave with the large box in his arms.

Thirty-Five

The grocery store's filled with the usual weekday chaos, cart wheels squeaking, fluorescent lights flickering overhead, someone's baby wailing in the next aisle. I just need milk and bread, but I let myself gallivant a little, drifting through the aisles and soaking up the rare feeling of having nowhere I need to be.

I'm sliding a loaf of bread into my cart when I feel the unstable weight of someone's gaze. My shoulders tighten before I even turn.

Jackie's standing by the end-cap display, a bag of chips in her hands, but her brown eyes are fixed on me. Unblinking. As if she were studying me.

I force a smile, my voice too bright when it leaves my throat. "Hey, Jackie—fancy seeing you here."

She counters back with an almost sarcastic edge. "I live around here. Where else would I be?" But the tension in her tone prickles along my skin.

We chat for a few seconds—nothing remarkable, just grocery store small talk, since we hardly know each other, but the whole time, I feel pinned, like she's cataloging every word, every movement. When I finally push my cart past her, relief hits me all at once.

I don't look back.

But as I unload my groceries at the checkout, I can't shake the sensation that she's still there, eyes tracking me, hidden behind the store shelves.

Still watching.

Thirty-Six

It's my first Thanksgiving as a single woman since high school, and I'm determined to indulge, eating all the Thanksgiving food I can.

My family gathers at my Grandma "Mom's" and Grandpa "Pop's" house. Thanksgiving has always been my favorite holiday, for the amazing food, cozy family vibe, and freedom from having to buy gifts (except for now, since it's Spencer's birthday).

After dinner, my siblings and I help clean up. There's always a flurry of activity since Grandma (the one we call Mom) did all the cooking; we let her relax while the rest of us divide ranks to restore her kitchen to order. Once I finish my share of the pan washing, I settle into the quaint, tidy living room. My phone has been silent all day. Of course, it would be. Everyone I need or want to talk to on the holiday is here—everyone except Spencer.

It's been a beautiful day. Perfect, in so many ways. As I sit reflecting, my phone unexpectedly rings. The caller ID reads "unknown." Hopeful it's Spencer. I excuse myself from the family room to answer.

"Hello?" I say... no answer.

"Hello?" I ask a second time—still silence from the other end.

"*Is anyone there?*" I say, still no answer... until, right before I hang up, there's a throaty, whispering mumble: "Fwaaah," accompanied by deep, rhythmic breathing.

I hang up, unsettled and a little creeped out.

While I try to shake it off, a part of me can't help but wonder... could Jackie have gotten my number?

I pause to take a breath and brush the thought of the strange phone call aside before returning to my family.

Later, I find myself at The Dog Shop. Linda took care of the dogs this morning, so it's my turn tonight. Outside, night has fallen early. It already feels like winter, and the once beautiful fall leaves now lend an eerie quality to the familiar building, rumored to be haunted, though I've never experienced anything myself.

In the living room, the dogs scamper about, burning off energy during free play. I need to use the bathroom, so I step into the foyer's small restroom. When I'm inside, the front door creaks open. I rush to finish up. I hurry so I can be sure no one is letting the dogs out.

When I emerge, everything seems normal. The dogs are playing and walking around just as they were before, and no one's there. I must be hearing things. I return to the task of caring for the dogs and securing the inside boarding door. Then, I suddenly hear the front door creak open once more. Startled, I whirl around.

"Spencer!" I exclaim. "Oh my gosh, you scared the crap out of me."

"How is that?" he asks.

"Fuck! Why did you open the door earlier and not saying anything?" I demand an answer, putting my hands over my heart, trying to settle its fast beating.

"Sarah," he responds, looking me in the eye quizzically, "This is the first time I've opened that door tonight."

"Really? You weren't here earlier?" I question, concern creeping into my expression.

He seems equally worried now. "No, is someone else here?" he asks, scanning the room with his eyes and craning his neck to check around the corners, making sure that no one is lurking in here with us.

"I don't know. The door opened a few minutes ago while I was in the bathroom, but when I came out, no one was there," I recount, puzzled.

"So what *are* you doing here?" I'm excited to see him but also confused.

"When I was driving back to my place from dinner at my mom's, I saw your car parked out front, so I took my family home. Then I came to get my tools for a 'service call,'" he responds, emphasizing *service call* with air quotes.

"Doesn't Nick do the service calls?" I ask.

"Usually, yes, but lately, it's been me," he winks, hinting at our secret side projects.

I press further, "and... Vanessa... what if she finds out?"

"She doesn't even know what a service call means. For her, work is work. As long as there's money, she doesn't care if I'm gone. I'm not lying either. I am on a service call. I'm here to service you." He grins and takes hold of me.

"But you never used to go on 'service calls,'" I repeat his air quotes. "Don't you think she'll start finding it odd that you suddenly need to be away?" I wonder aloud, not quite ready to shake the possibility that someone had come into the shop before Spencer.

Vanessa doesn't seem like the kind of woman who conducts her business in the shadows. When she came into the shop before, it was in broad daylight, but if it wasn't her, who was it? Maybe it was nothing. Or maybe I'm being watched.

He shrugs, "I don't think so. I guess I'll find out sooner or later."

I eventually let my guard down and fold into him.

"Hi," I say smiling up at him in a bid to start the conversation over. My voice is soft and laden with longing, "I missed you. I'm so glad you came to see me."

"Missed you too," he says, voice roughened by a smile, and then, with a playful grab at my ass, adds, "Happy Thanksgiving."

I kiss him on the lips and wrap my arms around his neck. Our mouths meet in a passionate, brief escape from reality. As his hands pull me closer to his pelvic area, I feel the outline of his bulge through his pants.

I'm wearing my royal blue smock, a thin, silky layer that keeps my clothes pristine.

"Hey," he teases between kisses, "are you ready for your date with Nick?"

THIRTY-SIX

"Why? Are you jealous?" I ask, a desperate note in my voice. I'm aching to know his true feelings. If I'm being honest with myself, it would be reassuring to know that he feels a faint sense of insecurity about the prospect of me dating another man.

He replies evasively, "Maybe... whatever you do, don't fuck him." It's a stern warning.

"Maybe," I tease, turning his own words back on him, leaving him to wonder. "Will I or won't I?"

"I'm serious! Don't fuck him!" He takes hold of me harder, his grip possessive, sending a clear message. I belong to him. It turns me on a little, watching him become territorial over me.

He spins my body around, swiftly pressing me into the door of my shop. With authority, he raises my hands above my head.

"Don't move." Slowly, he pulls my smock and my pants down to my ankles. Next, I hear the soft clink as he unbuckles his belt. The sound of it snapping against itself floods me with unease.

What is he doing? Is he going to hurt me? I silently question in fear. Is he teasing me—or is he truly going to use it.

He flicks the belt again, and I feel a light brush of leather against my ass cheeks. Nervously, I wait, and then a gentle whip strikes my right cheek. The tingling, burning sensation is unexpected. I'd never considered whether I'd enjoy something like this, being whipped by a lover, but I do. Next, Spencer drives a deeper lash across my left cheek, and my endorphins surge, intensifying my sexual desire for this new, exhilarating experience.

"Do you want more?" his gruff voice whispers close to my ear.

"Yes, I think so," I reply, my voice trembling with yearning and a hint of uncertainty. "Do I?"

"Do I?" he teases, repeating my words as he whips me harder.

This isn't quite what I imagined for tonight, but I surrender to the thrill. He delivers one final lash—louder, firmer, more intense, leaving my skin hot, sore, and completely turned on.

Still facing away, I lower my arms as he suddenly slides two fingers into me without warning. "Do you like being finger-fucked?" he asks, his tone sultry and teasing, a unique combination.

"Yes, I do." *What kind of question is that? Of course, I love this. Who wouldn't?*

He continues, his thumb moving over my soaked center, and then, with a playful edge, he questions, "Do you want Nick's fingers in you right now, instead of mine?"

"Maybe..." I tease, mirroring his vagueness.

"Maybe isn't an answer! Do you need another lashing to tell me the truth?" his words are stern.

I know full well that I have no desire for Nick, only Spencer. And yet, there's a dark thrill in teasing him, giving me a twisted sense of control. He wields so much power over me. More than he knows. I'm trying to preserve some power of my own.

"I guess I'll see...," I remark, giving him no certainty.

He quickly withdraws his fingers, then fills the empty space with his length as if he owns every inch of me.

"Don't fuck him," he warns darkly, "or I'll have to whip you harder."

I murmur a soft "Okay," though I know with complete certainty that I do not want Nick.

Without warning, he mounts me against the door, his thrusts growing harder and faster until the noise rouses the dogs in the back room into a cacophony of barking. Their yapping drowns out our moans, making it tough to focus, though Spencer seems unfazed. He fucks me mercilessly for only a few minutes before he finally empties himself inside me.

Pulling away, he steps into the tiny bathroom beside us and wipes himself off.

"Talk about a quickie," I joke.

"Sorry, I've got to get back to my family. It's Thanksgiving after all. I just couldn't resist seeing you."

Outside the bathroom, I pull my pants up and wait. "Happy birthday," I say from my side of the door, keeping my tone light.

He steps out and plants a soft kiss on my lips. "Thank you. I'm glad I could see you tonight. You've given me the best surprise a guy could ask for," he wraps his arms around me, kissing the top of my head as he prepares to leave.

"See you, Buster," I whisper, not wanting him to go.

"See you, Princess," he replies confidently, leaving yet another clandestine meeting with the bittersweet promise of more to come.

The shop is quiet with Spencer gone—too quiet. I pause mid-sweep, eyes drawn to the front door. There's nothing out of the ordinary, only the usual clicks of toenails on the floor.

But then I see something.

A single photo—taped to the outside of the glass.

One of me and Spencer, taken from a distance. Our hands are brushing.

My chest tightens. I pull it down and flip it over.

I see you.

My vision blurs. I don't hear footsteps. But when I turn—

I catch a glimpse of a woman with dark hair hurrying past. For a split second, I'm sure it's Jackie.

"Hey!" I call out.

But she doesn't turn around. Within moments, she disappears around the corner.

All that's left is a photo.

And a message.

Thirty-Seven

Winter 2004

Like clockwork, Spencer comes by every morning before work. He usually makes me breakfast including sugar sprinkled grapefruit, orange juice, and waffles, drizzled with his family's secret orange syrup, sweet with barely a hint of tang. I can practically lick the plate clean.

On Sundays, he never forgets to bring me a root beer. One soda a week has become our ritual, a tiny indulgence that can't hurt, I reason.

I love our new routine. It lulls me into a sense of safety, leaving me less worried about being caught and more secure in the little life we've built.

Dominic and I have settled into an awkward friendship. We pretend everything is normal. No one seems hurt and, thankfully, he's never found out about Spencer. The secrecy is essential to maintaining the status quo and allowing us to mingle with our friends at social gatherings.

Tonight, I'm preparing for the highly anticipated date with Nick. He's expected to pick me up any minute now, and despite everything, I feel a little on edge.

I reluctantly agreed to this date because Mike caught me off guard by asking me to go on a date with his brother. I didn't have an excuse ready, but it's turned a convenient way to test the waters with Spencer. His lack of reaction when Mike suggested I date Nick is what made me want to say *yes*. However, I can't help but feel guilty. I feel like I'm cheating, which is

THIRTY-SEVEN

ridiculous. Spencer's married. He's at Mike's Christmas party tonight—*with his wife*.

But I can't help the way I feel. The truth is, I don't want anyone else, only Spencer.

Nick is taking me to dinner and a movie—a classic first-date setup. When he arrives, he's put together in a well-fitted shirt, pressed jeans, his neat hair, and light blue eyes doing their best to distract me from the storm of feelings still tangled around Spencer.

"We're still headed to the movie, right?" I ask, trying to sound more excited than torn.

"Eventually," he replies with a grin. "I thought we could make a quick stop by Mike's Christmas party first. They've got games going on, and it's always a good time."

I stiffen. "Mike's party?"

"Yeah," he says. "He said a few coworkers were coming. No pressure. We won't stay long."

As we pull into the driveway, festive music filters through the front door, accompanied by bursts of laughter and the twinkling of string lights illuminating the entrance.

We climb the wide front steps dusted with snow, each step of my boots crunching abnormally loud. I count them without meaning to—one, two, three, four—as if I'm measuring out my courage in numbers. By the fifth step, my chest tightens. Crossing this threshold feels like re-entering a life I'm not supposed to step back into.

Nick doesn't knock. He doesn't have to. He swings the door open.

"Perfect timing!" Mike beams, ushering us in. "We're playing charades. Join us!"

I step inside, anxiety zipping back and forth beneath my ribs. Secretly, I'm ecstatic to be invited to such an affluent party, but the most enticing and discomforting part is, Spencer is already here. Laughing.

He's sitting comfortably on the arm of a couch, a drink in hand, his face crinkled with amusement as Vanessa pantomimes some elaborate gesture in the center of the room. He claps along with the others, his guard down, his smile easy and genuine—something I rarely see even when it's just the two of us.

She returns to her place standing beside him, gorgeous and relaxed in a wine-colored dress, her hand resting on his knee as she laughs too. He doesn't pull away.

The sight slices through me before I can stop it. Then, he sees me.

His smile falters. The laughter drains from his face like someone flipped a switch. His eyes lock on mine across the room—stunned. Like he's been caught doing something he shouldn't, even though we both know he's allowed to be here. With her.

He stands slowly, straightening, his features tightening in that familiar way I know too well—unsure of how to act. Vanessa follows his gaze, her brow furrowing slightly.

"Oh hey, Nick!" Someone calls out, breaking the tension. "You brought a plus one?"

"This is Sarah," he says, proudly. "She's a friend of mine."

The whole room welcomes me in, but I can't take my eyes off Spencer—how quickly he's recovered, how he forces a smile that I know isn't sincere.

A woman in a sparkly red sweater waves us over to the group. "We're about to start the next round. You two should join! We need fresh victims."

Nick chuckles and glances at me. "What do you say? Up for some public humiliation?"

"Sure." I take the only open seat on the opposite side of the room from Spencer and Vanessa, my pulse thudding beneath skin that feels too tight.

The game continues, light and energetic. People are shouting guesses, laughing at the gestures and the terrible acting. Nick pops up and mimes something so ridiculous it has everyone in hysterics, except me. I can't stop glancing across the room, hyper-aware of Spencer's presence.

Then Mike claps his hands. "Alright, you're up, Spencer."

Spencer rises giving nothing away, brushing his palms together. "Let's do this."

Vanessa hands him the next prompt card. He barely glances at it before launching into his act.

He throws his arm wide, stomping theatrically, then bends down like he's picking something up. Everyone's yelling out guesses: "Lion!" "Giant!" "Earthquake!"

"Titanic," I say under my breath. He pauses, his eyes flickering to mine across the room.

His lips twitch into the faintest smile.

"Correct."

People groan. "How the hell did you get that so fast?"

I shrug, feigning modesty. "He did the iceberg thing."

He moves onto the next one. He acts out holding something. He tilts his head and walks with an exaggerated limp.

"Pirate?" someone shouts.

"Captain Hook?"

"One-Eyed Willy?"

I narrow my eyes, watching the tilt of his hands, the slight flex of his shoulders.

"Jack Sparrow," I call out.

He freezes again for a second, then lifts two fingers in acknowledgment. "Yep."

Another wave of groans and laughter.

"What is happening?" one of the women laughs.

"Are you two telepathic or something?"

"No, I'm just a lucky guesser," I say, trying to remove suspicion from myself.

Vanessa gives a sideways glance, subtle enough to mask the weight behind it. She laughs, but her eyes don't match her tone. They're not watching the game anymore. They're watching me. Watching *us*.

Spencer keeps going. With each prompt, he barely needs to start before I call it out.

"Dirty Dancing."

"The Notebook."

The words fall from my mouth without thinking, as if we've done this a thousand times. Like there's some invisible thread tethering us.

He flinches at *The Notebook*. His gaze darts to mine.

It feels like we're locked in a private current while the rest of the room swims upstream. He acts. I already know. No one else stands a chance.

When he finally sits down, flushed and grinning, he avoids my eyes entirely. Vanessa leans in, whispering a secret in his ear, but her glance cuts sideways toward me. There's no mistaking it—she's uncomfortable. Suspicious.

Nick leans over with a crooked grin.

"So... you two used to date or something?"

"Will you excuse me?" I say quickly. I need air—space to breathe.

In the hallway, my phone buzzes. I grab it and press it to my ear, grateful for the distraction. "Hello?"

Silence.

"Hello?" I repeat, a little louder this time.

Still nothing.

Then, a slow, raspy breath filters through the static, followed by distorted whisper.

"I saw you..."

My stomach flips.

"Who is this?" I snap, my voice shaking now. "Is this some kind of joke?"

A low, breathy chuckle. Then—click.

When I finally manage to move, I slip the phone into my pocket and rejoin Nick in the living room. The game is still going, laughter bouncing off the walls. The kind of laughter that hides something. *What if the call came from someone in this room?*

They'd just been laughing about me and Spencer, teasing about our "telepathy." What if it wasn't just a joke? What if the whisper wasn't a stranger, but one of them? Watching. Waiting. Testing me.

I try to compose myself. Nick glances up, concern etched across his face. He's sitting exactly as he was when I left—at least that's how it looks. A small voice whispers in my head.

"Everything okay?" Nick asks, concern in his voice.

"Yeah. I received a call from a wrong number," I lie. "Creepy one, though."

"You sure you're all right?" Nick presses once more.

I nod, but my mind is still spinning. The phone call. Spencer. Vanessa's stare. The tension crackling between us is like a live wire no one wants to touch.

Someone calls out for the next game, but Nick leans in. "Wanna head out?"

I glance toward the couch. Spencer's laughing at something someone said, but he doesn't look over again. Not once.

"Yeah," I say softly. "Let's go."

The rest of the date is pleasant enough on paper.

Nick takes me to a charming restaurant strung with Christmas lights, the scent of cinnamon and roasted meat warming the air. He orders a peppermint hot chocolate for us to share and talks about his nieces and nephews, the charm of small towns, and how he's thinking about getting a dog.

I listen. I smile. Even laugh once or twice.

Every time he reaches for my hand, I picture Spencer's. Every time he leans closer, I see clear blue eyes that already know everything I'm going to say.

We saunter into the movie theater. Some romantic comedy is playing. I forget the name almost immediately. The theater's dim, the screen glowing against our faces. He holds my hand. I let him.

The evening couldn't have gone any better before Nick drops me off at my condo.

Well, maybe it could have, if we hadn't gone to Mike's party first. That unexpected detour left me rattled, Spencer's presence still clinging to my skin like static. It was supposed to be Nick's night, but the moment I stepped into that room, everything changed.

Still, I felt a pang of conflicted pleasure. For a moment, I even considered inviting Nick into my home, to extend the date, and if nothing else, drive

Spencer a little crazy with wonder. But I quickly dismissed the thought. I didn't want to lead Nick on; tonight, he's a stand-in, a prop to get Spencer's mind whirling.

Nick walks me to the front door. I lock eyes with him and thank him for the wonderful night. "See you at work," I say, as I hug him.

He stops me mid-hug to give me a quick, unexpected peck on the lips. I'm surprised, and though I reciprocate the peck, I know I must be clear. I don't want anything more. He's a genuinely great guy but I want to remain *friends*.

"Did he hurt you?" Nick asks, voice low.

My brows furrow. I'm taken aback. "What?"

"Spencer. The way you flinch when his name comes up... I've noticed it before."

Something shifts in Nick's gaze, protective, maybe. Or possessive. I can't tell.

I try to laugh it off, but the discomfort sits like a rock inside me.

"I mean, I like him. He's my boss, and a damn good one. But when it comes to his personal life—I think he's trouble," he adds, then glances toward the shadows at the edge of my building. "Some people are just wired that way."

I follow his gaze, but there's no one there. Just dark pavement. Just cold air.

"I appreciated tonight," I tell him, hoping to end the date now.

"Yeah, me too. I hope we can do it again."

He's waiting for a reply. He hasn't gotten the hint that I'm not that interested, but he's such a sweet guy. I can't bring myself to let him down, so I agree.

"Definitely," I say, stepping back ready to send him on his way. Silently, I hope he heads back to Spencer with a glimmer of light in his eyes, maybe alluding to something more having happened between us. I secretly hope it will send Spencer into a small frenzy of crazed thoughts—like the ones I endure regularly.

Inside, I bid farewell to the evening and prepare for bed, trying to avoid dwelling on my encounter with Nick. However, my thoughts keep drifting

THIRTY-SEVEN

to Spencer, and I can't help but wonder what he's up to and what he might be thinking. If we'd skipped the party altogether, maybe I could have given Nick a more fair chance.

But it's too late for that now.

This mental preoccupation drives me to exhaustion, and finally, I drift off to sleep.

Thirty-Eight

Spencer has a work trip to California planned close to Christmas, and he's asked me to come along.

It's short notice, and getting time off work during the holidays is nearly impossible. Everyone is traveling and leaving their dogs at my boarding facility. Spencer will drive there first since he needs his work truck, and I'll fly in for the last few days at the tail end of the trip so we can have a mini vacation together.

Linda agreed to cover my shifts for the boarding, but I had to reschedule some of my grooming clients to make this trip happen. I'll be working overtime when I get back, but it's worth it. Meanwhile, I need to pack and arrange pet-sitting for my own fur daughter, Evie. I also have plans to go out with Dominic and some of our friends.

Don't ask why I keep saying *yes* to Dominic. Maybe it's guilt settling in the back of my mind. Maybe staying friends makes it feel less like betrayal.

Lately, I've gone to church a few times. I know I need forgiveness for continuing to sleep with a married man. Surprisingly, I feel like I'm being given grace anyway, even though I have no intention of stopping.

Deep down, I believe God has his hands in our relationship. I don't know why God would give Spencer a wife and three children, and then toss me into the mix, but I feel like I'm meant to be here. Like God's steering my ship straight towards Spencer's. I'm grateful. But the course is messier than I ever imagined.

THIRTY-EIGHT

The house is finally peaceful. No Dominic. No blaring TV. Just quiet.

I've never been a big TV watcher, except for *The Bachelor* on Mondays, *Lifetime* movies on Sundays, and the occasional *Snapped* or *Dateline*.

I love a good murder mystery.

Tonight, lying in bed, a strange unease prickles beneath my skin. I don't know why—maybe it's the silence. The stillness. The weight of too much space.

I turn on the TV and flip through the channels until I find *Dateline*.

True crime calms me. Maybe it's the narrator's calming voice, maybe it's the illusion of control. That if I can spot the killer, I'll be able to see one coming in real life.

Eventually, I start to relax. My breathing slows. Just as my mind begins to drift into the hypnosis of the show... my phone rings.

I jump.

It's late. Too late.

I answer the phone anyway.

"Hello?"

Silence.

I hold the phone tighter, listening carefully. Knowing exactly what quiet like this means.

"Stop calling me!" I snap, and hang up.

Immediately, my phone rings again.

Frustrated, I pick up. "I'm going to report you!" I threaten, hoping it will scare them into stopping.

Instead, silence remains for a handful of seconds, my pulse pounds in my ears. And then, a deep, muffled voice whispers:

"I see you."

The line goes dead.

A wave of fear grips me.

I'm not easily shaken, but being alone and knowing someone out there is watching has me on high alert.

It's late. I know I'm breaking our no-phone-contact rule, but I need to know if it's Spencer. If he's playing some demented game to tease me or scare me, I need him to admit it or deny it.

I type, "Was that you who called me?"

Several minutes drag by.

My screen finally lights up.

"No, why?"

"I've been getting strange calls. I need to be sure it wasn't you."

Another pause.

"Nope, not me. I have to go."

That's it?

No concern, no follow-up.

Nothing?

He's either asleep with Vanessa or doesn't care that I'm being harassed.

I stare at my screen, irritation bubbling under my skin. Maybe I want it to be Spencer because the alternative is worse.

Someone else is watching.

"Alright, night, night," I type.

He doesn't reply.

My petulant mind goes unhinged.

I creep downstairs, barefoot and tiptoeing.

Check the front door—locked.

Then the kitchen.

Then the back sliding door.

All locked. Blinds are drawn.

Still, my pulse won't settle.

I sprint upstairs, slam the bedroom door shut, and dive into bed. I crank the TV volume up, drowning out everything outside my room.

I don't move. I don't breathe too loudly.

I remain locked in place, listening for footsteps that never come.

Thirty-Nine

My plane lands at LAX in the early evening. Giddiness bubbles inside me, like a child on Christmas morning, at the thought of spending days alone with Spencer.

I make my way to the passenger pick-up, scanning the line of cars, eagerly searching for him. For once, I don't have to hide. I don't have to worry about being seen with him. He's mine for this trip. Out in the open, no secrecy, no guilt.

His truck pulls up, and like the gentleman he is, Spencer hops out from the driver's side, striding toward me with the confidence I love. He swings open the passenger door before folding me into a hug, his arms wrapping around me in a way that's both settling and new all at once.

"Hey, Buster," I grin into his chest.

"Good afternoon, my gorgeous princess," he says. The way he says it makes my heart flip.

I can't stop smiling. For the first time, I feel like we're a real couple. No hiding. No watching over our shoulders. No secret rendezvous.

On top of that, maybe it's the fact that Spencer is eleven years older than me, but being with him makes me feel more mature, like I've stepped into the role of a woman—one who can finally be seen with him in public.

I sink into the seat as he shuts the door behind me. "It's hot here," I say, tugging at my shirt and fanning my chest. It's a stark contrast to the cold, snowy Utah weather I left behind.

"Should've warned you," he chuckles. "The seventies feel toasty when you're used to freezing. Let me take care of finding you an outfit that's more revealing." He throws a wink my direction.

We're staying at the Beverly Wilshire, a hotel Spencer's familiar with, though I've never been. I've wanted to. I trust it will be just as nice as he says.

"Before we head to the hotel, I'm taking you on a fun little ride," he says, flashing a smile that sparkles more than it should.

"How far?"

"It's on the way."

He drives while we talk, mostly about his Christmas party and my date with Nick. Apparently, Nick couldn't help himself and ran straight to Mike with the news. Word traveled fast.

"He told everyone you kissed," he says, "you really did something to him." Spencer's voice cracks. Then he glances at me and back at the road. "You were... stunning that night."

"At Mike's?" I ask.

"Yes, you walked in wearing that green dress, and for a second I forgot Nick was even with you. Hell, I forgot anyone else was in the room. You looked like a Christmas wish I wanted to unwrap."

I glance out the window, watching the palm trees pass by.

"You didn't seem thrilled to see me." I throw speculation at him.

"Are you kidding?" he says, glancing over again. "I was wrecked. Every instinct wanted to go with you, to touch you. But I couldn't. Not with Vanessa watching. Not with Nick sitting right beside you." He exhales through his nose. "I had to sit there pretending I was fine while you looked like that, sitting next to someone else."

I choke back. "Then you got up to play charades..."

He laughs quietly. "Yeah. That was me trying to distract myself." He pauses, eyes dark with memory. "But then you started guessing—one after the other—before I even finished the gestures. It was like we tuned into each other, and the whole room noticed."

"Vanessa appeared suspicious."

THIRTY-NINE

"She wasn't the only one." His voice softens. "But I didn't care. In that moment, when you shouted out those answers like you knew every corner of my brain... I felt seen. Like we weren't hiding anymore."

I smile at the memory. "I know you. That's all."

He doesn't answer for a moment, as if reflecting. "Since the beginning." Then his tone shifts, firmer now. "That's why you need to tell him no."

I blink, pulled back into the moment. "Nick?"

He clenches his jaw tight. "Yeah. He told me he's planning to ask you out again."

"He is?" I'm shocked to hear this news. "I don't know if I would... but maybe..." I say, dragging out the word, loving the way his grip tightens on the steering wheel. "I liked the date enough to consider it." I can't help but rub it in a little. I laugh, thrilled by the possessiveness in his tone. "I guess I'll decide if and when he asks me out again," I tease, with a mischievous smile.

"Stop playing games, it drove me crazy thinking about you with him all night." He exhales hard, shaking his head.

I take my opening.

My hand skims his thigh, fingers pressing into the soft fabric of his shorts. Smooth on the surface, but underneath?

He's anything but calm.

He's ready.

Waiting.

For me.

I pull the fabric aside, freeing him. His breath shortens as he leans his hips, helping me slide the shorts down just enough to expose exactly what I hoped for.

"Well," I drawl, letting a hint of mischief color my voice, "what do you want me to do with that?"

Spencer's knuckles go white on the wheel. "You know exactly what."

I smirk, dragging my fingers along his length, relishing the way his body tenses. "Maybe I just like watching you squirm for me."

His jaw clenches. "Stop teasing and put that pretty mouth to work."

"As you wish." I laugh softly but obey, lowering my lips to him, tasting the salt of his skin as I take him in. I scrape my teeth lightly over the shaft before rolling my tongue around the tip.

The truck hums beneath us, tires rumbling over the winding road, but my focus is locked on him—the way his breathing is uneven, the quiet curses that slip from his lips, the way his body pushes toward me.

I pull back enough to glance up at him. "Am I missing something important?"

He lets out a strained laugh. "Not yet. Keep going."

Instead, I sit up, smoothing my lips with the back of my hand as I twist toward the window. The road curves sharply, each turn slicing through the dark like we're chasing the edge of the city. Distant lights blink like scattered stars beneath the deepening sky.

"Where are we?"

"Mulholland Drive." He says, softly. "The first time I came here, I didn't expect it to be this beautiful. I immediately thought of you."

The darkness, the thrill of the unknown turns—it all feels electric, mirroring the tension between us. And I'm not done with him yet. A reckless idea sparks to life.

I reach for the button of my jeans, sliding them down my hips. Spencer watches from the corner of his eye, while maintaining his careful attention on the winding road.

"What do you think you're doing?"

He knows what's coming, but makes a show pretending to object.

I straddle his lap, pressing close, letting him feel the pulse of my intent.

"Making the drive more memorable." I say, drawing him into me.

"This is reckless," he warns, though he doesn't move a muscle to stop me.

I lean back, my lips brushing against his ear. "Then keep your eyes on the road, and let me handle the rest."

The truck carves a path through the bends of the canyon. I move with him to a reckless, intoxicating rhythm—one that matches the thrill surging through my veins. In this moment, nothing else exists, only us, the narrow winding road, and the intoxicating danger of wanting something we shouldn't have.

Spencer groans clearly pleased with my boldness. I revel in feeling the thickness of him. The fusion of sex and speed sends a jolt of adrenaline through me. Pushing me to spiral to new heights.

The fear of crashing and the thrill of the forbidden—it pushes me over the edge.

I cling to him, determined to drag him to the precipice, though I know he's still focused on the winding road.

This one's mine, but I'm willing to bring him along for the ride.

It's messy and chaotic, and wildly satisfying.

I slip off him, breath still short, reaching for something, anything, to clean us up. There's not much at hand, so I yank open the glove box and pull out a pack of crumpled napkins. I'm shocked there are any, since he's always so tidy. It's not ideal, but it'll do. I take the time to wipe away the evidence of our passion.

"That was scary," I admit, sitting taller, and proud of my little brush with danger.

"No, that was thrilling," he says, flashing a crooked smile.

"You liked it?" I ask softly, seeking reassurance.

"Liked it? I loved it!" He insists, his cool, collected demeanor bellying the wild rush beneath it. I wonder how he manages to stay so suave even in moments like this.

As he drives, the fences blur past. Despite the madness we just unleashed, he keeps one hand relaxed on the wheel, the other on me.

Fascination flickers through me as I take in the building's grand exterior. I glance over at Spencer, searching for a spark of recognition.

"You do know this is the hotel from Pretty Woman, right?"

"I had no idea," he says, but the sly smile and exaggerated wink tell a different story.

I shake my head, half-laughing. "This place is too fancy for me."

"Don't be ridiculous. Nothing is too good for you."

He's firm, his gaze doesn't budge. And before I can throw out some deflection, he pulls me in and kisses me like he means it.

We step into the grand lobby of the Beverly Wilshire. I pause, letting the moment settle. The chandeliers, the marble floors, the scent of fresh flowers—it's everything I imagined and more.

Spencer steers me toward the check-in desk, his warm hand at the small of my back. The touch is gentle, but it anchors me—protective and possessive all at once.

I scan the room: men in their polo shirts and tailored suits, women draped in designer ensembles—their sophistication stands as a contrast to my standard of living. Still, Spencer's words replay. *Nothing is too good for you.*

The receptionist greets us with a glossy smile and wasting no time checking us in. Within minutes we're in the elevator. A soft piano melody plays as we ascend, and I smirk—remembering Spencer still owes me the song he promised to play.

The suite is stunning.

A grand king-sized bed sits dressed in crisp white linens and decadent pillows—elegant even by Spencer's standards. The walls wear curated art and subtle accent lighting.

A velvet love-seat, silver tray of champagne, and crystal flutes wait nearby, though I won't be drinking from them. Spencer, on the other hand, might claim them as his.

I drift to the floor-to-ceiling windows, pulling back the sheer curtains to reveal the galaxy of blinking city lights below.

I step onto the balcony and inhale. The night air kisses my skin, cool and light—nothing like the sharp chill back home.

A bistro table and two chairs wait in the corner, suggesting quiet mornings or whispered confessions at midnight—if I can keep my eyes open long enough to see them.

Spencer appears behind me, his arms wrapping around my waist.

"Worth the trip?" he whispers at my ear.

THIRTY-NINE

I lean into him; an inevitable smile spreads across my lips. "I could get used to this."

He sets a kiss on my shoulder. "Good—because I'm just getting started."

The day begins to settle in, weighing down what's remaining of my energy.

We spend the rest of the evening taking it slow—unhurried, indulgent—letting the quiet luxury of the room, and each other, fold around us.

This man. This moment. This place.

It all feels right.

And still, I don't know how I got so lucky.

Forty

The sun has barely begun to sneak through the all-too-sheer curtains of our suite when Spencer leans down, pressing a soft kiss to my forehead. Recently showered, he smells like clean skin and cologne, and I breathe him in.

He's off to an important meeting, something about a high-stakes contract with the state of California, though he spares me the finer details. That's how he is—discreet, always juggling deals and businesses, yet never forgetting to leave a small gesture of appreciation.

This time, it's breakfast in bed. I smile at the thoughtfulness before drifting back into sleep, comforted by the plush, high-thread-count sheets against my skin.

By the time I wake up, the morning's mostly gone. It's already 11:00 a.m. The realization makes me stretch lazily, soaking in the luxury of having nowhere to be.

Spencer's still gone, but my hunger pulls me from my cocoon. My breakfast is a plate of waffles—my favorite—and half a grapefruit sprinkled with sugar. *I don't know anyone who would* ever *eat grapefruit without it.* Though the waffle's gone cold, I devour it anyway, the tangy citrus balancing perfectly with the sweet, syrup-soaked bites.

With no plans for the day, I take my time getting ready and head out to explore the hotel. The moment I step outside, the hotel's grandeur wraps around me like an old movie scene. I wander around the stunning

FORTY

Mediterranean-style pool area, where lounge chairs line the clear, glass-blue water, empty of swimmers this early in the day. I spend hours lounging, my iPod playing softly in my ears, lost in the pages of a murder mystery. The rays of the sun soak my skin, reviving the tan that's faded since summer.

By mid-afternoon, sun-drenched and recharged, I head back to the suite to shower and get ready for Spencer's return. I'm brushing through damp hair when the door opens. He's back, much earlier than expected.

"How was work?" I ask, barely finishing before he's on me, hands gripping my hips, pulling me close.

"Amazing," he grins, "I closed the deal, and I have a surprise. Get ready. We're going somewhere."

He loosens his tie and shrugs out of his shirt, left in black slacks that still carry the formality of the deal. The light spills across him, making him look less like a man celebrating and more like one unraveling beneath success.

For a second, I just watch him move through the space, too composed for the storm of excitement living inside him.

Suddenly, I'm scrambling to get dressed fast enough.

Within minutes, Spencer's leading me by the hand down the sidewalk, his stride brisk and sure. The afternoon light glints off his hair as he moves. His pace is clipped, his purpose clear. He always walks like the world's waiting for him to catch it.

And then we stop.

A sleek, modern building rises before us—floor-to-ceiling glass, sharp lines, and a quiet air of exclusivity. The sign near the entrance reads: *Mandarin Oriental Residences.*

"What is this place?" I ask, my heart hammering in my chest.

Spencer doesn't answer. Instead, he smiles, leading me through the glass doors into a bright, minimalist lobby that smells faintly of cedar and citrus. An open courtyard at the center spills with greenery and a calming water feature. Every surface gleams with sleek wood and pale marble.

He doesn't stop. We step into the elevator, rising fast. On the top floor, he unlocks the door and sweeps me inside, carrying me effortlessly over the threshold. Again, I'm struck by his old-fashioned chivalry.

When he sets me back on my feet, I'm breathless. The penthouse before me is beyond anything I've ever seen. The back wall is all glass, opening to a view that rivals the Beverly Wilshire's—an endless sweep of the Los Angeles Skyline, glowing in the haze of the afternoon light.

The windows stretch high and wide, curving slightly at the edges, giving the illusion that we're suspended in air.

The living room is a dream of quiet opulence, white curved sofa, soft lighting that glows against clean lines.

But what draws my eye is the black grand piano nestled in the corner, its lacquered surface reflecting the twinkling of white Christmas lights wrapped around a small evergreen.

Next to it, a guitar rests on its stand, propped upright, like it a corner made just for it.

Even the kitchen gleams, the scent of cedar and fresh linen drifting through the air. Every inch whispers money and restraint.

It's a far cry from my little condo. I can almost feel my old life shrinking behind me.

Why does everything here have floor-to-ceiling windows? I sweep the glass with my eyes, half in awe, half overwhelmed.

Even Spencer's house in Utah has them. It's such a him thing—letting strangers in even when he's trying to keep them out.

"Why are we here?" I whisper, still trying to process the grandeur.

"This is for us."

"For us?" I tilt my head, brows knitting in disbelief.

"I'll be visiting California more often for work," he takes light hold of my hands, his eyes search mine. "And I wanted somewhere to come that felt... right. For just us."

His voice dips lower. "It's our secret. Where we can get lost together without worrying. Tell me you'll come stay with me when you can."

The answer is immediate. "Yes!"

I throw myself into his arms. He catches me midair, spinning me in a circle. I can't stop laughing—dizzy with disbelief, with joy—from the sheer fairytale of it all.

"I was afraid you would say no," he admits, setting me down.

I shake my head. "How could I say no? Although..." I glance around. "You didn't have to do all this. I'd be happy anywhere with you."

"I know I didn't have to," he says with certainty. "I wanted to. I want to build a life with you. And this is how we start." He brushes a strand of hair behind my ear; his touch is tender.

"So does this mean you will finally play a song for me? You did promise me you would, after all." I tease, hoping he'll give me one more glimpse of the man beneath all that control.

"Sure." His tone is confident, lips curving. "What do you want to hear?"

"Surprise me."

Without fanfare, he strolls toward the tree, fingers seductively grazing over the piano, then drifting to the guitar. He lifts it, settles on the sofa, and locks his eyes on mine.

"I've learned this one for you. I hope you like it."

He begins plucking, testing the strings, as if he's checking their tune. The quiet notes swelling into *God Blessed the Broken Road*. Then he sings—his voice is beautiful and raw, filled with emotion. He's not performing; he's offering.

By the time the last chord fades, a tear slips free and I don't even try to stop it. It's the most beautiful thing anyone's ever done for me. My heart swells until it almost hurts.

How did I end up here—wrapped up in a story that feels more like a movie than real life?

He sets the guitar aside, watching me. For a heartbeat, neither of us moves.

Then he reaches out, brushing a thumb across my cheek. "You're crying," he says tenderly, a smile ghosting his lips.

"I can't help it," I whisper, laughing through the tears. "That was... perfect."

He pulls me close, his voice low against my hair. "You make everything worth it."

For a moment I let myself believe it—that this is the start of something real, something strong enough to weather the storms we've already survived.

What started as an unexpected encounter in a parking lot, a conversation about his *mistress,* has somehow become the story I never saw coming, my real-life fantasy. Something that could never have been planned, at least not by me.

After setting the guitar back on its stand, he wraps me in his arms. For a while, neither of us speaks. The silence is full, heavy with the kind of emotion that doesn't need words.

When I finally pull away, I start exploring the penthouse. Every room is meticulously designed. The bedroom, with its floor-to-ceiling windows and luxuriously soft bed, feels like stepping into a dream.

The bathroom, with its marble, glass, and gold fixtures, is pure indulgence.

I can't wait to tell Maya and Linda.

I never want this feeling to end.

His soulful voice pulls me from the depths of sleep. My eyes flutter open, and there he is—leaning over me, face close, grinning cheesy.

"Time to wake up, sleepyhead. We've got a big day in front of us."

I squint up at him, still foggy. Sunlight pours through the oversized windows—too bright, too early, but beautiful. The silk sheets beneath me feel impossibly smooth, a far cry from the life I usually wake up to.

"Where are we going?" I mumble, stretching beneath the covers.

"Don't worry about it, Princess. You'll see soon enough."

His words—*don't worry about it*—echo. They always do. He loves the mystery, the control, the tease.

Curiosity wins. I sit up and notice the outfit waiting for me on the end of the bed—new shorts, a fitted white tank, and a light denim jacket.

All my exact size.

Of course they are.

I roll out of bed and step into the cool marble bathroom, taking a quick shower before styling my hair and brush on light makeup.

FORTY

The bathroom is a dream, every inch exudes luxury. The heated tile warms my feet, a rainfall shower mists over me, and the vanity illuminates with perfect lighting.

Every small detail reminds me this is not my real life, yet somehow I'm living in it.

With my hair towel-dried, I grab my clothes from the edge of the bed, then stroll naked into the family room. I know Spencer is somewhere in the suite, but the thrill of walking around here in this massive, private space, sends a rush through me.

On the stone island in the kitchen sits a fresh blueberry muffin, a perfectly halved ruby-red grapefruit topped with just the right dusting of sugar, and a glass of freshly squeezed orange juice. It's the same breakfast he's made for me countless times at my condo. A subtle, thoughtful gesture amid all this extravagance. Proof that even in all his wealth, Spencer still notices the little things.

I slip into the outfit he chose for me, then move to the long wooden dining table with my breakfast he's so carefully crafted. Spencer appears from the balcony to join me. He sits at the far end, watching. It feels intentional, like he wants the distance to make me feel the weight of what he's done.

For me. For us.

Until it fully sinks in.

And it does.

I look around, taking in every detail of the sweeping views and faultless design. Spencer didn't just *buy a place.* He's building a life, a future—for us.

He's giving me permanence.

A commitment with gravity.

But then, he rises from his chair, the scrape of wood against marble echoing as he pushes the chair back. His eyes are locked on mine, no smile, no words, just that low-burning intensity that never fails to light me up.

He rounds the table like a man with a mission, his fingers grazing the edge of the stone island as he passes by it.

He's shirtless now; his skin catches the light, reflecting onto each fine muscle of his chest. The dark slacks hang low on his hips, businessman undone, temptation barely restrained. I stay seated, breath caught, heart hammering, as he comes to a stop behind me.

His hands slide over my shoulders, then down the curve of my arms.

"Don't move," he murmurs.

I freeze, every muscle tightening beneath is touch.

Then the scent hits me, citrus laced with musk. A moment later, something cold kisses the base of my neck. Grapefruit juice. I gasp.

Spencer's mouth follows. His tongue traces the trail with agonizing slowness, licking the sweet stickiness from my skin as if he has all the time in the world. An involuntary moan escapes me.

He moves to face me, grabbing hold of the bottom of my shirt, and pulling it overhead. "I bought this place for mornings like this," he says, voice husky. "So I can wake up and ruin you slowly."

Piece by piece, my clothes fall away until I'm bare against the cool surface of the table. He lays me back where the breakfast once sat, leaving only the half grapefruit in his hand.

He straddles me, and with no beats missed, a burst of citrus hits my chest, I jolt, half from the cold, half from the unexpected pressure. Eyes locked on mine, he squeezes, liquid streams from the fruit in a sudden rush, trickling between my breasts, breaking over my skin.

He lowers himself, mouth open, tongue chasing the trail as it travels downward. He drags a line through the center of me, pausing at my navel to drink from the small pool he's made. Then, with one hand braced beside my ribs, he continues his path lower, slower, unrelenting.

Every inch of me feels bared, exposed in more ways than one.

And before I can breathe, before I can beg, I break beneath him. Shattered under his touch once more.

Forty-One

We've been driving for a while, and I still have no clue where we're going. The suspense is delicious, but it's driving me crazy.

Out of the corner of my eye, I catch a glimpse of a road sign: *Disneyland Park—this way.*

I sit up straighter, my heart skipping a beat.

"Wait... are we going to Disneyland?"

Spencer hooks his lips upward, but keeps his eyes on the road.

"Maybe."

"Come on, tell me!" I beg, practically bouncing in my seat.

"It's a surprise," he teases.

"I knew it! We are! I haven't been since I was ten!" The realization washes over me, and I can't contain my excitement.

"Spencer, you're the best!"

He chuckles, glancing over with a playful glint.

"Shhhh. Don't tell anyone. They'll all want me."

I let out a small giggle, shaking my head. Only Spencer could make a trip to Disneyland feel like a VIP red-carpet event.

Stepping into Disneyland feels like stepping straight into a snow globe. Everything shimmers in holiday magic. A towering 60-foot Christmas tree stands proudly at the entrance, draped in thousands of twinkling white lights and perfectly placed oversized ornaments. Festive wreaths and ribbons hang wrapping every vintage lamp post lining Main Street's brick sidewalks. The storefronts are decked out with enchanting window displays. A horse-drawn trolley jingles down the street, bells dangling from the horses' necks.

Spencer laces his fingers with mine, anchoring me in the moment.

We pause, soaking it in, standing in amazement like little children exploring a park for the first time.

December at Disneyland smells like cinnamon churros and warm caramel corn. He pulls me into a quick embrace, and we snap a few pictures in front of the grand tree before plunging headfirst into the magic.

We share cotton candy—I feed him facefuls, and he's more gentle with the portions he feeds me. We skip from one nostalgic ride to the next, our fingers never parting. It's like we've stepped into the pages of someone else's perfect story, only this one's ours.

We don't race through it like tourists chasing thrills.

We wander. Drift. Let the day unfold at its own pace.

Still, there's this undertow, a push-pull of wanting to soak up every second but knowing the day won't last forever.

We find ourselves laughing until our cheeks hurt, and playfully argue over who gets to choose the next ride, until he gives in with a dramatic sigh and says, "Fine. But I'm picking the next snack."

It's A Small World has been transformed into a dazzling holiday wonderland, its exterior twinkling with thousands of colored lights. I love it, not only for the pull back to my childhood, but because it's a nice, long ride where I can rest my feet.

I lean my head on his shoulder, lulled by the warmth of him and the mild rocking of the ride. I curl up under his arm like I belong there.

And maybe I do.

By the time we reach *The Haunted Mansion*, decked out in full *Nightmare Before Christmas* glory. Spencer wraps his arms around me protectively in the darkened rooms, like he's shielding me from ghouls that don't actually scare me—except when he whispers, "boo," low against my ear, just to make me jump. I slap his chest with a breathless laugh, and he grins like he's proud of himself.

And, of course, not to be forgotten, *Pirates of the Caribbean* never disap-

FORTY-ONE

points. There's a draw to the ambiance of the dimly lit caverns and the scent of damp stone. The water laps quietly beneath the boats as we drift deeper into its caves. The animatronic pirates chant and sing their catchy anthem, the refrain looping just long enough for me to steal another break from the aching soles of my feet. Even here, in the dark, Spencer takes my hand—and I have his.

Between rides, we indulge in Disneyland's best treats. I savor a creamy corn chowder in a sourdough bread bowl, so far it's our favorite meal. Afterward, Spencer munches on a caramel apple and guards his churro like treasure.

Which is fair.

It's golden and crisp, with cinnamon-sugar that melts upon the touch of a tongue. Even the seagulls seem to know it. One daring bird swoops in and snatches it right out of Spencer's hand the moment he buys it. Spencer's face freezes in disbelief.

"That bird's dead to me," Spencer mutters, eyes narrowed.

I laugh so hard I nearly choke on mine.

A nearby cast member, clearly used to this, kindly replaces it for him.

I don't think I've laughed this much in my life. It makes my cheeks ache.

As the sky deepens into a velvety twilight, the park transforms again. Tiny white lights twinkle in the trees, and Sleeping Beauty's castle glows in lavender and royal blue, its turrets dusted with what appears to be freshly fallen snow.

Spencer and I duck into a quaint little shop, picking up new park hoodies to fend off the evening chill. My little jacket isn't doing its job anymore, and his long arms only cover so much. He chooses a classic black hoodie with a classic Mickey embroidered small on the front. I pick the most feminine one I can find, pastel pink, with a tiny stitched Minnie in the corner. We match—without matching.

Now layered and warm, me holding my steaming hot chocolate and him sipping a black coffee, we weave through the bustling crowd, searching for the perfect viewing spot in front of the castle.

I had never thought of Disneyland as romantic before. It was always for families. Childhood memories. Lines and too many strollers. But standing here, wrapped in Spencer's arms, surrounded by holiday magic, I see it differently now.

Tonight, it feels like the most romantic place on earth.

The first soft notes of the nighttime show begin. Gentle bells and sweeping orchestral music that glides through the air like magic. Everyone pauses, their faces glowing from the castle lights.

Spencer's arms tighten around my waist, pulling me closer, holding me against him as we watch the spectacle unfold. I rest my hand over his, our fingers laced together, my hot chocolate heating my free hand.

I don't speak.

Neither does he.

* * *

SPENCER

The crowd presses in, music, kids, colors spilling across the park—but none of it touches me.

She's all I see.

Sarah's face glows in the shimmer of the castle, her smile unguarded. There's wonder in her eyes that's real and unfiltered. The kind people lose somewhere along the way. She giggles at something tiny, and the sound hits harder than it should, knocking something loose in me.

I should be thinking about the penthouse. The contract. The risk. About keeping my head on straight. I built my life on logic, on control, not fairytale castles and wide-eyed girls who laugh like they still believe in magic.

I've got every reason to keep my focus anywhere else. But I don't.

Instead, all I can think is that I want this—her—again and again.

Her hand brushes mine in the crush of people, and right now it's the only thing that feels real.

This is what peace feels like. Not the numb kind I was raised to settle for, the hard-earned, transactional kind people pretend is love.

This is the kind that undoes you, makes you a better man.

And yet, even as the feeling settles into my chest, some part of me fights it, because wanting her this much? It's wrong. But not wanting her? That feels impossible.

And as I watch her light up in a place Vanessa would've called juvenile or beneath us, I know with gut-level certainty—

I'll never find this with anyone else.

* * *

SARAH

An array of colors shimmer across his face, and I swear, for a second, he looks like he's about to say the three words I've been longing to hear. But the moment passes all too quickly when the castle begins to come alive—dazzling projections and holiday scenes dancing across its walls, perfectly synchronized with the swelling music. The moment is overwhelming in the best way possible. Right now I'm reminded of everything I want and need in my life. Love. Family. Magic. It's all here.

And, more than anything, I want Spencer to be my family.

He has no idea I feel this way. I've only told him that I love him a handful of times, and he's yet to say it back. But tonight, in this moment, I hope he feels the same way.

The grand finale begins—a breathtaking fireworks display explodes above us, painting the sky in shimmering gold, silver, and red. Spencer rests his chin on my head as we watch in awe, our breath visible in the crisp night air.

And when I think the night can't get any more magical, it starts to snow.

Tiny, delicate snowflakes blow through the air, catching the glow of the twinkling lights as they drift down around us. The entire street gasps in wonder.

Spencer turns my body to face him. His eyes are locked on me, not on the spectacle.

The back of his fingers trace a soft line down my cheek, his touch *featherlight*, stopping to grab a gentle hold on my chin. "You're so beautiful," he utters quietly, making the entire world outside of us fade away.

He bends down, setting his empty coffee cup on the ground, never breaking eye contact. Then, as he straightens, he takes my left hand, cradling it between his two.

Slowly, he slides his thumb and forefinger to the very tip of my finger, holding it there for a moment, as if savoring the significance of what he's about to do. Then, with exact precision, he glides his fingers downward, tracing an invisible band along the length of my finger, stopping before the base.

He doesn't say the words, but somehow, this means more. This is his way of saying he sees a future—with me.

The way he does it... it feels like a promise, a silent question. My heart stutters, and I draw in air. *Is this truly happening?*

I hold still, afraid that if I move, I'll break the moment.

My eyes meet his in silent agreement, unable to form words, my emotions too tangled inside me from the magic of the moment. Right now, with him, is the closest I've ever come to a real proposal.

Dominic never proposed. Instead, he told me to purchase the ring I wanted, and he would pay me back. I went with Linda to pick it out. It should have been my sign to run, but I believed in him.

Spencer sweeps me into his arms, lifting me with such ease it steals my breath. He spins me slowly, positioning me so I'm facing the massive Christmas tree.

This moment, this man, this love—is more than I ever dreamed. Time alone would be enough, is enough, but his unspoken promise right now is too.

When he finally sets me down, the snow has stopped, and my imperial high comes back down into a focused reality. I rest my forehead against his chest, feeling his even, strong beat.

God led me to him. I know it.

FORTY-ONE

Disneyland is called *the happiest place on Earth*. And tonight? It truly is.

Forty-Two

***

SPENCER

The city buzzes below us, all neon arteries and scattered headlights. From the penthouse window it looks like a toy world, too far away to touch. Up here, it feels like nothing could intrude.

Sarah fell asleep curled up against my chest. She carried the magic of Disney into her dreams—the lights, the laughter, the snow falling from the sky. I thought she'd stay that way all night, weightless.

But sometime after three, the sound cuts through me like a blade.

She jerks upright, hair plastered to her temples, nightgown soaked through like she's stepped out of a storm. The sheets cling to her thighs in damp tangles, and I can see the shiver rippling under her skin even as sweat runs down her collarbones.

A cry tears from her throat—not a scream, but something worse. It's the kind you make when you're dying in your own head.

"Sarah." My voice breaks. I reach for her, but she recoils like I've burned her—eyes wide, glassy, unfocused. She doesn't even see me.

"He shot me," she gasps, the words torn from her throat. "I swear, I felt it. Dominic..."

It's not just a nightmare. It's a memory twisted with terror, playing out in real time. Her whole body thrashes, tremors jerking her so violently the mattress jolts under us, her breath hot and shallow against my neck, sharp with the salt of her sweat.

I wrap my arms around her, pinning her trembling body to mine, but she even fights that—weak fists pushing at my chest until they falter.

"No. You're here. You're safe," I whisper, strands catching in my breath. I speak her name, over and over, because it's the only rope I can throw into the pit she's falling through.

"You're not dying. Not tonight. Not ever. Not while I'm breathing."

She sobs, the sound breaking something in me I didn't know could break. I've seen her laugh in my arms, tease me until I wanted to lose my mind, melt into me with a kind of sweetness I didn't know existed. But I've never seen this—this raw wound she's carried, the ghost she hides when the sun's up.

And God help me, I don't know what to do. I can buy her the world, bulldoze every obstacle, but I can't fight what hunts her when she closes her eyes. I can't put a fist through a dream.

So I hold tighter. I whisper into her hair, nonsense and vows, anything to fill the silence between her broken breaths. Her skin is cold in places and fever-hot in others, as though her body can't decide whether to burn or freeze.

Slowly, painfully, her body softens, her trembling ebbs. She clings to my shirt, knuckles white, until her grip eases and sleep drags her back under.

But I don't follow. I can't.

The picture is still burned into me: Sarah thrashing, gasping, begging for a life she thought she'd already lost.

Even in her sleep, he's still inside her head. And I hate him for it. I hate that he still gets a piece of her I can't touch.

She won't remember this in the morning. She'll smile like she always does, downplay the shadows, maybe even tell me she slept well. But I'll remember. I'll carry it for both of us.

And for the first time in my life, I know without doubt—if Dominic ever comes near her again, if he so much as breathes her name—I'll end it.

And then, just loud enough to break me wide open, she whispers:

"Stay."

Just that one word—damn near undoes me.

I press her closer, her cheek damp against my chest, and even when her body goes still, I stay awake, watching the shadows crawl across the wall.

I whisper the only truth that matters:

"You're mine to protect. I will never leave you."

Forty-Three

***

Sarah

After a night neither of us will forget, I wake in our sanctuary, sunlight spilling through the curtains.

Yesterday had been long; we'd spent the entire day together, laughing, wandering, riding from one adventure to the next. So this morning, we let the world wait—lingering maybe a little too long in the luxury of doing nothing but existing side by side.

"This bed is amazing. Best sleep I've had in weeks," I say, turning toward him.

"Yeah," he says, softly. "You seemed... peaceful."

"Why do you sound surprised?"

"Because you don't know what I know." His smile curves slowly, confident.

I continue snuggling into him, tracing his superhero fluff with the tip of my finger.

"Let's get you a bed like this back in Utah," he suggests, casual but sure.

"You don't have to twist my arm to buy a new bed." I respond. "But only if we can pick it together!"

"Perfect," he winks.

"I'll buy it for you." His sarcasm lands heavy.

"No way! We both will. You've bought me enough already." I'm adamant that I have a say in what happens with the purchase.

He grins. "Deal." Then he leans in, brushing a kiss against my forehead as if to seal the promise.

I roll on top of him, my legs straddling his waist, stretching my arms above my head as I gather my hair into a ponytail. Spencer takes the opportunity to reach out, grabbing both my breasts with one unrepentant, greedy motion.

The diffuse light passing through the sheer curtains makes for the most whimsical morning. An intimate enigma settles over us, a quiet fog laced with the traces of past entanglements.

His scarred, calloused hands reacquaint themselves with my body, making slow passes down my sides.

"You are so soft," he whispers, voice tender with honesty.

Gently, he lifts me, guiding me down until he's inside me. A gasp escapes my lips. The feeling is intoxicating, perfect, seamless, ours.

As I move, he watches me, his gaze locked onto mine as if I'm the only thing that exists.

His hands find my waist, anchoring me to him, and we fall into a rhythm so natural, so instinctive, a wordless language of movement and trust.

A slow, consuming wave of feelings builds inside me. It's unfamiliar, overwhelming. I try to focus on the physical, to suppress the rush of emotion, but it surges anyway, and it's impossible to ignore.

He holds all my love and he has no idea.

I brace against his chest, my fingers tangling briefly in the soft scatter of hair that feels like home.

When I stare into his beautiful blue eyes, tears prick mine. I tilt my head back, willing them away, but of course, he sees.

His grip tightens at my waist, like he's holding me together.

Our movements intensify, our bodies colliding in perfect harmony until we both come undone, gasping in unison. I collapse onto his chest.

The tears escape and begin rolling from my eyes. I bury my face in the pillow beside him, hoping he won't notice the emotion that's managed to escape.

But he does. Of course, he does.

I love him.

My heart is screaming.

He doesn't know how deeply, how completely I am his.

I'm ashamed of my emotions right now. I never show feelings unless they are bubbly, happy, and positive. I'm the peacekeeper.

To keep everyone together, I've always had to stay evenly tempered. Crying is perceived to be a weakness. You can't be weak and be the youngest of seven children.

Finally, I build up enough courage to lift my head and meet his gaze. His endlessly deep eyes search mine, and then he speaks, to soothe me—to calm me.

"I feel it too," he whispers, his voice soft, reassuring.

"I love you so much," I confess in this overwhelming moment.

"I know," he says, and brushes away a tear with his thumb.

Who is this man? Strong, intelligent, and completely attuned to me in ways I can't explain.

Yet, still not saying *those three words* back.

How can he invest so much into me—time, energy, money and still not love me?

I accept our situation. Maybe that's why he gets rid of his mistresses.

He doesn't love them. And never will.

Maybe he will always *only* belong to Vanessa.

I roll back to his side and we lie quiet, still, until I fall asleep pretending I didn't cry.

Forty-Four

A perky voice calls from somewhere distant. "Time to get going." Spencer is already up, showered, dressed, put back together. I must've fallen back asleep again, alone in the wreckage of what we were.

"We need to head out, your flight leaves in three hours."

I yawn and stretch like I have all the time in the world. Because I do. Why would I want to leave this dream? I may not have bought it, but he considers it ours, so I do too. For now.

Now he lies beside me, brushing my disheveled hair away from my face, staring deep into my eyes as if he's deciding to tell me something.

Uncertain of what's coming, I look at him the same way.

"You are the most beautiful woman I've ever known," he says, speaking directly to my soul. "Don't ever change."

"I wasn't planning on it," I reassure him.

But I wasn't expecting just that. Not something soft. Not something final. I assumed he had more to say than that.

"Sit up," he politely commands.

So I do, exposing my bare chest. My legs dangle over the edge of the bed, the sheets tangled around them.

He stands on the side in front of me and slides the back of his hand along my cheek. I instinctively lean into his touch.

"Listen," he says.

His tone makes me uneasy. It's restrained. Like it's been rehearsed. He's never looked at me like this before. *Did he change his mind about me? Am I getting dumped?*

"I'm listening," I anxiously wait for him to spit out the words he's holding captive, bracing for the drop.

"I've been wanting to tell you this for a long time," he begins. "At first, it felt too early, too sudden. I didn't know if it was simply lust or something real. But now, I'm certain."

"Okay... what is it?"

My mind races, flipping through my entire life catalog of everything I could have possibly done wrong. Every buried secret, every mistake, every regret rears its head. I let him finish speaking, already halfway down the hallway of worst-case scenarios, but somewhere, deep down, I think I already know where this is going.

"You make me want to be a better man whenever I'm with you. You're the one I want stealing my blankets at night. You're the reason I wake up excited every morning hoping I'll see you. And I haven't told you I love you, because I don't."

My heart sinks. *Wait... what the hell is he doing?*

He's toying with my emotions.

But before I can react, he continues.

"I'm already deeply and madly *in love* with you, and I have been from the jump."

I don't wait a second.

"Oh my gosh, you scared the crap out of me!" I launch into his arms.

A huge, cheesy grin spreads across his face.

I couldn't feel more elated, or more relieved, than I do right now. He does feel the same way I do. We're both completely in love with each other.

"Phew! I was so scared. Don't ever do that again."

He lets out a deep, belly laugh.

I slug him lightly in the arm. "Ugh! You think you're so funny,"

"That's because I am," he's still laughing, clearly enjoying himself.

"We gotta get going," he adds, nudging me, trying to motivate me out of bed.

Reluctantly, I start getting ready, slipping into a comfortable outfit, pulling my hair into a cute ponytail. When I'm finally packed for the day, I head to the kitchen, where Spencer has prepared a perfectly fluffy omelet just for me, taking care of me, just like he always does.

We hold hands the entire drive to the airport, soaking in the final moments we have left. Inside, I'm dreading leaving him. More than that, I'm dreading returning to reality, knowing he's going to be back home with Vanessa, and that this entire fantasy is just that—fantasy.

The only thing I'm truly excited to return to is my sweet little dog, *Evie*.

As we drive, we sing along to songs, chat about our hopeful future, and pretend for a little longer that this moment will last forever.

Upon arriving at the airport, ever the gentleman, Spencer steps out and opens my door. He pulls me into a long embrace, whispering another, "I love you," before he reaches into his wallet and pulls out a wad of cash.

"For anything you might need," he says, handing me $500.

I hesitate before accepting it. I don't need his money, but I love that he feels the need to take care of me.

"I love you too," I say, sealing my words with a wet kiss.

"See you soon."

Then, the ringtone of my phone cuts through the moment. I pull it from my purse and answer.

"Hello?"

Silence.

The same heavy stillness I've come to dread stretches on too long.

I frown, unsettled. "It's the prank caller," I whisper, handing the phone to Spencer. "Say hello. See if anyone answers for you."

He holds the phone to his ear. His jaw tensing.

"Can I help you? Who is this?" His voice drops into a deep, assertive tone. Another long pause. Then, a gargled sound crackles, too faint to make out.

"What? I can't understand you. Are you okay?" Spencer's brows knit.

More silence.

Static charges the air, distorted and strong, like someone's breathing too

FORTY-FOUR

close to the mic.

Then, suddenly—

"She looks like her mother..."

Spencer's entire body goes rigid. His eyes sharpen. "What the hell did you say?" he snaps. "Fuck off." he says, his voice is cold steel as he ends the call.

I stare at him, dread settling like ice under my skin.

"Did you hear what they said?"

"Yeah. Don't worry about it. Let me know if they call again."

He shifts, his whole demeanor resetting as he hands the phone back.

"Well... what did they say?"

He hesitates.

"Nothing to bother you with. Travel safe."

I pause, my stomach tightening.

"Linda."

He blinks. "What?"

"That's what they said, didn't they? She looks like her mother. How would I even know that unless I heard it?"

Spencer doesn't answer. His expression remains guarded, unreadable.

"Maybe it was nothing. Or maybe they were trying to fuck with you. Either way, I won't let them get to you," he says—as if he can protect me when I can't.

He kisses my cheek one last time, ending the conversation for good.

I take hold of my bag and roll it behind me, forcing myself forward, step by step.

Leaving Spencer behind.

Forty-Five

The holidays have passed, bringing their usual mix of highs and lows.

My trip with Spencer was a huge high. But immediately after I left California, he took his family on a trip to the Canary Islands.

That was a low.

Another high moment—Spencer and I exchanged Christmas gifts. But then he bought his wife new couches, which landed like a low blow.

Through his family trip, Christmas, and New Year's, Spencer broke our *no-contact rule* more than once. He called me twice while on the islands and sent a handful of texts. I didn't want to come off as clingy or needy, so I kept my responses light—just enough to say I missed him and hoped to see him soon.

Meanwhile, life upon returning has settled back into routine. I'm back at work, and Nick was brave enough to ask me on another date.

I built up the courage to politely decline.

Nick and I had become good friends, and I felt like I owed him honesty. I trusted him to keep a secret, so I told him that Spencer and I are in a relationship. He was gracious about it. He admitted he'd suspected something for a while, having seen Spencer come in and out of my shop too often. He promised to keep it between us and didn't seem too bothered by the situation—which was a relief.

In other news, I finally ordered a new bed, and it's being delivered next week.

FORTY-FIVE

Spencer will be joining me the morning after it arrives. I can't wait to stop sleeping in my guest bedroom. I hadn't even realized how badly I needed a new one until our trip.

To pass the time over the holidays, besides work and family, I've been going out with Maya. There's a club in town that has an 18-to-21 section underneath the main 21+ level. She's invited me out a few times with her, Dominic, and Dustin. It's not particularly thrilling, but I want to support her and her interests.

We play pool and dance until the club closes. Some nights, I don't feel like dancing. Other nights, I give in, singing a song or dancing with a stranger.

Is that cheating on Spencer?

I don't know.

I never kiss anyone, though some of the men have tried. And since it's dark, Dominic hasn't noticed either.

But as long as Spencer is with Vanessa, *I'm not completely his to have.*

At least that's what I let him believe.

He still needs to worry about keeping me content. I have to be a little unpredictable. Keep him on his toes.

My new bed arrived yesterday around noon, and I've been stoked to share it with Spencer. It's been weeks since I last saw him, let alone felt his hands on my skin, his breathing against my neck. I even bought fresh linen sheets, the softest I could find—a pristine blank slate for us to imprint new memories on. Everything about this moment is new, clean, untouched, and it's ours.

Our relationship has evolved to the point where I don't need to greet him at the door. I wait. He lets himself in. He moves through my house like he belongs here. Most mornings, I stir to the sound of his steps on the stairs or the creak of the bedroom door, just before he slides into bed next to me.

But today is different.

He's late.

I stay still, my fingers loosely clutching the sheets, as my mind begins its slow descent into doubt.

Why isn't he here yet?

He should be—sneaking into my bed.

Then my phone rings.

It startles me so I grab it quickly.

For a moment, a wave of calm washes over me.

At the same time, the front door creaks open.

I hear the familiar rhythm of breathing.

Not Spencer's.

Heavy. Wet. A slow, deliberate inhale that crackles through the receiver like a sinister whisper.

I freeze. My grip on the phone tightens.

"Stop calling me!" My voice is sharp, worn down by too many of these calls. "I'm changing my number!"

But this time, they speak.

A distorted voice, muffled—like a voice pressed against fabric.

"I know who you're fucking! And I know he's there right now!"

The line goes dead.

And then—Spencer steps into the room.

His gaze locks onto mine immediately, his sharp blue eyes narrowing with concern. He strides toward me before gently pulling the phone from my shaking hand.

"You okay?"

I draw in a deep breath through my nose, forcing my shoulders to relax, trying to shake off the eerie feeling.

Spencer—trying to lift the mood flops onto the bed with a satisfied sigh, arms spreading wide across the fresh sheets, not waiting for me to answer his question. His lips curl into a lazy grin, as if completely unaware of the storm raging inside me. He usually pays such close attention to the details—but this time he lets them slip.

"Damn," he drawls, stretching luxuriously. "This bed is nice."

I do my best to brush off the anxiety. I slide onto the bed beside him, sighing, letting my fingers chase invisible patterns against the sheets. I explain to him what has happened.

FORTY-FIVE

"It was that person with the heavy breathing on the other end. But this time, they said they know you're here. Right now."

Spencer doesn't flinch. He simply exhales through his nose, calm to the point of infuriating.

His expression remains unreadable.

I press on, needing reassurance. "Do you think Vanessa knows? Or that someone's going to say something?"

He shakes his head before answering. "No, she definitely doesn't know. She thinks I've renewed my vows because I bought her a new couch." He rolls his eyes, his tone thick in disbelief.

I let out a dry, humorless laugh. "A couch? That's all it takes for her to believe everything's perfect?"

"Yep. That's it."

I wrap my arms around myself. "What if this person tells her? How did they even get my number?"

Spencer leans back and fluffs the pillows, unbothered and annoyingly serene. His fingers drum lazily against his own chest.

"Doesn't matter," he says, his voice smooth, dismissive.

"You only worry about what you can control, like us. Right now. In this amazing new bed."

I stare at him, waiting for something more, an ounce of concern, a plan, a protective instinct. But all I get is confidence—it's maddening.

I bite my lip, still unconvinced. "Fine," I concede, "but I'm changing my number. Just in case. I'll text you when it's done."

"Sounds good," he humors me.

Then his gaze darkens, turning hungry.

"Now, come here."

We get straight to the point of intimacy. It doesn't last long before we need to clean ourselves up and crawl back into bed to cuddle.

I take this stillness, this quiet space between us, as an opportunity to learn more about the man before me, beyond the present, beyond our relationship. I want to know what shapes him, what path led him here.

I relax and sprawl out across the bed with him.

But in the back of my mind, unease dwells, about the person who keeps calling me. I suppress those worries while I lie in this moment with him.

I don't ask him how his family trip over Christmas went, since it brings up jealousy and insecurity. No one can compete with the love for his children—nor should they, so I choose to keep that separate from our reality. Even if I wanted a child, he couldn't give me one.

He's told me what he wants me to know—about his family, painting a picture of his past. But the more time I spend with him, the more I realize the depth of him—the shadows he's tucked away in the corners of his life. There's a darkness there, something that haunts him in the way he moves, and the way he guards certain parts of himself. I speculate that his need for control extends far beyond me. It's woven into the fabric of his existence. It's in the way he structures his life, the way he dictates everyone and everything around him. But now, I wonder if that need is coming from something deeper.

Something painful.

At first, I test the waters, gauging how open he's willing to be with me. Spencer has been elusive when it comes to discussing money, so I cut straight to the chase.

"How much was Disneyland?" I ask casually, watching his reaction.

He shifts his gaze from the ceiling to me, his expression unreadable. "That's a strange question," he remarks before adding, "a dollar."

I roll my eyes, undeterred. "How much was the penthouse?"

"Two dollars."

That response—"a dollar"—means it was expensive, but "two dollars?" If it's very expensive.

I know better than to expect a truthful number. Realizing he won't budge, I change the subject. I don't expect much when I ask about his childhood, assuming he's already told me what he wants me to know.

But to my surprise, he doesn't deflect.

Instead, he begins to tell me a story.

FORTY-FIVE

Spencer exhales slowly before speaking, "I'll start at the beginning. I was born in California, but when I was about five, we moved to Utah. We lived on a pig farm for a year. Then we moved one town over and finally put down roots. We didn't have a lot. My dad worked for the county, and my mom worked at a local company. Money was tight. Always. There were six of us packed into a tiny two-bedroom house—my parents, my older brother, my younger sister, brother, and me. But my older brother and I didn't get a room inside. We slept in the cellar out back." His eyes stay fixed on the ceiling as if watching the past play out like an old film.

"I told you about the cellar before," he continues. "The floor was dirt, covered with a thin rug. The washer and dryer sat outside the entrance, with a drain in the concrete between them. To get inside, we had to step over that drain, push past a sleeping bag we used as a door, and crawl into our so-called bedroom."

A humorless chuckle escapes him, but there's nothing amusing in his voice. "I remember coming home from school one day, heading toward the cellar like always. But right before I walked in, I saw my dad—right there, fucking some stranger on top of our washer."

The words land between us like a stone dropping into deep water—heavy, irreversible.

I say nothing, afraid to shatter this rare moment of honesty.

"I saw things no kid should ever see," he continues. "My parents took us to nudist colonies—places full of old, naked people walking around like it was normal. At the time, I didn't question it. But looking back, it was... confusing. Especially since we were raised LDS, going to church every Sunday, hearing about purity and morality, even as we lived a life that contradicted it."

His jaw tightens, his gaze still unmoved.

"My dad wasn't just strict with his discipline, he was aggressive, and at times—brutal. My older brother took the worst of it, but I wasn't spared either."

I lean in, hanging onto every word, careful not to interrupt.

This isn't just a story. It's a confession, a glimpse into the foundation of the man lying next to me.

I stare straight up too, trying to picture it all.

A little boy stepping over a drain, pushing through a hanging sleeping bag, entering a world of struggle most wouldn't survive.

And yet, he didn't just survive.

He fought his way out, built an empire from nothing, and became the man lying beside me now.

I'm not only surprised by his honesty.

I'm in awe of his resilience.

But I can't help but wonder... *how much of him is still in that cellar?*

"The church has always been a foundation for me," he continues, "It kept me grounded, kept me on the right path. I went on my mission, and the very week I returned, I met Vanessa. We were married within the year, like I was taught to do. We made a mistake, we'd had premarital sex once. We went to our bishop to ask for forgiveness, hoping he'd grant us permission to marry in the temple. But he refused, and that was the first time my trust in the church was tested—nearly shattered."

He takes a deep inhale, the vulnerability clear in every word.

"I knew, even on my wedding day, that I didn't want to spend forever with Vanessa. But I didn't have the strength to back out. I felt trapped in what I thought I had to do, what I was supposed to do."

There's a long pause before he speaks again. His voice lower now. "Two years into the marriage, I learned something that changed everything. My father had been molesting my little sister. She was still a minor when she came to us and told us everything. I didn't have to think about what I was going to do. I called the authorities, he was arrested. He's been in prison ever since."

Spencer breathes the story out through his nose, the sound slow and methodical, as if releasing years of pain. We both turn our heads, the feeling made unbearably heavy with the weight of what he's shared. There's a silence engulfing the space between us.

"That's where he is today. It's where he belongs. The day he went to prison is the day I felt like he died. I grieved the loss of who I thought my father was... he was never the man I held in high regard. I vowed to myself I would become the very best version of myself. That's what has brought me to this level in my life."

A deep connection hangs between us, our eyes locked in silence, our bodies sprawled out and limbs intertwined.

"I'm so sorry," Spencer says softly, his voice tinged with self-reproach. "I guess I needed to get this all out, so you could understand what a fucked-up person I am."

Trying to comfort him, I respond gently.

"You're not messed up. Everything you've been through made you who you are. You broke free from your difficult past, and it made you stronger. You're more ambitious and courageous than I ever realized. Honestly, you sort of had me fooled. I thought you had a silver spoon in your mouth," I tease, hoping to lighten the mood.

He smiles softly, though his eyes remain heavy with the weight of his past.

"I don't see you as being defined by where you come from. People change, especially when they've had to overcome challenges like yours. You're amazing."

"My faith in God and Jesus Christ has helped me through a lot of pain. That's why I still attend church and why I bring my family there. It's part of who I am."

"I understand that," I reply, my voice sincere. "We all need something to hold onto—some way to cope, to keep hope alive. And it sounds like your faith has been a lifeline for you, more than most."

"It has been. Sorry for dumping all this on you. I didn't know I'd end up giving you my life story."

"Thank you, I'm glad you do," I say. "Although I'm sure there's more to it than that."

"Maybe..." he grins, before pulling the sheet over our heads.

Forty-Six

By some quiet mercy, I've started going back to church again: a different time, different ward, far enough away that no one asks questions.

It isn't about being seen; it's about remembering who I was before everything went blurry, before things became confusing.

The uncomfortable push, pull of Dominic. The draw to Spencer. The desire to make myself happy, instead of what others tell me is happy.

Now, the calls have started to come in again.

The first time, I changed my number and gave it out to everyone. I didn't think it could be someone I know.

The second time I gave it to fewer people, mostly those who I talk to on a semi-regular basis.

But the same voice still found me. Calling from the same blocked number.

So I changed it again. This time, I was careful. Only a handful of people have it now.

I tell myself not to panic.

The police officer next door brings a small comfort. Every night I double-check the locks, whisper a prayer, and try to believe it's enough.

Maybe it is. Maybe this is what faith looks like—trusting that safety you can't quite feel.

Still, when the phone sits quiet for too long, I catch myself listening for something I hope I'll never hear again.

Forty-Seven

Valentine's Day falls on a Monday this year—perfect timing for a secret night with Spencer. He spent the weekend with Vanessa, but tonight his "service call" buys us a few stolen hours. I left work early, eager to make them count, with steak, lobster, and candlelight waiting just for him.

The late afternoon sun fills the front room like a promise. Six taper candles burn low in the center of the dining table, their flames dancing in the quiet air, promising an intimate evening.

I didn't buy him much, just a few shirts and a cologne that smells like sweet heat. Still, my real gift isn't wrapped. Tonight, I plan to spoil him with more than dinner.

I slip into a blush pink dress, tight along my curves, layered over new crimson lingerie, silk, and temptation stitched together. The fabric clings, teasing, not meant for comfort or longevity. Spencer won't let me keep it on long, and that's the point.

The table gleams with clear plates, polished silver, and glasses catching candlelight. Apple cider replaces champagne, a quiet nod to our shared restraint. White napkins trimmed in blush soften the formality. The house smells divine— steaks searing, butter melting into potatoes and green beans on the right side. Dominic took the grill, but I've mastered the stove. Spencer loves bread, so I added warm rolls to finish the spread.

I sink into my chair, heart ticking with the clock as I wait for Spencer to walk through the door. The candles burn lower, their light trembling. He's later than I hoped. The food won't stay warm forever, and the anticipation begins to ache. Restless, I drift into the family room and scroll through the music channels until a slow classic station fills the silence. Soft melodies curl through the house, blending with the scent of vanilla wax and butter.

I hear the familiar click of the door. Spencer bursts in, energy sparking, arms full of small gifts. For a second, I feel the sting of guilt. *He didn't need to get me more.* But I know him. He wouldn't bring anything unless he wanted to.

I walk over to meet him, eager to help him find a place to set the gifts. When his eyes meet mine, my heart flutters. I can't help noticing how good he looks.

"I didn't think you'd change before coming over," I say, a small smile breaking through.

"Of course I would," he replies with sincerity. "It's Valentine's Day. Only my best for you." He takes a deep inhale, eyes sweeping the room. "Something smells incredible in here."

"I made dinner," I say, wrapping my arms around his solid frame.

"That's not what I meant," he pulls me closer and whispers, "You smell... delightful. Hopefully I'll get to taste some of you later?"

His words ignite a flutter beneath my ribs. Before I can answer, his mouth finds mine. The kiss starts slow, careful, savoring—before deepening, heat building between us. When we finally part, I tease, "Hopefully."

He grins. "Now, let's eat before the food gets jealous."

His excitement is contagious as he heads to the dining room, and I follow, my smile stretching wide.

Spencer pulls out the rolling chair for me, his movement fluid, effortless. He waits until I sit. Then, circling the table, he takes his seat across from me. The silence that settles between us is easy, the kind that speaks of comfort rather than absence. We eat slowly, savoring the delicious flavors of the dinner. The fact that he's enjoying what I made fills me with pride. This meal isn't something I do often, but when I do, I want it to be flawless.

Over dinner, Spencer mentions a work trip to California. He suggests that I join him. Then, as an afterthought, he asks if my stalker has stopped calling since I changed my number. His question snags the air between us. The energy shifts, a quiet tension threading the room.

"It's been quiet," I say, setting down my fork.

He nods, but his expression drifts somewhere distant, his usual spark dimmed. Something's off. Uncertainty flickers beneath his calm.

"You alright?" I ask, softening my voice.

"I think so." He forces a grin. "Do I not look okay?"

"You do," I reply, watching him closely. "You look damn sexy. But something else is off."

"No, not off... At least, not yet." He winks, and for a moment the weight of whatever is on his mind seems to lift.

We finish our meal, and after clearing the plates, we move to the family room to exchange gifts. I gesture for him to go first. He grabs the cologne I bought and mists it onto his neck before pulling on the baby-blue shirt. It hugs his shoulders perfectly, the color sharpening the blue in his eyes. I can't help admire how effortlessly he wears it.

Spencer seems pleased; his enthusiasm is infectious as he hands me my first present. A black, rectangular box is held between his fingertips, gleaming under the light. When I open it, I gasp at the tennis bracelet, diamonds catching the light just so. Overwhelmed, I can barely speak.

"Oh my gosh," I whisper, tracing my fingers over the elegant line of stones. "I've always wanted one of these. Spencer. I can't—"

"You absolutely can," he says, his tone firm but playful. "Now open your next one." He seems more excited to see my reaction than about the gift itself.

He clasps the bracelet around my wrist, his fingers brushing my skin, the gesture both tender and claiming. I marvel at its beauty before tearing into the second box.

Inside, something soft meets my fingers. I pull it free—a teddy bear. My first instinct is to laugh, though a flicker of confusion follows. *What does he think? That I'm twelve?*

Then I notice the details. The bear wears a tiny leather jacket, a bandanna wrapped around its head, boots, and sunglasses, clutching a bouquet of red roses. A grin breaks across my face. "He's adorable."

"Turn it around," he says.

I do—and freeze. Embroidered on the back is one word: Buster.

I laugh softly. "Now I understand the gift." The humor fades into something tender. "I love it so much, Spencer. It's so thoughtful."

"I'm glad you do," he says, pride flickering in his smile. "Now you'll always have a little reminder of me."

I lean in to kiss him, my lips meeting his as I settle onto the cool leather of the couch. But Spencer, with a mischievous gleam in his eye, gently pushes me back, sinking me deeper into the cushions. A playful spark crosses his eyes.

He gathers my dress around my waist, his fingertips eager yet gentle. I meet his urgency, undressing him in turn. Kneeling over me, his need is obvious, and I can't deny how completely I'm drawn to him in this moment.

He drags himself against me, the friction burning through the thin barrier between us.

His touch is purposeful, almost frantic, like he's trying to make up for every last second we've missed.

His passion is undeniable, like it's not just desire—it's possession. Each movement speaks of needing to claim every inch of me, too quickly, too completely.

The fabric of my dress yields easily as he lifts it over my head, revealing the lingerie I bought just for tonight.

"You have no idea what this does to me," he breathes a trail of kisses between my breasts.

He explores me with reverence, almost like worship, every brush of skin charged, unusually eager. "You're so damn sexy," he says it, but there's a kind of urgency I haven't felt before. His movements are faster, hungrier, as if he's afraid the moment might slip away if he doesn't take it all now. He pushes against me, the charge of his body burning through the fabric still between us. His roaming hands, now everywhere, are brushing over me like

I'm territory he's desperate to claim.

"You're the hottest woman I've ever made love to," he growls.

He rubs himself against me, the friction maddening. Then he pushes my panties aside and inserts himself.

"Do you like it rough, baby?"

"A little," I whisper.

He thrusts deeper.

"You drive me insane," he mutters. "I need all of you."

My body arches toward him, wanting. Needing. Lost to the pace he's setting.

"Aaah, that's all I can take." I whisper, the stretch catching me off guard.

His voice lowers. "Do you want me to stop?"

I shake my head instantly, breath shaky. "No."

"Then let me give you everything."

And he does.

Heat and hunger collide in rhythm.

Each motion more consuming than the last. I open to him, let him in, let him take. It's more than I expected, more than I'm ready for, and still, I want all of it. I want him to break me open. To stitch me back together with nothing but his mouth and his hands.

He tastes me like a vow whispered through clenched teeth. Like he means to keep it, or bury me with it.

He yanks my panties down and forces my legs apart, his hands firm as he spreads me. Then his mouth crashes into me—wet, exploring from the underneath, teasing dangerously close to my most sensitive areas.

His tongue works with wild hunger, messy and unrestrained, as if he doesn't care what it sounds like. He moans into me, and I feel it everywhere. He meant it when he said "he'd eat me later."

I hate how much I crave this kind of raw, filthy indulgence—how it shreds me apart inside.

A finger pushes into me, one at first, working in rhythm with the flicks of his tongue. My body clenches down hard, but he doesn't pull back. The way he moves, almost wrong in its confidence, makes it clear he knows exactly what he's doing. Then, another finger joins the first, stretching me wide, and he doesn't pause to check. He's ravenous. Merciless. And I give him everything.

I push into him, commanding, "more."

He obeys, pressing another finger in, dragging a groan from my throat as he fills me to the edge of breaking. It's almost unbearable. But I don't back away. "Give it all to me," I cry. "Let me see what I can take."

He doesn't wait. I spread wider, and he keeps going, hungry, worshiping me with every sloppy stroke of his tongue.

"Keep going," I pant.

He spits in his hand, quick, functional, then drives deeper.

"Do you want me to hurt you?" he asks with deep desire in his voice, as if that's exactly what he's hoping for.

"Yes," I choke out.

I'm already trembling, desperate to see how far I'll let him go.

He works his fingers deeper, shifting inside me until the pressure spikes, until I'm gasping, climbing at the edge of something I both dread and crave.

"Give it all to me," I cry.

He leans in, his breath hot at my ear. "I'm going to put my whole hand in you."

These words land like a challenge. Caught in hysteria, I whisper, "Do it."

A dark smile tugs at his lips just before he pushes forward again, slow, then brutal. I feel myself splitting open for him, already raw and shaking, already wrecked. And still—I want more.

The line between submission and control disappears. I let go completely, drowning in the overwhelming need to feel him filling every broken part of me.

His knuckles stretch me to the edge. The pressure is unbearable, exquisite. He keeps going, patient but unrelenting, testing my limits like they belong to him. He finally withdraws, slow, wet, gleaming with my surrender. I gasp at the loss. I never let anyone this far in, but I now know why I never got this far before.

He reaches behind me to unclasp my bra. The fabric slips away, leaving

FORTY-SEVEN

me completely exposed and open beneath him. Vulnerable. Taken.

He presses himself against me, groaning low, the sound rolling through his chest like thunder. "I love how wet you are." He grips my hips tighter, his ragged breath crashing through the room.

Then he says it. "Fuck yeah, now you're loose just like Vanessa."

He did it. He said her name. While inside me.

It should humiliate me. Instead, it burns. I want to shove him back. Hit him. Drag him deeper.

I'm going to make him forget she ever existed.

Instead of shrinking, I ignite. Rage coils into something hotter—possessiveness, desperation, lust. If he wants to compare us, fine.

I'll make damn sure he never says her name again. Not with me under him. Not when I am the one he's inside.

I tighten around him, my fingers clawing at his back, daring him to forget her in the way I pull him deeper.

He pulls into himself, lost in it, and I see the pleasure overtaking him. The surrender. The loss of control.

I don't want to be another woman in his bed. I want to be the one he can't sleep without. The one he wrecks his life for. The one he never forgets.

The one he belongs to.

The thought of him picturing her while inside me, is like a fire I can't contain—it spreads through me like war.

"Take me like I'm your wife," I demand, voice trembling with need.

Something dark flickers in his eyes when he hears my demand. He thrusts into me with punishing force, making my body quake beneath him. I take it. Every deep, relentless stroke, moaning, crying out, lost in the intoxicating mix of pleasure and longing.

"I'm going to screw you like I do Vanessa," he growls, teeth clenched. "Oh, Vanessa!" he calls out her name. "You dirty little girl," he sneers. "You love this? Being used just the way you need?"

My body seethes, torn between rage and heat. I shouldn't want this. But heaven help me, I do.

"Yes," I gasp. "Harder. Take me."

He does. He slams into me with merciless rhythm, his skin slick with sweat, his sculpted chest heaving.

I cry out again. Raw, broken, too far gone to feel shame. Every part of me tightens, my body coiling as the pressure peaks.

"Holy fuck," I scream, the words torn from somewhere unknown. And then I fall—shaking, pulsing, clenching around him as I break apart completely.

He moans from deep within his chest, grabbing my hips as he chases the last wave of it. "Take that come," he snarls, and I feel him jerk inside me, finishing with a violent shutter.

That was not what I was expecting for our Valentine's love-making. The rawness. The violent edge. My body still trembles, nerve endings singing. Spencer moves across the couch, lying spent—chest thumping, sweat cooling, silennce settling between us like smoke. We're both wrecked. Coming down.

"Damn," he finally mutters, "You keep getting better."

Curiosity sparks in my gaze. "Where did you learn all of this... kinky stuff?" I ask, sitting straighter. Then, I find the courage to question, "Why are you so rough?"

His eyes narrow.

"Because I'm fucked up," he says, "But I told you that a long time ago."

I wonder if he really understands the roots of his need to dominate, to control.

"You're not messed up," I say, "Outside the bedroom, you seem... normal."

He meets my gaze—haunted.

"I'm not normal," he replies quietly. "I've just learned to wear it well. Pretend. But escaping the kind of childhood I had? It doesn't really happen."

As we dress in silence, he finally speaks again.

"I've buried myself in my companies, building something real, something clean. It's how I escape the deranged life I once knew. I'm sorry if I come off perverse with you; I don't try to be, I just... can't shut it off at times."

He pauses, eyes on the floor.

FORTY-SEVEN

"That thing I said..." he finally mutters. "About Vanessa. About how you felt. That wasn't about you, Sarah. That was me, slipping back into something ugly I thought I'd buried. It came out before I could stop myself."

He brushes his fingers through his disheveled hair.

"You're not like her. Not even close. I need you to know that. I would never want to hurt you. But sometimes I forget I'm not still at battle with myself."

The layers of him keep unraveling. The depths of this man keep revealing themselves. I never imagined anyone could be so deep. I'm still processing it when I slip into my dress.

Then freeze.

The front door handle twitches.

Panic seizes me. I yank my dress down over my body.

Spencer, sensing my alarm, quickly pulls on his shirt. He strides to the door and opens it slowly, peering through the narrow gap.

"I can't see anything," he whispers.

"Open it all the way," I suggest softly.

We both step into the night.

"There's nothing. I see nothing," I say a little louder.

My pulse won't calm. The door handle just moved. Someone was out there.

Spencer scans further into the yard, easing slightly.

Then my phone rings.

Startled, I rush inside, expecting it to be my mom or sister, calling to ask about how Valentine's went with Spencer.

Instead, a deep, muffled voice grunts, "I know you're fucking your boy toy. And he's there right now." My stomach drops. The words are weighted with something darker than anger. But what are they threatening me with?

The line goes dead before I can say a word.

"Who the hell is messing with you?" Spencer's voice sharpens as he re-enters the room, locking the door behind him.

"I'm not sure," I reply. "I guess changing my number didn't work. They're watching. Whoever *they* are."

Spencer's brows pull tight, his concern deepening.

Trying to keep calm, I say, "Don't worry, I'll handle it. I'll call the phone company again and ask if they can trace the blocked number." At least that gives Spencer something to hold onto. Something to do besides worry about getting caught.

"Are you going to be okay after I leave?" he asks. "I hate the idea of you being here alone. Whoever this is... they sound more intense now. Like their obsession is escalating."

"I'll be fine," I say, but feeling deep down, fear coiling tighter.

"I hate to leave, but the time has come." He glances toward the door. He looks like he wants to rip up his plans and stay here.

"I know. I don't want you to go either." My voice cracks, and I force a small laugh. "I hate it when you leave," I admit, as I feel my clingy side take over.

He sighs, his expression softening. "I'll try to come over in the morning on your day off. Otherwise... I'll see you at work."

"I'll see you, too! I love you, Buster! Thank you for my gifts. The bracelet is out-of-this-world gorgeous and Buster Bear.... he's the best." I lift my wrist to catch the light, letting him see how much I adore the sparkling new bracelet.

"You're welcome," he says, "My gifts are great too. Stay safe. Call me if it's urgent."

With that, Spencer heads to his truck, disappearing into the night with his gifts in tow—leaving me alone.

With a sore body.

A racing heart.

And a lingering sense of something I can't quite name.

Not love. Not fear.

But the ache of wanting it all to stop... and not wanting it to end.

Forty-Eight

I pace behind the counter, wedging the phone between my shoulder and ear.

"So there's no way to tell who's calling me?"

"Not without a police report," the agent says.

I stop pacing. "Even if I've changed my number before?"

"Yes. We can't disclose that information without formal documentation."

I hang up frustrated. I'll change it again. But this time, I'll give it out slowly, one person at a time—starting with Linda. I know it's not her, but I have to rule people out. Someone's breached my privacy. And I need to know who.

I plan to file a police report later today.

But right now the chaos at The Dog Shop hums around me—check-ins, barking, bathwater, phones. My schedule is slammed. Amber swings by to chat, with not much on her lineup of things to do, and her presence helps the hours pass as Linda and I work through the consistent stream of dogs.

I'm towel-drying a golden retriever when I catch a glimpse of Spencer at the window—just a flicker of his hooked finger. A silent invitation to join him in the foyer.

Amber's distracted, watching Linda bathe a dog. Linda's laser-focused on work. Neither of them sees him.

I dry my hands, duck out quietly, and head for the bathroom, where Spencer waits, leaning against the doorframe.

"You've been on my mind all morning," he murmurs, with sultry in his tone. "Every time I blink, I see you."

I smile despite myself. "You're insane."

"Insane for you," he breathes.

He kisses me hard—no preamble. No space. No patience.

"We don't have time," I whisper against his mouth.

"I don't care," he growls. "I can't wait 'til Thursday to be with you again. Bend over." His tone is firm—commanding.

I barely glance at the door before he drops to his knees, tugging my pants down. He spreads my thighs, then buries his head between them. Face up. No shame.

Wet desire brushes my clit, making trails to my opening—then farther, deeper.

He lifts my shirt next, mouth leaving a trail of wet heat up my spine.

"Spencer—" I hiss, trying to catch my breath. "They could come in any second."

"Then be a quiet, good-girl for me." He positions himself behind me.

"You don't even know what you do to me," he whispers. "The way you look at me when you're pretending not to want this—I could explode just from that."

I breathe out, surrendering. "Then do it. But be fast."

He slides inside me, and I clamp a hand over my mouth, stifling a moan as my forehead hits the wall.

"I've never wanted anyone like this," he pants in my ear, voice ragged now. "I'd take you right here every damn day if I could."

"I'd let you," I say, through the jolts punishing me.

When he finishes, he withdraws quickly, cleans himself with water and toilet paper. We barely say anything. He pulls me in for one last kiss, a kiss tasting like cinnamon and everything I crave.

I whisper against his mouth, "You're going to be the death of me."

He grins. "Worth it."

My mouth locks on his until my chin becomes raw from the roughness of his stubble—a secret I cherish, something masculine and wild that turns me inside out.

Gathering my composure, I straighten my clothes and smooth my hair, trying to erase any trace of what just happened, and return to work—my legs still shaking.

That's when I notice Amber's strange look. She glances toward the door just as Spencer passes by. Her eyes narrow, and in that moment I realize: *I'm busted.*

"Were you making out with the landlord?" she hisses, arms crossed. "And he's married."

I try to lie, but her stare is unyielding. "What? No..."

"Yes, you were. Your mouth is swollen and your chin's all red." She points with a knowing smirk.

With no getting around it, I sigh and come clean.

"Fine. Maybe. Kind of." I glance down. "Yes. But you can't tell anyone."

"Well, I won't. But you better tell me everything. Right now."

"Deal. But you have to promise not to judge."

She raises her brows. "You're literally sneaking into a bathroom with a married man. Judgment's kind of inevitable. But go on."

Linda, still bathing a dog in the back, doesn't look up. But I know she hears everything.

I tell Amber all the details, recounting every memorable moment and secret rendezvous over the past several months. As I share the excitement of our hidden affair, I notice her expression soften. She doesn't flinch at the part where I affirm he's still married. In fact, her acceptance gives me the reassurance I didn't realize I needed. Until now, I hadn't come to notice how badly I wanted more than a few people to know.

"You guys are getting serious, aren't you?"

I nod, "I think I might love him. Even though it's completely wrong."

For the first time, her teasing fades.

"Well... if you're gonna wreck your life, at least let it be for something that feels real."

It's not a blessing. But it's not judgment either.

And that's enough.

I've been giving out my new phone number, one trusted person at a time.

I'm cautious, making sure only the people I *know* I can rely on have it. So far, the plan's worked. No strange calls, no blocked numbers popping up—just a peace of knowing that whoever was harassing me before doesn't have access to this number. And even if they know where I live, they haven't come back.

Spencer and I spend more time in California now. It feels like freedom. Like a life untouched by guilt. We've grown in ways I never expected, and our relationship is turning into a love story that could fill pages.

Do I believe we will get married one day?

Yes. I see it like a photograph burned into my mind—me in a soft white dress, standing at the end of the aisle. His eyes locked on mine the way they always are when we're alone.

I hope that day comes soon. I keep waiting for him to say it's done. That he's filed for divorce.

He's promised me, in no certain terms, that he *will*.

And I believe him.

But I also know his life isn't simple. He has children, a life that's tangled with Vanessa's in ways that aren't easy to walk away from. I try to be patient, to be understanding. But sometimes the doubt creeps in anyway.

What if I keep waiting, and he never leaves her?

The thought presses in on quiet nights. No matter how much I try to shove it down, it still resurfaces.

Today, he came home with the most beautiful bouquet of deep red roses—the kind that make the entire room smell like romance. He sets them on our dining table, a reminder of how much he loves me.

Then came the robe—hot pink fleece from Victoria's Secret. It's soft, snug, and feels like being wrapped up in him. After a long soak in our jetted tub, I slip it on and let myself believe that just for a moment, this is really my life now. I have a man who brings me roses and robes I don't have to buy for myself. He provides a home where I can finally rest.

He doesn't say much when he gives it to me. He just watches me open the gift bag and run my fingers over the fabric. *But I know him now.* I see the way his eyes trace over me when I put it on, the way his shoulders drop like he's finally done something right.

We make the most of every second we're given. We've become experts at stolen time. When we're alone, our love is fierce and quiet at once. There's laughter and longing, teasing and tenderness. At night, I curl against him, wondering *how a secret can feel this sacred.*

We've memorized each other's bodies, uncovered what makes the other tick. *But* there's still more to discover. And maybe that's what keeps me coming back.

Forty-Nine

I have dinner plans tonight with Maya, Dominic, and Dustin.

Maya continues dating Dustin, and thanks to the two of them, Dominic and I have managed to maintain a distant yet civil friendship. Since Maya planned the evening, I didn't have to coordinate with Dominic beforehand, which was a relief.

We're meeting at a sushi restaurant where seating is traditional—cushions on the floor, the meal served in an intimate, close setting. The atmosphere is comfortable, the conversation easy.

It feels strangely natural to be here with the same group I spent four years of my life with, as though nothing has changed, even though everything has.

Dustin raises his sake glass.

"To good sushi, better friends, and Maya pretending raw fish won't kill her."

Maya laughs, wrinkling her nose.

Dominic smirks, reaching for his chopsticks. "Maya gagging over raw fish, isn't that bad. I've had worse dates. My last one ordered a steak well-done at a teppanyaki place, and then asked the chef if she could... 'just microwave it instead.'"

Dustin winces. "Oof. That's a crime."

I glance up, caught off-guard. "Wait, you've been dating?"

"Yeah. Sydney. We met through a friend at work. It's been kind of a whirlwind, honestly. She's... different."

"Different how?" Maya asks.

He shrugs. "She's bold. Outspoken. Very... open-minded."

FORTY-NINE

Dustin barks a laugh. "That sounds loaded."

Dominic grins. "It is."

He quickly changes the subject. "Anyway, how's the dog shop, Sarah? Still drowning in golden retriever hair?" It's interesting he would ask me about the shop—when he had been so vindictive before—but that's not what catches me. I smile politely, but Sydney and "whirlwind" sticks in my brain like a pebble in a shoe.

Maya's eyes flick toward me.

She nudges her plate forward. "Is everything alright?" Her words are soft, not performative.

"Yeah," I say. "Just... processing."

She holds my gaze for a second longer. Her expression is layered in concern and curiosity.

I know she's watching me the way a friend watches a friend they've had to patch back together.

Maya leans over to grab another roll, her sleeve brushing Dustin's arm.

He glances at her, waiting. She hesitates, then pushes the roll toward him instead.

"Not hungry?" He mumbles, low enough that only I catch it.

She shrugs.

There's a long silence between them, the kind that feels full of meaning even when no one speaks.

The kind of silence only two people who have shared something unfixable can sit in.

Grief that doesn't need to be named but can still reside at the table.

Dominic clears his throat, loud in the quiet. "So, who's ready for dessert?"

Dustin answers too quickly. "Always. As long as it's not those weird bean things."

Maya laughs, breaking the moment.

I glance at Dustin's hand resting near hers. Not touching, but close. They still orbit each other. Same pull, different rules. Some things feel too fragile to sit on a plate between soy sauce and wasabi.

I'm glad Dominic is dating someone new. Truly. I want nothing but the best for him.

I, however, keep quiet about my own relationship status. As far as the guys know, I'm single, and I plan to keep it that way.

Part of me hopes this outing will spark up jealousy or insecurity in Spencer, to push him to work on finally making a permanent commitment to me. Maybe the thought of me with Dominic again will be enough to move his pendulum in the right direction.

After dinner, the guys order drinks. I pass. Not because of Dominic, though his drinking was a factor in our unraveling, but because some lines, for me, are still lines. They're boundaries I don't cross. Not even now.

When it's time to leave, Maya plans to head to Dustin's. Since I rode with her, Dominic offered to drive me home.

"You sure you're okay with him taking you?" Maya's concern is sweet, but unnecessary.

"Yeah," I say, even though I'm not. "Go have fun, I'll be fine."

I don't love the idea of riding with him after he's been drinking, but I also don't want to turn it into something it doesn't need to be. So, I slide into his truck and shut the door.

Alone, just the two of us, Dominic launches into a barrage of questions about what I've been up to since we last saw each other. I dodge most of them, offering vague answers and steering the conversation back to him.

He tells me about the new woman he's seeing, how he likes her, how things are casual, but how he can't stand the way she slurps her milk and eats while naked. Apparently, it disgusts him.

Without much hesitation, he shifts into something more personal, as if he couldn't wait to share this with me.

"She likes to be choked," he says, like he's commenting on the weather.

I blink, caught completely off-guard. "I've never heard of that. Why would she want that?"

I lie, remembering my first time with Spencer at his house, his hand closing around my neck, just long enough to draw a deep, aching pull out of me.

His brows furrow, as if he hasn't fully grasped the situation himself. "I'm not entirely sure, but she seems to be enjoying it. Honestly, I've begun to develop a liking for it as well. Occasionally, I initiate the choking before reaching my orgasm, and she reciprocates. This dynamic intensifies the climax. That's possibly the reason behind it."

I stare at him, stunned. *This is the same man I spent years with? The same man who used to be so plain and predictable in bed?* I never would have imagined him experimenting like this, let alone enjoying it.

It's strange. Learning something so intimate about someone I once knew so well, only to realize I didn't know him well at all.

The strange turn of events neither of us could have predicted has led him to a woman who wants to be choked, and me to a man who wants to claim me. Life's cruelly ironic like that. Both of us are a far cry from the mundane prudes we once were. But why is he sharing this with *me*? Maybe he's trying to make me jealous, like I've wanted Spencer to be. Maybe this is all to get a reaction out of me.

Whatever his intentions, I find it unsettling, too strange, and a little creepy. I don't have much interest in who he's been with, or what they do.

"Are you certain you haven't been with someone else you'd rather not tell me about?" His voice lowers, falsely tender, like he's trying to earn my trust.

"No, not at all," I say without flinching.

I detest lying. But then again, I don't want to hurt his feelings, and more importantly, I know better than to provoke him. His past reactions have taught me that certain truths are better left unsaid.

"Ha ha," he scoffs, clearly not believing me.

Suddenly, without any warning, he reaches his right hand off the steering wheel and clamps it around my neck, pinning me against my seat. I thrash, frantically trying to break free. Choking through the restricted air, I manage to croak out, "Let me go."

But he doesn't.

His grip tightens, clamping down on my windpipe, compressing, flattening. Panic ignites behind my ribs. I can't breathe. I claw at his wrist, tearing at his skin, but he doesn't flinch. My vision starts to tunnel, shrinking everything into a pinhole of light as the roar of my heartbeat fills my ears.

My lungs burn. Somewhere in the narrowing dark I think of baptism—the drowning before the rise.

I can't breathe. I can't scream.

For one sickening second, I'm certain this is how it ends.

He makes no effort to release me. Instead, he tightens his grip even further.

"You enjoy being choked, bitch?"

The same thing Spencer once used to arouse me, Dominic now uses to control me. The contrast hits me like a second blow. It's not about lust anymore—it's about power. About fear.

He has never actually laid hands on me before, not like this. Just threats. Flying objects. Slammed doors.

I keep fighting, but my mind is fogging, limbs weakening.

I think quickly, and see my last chance to make him stop.

I yank the steering wheel with a desperate burst of strength I didn't know I had.

Tires screech. The truck jerks sideways, swerving violently across the asphalt as Dominic shouts, "You stupid bitch!"

Those are the last words I hear before there's a blinding flash of headlights. Then a jarring crunch of metal.

The front end of the vehicle crumples like paper against a thick tree trunk.

The world explodes in noise and chaos. My head snaps forward. Glass shatters. A force slams me sideways.

Then... nothing.

Everything is soundless.

Almost... *empty*.

Then, slowly, it all returns in waves: a ringing in my ears, the copper tang of blood in my mouth. The icy sting of glass against my cheek.

I can't move. My limbs feel disconnected, floating somewhere far from me.

I blink hard, my vision returning hazy, the shapes around me slowly

FORTY-NINE

sharpening, until I notice the cracked windshield, crumpled dashboard—and the faint smell of gasoline.

I turn my head and immediately regret it. Pain pulses through my skull.

Dominic is slumped beside me, motionless. For a moment, I can't tell if he's breathing.

"Help," I whisper, but the sound dies in my throat.

Panic claws at me. I force my fingers to move, then my arm. I fumble for the door handle, but it swings open before I reach it.

A woman's voice shouts, and Dominic is yanked from the truck and pulled to the ground. Hands tug at me. A flood of light blinds me as someone leans in.

"Are you okay?"

I nod, because I don't know how else to respond.

"You don't look okay. You're bleeding from your head. Don't move—an ambulance is on its way. Here, put this on your head." She holds a sweatshirt against it, causing a searing pain to bloom.

"Really, I'm fine." I croak, trying to reassure her. "Is he...?"

"I believe he's breathing," she says. I'm unsure if she's being truthful or just trying to keep me calm, but I'm taking her words at face value.

The pain I'm in makes waiting for an ambulance seem like an eternity.

Finally, it arrives with medical personnel. They check Dominic first. Then someone approaches me. He asks me the same questions the woman did, but in more detail.

I reiterate that I'm okay, but they run tests anyway.

The paramedic reassures me:

"It appears you need a few stitches and suffered a concussion." He then notices the marks along my neck.

"What are these?" he asks, referring to the bruises from Dominic's hands.

My mind races to find an adequate response.

One word could destroy everything, so I stay silent.

"I don't know," I whisper, my fingers brushing the bruises on my neck. "I think I hit the dashboard. I blacked out after we swerved."

The paramedic studies me, clearly unconvinced, but doesn't press.

I make a silent decision: if Dominic survives, I'll let everyone believe it was just a DUI.

I'll let them believe I was lucky to walk away. It was an accident. He swerved to miss an animal.

The rest stays with me.

Fifty

The slow rhythm of the machine beeping irritates me, but not as much as the reason I'm lying here, in this hard-as-a-rock hospital bed.

Knowing Dominic is the one who caused this feels impossible to reconcile. *Why would he do this? How could he do this?* I don't know why but, even now, I hope he's okay. I don't think—*I don't want to think*—he would ever intentionally hurt me.

Or maybe he would.

Maybe the divorce wasn't as easy or unbothered as he made it seem. Maybe resentment didn't fade as cleanly as he implied. Could he have been harboring ill will against me this entire time? Was going out with me and friends a ruse—an act, a way to stay close?

If he dies, I'll never know.

If he lives, I may never get the answers.

Aside from a few stitches and a minor concussion, I'm fine. That's what the doctor and nurse tell me, anyway. I need to get out of this hospital. I didn't want to come, yet my choice was overruled. Emergency personal insisted—something about making sure I hadn't endured more damage than what could be seen.

"All right, It looks like you're cleared to get out of here," the nurse says, her voice worn thin. It sounds like the end of a shift that should have ended hours ago. Her hair is disheveled, her posture slack, her expression tired and indifferent.

"Is my..."

I stop myself before the word *husband* creeps out, like it's second nature.

"Is the driver going to be okay?"

I brace myself for the word *no*.

"I can't give you too much information, for privacy reasons," she says, stepping closer after entering notes into the computer. "But he's in surgery. I was told he's expected to make a full recovery. Broken bones heal."

My body slackens instantly, tension draining out after being held in too long.

Then the relief falters.

Why don't I feel happy that he's going to be okay?

I wouldn't want him to die. I know that. But this outcome doesn't feel right either. It feels unfinished. Like the truth has been buried beneath the wreckage, and whatever remains will never fully be unearthed.

***

SPENCER

The chapel smells of bread and paper programs.

Vanessa sits beside me on the bench, her perfume faint and uninspiring and her hand is folded primly over our son's. From a distance, we look whole. Maybe that's the point.

The organ hums the opening hymn. My throat tightens with the first verse, but I mouth the words anyway, afraid of what silence might betray. Around me, the congregation sways with certainty—voices sure, faces calm. I used to hold that kind of peace. Now I can't tell if I simply lost it or traded it.

The deacons rise. Silver trays shimmer like a king's platter. The bread comes first. Then the water. My pulse climbs as the young men move down the aisle, slow and methodical.

I tell myself I'll pass when it comes. That I'll have the strength to keep my hands in my lap, to show the discipline I once preached. But when the tray reaches the end of my row, I feel every gaze in front and behind me—the

FIFTY

bishop, my neighbors, men who shake my hand each week—as if my grip still means something.

Vanessa leans forward slightly, ready to take her portion. Her diamond ring glints as she reaches. Our sons watch me. Waiting. Mimicking.

If I pass it, they'll notice.

If I take it, God will.

The boy on my side passes the tray to me. It's lighter than I remember, too easy to lift, too hard to bear. I take a piece of bread between my fingers. It feels wrong, like holding a promise I already broke.

For a beat, I think of Sarah. The way she says my name like a prayer and sin all at once. I place the bread in my mouth before I can stop myself. It's dry, leaving it sticking to my tongue.

Swallowing feels like lying.

I stomach the lie.

For a moment my thoughts drift where they shouldn't. They return to the night Sarah told me about her accident. The careful way she explained it. I recall how precise she was. She was unusually careful in the way she explained it. That wasn't like her. She doesn't curate her words before she speaks.

The pauses stood out. So did the lack of details.

She said *it was only a deer, a slick road, bad timing.* She made it sound like it was nothing worth worrying over. She said it like she *needed* me to believe her. Not like she was telling me a story.

I remember watching her hands while she talked. She kept them folded in her lap. There was no gesturing to describe how it happened, she didn't even fidget. All of it felt rehearsed. As if she had read a script, memorized it, and then regurgitated the information.

Rage fueled inside me. Not at her. Not because of her. It was aimed at him—the man that made her question her worth. *Dominic.* I can hardly think of the man's name without fury igniting within me.

I extinguish the flames quickly, remembering I'm in the house of the Lord. But her words echo, *It was a DUI.* That was the story she landed on. It sounds clean enough. Simple enough. Something you could file away without asking more questions.

No matter, even then, I felt there was more. The small bruises along her neck didn't fit anywhere in the story. It didn't seem like she was lying, just omitting.

I didn't press her.

Instead, I did what I always do. *I watched her*, closely. Listened to her harder. I checked in more often, made excuses to stay around longer. I knew I needed to protect her from a truth she wasn't ready to handover.

If she wasn't going to tell me what really happened, then I'd have to live with the guessing.

And so I do.

But I'm patient, and eventually I *will* learn the truth.

Later, when the water comes, my hand trembles. The cup is so small it barely fits between my fingers. Clear, cold, pure. I stare into it and see nothing but a reflection—mine, fractured by guilt.

One sip.

That's all it takes to pretend I'm clean.

I lift it halfway. The rim touches my lip, but I can't drink. The air catches in my throat, sharp as confusion. I set it back in the tray, undrunk.

Vanessa doesn't look at me. She doesn't have to. She can feel it, the space between us, the lie we both agree to keep breathing—that we live a perfect life, with the perfect marriage.

The tray moves on. The silence of sacrament ends.

The bishop gives the closing remarks, smiling, reminding us of forgiveness and renewal.

Forgiveness.

Renewal.

I want both. But I deserve neither.

When the final "Amen" sounds, I stay seated a second longer than everyone else, my palms pressed to my knees like I'm holding myself in

FIFTY

place. My son tugs my sleeve, eager to leave. Vanessa whispers something about lunch. I nod without hearing.

As the chapel empties, I glance toward the pulpit. The bread and water are gone, cleared away, replaced by emptiness.

All that's left is me.

And the taste of holy bread I should not have touched.

Fifty-One

***

Sarah

My stalker has returned. Whoever it is leaves ominous notes on my door, each one more unsettling than the last. The newest one is a threat. They're going to tell Spencer's wife about the affair.

But how would they even know who Spencer's married to?

The fear swells inside me. The only people who know about both of us and the affair, are Nick, Maya, Amber, and Linda—and they've all known for quite sometime. But I'm absolutely certain it's not them.

Weeks have passed, and the calls have started again.

I was so careful. I gave my number out one person at a time, always keeping an eye out for any sign of trouble.

But whoever this is, they're patient. Cunning. They waited. They let me feel safe before striking again.

I call the police and file another report. Then I contact the phone company, determined to get answers.

After a frustrating amount of time and persistence, I finally reach someone who can help. They say they'll send a statement in the mail with the blocked caller's number—unredacted, of course. "Only if the investigation supports it," they add. It may take a while, but at least I'll have something. A lead. A

FIFTY-ONE

way to finally end this nightmare.

I'm desperate to find out who it is, anything to put an end to it.

It's been months since this started. But the threats aren't only about me anymore; Spencer's being dragged into it, too. And that's what scares me the most.

The stalker is getting bolder.

The latest note proved it. It contained details, intimate, disturbing details, about me and Spencer making love on Valentine's Day. Whoever this is, they were listening. Watching.

They knew that Spencer whispered in my ear that night—filthy, breathless words only lovers share.

It wasn't just the words they heard that night. It was the way I moaned when he said them. They knew too much.

"You like being my dirty little secret, don't you?"

The note quoted it word-for-word. Spinning our intimacy into something shameful. Turning his desire into a weapon.

Now they're turning it on me. I can't let them twist this into something ugly.

I think back to that night when the handle rattled. The night Spencer opened the door and saw nothing but darkness.

Now I know.

It wasn't just paranoia.

They were out there.

Of course they were. How else would they have known exactly when to call?

I replay the course of events over and over in my mind, trying to piece it together.

Every moment, every word, replays like static.

None of it makes sense. But the feeling does.

I don't feel safe anymore. I can't live like this, constantly looking over my shoulder, wondering if I'm being followed.

I have to do something.

I have to make them stop.

Fifty-Two

Spring 2005

Today is a day promised to be filled with romance. My brother James is getting married. And even better? Spencer has officially decided to be my plus one for the wedding. It's a *huge* step. This will be the first time my family hears about him, the first time they meet him. I'm excited to show off this tall, muscular, calm, sexy man to everyone. But we're both a little uneasy. After all, he's still technically married, and if that comes up, I have no idea how to explain it. For today though, he's taken off his wedding ring, just to avoid any red flags.

We stroll hand-in-hand into the LDS church. The moment we step inside, I'm hit with familiar, smiling faces and soft conversations.

While I scan the crowd for close family and friends, Spencer leans in and whispers, "Hey, I know that guy."

"What guy?" I lean in and whisper back.

He gestures in the direction of the man across the room. A man I know all too well.

"That guy," he says, pointing directly at my oldest brother.

Panic flutters in my chest. "How do you know him?" I ask, trying to sound casual and feeling anything but.

"We used to be janitors together in high school."

"Oh! High school. Cool." Silently I feel relief that their relationship isn't a current one that could burn us down.

I introduce the two of them as if it's their first time meeting, keeping it brief and unremarkable—exactly the way I want it. They exchange pleasantries, my brother making no mention that he knew Spencer previously, he must have forgotten, and we move on with our rounds to meet the in-laws and other guests.

The gymnasium has been transformed. Cream-colored fabric hides the basketball hoops and fluorescent lights, giving the space a warm, elegant glow. Reception tables are already set. A white silk aisle stretches through the center, lined with pastel spring flowers, roses, and baby's breath. Golden *Chiavari* chairs are arranged in perfect rows. As we take our seats, I can't help but admire the attention to detail.

At the front of the room, stands a stunning floral arch, woven with greenery and soft pink roses. The twinkling lights wrap the wooden frame, flickering like a *fairytale* overhead. The soft notes of a piano play in the background, saturating the room with a gentle, romantic ambiance.

It's a classic Mormon wedding, outside of the temple, a backup plan since the original outdoor venue was rained out. But despite the unpredictable Utah spring weather, my brother and soon-to-be sister-in-law have made the best of it.

I feel a sense of pride as I move through the room, walking beside Spencer, hand-in-hand. There's a thrill in being here with him, in public, in my home state, surrounded by my family. I'm eager to introduce him to everyone, to show him off.

We turn heads as we move through the venue. Maybe it's because he's so ridiculously good-looking. A small, amused thought crosses my mind—do they think he's my dad?

Nah.

I dismiss the idea quickly. No, that's not it. They're looking because he's a showstopper. His presence commands attention, effortlessly drawing people in. Even in a room filled with wedding guests, he stands out.

And today, I get to be the one standing beside him.

Everyone in my family is surprised to see me with a new man. I can see the curiosity in their faces. Some of them ask questions. But for now, I soak in the moment, thrilled to finally have Spencer here, in *my world*, where he belongs.

Spencer surrenders to being grilled with a million questions by my family. They are eager to gather as much information as possible in the short time they have with him. They want to know everything: where he's from, what he does, how we met, what his intentions are. It's relentless, but he handles it all effortlessly, answering each question with a cool confidence that only makes him more attractive in my eyes.

He's unfazed by the attention, never flustered or caught off-guard. Spencer is a man who knows exactly who he is, and it shows. His self-assurance borders on cocky—arrogant, even, to some. But I understand him in a way others don't. He's not putting on a show; he's simply comfortable in his skin. I admire that about him. It's a quality I love, which makes us the perfect balance. I don't enjoy being the center of attention, but he thrives on it, and I'm more than happy to let him take the spotlight.

Once the introductions have wrapped up, aside from the remaining skepticism from James, we take our seats for the ceremony. Spencer and I settle into the second row on the groom's side, behind my parents and grandparents. The siblings are scattered throughout the room, a sea of familiar faces among the wedding guests.

As the other attendees also settle in, the simmer of conversation dies down, replaced by the anticipation that builds before the music starts to play.

The ceremony begins with my little four-year-old nephew making his way down the aisle as the ring bearer, his tiny hands gripping the delicate satin pillow. My eight-year-old niece follows closely behind him, tossing pink rose petals, not exactly how a bride would want them tossed, sparse and outside the lines. They park at the altar, taking their places on either side, setting the stage for the bride's grand entrance.

FIFTY-TWO

The doors at the back of the room open, and everyone turns.

The bride steps in, glowing in a modest, lace-detailed gown that hugs her figure perfectly. Her long veil cascades down her back, trailing behind her as she glides forward. She's a radiant bride, lit from within.

I glance at my brother. His eyes glisten with unshed tears as he watches her approach, overcome with emotion. The moment is pure, charged with an unspoken promise that only they understand.

I sneak a glance at Spencer beside me. He's watching too, his usual composed expression unreadable. I wonder what he's thinking. Weddings tend to stir emotions in people, and this wedding is doing exactly that. I reach for his hand, entwining my fingers with his, giving a gentle squeeze. I'm not sure what I'm trying to tell him, but I know I'm saying something. Maybe I'm hoping, silently, that one day it will be *us* standing at the altar, exchanging vows and promises of forever.

Spencer squeezes my hand back, his grip firm and reassuring.

The room flows with love, faith, and devotion. It's everything a wedding should be. Everything a *marriage* should be.

My nephew is doing his best to stand while the vows are exchanged, but it's clear the task is becoming too much for a restless four-year-old. He shifts his weight from foot to foot, glancing around the room. I can almost feel his struggle, the effort it's taking to resist the urge to move.

Finally, the moment comes for the rings to be exchanged. My nephew straightens, stepping forward with a serious expression, determined to fulfill his duty. He lifts the ring pillow up to meet my brother's hand, but in doing so, he tilts it just enough for the rings to slip loose.

A collective gasp ripples through the room as both rings tumble to the ground, rolling beneath the rows of chairs. The guests shift in their seats, some crouching to find them, whispers rising through the space. My nephew's face flushes with embarrassment, his little lips pressing into a tight frown. When I think panic might set in, Spencer leans down, reaching beneath his chair. A second later, he straightens, one ring now resting safely in his palm. Someone a few rows behind us raises the other ring between his fingers, lifting it into the air for everyone to see.

The crowd erupts in clapping, and Spencer stands taking the ring from the gentleman and gently placing both of them in the brides palm. "I believe these belong to you," he says, smoothly. The room sighs in relief, a few chuckles, breaking the tension.

My brother ruffles my nephew's hair, reassuring him with a caring smile, and the ceremony moves forward as if nothing happened.

Spencer settles back into his seat, and when I glance over to him, his eyes immediately lock onto mine. The room, the wedding, the guests, all of it blurs into the background.

It's just us.

The weight of the moment settles deep in my chest, and I know he feels it too. The air between us is charged with an electric pull.

Something about this day feels bigger than us, like the universe is nudging us in the direction we're meant to go. I mouth the words, "I love you."

He gives me a look like he just might mouth the same words back but the intensity of our connection is too much. I glance down, breaking eye contact before anyone else can catch on. Spencer leans in slightly, "I think that was an omen for us." His words flood me with a tingle. I glance up at him again, searching his face. He truly believes it—believes that this moment, however small, means something for us. And maybe... maybe he's right.

The rings slide on their fingers, and my brother and his new wife seal their marriage with a kiss. The room erupts into cheers, clapping, and celebration. But even in the midst of all the joy, I can't shake the feeling that something profound has happened between Spencer and me.

Maybe today isn't only the start of their forever. Maybe, in some way, it is the start of ours too.

Then it's time for the reception.

The tables are arranged in neat, circular clusters, each adorned with elegant floral centerpieces and flickering votive candles. The decadent tiered wedding cake sits at the head table—buttercream and fresh flowers match the bride's bouquet.

The reception continues in full swing, with music and laughter flooding the room. We eat, we dance, and the atmosphere is light and joyful. I mingle among more of my family, catching up with relatives I rarely see. But somewhere along the way, Spencer and I get separated, and I suddenly realize I haven't seen him for a while.

I scan the room, looking for him, and finally spot him tucked away in a quiet corner with my sister, Amber. True to her middle-child nature, she's always been drawn to the center of attention, even if it means sidling up to Spencer. She laughs a little too loudly, her hand brushing his arm. Amber is the type who hates being left out of any conversation, especially if it looks important. But standing this close to him, her head tilted just so, it feels wrong. Too intimate. Too much.

I make my way toward them, trying to discreetly catch snippets of the conversation, but I can't make out any of the words. I move in closer, Amber notices me and her demeanor changes quickly.

"What are you guys talking about?" I ask, trying to mask my concern.

"Oh, nothing, I'm asking Spencer some questions about you guys," she says, wearing a big smile, brushing it off like it's no big deal.

Even though I trust them both, a nagging voice reminds me of something I've heard time and time again: *if they'll cheat with you, they'll cheat on you.*

I push the thought away, refusing to let insecurity creep in. Spencer is too invested in me, and the bond we share is something neither of us has shared with anyone else. There's no way he would throw that away.

He reassures me immediately, his hand on my back as he leans in close. "It was nothing, I promise," he says. "She was asking about us, that's all."

I let the feelings go, having faith in him, in a way I haven't had with a man before.

As the evening comes to a close, we make our way outside. The rain has stopped, and the sky has cleared just enough for the most radiant rainbow to appear right in front of the church. Everyone crowds together to take pictures, and Spencer and I join in. It's one of those moments that feels too perfect to question—like the universe is giving us its approval.

I draw in air, inhaling the sweet essence of spring flowers mixed with the fresh rain. It's peaceful. The rainbow glows in the fading light of the evening, and for a fleeting second, it feels like God's way of saying, "This is right—not only for my brother and his bride, but for Spencer and me, too."

Fifty-Three

My watch ticks while I wait for Spencer. I notice the trees have begun to settle into deeper greens and the spring blossoms have mostly fallen.

Evie rests beside me on the porch, my fingers looping through her hair.

It feels surreal knowing my family finally met Spencer, and approved. All except for my brother Shane. He'll come around eventually. His loyalty to Dominic still runs deep, and I get it. Choosing a side isn't easy.

The low rumble of an engine builds behind me, louder, closer. Just the sound lets me know it's him.

He rolls in, wearing full black leather, coat, gloves, and the new saddlebags I got him for his birthday. Bad-boy allure, turned up to eleven.

The painted silhouette of a naked woman on his helmet catches my eye. I snort. Of course.

As he pulls into the stall, he cuts the engine, drops the kickstand and swings off the bike.

I move before I think, rushing straight to him, arms looping around his neck, kissing him hard.

"Ready?" He grins.

"So ready. And stoked you brought the bike." I raise a brow. "Where are we going?"

"If I told you, I'd have to kill you," he teases.

"Do I need to bring anything?"

"Nope, I've got it covered. Put your doggie away," he says.

I sigh. Patience isn't my strong suit. But for Spencer, I'll try.

"Help me up? And strap on my helmet?"

He lifts me onto the seat. When he fastens the chinstrap on my helmet, a flicker of claustrophobia creeps in. It's not that I'm choking—just a tightness I hate.

Anything tight around my neck makes my pulse stutter. And reminds me of hands that once didn't let go.

I shake it off and force a smile, leaning into him.

Spencer presses the starter, and the engine roars awake. He kicks up the stand, eases us back, then revs the engine. I press close, fingers linking in front of him, and we launch into the evening air. I wonder what he's planning, but I trust him. After five to seven minutes, we pull into a park I don't recognize.

He pulls in near the tree line, where a narrow trail disappears into the woods. I follow as he hops off, stashing his gloves in the saddlebags I got him.

"I love them, by the way," he tells me, smiling down at the bags.

"I'm glad you're using them," I reply, my fingers brushing his as I take his hand.

"Follow me," he adds, eyes twinkling.

We meander on the trail, trees closing in around us. The air is crisp, clean. As we hike deeper, it starts to feel like a hidden forest. Towering trees rise like guardians, their thick trunks wrapped in shadows, their needles casting a peaceful shade. It smells like Christmas. I inhale deeply, lungs filling, mind settling.

It feels like a sanctuary, where time is slower.

Deeper in, the trees part into a hidden clearing, ringed by spruce, ponderosa pine, and scattered oak and aspen. The earth's awake and breathing.

In the center, a colorful patchwork quilt lies across the wild grass. The blanket's inviting, a stark contrast against the natural chaos of the forest floor. A second blanket sits folded in the corner. A wicker basket and closed laptop rest beside it. I could guess what he's planning, but I'm not entirely sure.

"Come sit with me," he says, patting the blanket.

FIFTY-THREE

I settle beside him, legs folded, facing him fully. His expression is focused, but there's something else in his eyes that makes my heart flutter.

Something about tonight feels different. The secluded setting, the picnic, the breeze swaying through the trees. It's unlike any other time we've shared.

"I brought you here tonight to spend time with you," he says, evenly. "But also... I need to tell you something important."

I startle. Panic prickles at the edges.

Is this it? Some final gesture before he walks away? I hate how fast my brain spirals, but that's me. I do my best to suppress the unwarranted thoughts.

"Okay... What is it?" I ask, bracing for the worst.

I grip his hand, my thumbs subconsciously rubbing over his skin in a nervous rhythm. By the time he lets go, his hand will probably be raw.

Spencer exhales, his eyes fixed on mine.

"When I first saw you at the shop... I never imagined starting something with you," he admits, his voice thick with truth. "I didn't even know if you were legal, and I wasn't looking to step out on Vanessa again." His eyes narrow, searching my face before continuing. "After that first night, I told myself it was a one-time mistake. I tried desperately to stay away, but I didn't have the willpower to quit you. I don't have the self-control," he admits. "My fate led me to surrender to you. I believe it's God's will. I don't know why this path was chosen for me, for my family, for you. But I do know what I have to do."

My brows lift. What is he saying?

When he speaks his voice is unwavering. "Sarah Vaughn, I freaking love you," he says, his words spilling out raw and unfiltered. "I love you more deeply than I've ever loved anyone. This isn't lust. It isn't infatuation. It's deeper, something I can't shake, no matter how hard I've tried."

He squeezes my hands, his grip firm, grounding me in this moment. "I need you. I want you. I have to have you." His voice cracks between words. "It was never a choice. I've fought it. I tried to be the man I was supposed to be. But every road, every decision—every damn moment—leads me right back to you."

His voice drops lower. "I don't want to wake up beside anyone else. I'm done pretending I don't know what this is. I'm done living a life without you at the center."

I sit motionless, trying to absorb the words I've waited so long to hear.

"I've thought long and hard about this. I know what I need to do.." His voice is certain, with an intensity behind it that makes my pulse quicken.

"The only way to be with you—the woman I'm soulmates with, the woman who knows me better than anybody, who I've been more honest with than anyone else... the only way—is to leave Vanessa."

His words hang in the air, leaving an indelible mark on both of us.

My breath catches in my throat, my chest tightens, and my mouth parts, but nothing comes out.

Did he really say it? He wants to leave Vanessa.

A rush of elation penetrates deep inside, a dizzying mix of disbelief, exhilaration, and something extremely close to fear. We're no longer playing house; he's serious.

I search his face, trying to process this moment—this seismic shift unraveling between us.

His gaze doesn't waver. There's no doubt. He's already made his choice. And in the charged moment, I realize everything is about to change.

I'm stunned by his admission. In all my imaginings, I never truly believed he'd leave her. He's hinted before, offhand, pleadingly, but never with real weight behind it. We never dissected the reality. And now, he tells it like it's already done. *Like he assumes I want it just as much.*

I narrow my eyes, masking the whirlwind of emotion stirring inside me. "What makes you think I want you to leave her?" I tease playfully, though there's a violent storm inside my chest.

Spencer's lips curl. "You don't want me to? Alright. Then I won't." His voice is teasing, laced with sarcasm, but the intensity in his eyes remains.

"Stop!" I laugh, the joy bursting out before I can question any of it. I launch myself at him, pushing him back onto the overgrown grass beneath the blanket.

He laughs in surprise, arms immediately closing tight around me. The

FIFTY-THREE

trees sway, the scent of pine and earth wraps around us like a cocoon. Nothing else exists—only us, tangled together, on the edge of something we can't come back from.

I attack him—kissing him with an urgency that leaves no room for doubt. I'm all in. I need him to feel it, so he knows that I want him just as fiercely.

Between kisses, my happiness spills out. "Yay, yay, yay! You're going to be all mine!" I squeal, giddy and wild with elation.

Spencer laughs, shaking his head at my childish enthusiasm, but his grin is just as wide. His joy is quieter, more composed, but it's there. He leans over me, that smoldering gaze flickering with warmth. "Alright, alright," he says, teasing. But I know he loves that I wear my heart out loud.

Reaching for the basket, he asks, "You hungry?"

"You know it."

Spencer lifts the basket lid, revealing an array of goodies. First, a small charcuterie board, already prepped with grapes, cheese, and slices of pepperoni, a snack that I love. My heart swells at the thoughtfulness.

Then he produces two plastic glasses, shaped like slender champagne flutes, along with a bottle of sparkling apple cider. I hold the glasses as he pops the top, the soft fizz breaking the quiet. He fills us both a glass until it bubbles over the brim.

"Cheers, to us, and to everything we thought we'd never have," I muse aloud, clinking my glass against his, before my eyes wander to the laptop. "What's the laptop for?"

He takes a sip before answering my question. "Remember that movie you wanted to see, the one about the couples? We never got the chance."

My eyes light up, recalling the movie he's referring to.

"That's the one. Watching it here is better than in a dirty old theater anyway," he says.

"It really is."

The rest of the evening we cuddle close, sharing kisses between bites of fruit and sips of cider. It's just the glow of the screen, our playful laughter, and me tucked in close to him under the blanket. It's perfect—unexpectedly, unbelievably perfect.

But even in the middle of this moment, my mind drifts back to the one thing. He's leaving Vanessa.

I shift against him, almost unable to process what he's revealed. "Are you absolutely sure you want a divorce?" My voice cuts through the movie, now just little more than background noise.

His answer comes quick. "Never been more sure than now."

"How did you decide? I don't want you leaving her for me, or because of me."

His fingers tighten around mine.

"It's not only because of you, I promise. You gave me the push, maybe, but I've been ready to walk away for a long time."

I exhale, relief loosening the knots in my chest.

"You just helped give me the extra boost of courage I needed to finally follow through," he continues. "Vanessa and I tried everything. We went to our bishop, to counseling, did every assignment they gave us. We took late-night walks, hoping we'd find a spark."

His voice gets lower, graveled with something new.

"None of it ever made me feel closer to her. The truth is, both feet have been out the door for years."

I let out a slow breath, my chest tight with a swirl of emotions. Relief. Excitement. The overwhelming feeling that this moment, his choice, is really real.

"You've shown me what love really is," he continues. "To give it. To feel it in return. And I'm not sure I've ever felt it before you. You don't need to feel guilty. You didn't break up my family. This is happening because Vanessa and I weren't right for each other. We never saw the world the same way."

"So... have you told her yet?"

He sighs, shaking his head. "No... not yet. The kids are finishing school, and I don't want to disrupt their last week. It'll be hard, but it's for the best."

I smile, choosing to let the moment be.

We curl back into each other, letting the final minutes of the movie play out.

I'd waited so long to see this film, but now, nothing on the screen compares to the reality unfolding in front of me.

When the credits roll, the mood shifts. Desire sparks between us again, undeniable, uncontainable. We give in, right here in the secluded clearing. The trees stand like silent witnesses, making me feel both exposed and held. We try to be discreet, but there's an intoxicating thrill in knowing we could be discovered.

Later, tangled in each other, Spencer reaches into the basket one last time. He pulls out a small container. Inside are chocolate-covered strawberries, my absolute favorite dessert.

I grin, shaking my head in admiration. "You really do pay attention, don't you?"

He gives a knowing smile, handing me one.

"Every little detail."

Fifty-Four

The phone rings unexpectedly. I answer uncertain who's on the other end.

"Is this Ms. Vaughn?" The voice on the other end asks with authority.

"Yes."

"This is Officer Smith. I'm calling in regard to your report about someone harassing you," he says. "We received the unredacted number from your phone company—the person who's been following you. The number is 555—530-0954. Do you recognize it?"

A cold rush of shock floods my veins. The weight of the moment is so heavy that it's hard to breathe.

"Yes," I reply, my voice trembling. "I know that number. Are you certain that's the person who's been calling me?" I must be absolutely sure before I let myself believe this is real.

"Yes, ma'am," the officer confirms, his tone firm but authoritative.

My blood leaves my face, creating a chill through me.

"So what's the next step?" I manage to croak out. "How do I make them stop?"

"The next step," Officer Smith explains, "is for me to call them directly. I'll let 'em know that if the behavior doesn't stop, charges could be filed, possibly even an arrest. Hopefully, that'll be enough to scare 'em off."

I nod, even though I know he can't see me. "Sounds like a plan. Thank you, Officer."

"You can reach out to me anytime if you require further assistance," he says. "I've been assigned to your case. Please keep a hold of your case number." He reads off a lengthy number, and I quickly write it down. "Ensure that you don't make any contact with this person in the future."

"I won't. I appreciate your help."

I end the call with a shaky breath, the silence around me suddenly deafening. My fingers are still curled around the phone, but it feels like it's no longer a lifeline, just a reminder of how close danger has been.

Something about hearing the officer's voice, knowing someone else finally sees this, makes it all feel real in a way it never did before.

The gravity of it all crushes me. The fear, the uncertainty—it all feels so overwhelming. But for the first time in a long while, someone I can't trust is finally taking control; he's doing everything he legally can. Now I have to pray that it will be enough.

The realization hits like a ton of bricks: the person behind all of this is someone I once loved. Someone I believed I could count on.

For a second, my brain fights it. This can't be happening.

I was so sure it was Jackie. That was the story that made sense.

The threat I'd built up in my mind.

For a while, I even wondered if it was Nick, which is why I never let myself get too close to him. The truth is, Nick was always just a friend, and I knew it. But the suspicion kept me guarded, even when he tried to be more.

But this? *Dominic? My husband?*

We've spent time with friends since the divorce, so he knows I wasn't honest when I told him I wasn't seeing anyone.

He knows about Spencer.

He knows about the affair.

And now I'm seeing it clearly. He's been manipulating me all along.

Playing me like a fool.

How can I have been so blind?

I should have known our marriage wouldn't end quietly, that he wouldn't settle for being just friends.

I ignored the signs, and he knew I would.

Now, I'm left reeling with the aftermath, keeping our accident a secret.

Covering for him. Leaving him with extensive injuries from fighting him off after he choked me wasn't enough for him to stay away.

I'm almost certain the officer's call will shake him.

That the threat of jail will finally be enough to make him back off.

But what will Dominic do now?

What kind of man is he really?

How do I keep from confronting him now? He'll know I know the truth. That I figured him out.

My thoughts race, but anger won't help. I have the upper hand now, and I need to keep it.

I reach out to Linda and then Maya. I tell them everything. Their calm voices keep me from unraveling.

"The officer will handle it," Linda says.

Maya echoes her, reminding me, "Focus on staying safe and let the law take care of the rest."

But how can I relax when the person harassing me—threatening me—once shared my bed?

I pretend to absorb their comfort, but inside I'm unraveling in slow, silent spirals.

I keep picturing Dominic's face if the officer actually calls him.

Would he laugh it off? Deny everything? Or would he finally realize I'm not afraid of him anymore?

I plan to tell Spencer when I see him next, but part of me knows he's already carrying too much.

I can't help but wonder where Spencer will go once he moves out of his house. I'm sure the pressure on him will only grow, even after he follows through with his plan.

So I won't burden him with this, with the news that Dominic is the one torturing me.

There's no use dwelling. For now, I'll act like nothing's changed.

This time, I'm walking with my eyes wide open.

Fifty-Five

Summer 2005

* * *

SPENCER

The house is too quiet when I step inside. My bags wait by the door, their weight matched only by the finality of what I'm about to do.

Vanessa sits on the sofa, the television casting flickering scenes across her face.

"We need to talk," I say. My voice is even, but my chest feels tight, stretched thin over nerves.

She turns when she hears me, and for a moment I see the hope she still clings to. Fragile. Exhausted. Worn thin from everything we've been pretending not to feel.

Her forehead creases. "About what?"

"Us."

The word is enough. She goes still, then shakes her head. "Don't do this. Not now. Not after everything we've been through."

"I can't keep pretending. We're not the same people we were eight years ago. And we've grown apart, not together. That's not failure; it's just truth. We've had a good run, Vanessa."

Her voice cracks, splintered by tears. "We made vows, Spencer. Before God. You don't get to walk away from that."

She stands, pacing. Tears streak down her face, then twist into rage. She snatches the remote from the table and hurls it hard against the wall. It shatters like the moment between us, scattering plastic across the floor.

"You think this fixes anything?" she spits. "You think leaving us will make you whole? You'll regret this. You'll wake up alone and realize you destroyed the only person who ever stayed."

The words strike my core. My hand clenches tight, every feeling I've been avoiding collapsing inward, crammed into the tiny universe trembling inside my grip. "I'm not complete here. I haven't been for a long time."

She holds her fists to her temples, rocking slightly now, crying harder. "You can't just erase a life together, Spencer. You can't just…"

"I'm not erasing it." My voice sharpens. "I'm saying it's over."

She breaks. Her sobs tear through the room, a guttural sound I'll never unhear.

And still, there's nothing left I can give her.

* * *

SARAH

The rain's coming down hard, pelting against the roof of my condo. I'm curled up on the couch, wrapped in the Chanel blanket Spencer bought me during my last trip to California, my arm drapes over Evie. An intense murder mystery plays on the TV, and sound of rain taps against the windows.

Then, there's a knock at the door. A sharp, urgent knock that disrupts my quiet. I wasn't expecting anyone, and for a moment I feel a twinge of annoyance at being pulled from my peace.

Until I open the door.

Spencer is standing there. Soaked. Pale. Worn. Like he's been dragging a weight through the storm for miles.

"What's wrong? Come in!" I rush to pull him in, quickly wrapping my blanket over his shoulders to warm him.

"I told her," he says, uncomfortably pulling the blanket back down to his waist.

"Told who what?" I ask, not fully knowing, but the sinking in my gut answers my own question before he says another word.

"Vanessa," he confirms, his eyes heavy with the burden of his confession.

My heart quickens. He did it. He actually told her. I wasn't sure he ever would, and now, here he is. Soaked in rain and grief, but finally here.

I feel a mix of empathy for him and anticipation for what comes next. But the stress in his eyes tells me this wasn't easy.

"How did she take it" I ask, even though it's obvious. I want to know everything, and yet I'm afraid to hear it all. "You look, awful," I whisper, my concern overriding everything else. I can't stop staring at him. He's gutted.

"Not good," he says, flustered, his voice shaking. "She pulled pictures off the walls. Woke the kids up. Started screaming words I've never heard her say before."

He drags a hand down his face. "It didn't go the way I hoped. Not at all."

I see it in his eyes—this wasn't just a conversation. This was an explosion. A final, splintering blow to a life he's been quietly trying to escape for years. This is the fallout. The cost of choosing himself.

I ache *for* him.

I pull him into my arms, holding him as if I could absorb the pain he's feeling. His breath is uneven. The tension in his body rises as though he's teetering on the brink of a breakdown.

It's a rawness I've never seen from him before.

Spencer, the strong one, is now so fragile—so meek, on the verge of tears. This vulnerability is jarring.

The gravity of the moment, the feelings pouring from him, encompasses the room and render everything else trivial. I don't know what to say, so I don't say anything. I hold him, letting him know I'm here, no questions, no judgments.

"I'll be fine," he finally admits, pulling away just enough to reassemble his composure. He sits halfway on the armrest of the couch, but the space between us suddenly feels like miles.

"What can I do for you? Do you need a place to stay?" I ask, wanting to ease his burden. Even if it's just for tonight, I want to soften the fall.

"No," he says, shaking his head. "I'm going to stay at Ken's. He offered his guest house while I figure out what comes next."

I nod, trying to keep the disappointment from showing. "That sounds like a great plan."

I take a few steps back, giving him space, but my eyes can't leave him. There's something about the way he looks right now—vulnerable, undone—sitting there in that baby blue shirt I love on him.

But I see past the clothes and for the first time I see all of him. Not the confident man I once knew. Not the cool, composed version that kept everything locked behind humor or restraint. This. This is the real Spencer.

He's simply... human. And somehow, that makes him even more irresistible.

I'm pulled in a way I didn't expect. I've never wanted him more—not just physically, but emotionally, too. Seeing him so unguarded only intensifies my feelings for him.

It's as if the walls he built around himself are finally cracking, letting me see the man underneath. And that man? *He's worth everything.*

He sits quietly, lost in thought. I want to reach for him again, but I don't. I don't want to scare him off or make him feel like I'm expecting anything.

After a long pause, he stands. There's a change in him. Not quiet resolve, but something close.

"I should go," he says, solemnly, avoiding my eyes.

"I understand." My voice rests easily.

I want to say *stay*. I want to pull him into me.

But I don't.

Fifty-Six

He opens the door and steps into the pouring darkness of the night. Immediately, I freeze. Panic zips through me as Vanessa's voice slices into the ominous air, seething with fury. Her words hit like a brick, creating a surge of terror within me.

How did she find us?

How did she find my home?

I feel the shock spread across my face as my mind scrambles to make sense of what's happening.

Spencer stands in the frame, his back to me, his entire body rigid with shock. He looks like a man trying to hold back a storm. Every word Vanessa hurls at him cuts deeper than the last, and I feel the sting of each one as if they're hitting me too. Her feral anger ricochets all around us.

"I knew it, you bastard!" She explodes, leaving nothing untouched in her wake. I can see the fire in her eyes as she barrels toward us.

Spencer tries to remain calm, but there's a crack of desperation.

"Oh shit," he mutters.

I can't tell if he's talking to me or to himself, but I feel the tension pulsing through his body. He's trying to reason with her, but she's not having it.

"I'm not fucking anybody!" he snaps, his frustration splintering out of him. But Vanessa is beyond reason now. Her accusations are louder, more venomous.

"Yes, you are! Jackie told me it wasn't her!" she shouts, pointing directly at me.

"But after meeting *her*, I knew it was!"

"No, it's not like that," Spencer pleads, his voice deceptively calm.

I want to say something, anything, to defend him, to defuse the bomb going off before me—but I'm paralyzed.

Vanessa's eyes cut to me like a blade. "It's her, isn't it?" she spits. "You've been sneaking around with *her* this whole time."

"Sarah? No. I told you, I'm not fucking anybody!" Spencer's words are desperate, defensive. It's too late. My name is a match to gasoline.

"Why are you here, then?" Vanessa hurls the question at him like a weapon—accusing, demanding, relentless.

She balls her hand into a fist, lunging past Spencer to swing at me. He catches her arm mid-motion, then lets go. She tries again, bulldozing toward me.

Spencer moves on instinct. He finds a way to hold her back—using the door as a barrier, wedging himself between us.

He's a wall, leaving her in the storm while holding us inside.

Then thunder detonates around us, as if the sky itself is reflecting the chaos too.

Vanessa's voice erupts again and I realize with a sinking certainty that nothing will ever be the same after tonight.

Spencer braces himself against the door, his face a mixture of exhaustion and resolve.

He's not just holding her back. He's holding back the life he's about to leave behind.

She's out there, fuming with rage, and I can't help but hurt for him.

This isn't how he thought his night would end.

It's not how I imagined mine, either.

Vanessa's voice, muffled from behind the door, still rings in my ears.

I can only imagine the anger she feels, the way everything is breaking beneath her feet.

And in that sense, I sympathize.

However, I can't deny the relief washing over me. Spencer took the first step toward his freedom. Toward us.

But how do we move forward?

Spencer pants, his eyes locked on mine.

But there's a quiet desperation there. A silent plea.

Maybe just to stay.

Maybe for me to tell him everything will be okay.

But words feel useless against the weight of what he's carrying.

His marriage is crumbling. He's hurting.

And still, he's shielding me from Vanessa—protecting me.

While he leans against the door, I wonder how much longer she'll stand out there.

Finally, he breaks the silence.

"As soon as she leaves, I have to go."

I nod in understanding, but I don't want him to leave. Not like this. Not with everything unfinished.

But I don't say that. There's nothing I can say to make this better.

There are no answers for what comes next.

The sparkle that was in his eyes is gone—hope, future, passion—all of it is snuffed out.

It's unsettling.

Spencer has always been so full of life, his energy infectious. Even in darkness, he keeps things light.

But now... he looks hollow.

It's a new look for him, this emptiness.

And I can't help but feel like I'm witnessing a transformation in real time.

Will this break him?

Turn him into someone I won't recognize? Maybe everything he thought was strength was tethered to Vanessa all along.

And now that she's gone...

He's unmoored.

Damn it, I hope not.

But I'm not naïve enough to count it out.

The silence between us is suffocating, but neither of us moves.

We just stand there.

Waiting.

Watching.

Listening.

Then a sound—what we think is her car door slamming shut.

We both exhale in sync, like we've been holding our breath the whole time.

Spencer moves first, peeling his gaze from mine and stepping toward the window. He peers through the wooden slat of my blinds, cautiously.

A few seconds pass before he motions, "It's her. She's leaving."

His voice is quiet.

Flat.

No relief. No certainty.

Just a fact.

This is it. The moment I dreaded, yet always knew was coming.

"I have to go now," he says, and there's a finality in his tone that tightens something in my chest.

I search for something, anything, to say.

Something meaningful. Something comforting.

But all I manage is a simple, "I'm so sorry."

His lips press into a thin line. "Me too."

And then, without another word, he opens the door and slips away—vanishing into the storm, into the unknown, into a moment in time neither of us can ever take back.

Fifty-Seven

The fallen dominoes in Spencer's life are steadily re-stacking themselves. His tumultuous separation from Vanessa was a quick meltdown and a slow rebuild, but now, with time and space, he's starting to find some sense of peace.

He's been traveling far and wide, working to rebuild himself after everything that's happened. I've had the rare privilege of joining him on those trips, watching him heal as he becomes someone new.

California became a refuge for us. A place to outrun the chaos and carve out something that felt like peace. He's tying up loose ends, finishing work, and preparing for the next chapter. He's hopeful now, trying to ensure Vanessa gets a large payout for the Utah home so she'll never dig deep enough to learn about the California retreat—the one where he and I have built a different reality, a truth that stands as solid as a rock.

The aftermath of that chaotic night has been harder than I imagined. There's no manual for how to navigate this, and I hadn't realized how much the reality of it all would take a toll.

But in some ways, it's brought Spencer and me closer. Our bond has deepened since that night; the walls between us, fear and secrecy, have come down.

We can be us now, free from the threat of being discovered. That shift has allowed our relationship to blossom in ways I didn't expect. We've embraced public affection, shared normal moments in our hometown, and settled into something that finally feels simple.

But it's also changed things. *Spencer's different now.* I've seen it in how he interacts with me, how he shows affection. There's a hesitancy in him, a vulnerability that didn't exist before. It's as if the walls have come down, but they were replaced by something even more fragile.

This divorce, this journey he's taking to rediscover himself, has changed him in ways I didn't account for. *How could I have?*

And I wonder, *will he always be this way? Is this transformation permanent? What happens to the man I'm falling deeper for if it is?*

I don't know the answers, but I know this much: whatever changes lie ahead, I want to be beside him as he rebuilds, just as I'm learning to rebuild myself.

Although Spencer is still loving, there's something in the way he touches me, speaks to me—and the hardest one to admit—looks at me, that has changed. His affection remains, but it's something that was once whole, and is now partly missing.

Sometimes he'll stare at me blankly, as if his eyes are seeing through me but don't quite land. The look is hard to read—not vacant, but guarded. As if something is hidden behind it.

And it leaves me questioning where I stand. The spark that once danced in his eyes—gone.

We're closer in some ways, certainly. We share deeper conversations, softer touches. A quiet understanding that feels rare.

We now share the fallout of divorce, and that, in itself, is a bond.

But at the same time, there's an emotional distance that I can't ignore. His words spin dances about love and the future, of promises and dreams.

Yet, even as he takes me on breathtaking adventures, showering me with beautiful gifts, something feels off.

We're no longer walking in the same direction. He's heading sideways— away from me, even while I stand right beside him.

I keep trying to decode his mind, to trace the thoughts running behind his eyes, but I can't catch them.

FIFTY-SEVEN

This trip to Monaco, on the French Riviera, should have been our pinnacle. It's one of the most beautiful places on Earth. The city exudes a luxurious and wondrous aura, making it feel like a realized dream.

Today, the brunch at Monte Carlo Casino is nothing short of lavish. It's designed to indulge every sense and immerse us in Monaco's refined elegance. The restaurant is perched on an outdoor balcony that offers sweeping, panoramic views of the Mediterranean.

The sunlight glints off the sea below us as we sit on the casino balcony, the whole harbor unfurling like a painting. Spencer's hand brushes mine against the table; his laughter is easy.

The morning should be flawless—linen-draped tables, croissants still steaming, hot chocolate rich enough to spoil me for anything else.

Yet, when I look up at him, just for a second, his gaze is elsewhere. It slides past the horizon, someplace I can't follow.

"What are you thinking about?" I ask softly.

He blinks, returning to me. "Just... how fast this all goes. How sometimes you don't know you were in the best part until it's already gone.'"

I reach for his hand. "We're still in it."

He squeezes mine back. Then catches me watching and leans in to press a kiss to my forehead as if nothing has slipped. I must be imagining it.

"You okay?" I ask.

He forces a tight smile, then says, "This is everything I hoped it would be."

Jet-lag or guilt has carved the shadow in his eyes. But even surrounded by the glamour of Monaco, a sliver of fear lodges under my ribs, the quiet sense that part of him is already drifting away.

Throughout the meal, Spencer and I exchange soft glances, basking in the fleeting beauty around us.

It's clear—we both understand the weight of the moment, a rare, once-in-a-lifetime experience we're trying to savor.

After our indulgent brunch, we venture into the narrow streets of La Turbie. As we glide along the winding roads of the hilltop village on our Vespa, the wind tangling through our hair, I feel like we've stepped into a world untouched by the noise of everyday life.

I squeeze his waist and shout over the wind, "Let's never leave."

He laughs. "Deal. We'll stay until they throw us out."

A beat passes, then he adds, quieter, "We deserve this. After everything."

La Turbie stands as a perfect contrast to the opulence of Monte Carlo—where time seems to stall, and the hustle and bustle of modern life can't reach us.

The village is a maze of cobblestone streets that twist and turn as they climb up the hillside, the views getting better at every bend. The buildings are a charming mix of weathered stone and brick.

The streets are lined with quaint cottages, each unique, their façades draped in ivy or perfected with vibrant flower boxes.

There's a timeless quality to this place. Like it's frozen in time, untouched by the march of progress.

We meander hand-in-hand through narrow streets thick with the smell of fresh herbs and wood smoke spiraling from chimneys.

The town is peaceful, the only sound is a gentle buzz of conversations and the occasional clink of a teacup on ceramic. There's no rush, just the rhythm of life moving in perfect harmony with the land.

The view from the top of the hill is breathtaking. The Mediterranean spreads out before us, its water sparkling in the afternoon sun, while the distant hills of the Alps rise in the background, their peaks kissed by the faintest trace of snow.

The contrast between the rugged terrain and pristine water is nothing short of mesmerizing. We stand near the edge of the world, looking out over a land steeped in history and beauty.

It is a perfect day, a stillness in the storm of emotion we've been weathering. We've stepped out of our lives for a while, into something simpler. We're here, in this moment, fully present. And this day has become one we'll carry forward, pressed into a memory like a keepsake.

Spencer seems more relaxed, and for the first time in a long time, I feel

FIFTY-SEVEN

something like freedom.

Even in this fresh start, a persistent worry lives in my mind, tucked deep into the corners.

I can't quite pinpoint the reason, only that it's lodged in my gut, an unshakable feeling I can't ignore.

I've tried to bring it up, but without a clear reason, he doesn't see it.

He simply reassures me everything's fine, reminding me daily how beautiful I am, and how happy he is to be starting this life together.

"You know I'd do this all again just to end up with you, right?" he tells me, brushing my hair back.

"Even the mess of it?" I question.

"Even the mess."

What more could I want in a partner?

To deepen our commitment, he gave me the pin-code to his phone, and I gave him mine. A symbolic gesture. Another step toward something real, no secrets between us.

We're not fully merged, no shared accounts or intertwined lives, but this was something tangible. Something a man who means to stay would do.

A little cheesy, maybe. But real.

And he's been making payments on my new bed, a quiet promise he's not going anywhere.

Tomorrow, we leave the opulence of France, and Spencer is right when he said the romance here would reach another level. From the dreamy brunch on the Monte Carlo Casino's balcony to the exhilarating Vespa ride up the winding road to La Turbie, every moment has felt like a fantasy.

I love him. I've fallen so deeply for Spencer that if he asked, I'd give him a child. Me. Sarah. The woman who never wanted kids, who has always claimed she didn't understand why anyone would. Now, I do.

If we were married, I can only imagine how much stronger this desire would be.

But I know Spencer is done having children; he's made that clear.

If he knew what I was feeling, I'm afraid it would scare him away.

So, for the first time, I'm keeping something from him.

I don't blame him for not wanting more children, three kids is a lot.

But my twenty-year-old heart still wonders, still dreams about what could be. And honestly? I love it. I love imagining what our future might become, what it would mean to share a home, a future, a family.

"What do you see, when you think about our future?" I whisper, as we lie in bed.

"You. Always you. Somewhere quiet... maybe a garden. You laughing." he answers immediately.

"Kids?"

He pauses. "No more. I don't have that in me again."

I shrink into his chest, pressing against him to hide my ache.

What anchors me is our shared faith in God and *His* plan.

I believe with everything in me, that we're being guided in the right direction.

That if we cling to that faith, everything will align exactly as it's meant to.

I know God has something beautiful waiting for us.

Fifty-Eight

Fall 2005

Returning to a regular schedule after the trip with Spencer is bittersweet.

I missed my doggy customers and the comfort of my own space, but being away with him felt like a dream.

Luckily, Linda has been incredible, keeping the business running while I've been off gallivanting with Spencer. She understands how much I want to build a future with him.

Linda and I have had a little more freedom at work—mostly because the remodel on the shop is finished. Occasionally, we let the dogs dry while she and I drive through the hills, admiring the beautiful homes—a small treat to ourselves. Today is no different.

As we pull back into the shop, I notice a sleek, jet-black Dodge truck parked out front. There's only one curbside parking spot—reserved for customers who need easier access—and I don't recognize the vehicle. Most of my customers are regulars, and I've memorized the cars and schedules.

What the hell?

I freeze, unsure what to do. Panic flutters inside me.

Linda glances at me. "Do you need me to stay close?"

"No, it's fine," I say.

She doesn't know the full extent of what he did to me that night, when we ran into the tree. I told everyone he swerved to avoid a deer. That's why I had the scratches on my face and needed a few stitches.

I don't know what happened with Dominic's DUI, or if anyone even found out about it. But clearly, nothing too serious was charged. He recovered from his injuries too.

Linda hesitates before walking past the truck and into the shop.

I take a deep lungful of air and step onto the sidewalk. I wait as Dominic gets out of the truck.

I go rigid, my posture instinctively defensive. The autumn sun reflects off the sleek black exterior, casting a glare so sharp I have to shift my body slightly to avoid it—the movement making me look even more disinterested.

Which, in truth, I am.

He rounds the front of his truck one foot at a time, indifferent on the outside, wired tight beneath it. He steps onto the sidewalk and stops directly in front of me.

Is this why he's here? To show off his new truck? Impressive. Not.

"Hey," he calls.

"Hey," I reply, my tone devoid of affection.

"I wanted to see you," he says. "Since I can't call you anymore, I thought I'd stop by."

My patience snaps tight.

"Why?"

He exhales, as if racing for impact. "I miss you. I'm sorry for the night we crashed. I shouldn't have been drinking. I don't know what got into me, and I'm sorry I scared you with the calls. I just... I wanted to hear your voice."

I narrow my eyes. "You could've called me like a normal person, you have no problem getting my number. Or, we could've met around friends. Instead, you stalked me with blocked numbers and tried to kill me. Why?"

He rubs his hand across the back of his neck. "I can't explain what got into me that night, Sarah, I'm sorry." A silence stretches between us before he adds, "I saw you one day, walking into your condo. With him. I wasn't ready for that. Seeing you move on... it drove me insane. So I called. And when I did, I could hear if you were with him or not." He looks down. "Sometimes."

A slow, uneasy chill sweeps over me, but I refuse to let it show.

"So you just happened to be driving by my house?"

His gaze flickers up. "To be honest? Yeah. I wanted to see you." He swallows. "But I wasn't prepared to see you with someone else."

I cross my arms over my chest.

"Look, I'm not going to stay angry forever, Dominic. But I can't have you in my life. Whatever we had—it's over."

His expression hardens for the briefest moment before softening. It is something like reluctant acceptance. "I understand," he says. "I needed to clear the air."

"Thanks for doing that. I appreciate it. But I need to get back to work."

"All right. I'll see you around."

He turns back toward his truck, and as he's about to climb in, I call out, "Hey, Dom... I'm glad you're okay. Oh, and nice truck!"

He pauses, glancing over his shoulder. A grin breaks across his face, pride lighting his eyes.

"Thanks," he says, running a hand along the door, "I'll see you."

Fifty-Nine

I make my way back into The Dog Shop, feeling Linda's eyes on me, full of curiosity and concern. She's eager to hear why Dominic showed up, especially after the police had warned him to stay away.

Trying to shake off the encounter, I make my way over to one of the kennels and pick up a silver and white schnauzer. They've always been my favorite breed to groom. I love how polished and perfectly manicured they look when I'm done. Luckily, there's no shortage of them around here. I run the clippers along the dog's back; the rhythmic hum is soothing, but my thoughts remain unsettled.

"I'm still not sure why he came," I admit to Linda. "He said it was to apologize, but honestly, I feel like he was showing off his new truck, like he needed to prove something." Then I add, "Or do you think there was something... darker behind it?"

"Yes! I don't believe he was being innocent," Linda says firmly, her voice edged with conviction. "He's got some nerve showing up here after everything—those calls, the notes, the way he scared you. I don't trust him, and you shouldn't either."

I take her words in, knowing she's probably right. If there's one thing I've learned, it's that my mom is almost always right.

We both focus on our work, distracted by the routine of grooming. The shop buzzes with clippers and fans, stirring the space with the familiar barking and chaos of our daily life. Then—suddenly—Linda lets out a startled scream and spins around. I freeze mid-motion, eyes darting around the room.

Then I see Spencer crouched under the front counter, gripping a broom, grinning like a mischievous child. With all the background noise, we hadn't even heard him sneak in.

"Spencer! You scoundrel! I could beat you!" Linda shrieks, her face flushed as she laughs, scolding him.

Spencer is doubled over, laughing so hard he can barely stand. Linda looks like she's about to throw something at him.

"What happened?" I ask, trying to resolve my confusion.

"He scared me half to death!" Linda exclaims, still glaring at him.

"How?" I glance at Spencer, still thoroughly amused. He loves pulling pranks when he can startle someone; it makes his entire day.

"He slid the broom up my arm, and I thought it was some huge bug crawling on me," she explains, shuddering.

I smirk, shaking my head. "Okay... that is kind of funny," I admit, grateful I wasn't the one he picked as his victim. I hate being scared.

Linda sighs dramatically. "All this talk about Dominic being obsessed and dangerous must've had me on edge. Your timing was impeccable, Spencer."

He straightens up, his grin fading to curiosity. "Wait, what do you mean?"

I fill him in on Dominic's surprise visit. As expected, his jaw clenches with disapproval.

"He shouldn't be coming around here," he says, glancing toward the front like Dominic might suddenly reappear. "If he shows up again, you have to tell him to stay away. After what he did to you... driving drunk..." He doesn't finish.

Spencer was so worried when he learned I was in an accident that he dropped everything to be by my side.

I agree, grateful for his protectiveness.

Stepping away from the dog I'm grooming, I move into Spencer's arms, embracing him. His body against mine reminds me how much has changed in such a short time. I'm so happy we don't have to hide anymore; now my mom can finally see our connection with her own eyes, instead of hearing me gush about it on repeat.

I cherish that he comes to see me at work whenever he's in town, slipping in like he belongs here—because he does. He is *my* landlord after all.

I love that we are able to start our mornings at my place and end our nights the same way, free to be seen.

I finally get to have *all* of him.

And I wouldn't change a thing.

Lately the exception to him coming over on Sunday's, is his kids. He still takes them to church on his time. I adore that he still takes them despite everything, and that he remains a man of faith, committed to going to church even when it's hard.

I love that he loves me, even though I haven't been able to join him at church, yet. And more than anything, I love that he's protective. He doesn't want to lose me. He doesn't want to see me hurt.

Spencer wraps his arms around me in a protective hug, then chats briefly with Linda before heading back to his busy workday.

Later, Linda and I finish up our own tasks and head home.

With no plans for the evening, I try calling Spencer just to hear his voice. It's his night with the kids, so he doesn't answer. Although I've met them briefly at the shop, they don't know about *us*. He wants to give them time before introducing me as his girlfriend, making sure they don't feel overwhelmed by one more change. Besides that, it hasn't been long since he left.

The kids already bounce back and forth between Vanessa and Spencer several times a week.

For now, he's staying at Ken's, but probably not for long. He recently put an offer in on a place in the country. I'm sure it's as lavish as his last.

When he doesn't pick up, I leave a voicemail asking him to call me back. Relentless and curious, I check his voicemail using the pin-code he gave me in France.

I don't even know what I'm hoping to find.

Maybe just his voice.

FIFTY-NINE

Instead, I hear four work-related messages and one from Vanessa, letting him know she'll be picking up the kids a little late.

Nothing unusual.

I hang up. Spencer doesn't call me back the rest of the night, so I settle in with a murder mystery and some dinner. Eventually, I head to bed.

Sixty

Hunting season has arrived once again, and while Spencer is eager to head into the wilderness, I can't say I share the same enthusiasm.

For one, I don't love the time it takes him away. And as an animal lover, the idea of hunting doesn't sit well with me.

However, Spencer is a responsible hunter. He only hunts what he can eat. That's something I can at least appreciate.

I sweep out the trailer and start stocking it with towels, dog bowls, and extra blankets, thinking about how someday this little space might carry more than just things.

I met his kids a few times, briefly, during a quick stop at the shop when he dropped off supplies. They were quiet, curious. One of them smiled at me.

When I help him pack, I take in the size of his newly purchased trailer. It's massive, with three pop-outs, making it spacious enough for all of us—him, his kids, and me—to take comfortable trips together. That's the plan, anyway. Our family.

For now, though, I won't be joining him. Since I don't hunt, he's heading out with his oldest son and his friend Ken, making their way to the Uintah mountains in Utah.

The Uintahs, awe-inspiring and rugged, stand tall with snow that lingers

SIXTY

into summer. Golden aspens and fiery red maples flare against the deep green pines, while rivers twist through valleys like veins.

The vast and wild hunter's paradise is unforgiving, even for seasoned outdoorsmen who can easily become disoriented in its endless terrain.

Spencer is no stranger to the wilderness, but the thought of him getting lost, or something going wrong, always sits in the back of my mind.

Saying goodbye is never easy. I can't imagine my world without him anymore. My love for him feels deeply rooted, as if my soul has known him forever.

Sensing my worry, he reassures me that he'll be safe.

"This trip," he tells me, "will be easier—my son will be with me." He tries to comfort me with logic, before adding, "so it won't be anything too extreme." In a simple way, I do feel a little more at ease.

We finish loading the trailer with all the essentials: bedding, cookware, towels, propane tanks, clothing, and, of course, hunting gear.

As excited as I am for him and the adventures he'll have, *I can't help but feel a little sorry for myself.* This is the trailer's first trip, and *I won't be on it.*

I smooth the plaid comforter over the bed inside, stepping back to admire the quaint little space we've put together.

"All finished," I say, with a satisfied smile.

He shakes his head, a playful glint in his eyes. "No, you're not."

Before I can respond, he scoops me up into his arms and places me in the center of the bed.

My breath hitches in my throat as he hovers over me, his gaze darkening with intent.

"I'm not?" I tease.

"Not even close."

With little time between words and action, his hands grab hold of me, slipping my shirt over my head. Followed by fingertips trailing heat down to the waistband of my jeans before yanking them off.

He pauses, taking me in, before warm fingers brush the lace of my lingerie—their touch seeping into my skin.

"We need to christen the trailer," he says, the corner of his mouth lifting into a smirk.

"I agree."

Wet lips graze my collarbone, as he pins my hands gently against the mattress.

His breath trails lower until it hovers over my most sensitive area. Then he blows cool air over me, cinnamon-scented and maddening.

"Spencer," I whisper, breathless.

He giggles against my skin, his grip firm enough to remind me who's in control. "Patience," he licks his lips, before finding mine, striking a slow-burning fuse inside me.

He undresses us both before rough but tender hands move along me, like they've done so many times.

Then he drags the length of himself over me, teasing, testing, savoring. Each slow, measured movement tears me at the seams—the pressure and friction perfectly balanced, softly unraveling me.

His body flows with mine, effortless, tuned to my every reaction. The rhythm builds, unspoken but understood, a language only we speak.

At first he's unrushed but soon his pace quickens, urgency mounting, each thrust giving way to something more primal.

My chest moves in time with his, and my breasts bounce wildly until his hands find them. He cradles them, as if they were made to fit perfectly in his grasp.

"I don't know how it's possible but you keep getting more beautiful," he's tender with his words.

The heat in me rises. The trailer lights cast a glow across our skin, making it impossible to hide the effect his words have on me. I will never tire of hearing them.

"And you're the sexiest man I've ever loved," I confide, pulling him closer. His body moves over mine, pressing me deeper into the mattress. Each movement grows more intense. The scent of cologne and sweat drenches the air. I breathe him in as if it's the first time, never wanting to let this part

SIXTY

of him go.

I savor the feel of his skin against mine drowning in him, his strength, his love. He is the only man I ever want to experience this closeness with.

The depth of my emotions pushes me over the edge faster than I expect. My body tenses as pleasure overtakes me, my thoughts dissolving into white-hot bliss.

"I'm coming," I gasp, clinging to him.

"Me too," he groans, his body perfectly synchronized with mine.

As the last echoes of pleasure fade, our bodies slow, leaving us stunned and entwined in the radiance of our shared euphoria. He collapses beside me, our skin still touching, our gasps uneven.

For a moment, we simply lie motionless, lost in each other—two souls *intertwined*, exactly where they're meant to be.

"You feel like home," I say, before I melt into him. "I can't imagine my future without you."

"I feel the same," he says, his voice flooded with sincerity. "You're so beautiful. You know me better than anyone, and if the world were mine to give, I'd give it to you."

His fingers lace through mine. "In so many ways, you've saved me." he says.

"You've given me courage I never had. For the first time, I feel like I'm truly living, the way I always hoped I could. Divorce and custody battles are hard, but I feel richer than I ever have. You and my children are my life. And our future, it's finally here. Keep being exactly who you are," he encourages, "because you're everything I need."

His words settle deep in my core, reassuring me in the way I've needed ever since the night his sparkle dimmed, after the rage of Vanessa tore at him.

We hold onto the moment a little longer, before reality calls us back.

Together, we load the last of his gear, securing the trailer to his truck. The evening is slipping away, and he needs time to pick up his son.

As always, I don't want him to go. I hold tight, reluctant to let this moment end.

"I love you," he whispers into my ear, his voice rich with emotion.

"I love you too, Buster," I whisper, holding him tighter.

With one last lingering look, he releases me and climbs into his truck.

I watch as he drives away, already missing him.

The house feels empty in his absence.

Like the breath's been sucked out of it.

His goodbye was soft, simple, and certain. There was no tension. No begging or bargaining. He left... and I didn't fall apart.

"Just a few days" he'd said, brushing a kiss to my temple.

But now that he's gone, the quiet settles in. I don't want to sit with it. I want to move.

I throw on leggings and trail runners, grab a hoodie, and head for the foothills.

The road winds familiar like nostalgia.

My phone stays behind in the passenger seat.

No music. No distractions.

Just breath and forward motion.

At the trailhead, the wind nips at my neck. Aspen leaves shimmer like silver coins. The path narrows quickly beneath me. I start to slow, letting my body settle.

The first incline burns in that satisfying way that tells me I'm alive.

I run.

Not from anything—but toward something.

Clarity. Stillness. Myself.

Each step knocks loose a thought I didn't know I was holding:

How safe I felt in Spencer's arms last night.

How terrifying it is to feel safe again.

How long it's been since I trusted my own instincts.

I pause at the ridgeline and stare out over the valley. For a fleeting second, I see myself somewhere else entirely.

SIXTY

I picture the other Mormon girls I grew up with, their hands folded. Their smiles beautiful as they stepped into the temple in white. They were everything I was told I should want to be—pure, worthy, chosen.

And yet, watching them from the outside, I always felt like I was pressing my nose to glass, aching for a life I couldn't quite touch.

I've tried so hard to wear that image.

To be what I was told would make me complete. But here, with the dirt under my shoes and my lungs burning from the climb, I can admit it—*I never really fit inside that picture.*

Maybe I still want pieces of it, the comfort, the belonging.

But what I feel now, standing on this ridge with my chest heaving, is something those white walls never gave me:

Freedom.

My chest burns, but it's the good kind of pain.

The kind that reminds you you're doing something hard, and doing it anyway.

He'll be back soon.

But even if he weren't, I'd still be standing here.

I'd still be breathing.

I'd still be me.

I smile, just a little, and begin the jog back down.

I toss my hoodie near the door, my shoes leaving faint prints on the mat.

The trail dust is still clinging to them like a badge—something earned.

Everything feels a little softer.

I stretch out on the couch with Evie, muscles twitching in quiet protest.

I tilt my face toward the ceiling.

My heart beats calmly.

My thoughts aren't racing anymore.

The tension has dissolved—mile by mile, breath by breath—along on the trail.

I think about the way Spencer kissed me before he left, his voice was relaxed and unhurried. Leaving me with a sureness I haven't known before. With no feelings of needing to chase him anymore.

Just love.

It's strange—this feeling of trusting someone and not waiting for the other shoe to drop.

I pull a blanket over my lap, still in my damp sports bra and leggings, and press my palm flat to my abdomen.

"I'm okay," I whisper. "I'll be okay."

Outside, a bird chirps from a branch.

I close my eyes and let the quiet hold me.

Spencer will be home soon. *And for once, I'm not afraid to let someone come home to me.*

Sixty-One

The drive home from town is quiet. I sing along to the radio, my hand resting on the cool steering wheel as I glance at the fading light over the hills. Evie's head hangs out the window, ears flapping in the breeze, her tail thumping against the seat. There's a strange calm in the air—one of those rare moments where life finally feels settled. Maybe like things are beginning to shift in my favor. It feels good to be seen. To be wanted. To have people in my life who don't make me feel like a burden.

I pull into the driveway, still humming under my breath, and scoop Evie against my chest as I head for the door. But the second my eyes catch the glitter of broken glass on the ground, my body goes stiff. Carefully, I lower her onto the porch, away from the shards.

When I open the door, the sight knocks the breath out of me. Drawers hang open, clothes and papers flung across the floor like a storm tore through the room. Shards of glass crunch under my shoes as I step inside, the sharp crack echoing in the hollow silence. The air smells of dust and something metallic, as though the violence that ripped through this room is still hanging there, waiting for me to breathe it in.

My every nerve screams that this isn't real, that this can't be my home.

My knees threaten to buckle, but I claw at the door frame, forcing myself to stay upright. My pulse hammers in my ears so loud it drowns the silence—panic rushing through me like a flood. Every instinct screams to run, but my feet won't move.

What if he's still here?

The thought slams through me, sharper than the broken glass beneath my shoes. My gaze jerks to the shadowed corners, the kitchen beyond, waiting for something—someone—to move.

This deliberate chaos tells me that Dominic has been here.

This wasn't supposed to happen. I thought I was safe, that everything was fine. But now, standing in the middle of the wreckage, dread coils in my stomach like barbed wire.

The realization sinks in slow, chilling me to the bone: *I never imagined I'd have to be afraid in my own home.*

The emotional toll, the destruction, and the invasive feeling of being violated in my own space are unbearable.

He knew what this would do to me.

He knows what it cost me last time.

Only now, there's no pretending I don't know who's behind it. No excuse left to believe the damage was random or harmless.

This time, I see him clearly.

Why would he do this?

What was he looking for?

The thought of it makes me sick.

I stand in the wreckage, my hands shaking, but I don't feel helpless. *Not this time.*

I grab my phone.

There's a tremble in my fingers as I dial the number.

"Non-emergency dispatch, how can I help you?"

"I've just walked into my house," I say, overtaken. "And... it's been broken into."

"Is anyone in the house now?"

"I don't think so."

My eyes sweep the room again, carefully.

"Everything is torn apart."

"What's your address?"

SIXTY-ONE

I give it to them.

"Do you have any idea who might have done this?"

"Yes, I do," I say.

A beat of silence passes.

"Officers are on the way. Stay outside the home if possible."

"Got it."

I end the call and sink onto the bottom step of the staircase, phone still in my hand.

Outside, the sun is still shining. The world hasn't stopped.

And maybe that's the strangest part.

Because despite the mess—despite the violation, the fear—I feel something different settling in my chest.

Control.

Not because someone is coming to fix it. But because I picked up the phone. Because I didn't run or hide.

I sit there, calm in the chaos, and wait for the sirens.

This is only the beginning.

A restraining order is coming.

More questions will follow. Maybe more fear.

But also: answers. Boundaries. Closure.

Overwhelmed, still trying to gather my thoughts, I'm unsure of where to begin. But I force myself to move.

I take a deep breath and slowly begin picking up the scattered remnants of my life.

My body is heavy with exhaustion, and my mind is a scramble.

While I try to push the fear down, it persists, clawing at the edges of my thoughts, a constant presence that won't let go.

Despite the urge to cry, I dial Spencer. My heart pounds as it rings once, twice...

Voicemail.

I should hang up.

But desperation holds me there.

I tap in the code he gave me, clinging to the hope of hearing something—anything—that will pull me close to him again.

My fingers tremble as I listen to the first voicemail. It's someone from work. I skip it.

The second is from Mike. I skip that one too. The tension builds with each passing second. *Why am I listening to these?*

Then the third voicemail plays.

Her voice.

Vanessa.

"Hey, Spence... I just dropped the little ones at the sitter so I can head up this weekend. I'm glad we're moving past the awful fall out at Sarah's. The kids have missed you, and Ken says he's excited to see us together as a family again. I can't wait to spend the weekend with you and our boy in our new trailer. This feels like the fresh start we've needed. I'll see you soon. I love you."

The words hit me like a physical blow.

My whole body locks in place.

She knows.

She knows about me—about us.

And she's still forgiving him.

Still taking him back.

And worse, his son, his friends, his whole circle are part of it.

It's not a decision he's making—in progress.

It's already done.

He's hers.

The world doesn't tilt or crash.

It just... ***stops.***

For months I prayed for peace, and He sent me truth instead. Maybe faith was never about saving me—but about showing me when to walk away.

SIXTY-ONE

Spencer isn't mine.

Not anymore.

Maybe he never was.

I finally understand the blankness in his eyes.

He already knew.

He had already chosen.

Her.

And I'm left standing in Dominic's wreckage, Vanessa's words echoing in my ear, realizing everything I believed—about love, about trust, about him... has shattered.

The truth cuts deeper than betrayal.

He didn't just return to her.

He never truly left.

I was the pause in his story.

She was the sentence he never stopped writing.

The voicemail ends.

Silence returns. But it isn't quiet.

It *roars* in my ears.

In the pieces of the life I thought we were building.

And all that's left is me...

Standing in the wreckage of a story I never belonged to.

Continue the Series

Book Two: Spiral

She left her husband behind.
   She stepped into freedom.
   But freedom has teeth.

A past love returns.
   Temptation rewrites the rules.
   And the girl who thought she knew herself…
   is about to spiral into someone new.

Coming soon.

A Note From the Author

Thank you for reading *Entanglement*.

If this story moved you or stayed with you after the final page, I would be incredibly grateful if you would consider leaving a review on Amazon or Goodreads. Reviews help readers discover books like this and make a meaningful difference for independent authors.

Even a short sentence or two about how the story made you feel is more than enough.

If you'd like to stay connected, receive updates about future books in the series, or get behind-the-scenes glimpses into The Landlord Series, you can find me online or sign up for my mailing list.

Thank you for supporting my work—and for spending your time inside this story.

With gratitude,
　L.L. Loveland

About the Author

L.L. Loveland writes about love, conflict, and the quiet strength found in rebuilding the most vulnerable, broken parts of ourselves. Her stories dig into desire, identity, and the difficult truths that reshape lives.

When she's not writing, she's homeschooling her three boys, attempting to grow a garden, and daydreaming about her next book. None of it would be possible without the steady support of her husband, who gives her the space to chase her dreams.

Let's stay connected
https://authorllloveland.wixsite.com/my-site-1
https://x.com/ll_loveland
http://facebook.com/author:l.l.loveland
https://www.instagram.com/l.l.loveland
https://www.tiktok.com/@l.l.loveland
https://subscribepage.io/4lI9DR

www.ingramcontent.com/pod-product-compliance
Lightning Source LLC
LaVergne TN
LVHW091622070526
838199LV00044B/902